THE LESSER OF TWO EVILS

What if the United States Fought
and Defeated Japan 'First' in World War II
— *An Alternative WWII*

JOHN M. MENTER

Dedication

This book is dedicated to my wife and best friend Jeanette, who as my conscience and editor, has followed this project for the past five years, urging me on, and my daughters Rachel and Kathryn as well as her husband Harold.

It is also dedicated to those professional trainers of the Mission Command Training Support Program (MCTSP) Warfighting Functional Area Team, who spend countless days travelling across the United States, training U.S. Army units deploying overseas in pursuit of freedom and liberty.

I consider myself extremely blessed to have the honor to work with some of the finest soldiers and professional trainers in the history of this nation.

Forward

Dr. John Menter's newest book, 'The Lesser of Two Evils' is a must read for anyone interested in World War II military history and what might have been. Base on little known, but actual critical events such as a German long range bomber reconnaissance over New York City in 1944; the detonation to two atomic devices other than on Japan; the compromise of our actual 'Rainbow Five' Warplan by the Chicago Daily Tribune and the Washington Times Herald; and Germany's use of superior new U-Boats, John presents an amazing alternative version so real that the reader is able to see what might have happened.

The Lesser of Two Evils clarifies historical facts and provides the reader with many new intriguing ones. Today, many Americans believe the United States declared on Germany at the same time it did with Japan, but in reality, Hitler declared war on America – four days after Pearl Harbor! Many of his ministers and key military advisors were mystified by this action; coming as his summer launched campaign 'Operation Barbarossa' was grinding to a halt in the wake of a Soviet counter offensive outside Moscow.

Using a commercially available geo-political simulation software in addition to the employment of newly released material from the Kremlin archives, Dr. Menter portrays a refighting of World War II starting with America's immediate reaction to the attack on Pearl Harbor and the use of another Rainbow Warplan – 'Rainbow Two' (basically a reworked War Plan Orange that US Naval strategist had yearned to conduct since the early years of the 20th Century), a plan that takes the war right to Japan's very doorstep, culminating in an invasion of the home islands less than two years after

Pearl Harbor. Meanwhile, unhampered by an American air offensive, the German's continue development of a whole new family of wonder weapons with devastating effects. Would an eventual American entry in the war after the defeat of Japan still win it for the Allies?

In his book *The Rise of the Fourth Reich* by Jim Marrs, Jim discusses in great detail how many key Nazi scientists that America imported at the end of World War II in a covert operation known as '*Operation Paperclip*' became in twined within our space and various defense programs. However, most readers are unaware of our acquisition of 560 kg of enriched U-235 material from the German U-Boat U-234, and how it may have contributed to the success of our Manhattan Project and ultimately the dropping of two atomic devices that ended the worst conflagration to befall the 20th Century. Doctor Menter uses these and other obscured war facts combined with colorful characters to captivate his readers.

To fight and win the Second World War, approximately 15 million American soldiers, sailors, and marines fought for the United States, with 418,500 making the ultimate sacrifice. **The Lesser of Two Evils** asks the question "Would this have changed if Japan had been defeated first and what would such a post-World War II world look like?" Dr. John Menter sees a very different world and after reading his book, you candecide for yourself.

Thomas J. Sullivan
Brigadier General,
USA, Retired

Preface

*"History is the version of past events that people have decided to agree upon... it is a
set of lies agreed upon by the victors"*
Napoleon Bonaparte, French general and politician (1769 - 1821)

It has been a little over sixty-five years since the men and women of what
Tom Brokaw termed *"greatest generation"* undertook the greatest crusade of the
twentieth century to rid the world of Italian fascism, German Nazism, and
Japanese militarism. In terms of perspective, we are further along in time
from the events of December 7, 1941, than the people of 1941 were from
Custer's Last Stand on the Little Big Horn River, or Theodore Roosevelt's
tumultuous ride up San Juan Hill during the Spanish-American War.

Yet, strangely enough, the Second World War remains a fixation in everyone's minds; there isn't a day that goes by without some mention of this
historical event in the form of a new book, a movie on Turner Classic Movies,
or an obituary of a deceased veteran. We as a nation of 300 million are still
obsessed with what happened from that "day of infamy" in December 1941
to that equally notable time when Japan formally surrendered in the wake of
the dropping of the second atomic bomb.

Events during this greatest of endeavors' played out per a hastily written
script, but few Americans know that this outcome might not have occurred
had two little understood events, occurring one week apart, changed. This
book examines through fictional characters, immersed in a transition of actual

historical events and facts (many unknown to the American public), what might have occurred had those two critical events occurred differently.

The first event occurred in the afternoon of December 4, when the *Chicago Daily Tribune* and the *Washington Times Herald* – both owned by notorious anti-Roosevelt publisher Colonel Robert McCormick – published America's war plan (or Victory Plan). Such a revelation would undoubtedly require war planners to scrap it for obvious reasons; additionally, its publication would serve to greatly embarrass the Roosevelt administration because it revealed the desire to steer this country toward a course *nearly nine out of ten Americans* did not want to pursue. Yet, strangely enough, no one was ever charged with treason or sedition, nor was "Rainbow Five" as the war plan was called, changed or dropped.

Chicago Tribune – December 4, 1941

It should be noted that for thirty plus years, Army & Navy War Planners had focused their energies on what many believed was the pending war against Imperial Japan. So inevitable was this that in April 1925, Hector C. Bywater, a reporter for the *New York Herald*, wrote a stunning book on a fictional naval war between the Japanese and the United States titled *The Great Pacific War: A History of the American-Japanese Campaign of 1931-1933*. He wrote of the "inevitable" war in the Pacific between the United States and Japan if the naval treaty between the United States, the United Kingdom, and Japan hadn't been signed in the 1920's. He predicted with amazing detail actions taken by both the Japanese and American Naval forces fifteen years prior to the 1941 bombing of Pearl Harbor.

This book, needless to say, was an overnight best seller and remains in print to this day. Concurrently, an upstart US Army air corps officer, Brigadier General Billy Mitchell, published his own 324-page book called *Winged Defense* in 1925, also predicting a future war with Japan, starting with a surprise attack on Pearl Harbor.

Yet in the early 1940's, Roosevelt (through the increasing influence of Britain's Prime Minister Winston Churchill) directed development of a "Germany First" warplan contrary to the opinion of the American public, many congressmen, senators, and Corporate America. In 1939, nine out ten Americans did not favor getting involved in Europe's latest war, while Corporate America cringed at the possibility of their investment in the Third Reich coming to ruin. To the average American on the street, the "Japs" were our future enemy, not the Germans. As for the British, American public opinion at the time was said to be "Anglophile" in culture – "Anglophobe" in politics.

In spite of an undeclared naval war against the German U-Boat force in the North Atlantic in 1940 – 41, most Americans felt we had no business sticking "our noses where it did not belong". Many Americans would be shocked at the correspondence that flowed behind the scenes between FDR and Churchill, which culminated in the esteemed Prime Minister's receiving of Roosevelt's blessing of a "Germany First" strategy during the famed meeting off Newfoundland in August 1941.

Such was FDR's tactics in getting Hitler to make the first move; they failed. When war came, it came at 7:49 am (Hawaiian time) December 7, from our predicted enemy: the Japanese. Roosevelt, much to his frustration, had no choice but to ask for war against the Japanese, something he could not do against Germany. Worse, he had no plan thanks in large part to the *Chicago Tribune!*

The second major event in the unfolding of the our involvement in the Second World War occurred one week later from the publication of the "Rainbow Five" war plan. In Berlin, Adolph Hitler announced to the world during one of his speeches of his "declaration of war against the United States." While this was not too much of a shock to Americans, it was to the average German who, for the most part, still had memories of the United States' intervention in the First World War and how the introduction of 2 million doughboys into France during late 1917 to 1918 robbed them of that last opportunity for victory.

No one knows why Hitler did this. Many of his closest advisors (such as Minister of Propaganda Dr. Joseph Gobbles) wrote in their diaries of their surprise and shock in this action by Hitler. Many Americans today believe (incorrectly) as well as my own mother-in-law (a native German raised under Hitler's regime), that the United States declared war on Germany as well as Japan on December 8. Nothing could be further from the truth.

Hitler's declaration of war came as an immense relief to the dilemma in which Roosevelt (and indirectly, Winston Churchill) had found himself in the wake of Pearl Harbor. "Rainbow Five" was back on with Germany as the main effort, but the American public, in the wake of Pearl Harbor, would be kept in the dark about this decision for some time to follow.

This brings me back to the original premise of this book: what would have happened had the president directed a new war plan and Hitler, in a sane moment, had not declared war on the United States? What would our world be like today if we had defeated the Japanese *first*, then turned all our energies toward eliminating Nazi Germany?

The "Greatest Generation" of America produced approximately 15 million soldiers, sailors, and marines in uniform, with 418,500 making the ultimate sacrifice. For this titanic effort to eliminate fascism and restore democracy to the world, their efforts were rewarded with the civil war in China, unrest in Asia, the Korean and Vietnam Wars, countless brush wars, and the advent of a forty-plus-year cold war with the Soviet Union, consuming hundreds of thousands of lives and countless billions of dollars in national treasure.

Would all this have changed had Japan been defeated first? I believe so. Hopefully you will conclude the same when you finish reading this counter-factual story, which simply uses many unknown facts and event about the war effort, taking the course of the Second World War as we know it in a different direction.

"History is written by the winners" — Alex Haley, Author of Roots

Contents

Chapter 1

A Visit to Ford's Theater

Fact: On May 20ᵗʰ, 1940, Officers from the British Counter-Intelligence Service known as "MI-5" arrested 29 year old Tyler Kent, an American cipher clerk working within the US Embassy, London. Within his apartment, MI-5 found over 1,900 official documents to include the private correspondence between then First Sea Lord of the Admiralty Winston Churchill, and President Franklin Delano Roosevelt. As a cipher clerk within the American Embassy, Kent intercepted hundreds of diplomatic dispatches between the embassies in Europe and the State Department in Washington, quickly learning that President Roosevelt was doing everything in his power to subvert the law and deceive the American people in order to get the Unites States into war. He decided to make copies or summaries of diplomatic dispatches documenting Roosevelt's secret policies and somehow bring them to the attention of sympathetic congressmen and senators. He made verbatim copies of most of the messages and paraphrased summaries of the rest. The most important and incriminating of these was the top secret correspondence between Roosevelt and Winston Churchill, which began with a letter from the President, dated 11 September 1939. It is unknown to this day whether all documents made by Kent were ever totally accounted for....

Fords Theater
Washington, D.C
2300 hrs, 8 December 1941

1

J ay Hill felt so out of place. For the last 18 months, he had been working virtually non stop as Harry Hopkin's aid, who in turn was probably the closest advisor and aid President Roosevelt had, closer perhaps than his wife Eleanor. From Jay's position, he could see up close the wheels of government turn – rightly or wrongly. And wrongly he had seen. For months, he had witnessed as Hopkins and Roosevelt would plan on ways to circumvent the law in providing aid to the beleaguered British. Lend lease, loans, call it what you may, Hill thought all these measures were sure to get the Americans back in a shooting war in Europe. "Hadn't we learned our lesson the first time around?" he thought as he rubbed his arm where 23 years earlier he took a bullet as a soldier in France with the American Expeditionary Force while in France.

But his luck was about to change or so he thought. Over the past few months, he had read in the Washington Post about the many demonstrations taking place across the country protesting American involvement in European affairs. He even had in his pocket an old post card from the "America First" committee advising the US to stay out of the war. This polyglot group of isolationists, anti communists, pacifists, and simple down to earth "Roosevelt haters", had grown over the past year to over one million members and over 700 chapter's nation wide. Hill was impressed at the many public notables involved such as the famous aviator Charles Lindberg, Henry Ford, and the arch conservative Robert McCormick of the Chicago Tribune. He was especially fond of Lindberg, after listening to him on the radio two months ago publicly stating that "only three groups want the Republic to go to war – the British, the Jews, and the Roosevelt Administration".

Months of working nights and weekends for a workaholic who scarcely expressed any concern for him was about to pay off. In Jay's possession were letters written between Roosevelt and Churchill he obtained secretly from a friend of his in London before his arrest by the British. In his hands were copies of diplomatic messages about plans to support the beleaguered British and get the Americans into "a shooting war", and he knew just the guy to give these to. For $10,000, he would not only stop Roosevelt from what Jay thought was wrong, but make a tidy "early retirement" in the mean time. That time was fast approaching.

Midnight at Ford's Theater. Here, in 1865, one President was murdered and tonight, 76 years later, another one was going to have his political career "killed".

"Do you have the package?" a voice called out from just outside a side ally. Hill was initially startled. "Where did he come from?" he thought. "Yes, I do", he replied. "Where's the money?" As Hill stepped closer, he thought he recognized the man's voice. It reminded him of a voice he heard over the radio a few weeks prior making some sort of political speech. Hill stepped up to the man in a brown full length coat who was raising his arm with a brown grocery sack, then dropping it out in front of Hill. "Your money, Sir" he murmured, "and now the letters." Jay reached into his coat pocket and pulled out the bundle, wrapped tightly to protect it from the elements. He stepped closer, handing the packet to the stranger in the process getting a better picture of him. "He's a god damn Senator!!" he said to himself, stepping back to pick up his retirement grocery bag. But that was his last thought, as he felt a strong arm grab him around his neck. Within moments, Jay Hill had achieved his "retirement" on a Washington Street with a knife in his back. The snow started falling shortly, forming his retirement "villa".

Chapter 2

The Old Executive Office Building

Fact: Prior to America's entry into the Second World War, the U.S. Army Chief of Staff, General George Marshall, removed thirty-one Division, Corps, and Army commanders, all of whom he deemed unfit for further command of units.

Old Executive Office Building
Washington, D.C.
1300 hrs, 9 December 1941

Colonel John Reynolds could not believe his luck—or, rather, his lack of it. Two days prior, he was down at Fort Benning, Georgia, in the warm sun, enjoying life back in the States after completing a hectic, eighteen-month tour of duty as the U.S. Army's attaché in Berlin. *Uggh*, he thought, *now I'm in Washington in December, of all times. This place can be as cold as Berlin.*

Once he picked up his baggage, Reynolds quickly left the brand new National Airport terminal and hailed one of the many taxi cabs loitering immediately out front.

"Where to, General?" the cabbie inquired. Reynolds, somewhat flattered by the cabbie's error, quickly educated this man with obviously no prior military service.

"It's Colonel, and I need to go to the Old Executive Office Building on Seventeen Street, Northwest."

"Sorry 'bout that," the cabbie responded. "I've been picking up and delivering so much brass these last few days—what with Pearl Harbor and all—I wouldn't know a sergeant from a major. Old Executive Office Building it is!" he said and pulled his flag down.

For as many times as he had been to Washington in the past as a staff officer working for the War Plans Division (WPD), as the taxi drove Colonel Reynolds north from National Airport he couldn't help but notice a massive project with thousands of construction workers moving like ants on a gigantic pile of dirt just south of Arlington National Cemetery.

"What's going on over there?" Reynolds inquired, pointing over the cabby's left shoulder.

"I don't know, but it's something big and something to do with the military. I think it's some military building or fort or something like that. Funny thing, one of my cabby buddies was telling me that when it's done, it'll have five sides. What kind of crazy Army building has five sides...?" Reynolds, though curious, was at that point too tired to pursue the conversation further and fell back into the seat. At this point, he really didn't care.

As the taxi continued up the Jefferson Davis Highway and began to cross the Potomac River over the Memorial Bridge, John couldn't help but notice the emerging similarities between Berlin and the post-Pearl Harbor nation's capital. The presence of the military was everywhere. Soldiers. Everywhere he looked there were troops posted. As the taxi drove over across the Potomac River and into the District of Columbia or "the District" as its residents called it, it became all to apparent that in front of all key government building and historical sites were soldiers—at the Lincoln Memorial, walking a post within the Capital Mall, manning checkpoints at key locations and street intersections. *Come to think of it*, he thought, *National Airport had soldiers there as well.*

As the taxi turned onto Seventeenth Street, he could make out the left shoulder patch of the many young lads on duty; the patch was composed of the blue and grey "ying-yang" design of the Twenty-Ninth Infantry Division, a Maryland and Virginia Army National Guard unit that had been activated last February and posted to nearby Fort Meade, Maryland. *Finally, a good use for the National Guard,* he thought to himself, *rather than sitting on their duffs at Fort Meade waiting for God knows what.* If the Twenty-Ninth Division was out guarding Washington, shouldn't he be out working with a unit getting it ready for war against the Japanese? His immediate supervisor couldn't answer his question when he informed John he was to report immediately to the Army Chief of Staff "ASAP"!

The taxi stopped for a light at the corner Seventeenth and F streets; John noticed a group of soldiers in front of a local theater. *Interesting,* he thought. Citizen Kane *with Orson Wells is showing along with John Ford's* How Green is My Valley. *Now that's a way to spend an afternoon.* Reynolds didn't think Marshall would be too keen on him taking a little time off to play a little hooky. He envied those troops, standing out front and getting an afternoon break from the everyday chaos of Washington life. For him, he had the top Army general waiting. *I wonder if the president takes any time off?* he thought as he look toward the right side of the car at the brilliantly lit-up White House, now being eclipsed by the Old Executive Building as they closed in.

If nothing else, over the last twenty-five years the Army taught him to be a good soldier and obey. His curiosity as to why General Marshal, the Army Chief of Staff, sent for him was always in the back of his mind.

John thought back to his first time to the capital. In 1939, he was assigned to the Joint Planning Committee, which was a collection of Army and Navy "thinkers" tasked with coming up with defense plans for the United States. More than an organized mob, but less than a cohesive group, this "committee," under the direct supervision of Lieutenant General Stanley D. Embick, Chief of the War Plans Division, eventually hammered out a series of war plans named the "Rainbow" series, five plans in all, out of the old color code plans.[1] John as a major at the time was the chief architect of the plan that would eventually carry the rather unglamorous name "Rainbow Two."

I thought the "Rainbow Five"[2] guys would win out, he thought, in reference to the plan's preeminence to fighting both the Germans and the Japanese simultaneously. That plan's author was Colonel Albert C. Wedemeyer,[3] who, like John, had been given the same planning considerations; an American Army of some 215 divisions or 8.8 million soldiers, with plans for approximately 5 million overseas against the Japanese, Germans, or both. That all changed just two days ago with the Japanese attack on Pearl Harbor.

Yesterday, the president asked and got the Congress to declare war on Japan; as John listened to the speech just after 12:00 noon over the radio down at Fort Benning, he understood that, strangely enough, war was not declared against Germany. This all in spite of the indirect coordination between Churchill and Roosevelt that John had heard about from his friends on the General Staff.

Well, you can plan all you like, but when reality hits, you have to do what you have to do. After all, no plan ever survives contact with the enemy, he mused. Still, what did Marshall have in mind for him....

The taxi finally arrived at 639 17th Street, pulling in front of the massive, old, gray building, now the nerve center for the U.S. war effort.

"Three dollars and ten cents, Colonel." John smiled knowing that the cabby learned something today. Pulling out four dollars from his wallet, he handed the money to the cabby, telling him in the process to keep the change.

---

1 Prior to the "Rainbow" plans, war plans were color-coded, depicting the particular country that plan was designated against. For example, War Plan "Orange" was for operations against Japan, "Black" against Germany—even "Red" for operations against Great Britain.

2 Also known as the "Victory Program."

3 Lieutenant General Embick also happened to be Wedemeyer's father-in-law.

"Thank ya, Sir. And you try and have a Merry Christmas." *Christmas? Never really thought about it.* Alas, until he could cash a check, there went his lunch money with that leftover change he gave the cabby.

"Same to you, too" he replied in turn as the taxi drove off.

The Old Executive Office Building

As John turned away from the taxi, he was immediately confronted by a small group of Twenty-Ninth Division soldiers manning a checkpoint outside the building; their mission was to check the identities of everyone desiring to enter the building. *These are chaotic times,* he thought. *After Pearl Harbor, maybe a little paranoia is a good thing.*

Colonel Reynolds smartly walked up to the group of soldiers, who immediately stood up, snapped to attention and saluted. John quickly returned their salute, at which time the Non-Commissioned Officer (NCO) in charge asked Reynolds for his ID and orders.

"Give me a second," he said as he fumbled through his light brown Army trench coat looking to the worn pieces of paper that served as the orders that brought him to Washington. He found the folded orders, unfolded them, and handed them to the staff sergeant. The NCO immediately whirled around and called for his superior officer.

"Sir," the NCO called out, "this man here is to see General Marshall." At this time, a big burly no-nonsense Virginian stepped forward to see what exactly the NCO was talking about.

"Sir, as you can see, these orders have him reporting directly to General Marshall." In a pure southern drawl, the Virginian looked at Reynolds, saluted, and introduced himself. "Sir, I'm Lieutenant Colonel Kenny Smith, Co-man-da of the First Battalion, IIIth Field Aw-tillary Regiment. Beggan ya pa-dun, Suh, for what purpose do ya'll"

Reynolds was somewhat taken aback. "Colonel Smith, aside from a need to know, which you do not need at this time, if I knew, I still wouldn't tell you. So I suggest if you desire to make full colonel in this war, you had either let me in or call General Marshall and tell him you have no desire to let me pass through your checkpoint. Either way, Marshall has a right to know, one way or another." John thought maybe he might make the double-feature movie after all.

Smith looked dead on at Reynolds and then cocked a slight smile. "No, Sir, I guess not. I sure wuddan't want to make that general mad. Just doing our job here. Never know when those sneak yellow Jap bastards might pull somethin' here, like blowin' up the buildin' or somethin' like that." With that, he handed John his orders back, snapped again to attention, and saluted. "Sir, you may proceed, and ya'll have a good afternoon. General Marshall's office is on the fourth floor. Y'can't miss it." Reynolds returned the salute, pocketed his orders back into his trench coat, and entered the building. Washington was sure different this time around.

As he entered the chief's outer office, he was at once taken by the chaotic atmosphere within the immediate area. Majors, colonels, and generals were all buzzing around much like a beehive but in complete, random disorder. He approached General Marshall's SGS, Secretary of the General Staff, introduced himself, and informed him he had an appointment to see the Chief of Staff as soon as he arrived in town.

"May I see your orders, Colonel Reynolds?" Colonel Butch Watts inquired. Reynolds reached into his overcoat, pulled the orders out and, with the flick of his wrist, unfolded and presented the incredibly worn copy to the SGS. Watts, looking the orders over, seemed pleased they were the real McCoy and handed them back to Reynolds. Then picking up the phone, he dialed two numbers and informed the voice on the other end, "Reynolds is here, Sir." John could hear the low, gruff voice on the other end, but could not understand what was being said. Watts then concluded with a crisp, "Yes, Sir. I'll inform him," and hung up.

Standing up, Watts motioned John to take a seat and informed him, "General Marshall will see you in a few minutes." With that, he took the first open chair and sat down, grabbing an abandoned newspaper in the process. Usually when the chief's secretary says "a few minutes," it means it will be a while.

Reynolds was immediately depressed reading the front page. The Japs were on the move everywhere: Hong Kong, the Philippines, Wake and Guam islands, all invaded. *I hope General MacArthur stops them in the Philippines. God knows we spent enough time putting a plan together.* He was less sympathetic to the British down in Malaysia and Singapore. He knew with all the troops Churchill was using in the North African desert to stop Rommel, he had to pull them out from somewhere.

Looking at local news, John's eye caught the attention of a name in the police arrest reports section of the paper. A Jay Hill was found stabbed in an alley next to Ford's Theater. *I know this guy*, he thought. *He works for Harry Hopkins and the president. What the hell was he doing there last night?* The police report went on to say there were no suspects. *I'll bet he was looking for a little late-night excitement. Being a bachelor, he probably went out looking for a call girl to have some fun with. Strange, though. . .Ford's Theater is not the place to go looking for a good time.*

"General Marshall will see you now," Colonel Watts stated as he came out of the chief's office. As John stood up, he could see another officer, a bald-headed brigadier general, just inside Marshall's office. As the aides left the office, Colonel Reynolds turned to the chief and saluted smartly. "Colonel John Reynolds reporting as ordered," he said almost robotically. Marshall returned the salute. "Please, take a seat," he directed.

"Before we move on," he began, "it's important to introduce you to your new boss here at War Plans. You'll be working with Brigadier General Dwight Eisenhower and responsible for putting some meat on this 'Rainbow Two' concept you developed a couple of years ago." John was stunned. *Whoa,* he thought. A concept was one thing, but putting together a plan was something entirely different.

Marshall continued: "Eisenhower is a cracker jack planner as you may have noticed during this past fall's Louisiana War Games, but he'll need your help with the Army's portion of a Pacific Plan. I don't know if you heard Roosevelt yesterday afternoon on the radio, but this is looking like a long war, and everyone wants that Jap Prime Minister Tojo's head on a platter."

Reynolds smiled. Even though a Pacific War would be a Naval Planner's wet dream, he would be able to write the Army's "script" in this larger-than-life, combative, Broadway production. *But was the Army up to it? In 1939, the U.S. Army had only 225,000 soldiers—hell, Yugoslavia had a bigger army than we had and they got whipped by the Krauts in just one month last May,* he thought.

But now, at 1.5 million Army and Air corpsmen and growing, it was not even adequate to execute "Rainbow One," the defense plan for the western hemisphere. So much so that Reynolds had recently read a report that even as late as last September, the War Department reluctantly admitted that only one infantry division, two bomber squadrons, and three fighter groups were even ready for combat. Still, Reynolds could not help but marvel at what Marshall as the Army chief of staff had done in the last two years, even though many other Army officers, far more senior than him, disagreed. Shortly after Marshall became chief of staff, he culled the ranks of officers of the Army's senior leadership, sacking many who were too old or too set in their ways to deal with the way modern warfare had evolved from the static days of the First World War. Those who found themselves unfavorably listed in his little "black book" soon found their careers suddenly stalled. But for Reynolds, Marshall had a mission for him.

"You have your work cut out for you, Reynolds," Marshall snapped as if to wake him out of his trance to write history. "You and Dwight here have until 1300 hours tomorrow to get the concept put together to brief both the boss and the rest of the 'Big Boys.' Have you ever met the president before?" John was again stunned and twice in one day. *So much to do and so little time.*

"No, Sir. Never been given the opportunity." When he heard the term "Big Boys," he surmised that the secretaries for War and Navy would also be present along with Admiral Stark, Chief of Naval Operations and Marshall's counterpart on the Navy staff.

At that time, the phone rang. Marshall looked annoyed as he picked it up. "I thought I told you I didn't want to be disturbed," he quipped at his secretary.

"Sir, it's the Secretary of War, Mr. Henry Stimson."

"OK, patch it through," he said. Reynolds wondered who was really in charge, the Secretary of War or Marshall.

In that constant professional if dull monotone voice, John heard the familiar "Yes, Sir…No, Sir…I didn't know that, Sir…I'll advise the staff immediately." With that, he hung up.

"Well, if you hadn't guessed, that was Secretary Stimson. He just informed me that Mr. Churchill wired the president today and wants to set up a coordination meeting between us and the Brits."

"I'll be damned," said Eisenhower. "Trying to get us to fight the Germans with them when it's the damned Japs that bombed us in the first place."

"Have the Army's 'Rainbow Two' revised concept plan together tomorrow at 1300 at the White House. I've gone ahead and passed on your clearances to the Secret Service. Class A's tomorrow. Any questions?"

Reynolds couldn't resist the temptation to have one last word with the CSA. "Sir, I couldn't help but notice the massive construction project going on just north of National Airport. The cabbie I rode with told me it's a military project. May I ask what's being built?"

With all that was going on, Marshall's ever-present chief of staff scowl quickly blanked, then changed ever so slightly to the faintest of smiles. "Well, why not, you'll find out soon enough. When you walked in, did you notice just how congested this building is?

"Yes, Sir," Reynolds responded. "I didn't want to ask, but I couldn't help wonder how you'll get anything done around here."

"Well, Colonel, what you are seeing being built is the world's largest office building, only it is for the War and Navy departments. When it's finished, it will be called the *Pentagon*. Any more questions, or are the two of you going to stand there for the rest of the afternoon?" Both Eisenhower and Reynolds simultaneously snapped out a crisp salute and chimed, "No, Sir!" Marshall couldn't resist having the last word. "You're both dismissed…and don't be late." Never did the chief's door ever look so good.

Chapter 3

The White House

Fact: On Thursday, December 4, 1941, the *Chicago Tribune* and its sister publication, the *Washington Times Herald,* printed the Army's top-secret "Rainbow Five" war plan. This was the war plan selected by Roosevelt in March 1941 for use in the event that a war broke out. It was top secret and fewer than a dozen copies of the plan were ever produced. Amazing as it may seem, despite an FBI investigation, no one was charged with treason or sedition.

The Presidential Oval Office
The White House, Washington, D.C.
1245 hrs, 10 December 1941

"Twelve Forty-Five, Dwight. We're 15 minutes early," Reynolds quipped as the two of them were lead into the Oval Office by one of the many presidential aides. They already knew that Marshall had arrived, having stopped his official staff car out in the VIP parking area. As they walked through the corridors, they couldn't help but wonder who else of "VIP" stature would also be present at this concept briefing. And, if that wasn't enough, both were exhausted having worked well through the night and early morning preparing to brief the president. When they finished at 0500, Eisenhower invited Reynolds to spend the night at his quarters at Fort Myer, which was considerably closer than his hotel room in Alexandria.

As they were lead into the Oval Office, both were immediately taken by the audience assembled; there were the Secretaries of War and Navy, Henry L. Stimson, and Frank Knox respectfully, the Chief of Naval Operations,

Admiral Harold R. Stark, Chief of Staff of the U.S. Army General George C. Marshall, Commander of the Army Air Corps, General Henry H. "Hap" Arnold, and finally the old navy curmudgeon in the form of Admiral Ernest J. King, a man nobody wanted to cross. Reynolds, Eisenhower, and a couple of aides busily assembled their maps and briefing charts in the short time allotted before the president was to arrive. Usually, Roosevelt was late.

As the two war planners put the finishing touches on their presentation, Marshall strode over, commenting that in spite of this being a mostly naval operation, the U.S. Army would have a major say and part in executing the operation. Eisenhower winked at both Marshall and Reynolds, stating, "Of course we will—ships can't hold land."

"Well, be advised," Marshall responded, "ole' Admiral King over there would just assume to write us out of the plan entirely."

Reynolds couldn't resist the chance to comment. "After all, it's pretty hard to conduct a major strategic bombing campaign against the Japs with just carrier fighter planes." Reynolds knew that land-based "Army" aircraft will have a major if not critical role in bringing the war to the Japanese and avenging Pearl Harbor. He had spent many an hour discussing this with General Hap Arnold and knew he could count on his support for "Rainbow Two" to work.

With that, a side door suddenly opened up with Alonzo Field, the supervisor of the White House staff, announcing in a calm but reassuring voice, "Gentleman, the President." Immediately, the room became silent as twenty senior officers and staff immediately stiffened to attention, standing in the direction of Alonzo's voice.

Before Reynolds's very eyes was Franklin Delano Roosevelt. But this was a different Roosevelt than the one he had seen in the newspapers or on the silver screen newsreels before the movie started. Here was the six-foot-two president with polio being wheeled in, looking more like a sack of potatoes than the leader of the most prosperous country in the world. A far different version than the one crafted for the public. And yet, in spite of his affliction, he came in with his head thrown back, a large, broad smile, as if serving as a fulcrum for his pince-nez eye glasses cocked on his pear-shaped nose, his eyes sparkling with the ever-present, ivory, cigarette holder thrust upward at a jaunty angle. Behind Roosevelt was ever-attentive Harry Hopkins followed by another man whom Reynolds didn't know.

"Please, everyone: take your seats," the president commanded in a whimsical manner, completely at ease in his role as the nation's commander-in-chief. "Gentleman, before we get started, I have three announcements I would like to make. First, the British Prime Minister, Mr. Churchill, desires to meet with me and have both the British and American staffs come up with a plan to coordinate our activities in light of what happened at Pearl Harbor last Sunday."

John couldn't help but hear Admiral King suddenly cough, mocking out the words "bull shit" under his breath. Admiral King was known throughout Washington circles for his adamant Anglophobic thinking. A few years prior while at the Army War College, Reynolds read a paper written in 1932 by then Captain King while at the Naval War College, depicting the Royal Navy as a potential enemy, with a war being fought over trade and naval might. Clearly, King was not the kind of officer to welcome Churchill, much less the British Imperial General Staff to Washington with open arms.

Roosevelt continued. "I need a recommendation as to what to tell Mr. Churchill. Second, I am saddened to pass on the news that two British battleships the *HMS Prince of Wales* and *HMS Repulse* were sunk today off the Malaysian coast near Kuandan by Japanese planes. FDR paused for a moment if not to reflect that he had been on the *Prince of Wales* only last August for his historic first meeting with Winston Churchill.

"What a loss of a magnificent ship," FDR added. He knew this was a major loss for the British in Southeast Asia. "For my last comment, a little good news: I am pleased to announce the appointment of Mr. Jerry Curry to succeed Jay Hill as Harry Hopkins's executive assistant. Jerry comes to us from the great state of Kentucky and brings a wealth of knowledge in construction and heavy industry, two areas I know we are going to need experience in the upcoming months. His credentials are impressive and he brings a great deal of connections with our British cousins to the table," Roosevelt added. Hopkins then chimed in as FDR finished, briefing everyone as to what happened to Jay Hill and that the Washington police still didn't have any suspects.

"I hope you don't have any peccadilloes in your closet," laughed Roosevelt as Jerry sat down.

Reynolds was thinking about his and Eisenhower's upcoming briefing, but his first impression of Curry really threw him. He didn't know what to make of the six-foot, four-inch, slightly balding man. By looking at him, he could simultaneously be your favorite Dutch uncle or the ambassador to Shangri-La. Either way, he sensed that there was a lot more to Curry than met the eye.

With a telltale tilt of his cigarette holder, Roosevelt signaled he wished to begin. "Gentlemen—and I do use that term figuratively—now down to business. We have a problem. As you know, I have worked with our fine, esteemed, British allies on a policy that many of you here present do not agree with, and that in event that should a war break out between the United States and the Axis powers, that the defeat of Germany would be the first priority. I also know that you have spent considerable hours developing many war plans culminating with my selection of one 'Rainbow Five' last May or June. Well, Harry Hopkins recently has informed me that last Thursday, December 4, ole' Colonel McCormick's *Chicago Tribune* and the *Washington Times Herald* printed this war plan on the front page for all its readers, calling it 'FDR's War Plans' and how I plan on getting Hitler!

"Based on General Marshall's advice, I informed him it's back to the drawing board for a new plan. Can't fight a war against the wrong enemy, especially if he knows what your plan is, eh? Besides, with Senator Wheeler and his 'America First' crew, I don't have a chance in Congress of fighting a war against Hitler and his pack of vultures after what the Japs just did to us in the Pacific."

Reynolds was not a bit surprised: both the *Chicago Tribune* the *Washington Times Herald* have both been bitter anti-Roosevelt platforms for years. *But how on earth did ole' McCormick get a copy of our most current war plan? J. Edgar Hoover over at the FBI must be creaming over the chance to investigate this one.*

Roosevelt continued: "With Mr. Churchill and the Brits desiring a conference with us shortly, I need to know if it's worthwhile for him to come over or do we just fight the Japs by ourselves and, if so, what will be our revised strategy? George [referring to General Marshall], what do you say?"

Marshall reflected a sour grin. The Army's chief of staff was a man who hated having his boss refer to him by his first name but, before he could stand, Admiral King beat him to his feet.

"Mr. President," King boomed like one of his twelve-inch battleship cannons, "we don't need the damned British in any way, shape, or form. They have their own damned problems, and we don't need to be bailing them out again like the sucker job they did to us back in '17. We have the whole Jap fleet to take on once we get back on our feet.

"Respectfully, Mr. President, you should tell him: don't call us, we'll call you." Roosevelt was keen enough a politician to immediately sense that this was the consensus view of the assembled audience.

"Remember Pearl Harbor, Mr. President!"

FDR could hear a dozen voices murmur that very saying: "Remember Pearl Harbor!"

"You know, he's right, Mr. President," Marshall finally chimed in once King stepped off his philosophical soap box. "Besides, with the vast majority of the German Wehrmacht stuck in deep Russia, what's the real threat to Britain other than a few lousy U-Boats? From what we hear from the embassy, looks like ole' man winter has them stymied," Marshall quipped.

FDR still appeared disheartened about the news of the unauthorized war plan release. "Who authored that one, George?" Marshall, visually pained, responded, "Mr. President, 'Rainbow Five' was authored by Major Albert C. Wedemeyer."

Roosevelt reacted as if he knew him. "*The Major Wedemeyer* who was the first American Army officer to attend the German War College?"

"Yes, Sir," responded Marshall.

Hopkins, at that moment, asked Marshall how many copies of "Rainbow Five" were available. "Sir, fewer than a dozen were ever printed. I'll have War Plans immediately run down and account for every copy." Simultaneously, both Hopkins and Curry moaned, "astonishing." John was equally stunned as well. He was thinking of being in Marshall's outer office the other day. Despite being a smart staff officer, Wedemeyer was known for his close friends in the America First group and remembered Albert telling him about his recent opportunity to escort Charles Lindberg throughout Germany while functioning as his interpreter.

Some circles heard that Wedemeyer also claimed to be close friends with the German Chief of Staff, General Ludwig Beck, until he was sacked by Hitler in 1938. The guy simply wasn't "Nazi" enough for the Fuehrer. But was Wedemeyer crazy enough to leak out this top-secret document to the press?

Marshall continued. "Mr President, I have asked Brigadier General Eisenhower and Colonel Reynolds both from War Plans Directorate to brief you on an alternative plan that they have worked on along with 'Rainbow Five,' recently named 'Rainbow Two,' which basically is a 'get the Japs first' strategy."

That was Eisenhower's cue to stand. Nearly a split second later, Reynolds was on his feet, too, both officers moving to their briefing positions like they were occupying a defensive position as part of a well-rehearsed battle drill. Eisenhower began.

"Mr. President, secretaries of War, Army, and Navy, General Marshall, Admiral King, esteemed colleagues, gentlemen: good morning. This is a combination informational and decisional briefing pertaining to the defense of the United States and the conduct of offensive operations against Imperial Japan, code named 'Rainbow Two.'

"The first part of this plan basically calls for the defense of the western hemisphere south to the bulge of Brazil, located here at about ten degrees south latitude."

Reynolds instinctively acted as Eisenhower's assistant pointing to a map of the western hemisphere where Brazil juts out into the Middle Atlantic. "Our first and major concern in this war plan, as in 'Rainbow Five,' is the enforcement of the Monroe Doctrine, basically a restatement to any European power, primarily Germany, that the Americas are still hands off and they need to steer clear of this side of the world."

King couldn't resist the urge to chime in adding, "Mr. President, we don't need any Nazis or Brits minding the Panama Canal." Roosevelt nodded in agreement, signaling Eisenhower to continue.

"The basic planning assumption of this war plan is that the United States is working in concert with Great Britain and France, and that the United States will not be providing maximum effort in Europe, but instead to the Far East, where Japan is our greatest threat; Pearl Harbor made that quite evident," Eisenhower stated. Reynolds added, "Sir, the only real change of this plan is the fact that Germany knocked France out of the war early last year."

At this point, Admiral King grinned and slowly rose to his feet to make a statement as if he didn't want the Army briefing team to have all the fun. "Mr. President, what you also must know is that there are a lot present here who quite clearly remember how we got into the last world war and the sucker job we got at the behest of our distinguished 'allies.' This war plan allows us to support the British from a distance, but not to the extent they would like us to." King had that glimmer in his eye, as if he had personally shot down Roosevelt from making any outlandish promises of support.

Roosevelt was clearly annoyed, but waving his cigarette holder, motioned for the briefing to continue. At this time, Reynolds took the lead. "Mr. President, after mobilization of approximately 300,000 soldiers, we will begin the initiative in the South Pacific, staging in either Australia or the Dutch East Indies. The U.S. Navy will move out and seek contact with the Japanese fleet. With Army moving into Indonesia and Borneo, we will cut off the Japanese home islands from oil, while rapidly re-securing ourselves back into the Philippine islands.

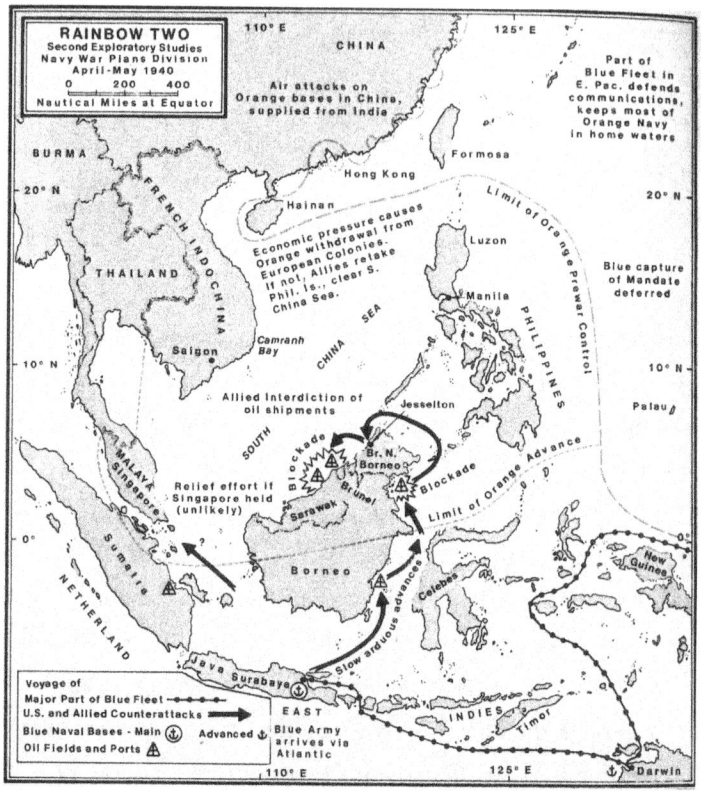

'Rainbow Two' Operational Concept

At this time, Reynolds then drew the assembled audience over to a map that Eisenhower quickly placed on the easel. "Gentlemen, as you can see, once we have secured the Dutch East Indies, we then move to Borneo. From there and the Philippines, we can then cross the South China Sea and begin to conduct operations on mainland China, thus lifting the pressure the Japanese have on the Nationalist."

"How many troops do we have available now to begin this?" Roosevelt inquired. Marshall quickly opened his briefcase, pulled out a file and produced a single sheet of paper. "Mr. President, we have approximately 132,000 soldiers ready to disembark, 20,000 of which are ready to sail to Iceland, and the remainder to Australia and New Caledonia. Of these, we have the Twenty-Fifth Infantry Division in Hawaii on full alert, followed by the Thirty-Fourth Infantry and Twenty-Third Americal Divisions ready to ship out of San Francisco near the end of the month. By March, we expect to have two additional divisions, the Twenty-Seventh National Guard out of New York and the Forty-First National Guard out of Oregon and Washington State."

"What about the Navy?" Roosevelt asked. Ernest King was never a man with a lack of words. Again, he rose up, looked at Roosevelt and, with an air of authority, stated:

"With the British on their own, we transfer the bulk of the Atlantic fleet over for protection of the West Coast. We immediately rebuild the Pacific Fleet out at Pearl, and then we go out, hunt the Japs down, and we kick their ass in, Mr. President."

Admiral Stark, who up to this point opted to remain low profile since the disaster at Pearl Harbor, finally decided to stand up with his fellow sailor.

"Mr. President," Stark chimed in, "in lieu of the disaster in the Pacific, we should be thankful that we didn't sortie the fleet out and met the Japanese head-on. In the mud bottom of Pearl Harbor, we can easily conduct salvage operations and have most if not all those ships raised and repaired within no time, since the Japanese attack didn't touch the dry-dock repair facilities. Out in the middle of the deep Pacific, however, those ships would have been lost for good." At that point, both King and Stark sat down, feeling good their point found home.

Roosevelt felt satisfied and began to lean back in his chair. "Harry, what do you think, and how will Mr. Churchill react to this?"

Both Harry and Jerry looked quickly at one another, and then mutually nodding their heads. Hopkins began to speak. "Mr. President, I believe I can safely say that on one hand, the Chinese leader, Chaing Ki Sheck, will be elated knowing that eventually we will come to his aid, throwing the Japanese out.

"While Mr. Churchill will not be a happy man that we're not joining his fight, it really is the only thing we can do at this time, since we are not on a war footing with the Germans."

Suddenly, Hopkins began coughing; trying to stifle it at first, it grew louder, as if trying to posses him like a demon. Everyone present looked at one another, wondering if he was going to choke. Roosevelt waved to Alonzo: "Alonzo, get Mr. Hopkins a glass of water before he coughs himself to death." Alonzo raced over with a glass handing it to Hopkins, who was still coughing, but not as loudly at this point. Harry downed the water, and then politely excused himself from the meeting, looking pale and shaken. That was Curry's signal to take over, once Hopkins was out of the room.

Jerry Curry then added, "My sources within Germany tell me that Hitler does not want a war with the United States, especially since he's gotten himself into some unfinished business in Russia. My best guess is he'll continue to harass us with his submarines, more or less maintaining the status quo in the Atlantic…especially if he thinks it will keep Lend-Lease equipment from the Brits. But, ultimately, he won't make the go."

"Speaking of the Soviet Union, how is ole' Stalin holding up?" the President asked. General Marshall replied, "From what we hear from Colonel

Truman Smith, my German specialist within Army G-2, and our attaché embassy folks, Stalin's gone over onto the offensive and appears to be throwing the Wehrmacht back from the gates of Moscow, largely because of their supply system and old man winter. We don't know how much of it is true or what actual German losses are, but it appears they have gotten their first bloody nose. If I were a betting man, I'd say you have a replay of Napoleon in Russia all over again. At either rate, he isn't ready to take the United States on at this time."

Reynolds thought to himself, *Well, Truman is back in Washington. What an interesting coincidence, especially in light of the publication of the "Rainbow Five" war plan.* Colonel Truman Smith was the Army's military attaché in Berlin for four years and, at the same time, Wedemeyer was in Germany escorting Lindberg around. If anybody from the American perspective knew the Fuehrer's mind, Truman would. Interesting that he was now serving as Marshall's "German" expert.

Alonzo Field returned to the room having escorted Hopkins out, walked over to the president, and handed him a note. Roosevelt quickly looked at it, appeared startled, and asked Alonzo to call the gentleman back, telling him he will return the senator's call once the meeting was finished. Suddenly, it looked like the president had other things to attend to rather than the war.

"Well, gentlemen," Roosevelt concluded, "We now have a new plan and a war to fight. You all know how I feel about Hitler and that he is the greater menace in the long run, but for the time being, *we must deal with the lesser of the two evils.*"

Chapter 4

Winter Nights

"Naturally the common people don't want war; neither in Russia, nor in England, nor in America, nor in Germany. That is understood. But after all, it is the leaders of the country who determine policy, and it is always a simple matter to drag the people along, whether it is a democracy, or a fascist dictatorship, or a parliament, or a communist dictatorship. Voice or no voice, the people can always be brought to the bidding of the leaders. That is easy. All you have to do is to tell them they are being attacked, and denounce the pacifists for lack of patriotism and exposing the country to danger. It works the same in any country."
— *Reich Fuehrer Herman Goering, 1940*

Fact: On November 30th, 1941, an engineer assault party from the 2nd Panzer Division, pushed to within 18 kilometers of Moscow, viewing the onion shaped Kremlin towers in the distance. This would be the closest the German Wehrmacht would come to the Soviet capital in 1941.

Outside Solnechnogorsh, Russia
2300 hrs, 11 Dec 1941

"Mein Gott, how much colder can it get here" thought Hauptman Eric Lampon, Commander of the 1st Kompanie, 38th Pioneer Battalion, 2nd Panzer Division, XXXXI Panzer Corps as they returned to the warming barn from a day of slow retreating, retreating due to the recent Russian offensive, now a little over one week old. Yesterday, it was -25F with no sign of it getting any warmer. Eric could not believe what had happened to him and his unit much less the mighty Wehrmacht since late November when out of nowhere in the dead of night, Soviet tank and infantry formations were everywhere. How could this be? He along with everyone in his unit thought the Russians were finished — why, when they took the city of Krasnaya Polyana, just 18 kilometers from Moscow, he could see the spires of the Kremlin from his forward command post just a fortnight ago. But in thinking back, it seemed kind of strange that for every Russian unit they smashed, another two seemed to take their place. The curse of Napoleon he thought...

Once his unit was secure within the barn and the sentries were posted, he looked up into the clear sky and marveled at how bright the stars shown. This was the first time he noticed the night sky in some time — the last few days of overcast brought more snow than he had seen in the last couple of years in southern Germany. But tonight — the night was clear and beautiful — not even the occasional red flares the Russians used in a clumsy attempt to signal a counterattack. In the distance, he could hear the faint thump-thump of a heavy mortar unit firing. "Ours or their's" he wondered out loud? Lampon quickly entered the barn and headed straight to the fire to warm his hands. In the corner, Leutnant Hans Menter, the Infantry Kompanie Commander assigned to protect Hauptman Lampon's Engineers was checking the latest communiqué from the Regimental Headquarters, pondering how far Regiment will have them   retreat the next day.

"Hey Eric," Menter shouted, "Der Furher is giving another Reichstag speech in a few minutes — maybe he'll declare victory in Russia and have us return home." In peace time, that comment could have meant a visit from the local Gestapo official, but here in Russia after six months of fighting — nobody really cared at this time. Lampon grabbed a cup of coffee from an orderly and sat down. He was utterly exhausted and cold. The only thing he wanted to hear was that maybe there was an end to this madness...

The static of the radio was loud. "Can't you make it come in clearer?" some on in the back yelled.

"Why" Feldwebel Kopas chimed in? "What's "Der Furher" going to say to make the Russians go away?"

"Quiet" Menter snapped, "Let's hear what he's got to say."

Over the radio, the soldiers could hear the all too familiar chorus of applause and the voice of Herman Goering announcing the leader of the German people – Adolph Hitler. Hitler, confident and full of his usual vigor, spoke glowingly to an audience of thousands in Berlin of the victories the mighty Wehrmacht had achieved in the past year over the British in North Africa, the Greeks & Yugoslavs and in its conquest of the Soviet Union.

"Humm" Kopas commented, "Someone should ask him if we've won, why we are retreating?"

"Sheessh" came from a soldier in the back. Der Fuehrer droned on and on, to the point where the assembled soldier audience began to nod off, after all while it was 2100 hrs in Berlin, it was nearly 2 hours later approaching midnight, Moscow time. Hitler then started to talk about "that person with his fireside chats" and everyone within the room knew he was referring to the talk about the American President Franklin Delano Roosevelt. The various soldiers huddled closer around the radio and fire started to look at one another. What's America got to do with the war they mumbled? Der Furher continued on...

"Deutches Volk,...Germany and Italy will morally support Japan's waging of the common war forced upon her by the U.S.A. and England with all the means of power at her disposal, to a victorious conclusion. Germany has always sought to have peace with America and at this time will make herself available as an arbitrator should President Roosevelt seek to end his conflict with the Japanese Empire. Our enemies must not deceive themselves-in the 2,000 years of German history known to us; our people have never been more united than today. The Lord of the Universe has treated us so well in the past years that we bow in gratitude to a providence which has allowed us to be members of such a great nation. We thank Him that we also can be entered with honor into the ever-lasting book of German history"!

The men were shocked – Japan and America were at war? Rumors had been running rampantly at Regimental Headquarters about a massive attack in the Pacific. Was it Hawaii, the Philippines, Timbukto? Concurrently, the men of the 1st Companie were also relieved. "Did he say what we thought he said?" they all wondered.

"Now that's the first thing ol Schkelgruber's said in recent memory that makes sense" Kopas commented.

"It's bad enough we have the Russians and the English as our enemies, thank God he has the sense not to take on the Americans on as well!" Leutnant Menter stammered.

Hauptman Lampon just sat there and stared into his coffee thinking to himself "If we were to take on the Americans as well, will God have mercy on us ..."

Lampon's commiseration was short lived. Outside, the noise of German command staff cars known as "Kubelwagons" stopped outside the hut. A tall but worn Wehrmacht Panzer officer in his traditional black panzer garb climbed out of his vehicle, straightened his tunic, and once he had put his gloves on, strode over to the hut as if he was on parade in Berlin. With him, two aides followed exactly two steps behind. Eric knew this wasn't room service from regimental headquarters.

"Who's in command here?" the officer bellowed. "I am" Lampon replied, slowly standing to attention. As the rank of the black dressed officer became apparent to all the soldiers within the room, they too stood at attention, but more quickly. "Hauptman Eric Lampon, Commander, 1st Kompanie, 38th Pioneer Battalion at your service, sir. And who might I be addressing?"

The tall officer looked around the room at the various soldiers present, took off his cap. "Hauptman, have you men stand at ease. I am Oberst Johann Bernatz, newly assigned commander of the 3rd Panzer Regiment, 2nd Panzer Division. We just happened to be in this area when we saw some light coming from this, how do you say it, haven from the cold". Only 4 months prior, Bernatz and the Division were sunning themselves in warm Southern France, refitting from their Balkans adventure. Lampon quickly motioned his men to stand at ease and asked Bernatz if he and his men would like to bunk down at his humble hut for the evening. Deep down, the thought of having a Colonel spending the evening was not on the top of his list of pleasurable events, but better not to make an enemy of him. One day, he thought, I might have to provide engineer support to his regiment and where the panzers were, so was trouble. "How would you and your men like some coffee?" the Hauptman asked. "It's not exactly Berlin's finest, but in this, anything warm inside you will get you though the night". Eric's comments were interrupted by the dull thud of an artillery round exploding nearby. Hearing the constant sounds of artillery or mortar rounds had become so common place on the Eastern Front that you soon ignore it, except when the sound and immediate concussion begins to shake your personal items off your shelf.

Oberst Johann Bernatz

"Ya, danke, three cups will do nicely Hauptman" Bernatz responded. Eric motioned for Kopas to grab three cups of coffee for their esteemed guests.

"So, what brings you to our little slice of heaven?" Lampon asked. "I am en-route to take command of the 3rd Panzer Regiment from Oberst Fritz von Boxberg who was recently killed in a Russian counter attack. Currently, 2nd Panzer Division is holding its position, but I had no idea it was that bad down here. I was coming down from Corps Headquarters and seemed to have lost my way" Bernatz responded. "Leutnant Menter" Lampon whirled around "weren't you just at the panzer regiment headquarters a couple of days ago?"

"Ya-voll" Menter quipped. "They were just 5 kilometers down the road, set up within the town of Krasnaja Poljana, but with all the Ruskies in the area, I think they've un-assed the area and are heading to the town of Radomia"

"Map!" Bernatz barked to one of his aids who quickly scampered to the kubelwagon, returning within a moments notice. As the map open up on the table, Leutnant Menter pointed to Krasnaja Poljana, then up the road 15 km to Radomia.

"Mein Gott" Bernatz mumbled, the Ruskies are certainly on the move. "My compliments on your hospitality Herr Hauptman, but we must be on our way. Gentleman – Heil Hitler" and with that, Bernatz and his crew spun around and departed to his vehicle. Most of Lampon's men just gave a short half wave – too tired to care, nearly asleep, but very grateful their house guest had other plans. Only after Bernatz's kubelwagon cranked on and moved out did they finally settle down to relax, thinking what horrors would await them this new day.

"At least we won't have the horror of 1918 in facing the Americans again" Lampon thought as he drifted off.

Men of 1st Kompanie, 38th Pioneer Battalion

While Lampon and the troops of 38th Pioneer Companie gave short thanks that maybe Hitler was coming to his senses in finally not declaring war on someone, a continent away on December 12th 1941, Winston Churchill, the English Prime Minister, sensed that this day was going to be more depressing than at any time since the war started back in 1939. He was beginning to realize that the great plans President Roosevelt and he had laid down last August off the coast of Newfoundland in the form of the Atlantic Charter reiterating the March 41 American-British Conversations or "ABC-1" staff recommendation of a Europe-first strategy may not happen. On December 8th, the United States Congress, on Roosevelt's behest, declared war on Japan - Germany unfortunately for Great Britain, was never mentioned. America's focus will be solely against the Japanese and with a thirst for revenge for their dastardly surprise attack. In a spirit of comradeship, Britain also declared war against the Japanese on Dec 9th, but Churchill's elation that America might join his war against Hitler and the despicable Nazi's became more remote with each passing day. Today, he felt sullen – he still had not heard from Roosevelt since cabling him a couple of days prior on his proposal for a meeting on the current situation the two of them faced, tentatively codenamed "ARCADIA", named after the Greek character Arcas who was the son of the great god Zeus and Callisto (the goddess of the Great Bear, known as Ursa Major).

A knock at the Prime Minister's door suddenly brought him to the reality of the day.

"Com-inn" ol Winne growled. It was the First Sea Lord of the Admiralty - Admiral Dudley Pound. He looked grim and Churchill knew from his facial expression it wasn't good news. "Com-in Admiral and tell me what news you have from Admiralty."

"Mister Prime Minister, I regret to inform you that late this morning off the coast Kuandan, Malaya, the HMS *Prince of Wales* and HMS *Repulse* were attacked by a strong force of Japanese high-level bombers and torpedo planes from the 22nd Air Flotilla based out of Saigon in French Indochina. Both heavy ships were hit several times. *Repulse* sank at about 1230 hrs. *Prince of Wales* capsized and followed her to the bottom less than an hour later."

Churchill was stunned and visibly shaken. The very ship he and Roosevelt met on and concluded the Atlantic Charter on August 12th was gone and as a bit of irony – so was any America's entry into the war against the German's. "How did this happen?" he asked half disbelieving.

Pound reached into his pocket with one hand to pull out his reading glasses and with his other hand, pulled out the message he just received from the Fleet HQ's in Singapore. "Apparently the *Prince of Wales's* surface scanning radar was inoperable, denying the fleet with one of its most potent early-warning devices. Once the Japanese torpedo planes found her, the *Prince of Wales* was disabled by a lucky torpedo hit where the propeller shaft entered the hull, which caused severe flooding, rendered the rudder useless, and cut the power to her 5.25 inch DP guns. Two further torpedo hits struck her weakest section, the area damaged by the German bombing in 1940 and never completely repaired. Altogether, she suffered 6 torpedo and 1 bomb hits. I believe several hundred men were killed when the ship sank with Vice-Admiral Phillips and her skipper Captain Leach being among those lost when they chose to go down with their ship. However, the stronger hull of the *Prince of Wales* enabled much of the crew to be saved, in stark contrast to the older *Repulse* which suffered a heavy loss of life."

"And where were our aircraft?" Churchill quipped. Pound folded up the message, removed his glasses, and once he put everything back into his pocket's replied, "No where to be found?" Historical ironies came be bittersweet Churchill thought. "Today, we just witnessed the loss of two majestic ships of his majesty's fleet on the high seas solely from airpower, a feat we've never seen before. What more will this war offer ….?"

Pound quietly turned around and left the Prime Minister to his thoughts.

Poster commemoration the attack, 1942

Chapter 5

A Presidential Quandary

Fact: Aluminum is the all-essential metal required for aircraft production. In the United States, aluminum production was controlled by a virtual monopoly held by the Aluminum Company of America (ALCOA). Not only did ALCOA own almost all of the plants that produced this metal, but it also controlled most of the high-grade bauxite ore, ensuring a cost fixing on production. In addition to owning production and ore, aluminum production requires massive amounts of electric power and Alcoa controlled much of the hydropower required. In the early 1940s, as America prepared for war, there was only one aluminum refiner: ALCOA.

The Presidential Oval Office
The White House, Washington, D.C.
1600 hrs, 10 December 1941

The strategy staff meeting had broken up with only a few civilian and aides still present. Jerry Curry decided it was time to retire for the day and catch up with Harry Hopkins, see how he was doing, and fill him in on what he had missed. "Jerry," the president quipped, "don't leave just yet. We still have things to talk about, and I'd like to get to know ya' better."

Jerry immediately wheeled around and stood directly in front of the great man's desk. "Please, Mr. Curry, have a seat." Jerry grabbed the first chair available, the one held by Admiral Stark during the "Rainbow Two" war plans meeting.

"We need to talk about two things: first, you have a great deal of knowledge and connections about production. You know, with a war on, we need to have someone who can advise me as to how we can synchronize our war production. Harry has been very usefully to me for the last few years in this regard, but your background is most impressive. My interior secretary, Harold Ickes, speaks very highly of you in addition to Harry, and I want to welcome you to the team with open arms. And, as with Ickes, it isn't too often I can find a Republican who's willing to work with an ole' New Deal Democratic such as myself." Jerry knew he was dealing with a first-class politician, perhaps the wiliest within the country.

"Well, Mr. President, I'll do what ever I can within my power."

Roosevelt continued. "I am most impressed as to how you an Ickes handled that ALCOA aluminum problem last year. You know, I don't need war profiteers dictating to me how and when they'll produce aluminum so we can build up our Air Corps. I haven't pressed Ickes about it, but give me the background on that situation and how you resolved it."

Jerry sat back relaxed and crossed his leg. "Well, Mr. President, as you know, there is considerable resistance in Corporate America to a number of your programs. A great deal of these corporations are headed by Republicans who in their opinion see you as doing anything to get America into a European war. Last year, Ford Motor Company rejected a contract by the British to build Rolls Royce engines for the Royal Air Force. But that was nothing compared to the virtual monopoly the Aluminum Company of America had on the production of aluminum in the States."

"Virtual monopoly?" Roosevelt suddenly sat up and took notice. "Ickes never told me that. What on earth do you mean?"

Curry leaned forward; he was somewhat surprised Roosevelt didn't know the extent of ALCOA's hold on the defense industry much less the American public. "You see, ALCOA owns not only all the plants that produce aluminum, but it also controls most of the high-grade ore from which it derives—an ore called 'bauxite.' Now, to produce aluminum, you need tremendous amounts of electric power. And who is the largest land owner and hydroelectric power plant generator along the Saint Lawrence Seaway on both sides? Our friend, Andrew Mellon."

Roosevelt slowly leaned back uttering "My God!" Curry continued. "Mellon not only controlled the production of aluminum through ALCOA, but he also sought to prevent all others from entering production through his cronies in the Office of Production and Management (OPM).

"You remember E. R. Stettinius, chairman of the board of U.S. Steel, who headed the OPM and was in charge of the Industrial Materials Section. Once a month, Stettinius issued his glowing reports, assuring that an adequate supply of raw materials was available. Many of the materials such as antimony, manganese, mercury, tungsten, nickel, chromium, and tin came from South Pacific islands and Malaysia and would be vulnerable to a supply cutoff. Nor were the stocks on hand adequate for a two-year supply, as purchasing of the materials didn't begin until 1940.

"Last May, the truth of these shortages was brought to light in a report from the Metals Reserve Corporation. The report detailed the amount purchased, the amount in transit and the amount delivered. In the case of mica, the report showed a purchase of 500 tons from India but, as of the date of the report, none had been shipped.

"In the case of zinc, a vital material in producing brass cartridges, the report was dismal. The only amount ordered was from Newfoundland for 50,000 tons (less than a month's supply). Zinc was being consumed at 70,000 tons per month (7,000 tons more than domestic production). To make 1,000 rounds of .30-caliber shells would consume sixteen pounds of zinc; for 75-mm shells, 1,000 rounds would consume 3,800 pounds of zinc. But perhaps the best example of how Stettinius and Mellon tried to hinder our preparation for the war effort is aluminum. Up 'till early this year, there was only one aluminum refiner: ALCOA. To date, ALCOA produced a maximum of 642 million pounds of aluminum in one year. But, Mr. President, the plan you worked out with General Marshall to expand the Army Air

Corps plan to produce bombers, this nation will require 1.6 billion pounds a year." Jerry was in his moment with Roosevelt transfixed, utterly trying to absorb Curry's statistics.

"So, how did Secretary Ickes and you circumvent the mighty ALCOA?" Roosevelt queried.

"Well, Sir, I knew of a small startup company named Reynolds Aluminum. Reynolds was a small manufacturer of aluminum products and has never cast a single ingot of virgin aluminum. Since ALCOA tried to create a shortage in aluminum, Reynolds agreed to mortgage all of his property to start refining in his own plants if we, the government, would lend him the money. Secretary Ickes checked with the Reconstruction Finance Corporation (RFC), who in turn approved Reynolds Aluminum's loan within thirty days for $20 million. Immediately thereafter, Reynolds soon had a plant at Lister, Alabama, which produced nearly 40 million pounds and shortly had another plant in Longview, Washington, producing 60 million pounds. We thought for sure we had beat Mellon, but things oftentimes don't work out quite so nice."

Roosevelt had the look of a Naval Academy football coach who knew they were winning the game in late fourth quarter, landing the ball on the Army five yard line, and then suddenly losing it. "What do you mean by that?"

"Out of the blue, we found out that considerable pressure was brought against Reynolds Aluminum's loan application. W. Averill Harriman and a delegation of war department officials pressured both Secretary Ickes and I to deny Reynolds an allocation of electrical power from Bonneville. Stettinius and his consultant, Grenville Holden, stepped in to oppose Reynolds's entry into the refining of aluminum vigorously behind the scenes.

"Although Reynolds persevered, despite the objections and backroom dealings of Stettinius and Holden with the help of Secretary Ickes, others failed. To protect his buddy Mellon and ALCOA, Stettinius and Holden blocked others from producing aluminum and from using new methods.

"Last March, the Bohn Aluminum Company sought a loan to produce aluminum and was denied by Holden. Although OPM had been ladling out millions of dollars to help businesses expand for the war effort, we found that Holden replied to Bohn Aluminum stating that '...the Army is not disposed to finance expansion of industrial capacity with government funds as long as any company is prepared to expand with private funds.'

"Incredibly, Mr. President, Holden was uninterested in expanding aluminum production even when a private company from Switzerland sought to enter the market. Holden also opposed the use of low-grade ore in an effort to protect ALCOA, while allowing ALCOA to maintain control of all the high-grade ore. We expect with such an increased demand for aluminum production for Army Air Corps aircraft that all the North American high-grade ore will be exhausted by 1943.

"Finally, going back to where we started this conversation with ALCOA, through my connections in Europe, we found out that the president of ALCOA, ole' Andrew Mellon, signed a cartel agreement with some German interests back in the late 1920s. But the bottom line, at least in the case of Reynolds Aluminum, is that with RFC's help, we won one, but there is a lot of resistance to you within Corporate America, many of which have hidden Nazi connections and are not at all supportive of a 'Europe first' war effort as discussed during last March's ABC-I meetings.

"Let me put it another way: its not that Corporate America is against a war. They are just not against the Germans and are at the risk of their losing tremendous investments. Quite frankly, Mr. President, I think with the mood the American people are in with the Japanese due to Pearl Harbor, you couldn't sell them on a war with Nazi Germany and have Corporate America support it to boot."

"You have a point, Jerry and, as you may have noticed, the chiefs and the secretaries of War and Navy were silent on the subject of my meeting Mr. Churchill," FDR commented. "Should I meet with the exulted British Prime Minister?"

Jerry shifted uncomfortably within his seat. This is the kind of question that requires a Harry Hopkins who "knows how FDR has thought for the last twenty years" type of answer. He felt flattered, yet unsure where it was his place to offer a strategic-level-of-thought answer.

Curry cleared his throat, buying time to think of what to say. "Well, Sir, here's how it looks to me. If you meet with Churchill, you might give the impression to both the British and the American people we are going to execute the very plan that was recently published in the *Chicago Tribune*, lending credence to the suspicion that maybe what McCormick wrote was true. That will be devastating to your administration, not to say your very credibility. I don't think many, if any, Americans are aware of what deal was cut with the British during last March's American-British Coordination conference or when the two of you met last August off Newfoundland. On the other hand, what kind of message are you sending to the British if we are to politely but firmly decline meeting until another time?"

"What are you saying Curry...no Churchill and no aid to the British?"

Curry continued. "Maybe not at this time, but if a small, discrete, British staff delegation was to come over and meet with the chiefs and the secretaries, maybe a common policy toward Japanese actions in the Pacific can be hammered out, or at least leaked to the press as a cover. But to meet to plan a general war against Germany, especially in light of Pearl Harbor...well, if that was to get out, especially to the Senate Foreign Relations committee... well, it could possibly be an impeachment of you and a fond farewell. You have a lot of enemies over there. But please remember, Mr. President, this is strictly my opinion."

Roosevelt by this time had a sour grin on his face; he stopped and took note. Once his cigarette holder was in the "up" position, like a flag pole being erected, Jerry knew Roosevelt was somewhat deflated, but ready to continue.

"I see, Mr. Curry. Which brings me to my next point of discussion. In listening to you, I am also very impressed with your connections within Europe in general and specifically Nazi Germany. I heard you've met with some key figures such as their Air Force Chief Herman Goering and Labor Minister Fritz Todt. Are the Nazis that good with their production?"

Jerry suddenly felt odd. *Who on earth told the President about these meetings?* "Mr. President, I believe I can safely say that Goering is a rather comic figure within the Reich today, both to us and the Germans, especially after blowing the Battle of Britain last summer. I believe the common joke I heard was Goering telling the Fuehrer if one bomb was to fall on Berlin, you could call him Meyer, but once the Royal Air Force did that, the first person who did was shot."

Roosevelt revealed a grin to replace his earlier grim smile. Jerry continues. "But Herr Todt bears watching. I don't know if you've been informed, but in 1938 with Hitler's blessing, he founded the Organization Todt (OT), which joined together government firms, private companies and the Reich Labor Service, all without having to worry about labor or strikes. This organization is largely responsible for the construction of the "West Wall" Germany's answer to France's "Maginot Line," a wall someone is going to have to face one day. Yet at this time, with what's is going on in Europe, especially with the debacle on the Eastern Front, my sources tell me the Germans as yet still have not gotten a total war footing."

"Your sources?" FDR queried. "Who might they be? Anybody in particular?"

"Mr. President, I've met so many people over in Germany: some pro-Nazi, but many others either neutral "fence sitters" or even anti-Nazi. The Russian Campaign will not endear him with the Germans if it continues to go bad."

"What are you saying?" Roosevelt wondered. "Do you think they would overthrow Hitler given the right circumstances?"

Curry responded. "On my visit last summer, I briefly met the former German Chief of the General Staff, General Ludwig Beck. A most charming and intelligent man and one who is still bitter toward Hitler. He resigned in disgust when Hitler took his army into the Sudetenland of Czechoslovakia three years ago. He introduced me to a close friend of his, a contact known as "Iceman," who I was led to believe is connected to an underground anti-Nazi resistance. Don't know how strong, or how organized, but a resistance nevertheless that includes businessmen, university intellectuals, disgruntled Wehrmacht officers, and others who strongly disagree with what the Nazis are all about. I got the impression this chap had quite a few connections all across Europe."

Roosevelt again asked the question more pressingly, "But, Curry, do you think the Germans would overthrow Hitler?"

Jerry looked down, shook his head, and said, "with what he's done to date from occupying the Rhineland, overthrowing that ridiculous Versailles Treaty, to defeating the French last year, unless something catastrophic happens, I don't thing so. It's just not in their blood".

"Humm, the Versailles Treaty,[4]" Roosevelt commented. "It not only humbled the Germans, it damned near destroyed the Democratic Party here in the U.S. in 1920. That was the first time I can ever remember where we lost not the presidency to Harding, but the whole Congress went overwhelmingly to the Republicans. Did you ever think the Irish in Boston would ever vote Republican?"

---

4   The formal document approved and signed in late 1919 called for the creation of numerous countries out of the former German, Austro-Hungarian, and the Ottoman Empires, but did not apply to the British in regard to Ireland or India. President Wilson lobbied for the U.S. Senate to approve and join the Treaty's "League of Nations," but he was overwhelmingly rejected. Wilson soon suffered a stroke and died shortly thereafter.

Curry remembered during the heady days of late 1919 and early 1920 when then President Wilson drove himself to a heart attack campaigning for support of a treaty so flawed as to be a joke. It was a treaty where the many polyglot nationalities from the former Austro-Hungarian and German empires were given their own independence, but when it came to the question of independence of Ireland, the British ever so coolly took it off the table. Not a subject to bring up at Finnigan's Pub in Boston. It was not only ironic it went down in flames with the Senate, but also swept the Republicans into power for the first time since the end of the Civil War, fifty-five years prior.

Roosevelt continued. "Had it not been for Hoover's incredible bungling at the start of the Great Depression, they'd still be in power. I still have to deal with a Republican-dominated Senate Foreign Affairs Committee dominated by that damn fascist from Montana," referring to Senator Burton K. Wheeler,[5] whose acerbic attitude toward the Roosevelt administration's foreign policy made for a living hell, especially last January when he personally debated on the Senate floor the poor merits of Roosevelt's Lend-Lease policy toward the British.

"Every time Secretary of State Cordell Hull or his assistant, Sumner Wells, have to testify to that committee, especially when it comes toward Europe, he makes us all look like fools. And if it isn't Wheeler, then it's his colleague, Gerald Nye from North Dakota."

"Is this the same Nye who stood on the Senate floor last January and made the ridiculous charge that it was not German submarines that were torpedoing American ships off the Atlantic coast in order to get us into war?" Curry inquired.

Roosevelt leaned back in his chair and grinned. "Yes, it's the same man. North Dakota deserves what they elected. Eventually, he recanted, but he can

---

5   In Sept 1940 Senator Burton Wheeler helped Charles Lindberg and Norman Thomas to create the "America First" committee, soon the largest and most powerful isolationist group (approximately 800,000 members) campaigning for the US to stay out of European affairs.

always be counted upon along with Wheeler to take pot shots at our foreign policy."

"From what the American people hear from these closet fascists, it's no small wonder they don't want to get involved in another 'screw' job from the Allies, like we did in the First World War. Why, Jerry, did you know the Service Training and Selection Act passed last September by only one vote, 203 to 202 in the House of Representatives?

"In the Senate chamber, I heard there were all sorts of women dressed in black veils and dresses, weeping and wailing about extending the draft. I'll bet you a dollar he had something to do with the leaking of the 'Rainbow Five' war plan to his buddy McComick at the *Tribune*."

FDR's face winched as if he had either eaten a rotten egg or had an incredible pain in his ass. At any rate, it was apparent he did not have a fond relationship or positive opinion of the two senators who were making his life and presidency ever more difficult.

"Well, Jerry, enough digressing. It is what it is. Since it is apparent the American people or Congress will clearly not support a war against the Nazis at this time with what the Japanese have just done in Pearl Harbor, I have no choice but to 'back burner' Germany. And, in conjunction Mr. Churchill, until such as time where the situation is more in our favor. For now, with Harry laid up, there are two things I would like you to do for me."

At that point, Jerry sat up and began to take mental notes.

"First, I want you to quietly get over to State and the War Department and have the secretaries cable White Hall and Churchill to send a small delegation for the purpose we just talked about. I don't need the publicity from the press to upset the Germans, much less our fascist senators. I'll call Churchill and send him my regrets that we can't meet at this time.

"Secondly, and most important, last August, I created the Office of Coordinator of Information, or *COI*, and made William Donovan its chief. You've probably heard of "Wild Bill" for the exotic exploits he's done in the past decade. Since he's a Republican like you, you two might have something in common. His duties as the coordinator are to collect and analyze all information and data, which bears upon the security of this nation, screen it, and then present it to me and those departments to which I see fit to receive it. For the COI to work, I need you to keep your German contacts open—I need all the information you have on what's going on in Germany.

"Since we still have diplomatic relations with them and the Vichy French, it shouldn't be too much a problem getting in. I want you to work with Bill and Harry on this, keep us all informed, and come back to me with any comments and suggestions. I'll have Harry set up an appointment for you to meet with General Donovan."

It suddenly dawned on Jerry it was dark outside the White House, much darker than normal due to the current wartime blackout conditions. With the exception of a couple of lamps turned on during the afternoon war plans briefing, the Oval Office was largely cascaded in shadow. Jerry's thoughts were suddenly interrupted by a knock at the door.

"Come in," FDR said in his commander-in-chief voice. Alonzo Field meekly entered the room. "Mr. President, Mr. Hopkins has recovered from his attack and wishes to know if you have anything for him before he retires upstairs for the evening."

"Of course. Have him come in." Hopkins entered, flushed and pale with the ever-present cigarette in his hand, taking a seat next to Curry on his left.

"You gave us quite a scare Harry. Are you all right?" Alonzo followed behind Hopkins and began turning on additional lights within the Oval Office. When he was done, FDR thanked him and let him know he may go. Once the door was closed, Roosevelt spoke.

"Yes, Franklin," Hopkins coughed. "These things come and go, but I'm all right." Curry was surprised and shocked that Hopkins called the mightiest man in America by his first name. But, then again, Harry was FDR's closest if not most trusted advisor since his halcyon days as governor of New York.

"Well, Harry, Jerry and I have had a most delightful discussion and I'm sure he will fill you in later on. I think you've picked an excellent man—certainly a step up from the last one, a Mr. Hill was it? I have to tell ya, I never really trusted him. What on earth was he doing at Ford's Theater that late at night? Have the police found anything yet?"

"I haven't heard anything, Sir, from the District police investigating the scene but, if I do, I'll let you know. We have some friends on the force that will keep this hush-hush and out of the press as much as possible," Harry said, his voice improving but still scratchy.

"Harry, I want you to set Mr. Curry up for a short meeting with General William Donovan over at COI. I believe Jerry has the right connections within Germany that Donovan is looking for. I may not be able to fight the Nazi's directly, but we can sure hit them behind the scenes. No one senator is going to stop me from fighting Hitler..."

Suddenly, Roosevelt caught himself mid-sentence and the Oval Office became silent.

"He called again, didn't he?" Hopkins queried. Roosevelt by this time was pale, but wasn't going to let it spoil the mood. "He did, but I didn't talk with him. I believe he'll call later on to see if I got the message. I'll discuss this later with you, Harry. I don't want to keep Mr. Curry any longer than possible."

Hopkins responded. "We have our folks looking into it at this very moment. Hopefully, they'll turn up very soon." *What is going on?* Curry thought to himself. What on earth are they discussing involving his predecessor, Jay Hill? Police cover-ups?

With FDR finally looking relaxed and smiling, reassured that Hopkins was back on the team, Jerry dismissed for the time being what he had just heard, sat back, and smiled.

"Do you see the global irony of all this, Mr. President? We are now at war with the Japanese who are treaty bound with the Germans through the Tripartite Pact,[6] the Germans, who are not at war with us and still have diplomatic relations with the United States. The Russians are fighting for their lives against the Germans, but are at peace with the Japanese, who are sitting out the Eastern Front calamity just when the Germans need them the most. And stuck in the middle are the British, fighting the Germans, the Japanese, and the Italians, if you're to count them, too. No wonder they need our help in the worse way. So much for *Pax Britannica*."

With that, FDR wheeled out from behind his desk toward the Oval Office bar and tucked to the left and behind Curry. "I think its time for a couple of my special dirty Martinis, boys! What do you say?"

"Make it a double, Mr. President," Jerry quipped. "I think I'm going to need it." He had his marching orders.

---

6   Japan formally joined the Pact on 27 September 1940

Chapter 6

A German Problem & British Dilemma

"The little affair of operational command is something anybody can do..."
—*Adolph Hitler, Dec 1941*

Fact: Contrary to the popular belief about the Wehrmacht's first winter campaign in Russia, Hitler did not forbid the issuing of winter clothing. Due to the limited rail capacity of lines going into occupied Russia, winter clothing was issued a lower priority than fuel or ammunition, leaving much of this clothing stockpiled in depots in Poland awaiting transport.

Outside The Reich Chancellery
Berlin, Germany
0900 hrs, 12 December 1941

A light snow had fallen on the German capital overnight, enough to give a pure clean, almost surreal vision of a city at war. To a visitor in Berlin, the city had an almost festive mood. Christmas was just less than two weeks away; the festivities were interrupted by the occasional drone of Luftwaffe aircraft taking off from nearby Templehof Airfield. Germans civilians and military personnel made their way through the busy streets giving the casual observer the appearance that the war in the east was a long way off and would soon be over. What a Christmas present that would be to many German folk to have their husbands and sons home. Home to finally enjoy the peace Hitler had spoken about. To many, the horror of recent events they heard going on deep in Russia were rumors—chatter of British propaganda some folks had heard listening illegally to the British Broadcasting Company or "BBC."

Traveling east along Leipziger Straße, a large black Mercedes Benz displaying the banner of a high general officer was making its way briskly toward the center of Berlin. Inside Major Pierre Massar was preparing Field Marshal Wilhelm Keitel, Chief of the Oberkommando der Wehrmacht or "OKW," for the morning situation staff briefing with the Fuehrer at the Reich Chancellery. Working long throughout the night down at OKW headquarters in Zossen, Massar had collected the situation reports from various Army commands, paying particular care to those units operating on the Eastern Front, consolidating them into short situation briefs for his boss to use in briefing Hitler. Throughout the thirty-minute drive from his quarters, Keitel would quickly review these reports, make comments in the margins, and then hand them back to Massar who would secure them within his ever-present brown leather staff officer briefcase.

"Shit," Keitel repeatedly said. "Things are going from bad to worse in the east. One week ago we were at the Gates of Moscow, then suddenly... shit!" Massar, exhausted from the night's activity could only muster a modest "*Ja-wohl, Herr Feld Marshal.*" Keitel decided to change the topic of the war in the east; it would be too depressing discussing it with Hitler much less in the staff car with his aide-de-camp.

"How is your mother doing these days, Pierre? Do you see her much?" Keitel asked.

"I was hoping to take some Christmas leave and visit her in Gottingen, but I think, with the present situation in Russia, I didn't think you could let me go," Massar responded.

"Ah, Gottingen. I can tell you some stories about your father and me during our Academy days there and all the trouble two students can get into. Your father was really a clever man. We joined the ole' Sixth Lower-Saxony Field Artillery Regiment together on a whim. One of these days, remind me to tell you of the day we raided a farmhouse in Flanders looking for chickens for the Forty-Sixth Field Artillery Regiment. French women can get very nasty when you take their chickens from them." The Field Marshal smirked. Massar noted it was the first time he saw the field marshal smile in the last two weeks. "I do miss the old man; he would have made an excellent regimental commander had he survived the war."

Pierre thought for a second bringing up the memory of his father. The last time he saw his father, Lieutenant Gunther Massar, he was a young boy of eleven, waving goodbye as his unit marched off for France in August 1914.

"Do you miss combat?" Keitel said, breaking the silent reflections Pierre was experiencing.

"Herr Feld Marshal, there are some things I miss, like the excitement of being with my Panzer regiment in action in France, moving twenty to thirty kilometers a day and seeing the English Channel at Abbeville. In Yugoslavia, it was pretty much the same thing: move, attack, and then move again. They really didn't put up much of a fight. As the Ib Quartermeister Staff Officer, I had my hands full coordinating supply for this regiment. Life, if anything, is not boring. There's nothing like it".

"Weren't you with the Third Panzer Regiment, Second Panzer Division?" Keitel asked.

"*Ja-wohl, Herr Feld Marshal*; are you familiar with it?"

Keitel paused for a moment. "I knew your old commander, Oberst Fritz von Boxberg. A true professional soldier. A hero. I'm sorry to tell you that he was recently killed in action near Krasnaja Poljana a few days ago."

Massar was quietly stunned. Boxberg had selected him for his regimental staff assignment during the winter of 1939 and the two of them became close, even exchanging letters once Massar left the regiment that past summer while it was in Poland conducting rest and refitting from the recent Balkan Campaign. Shortly thereafter, Boxberg wrote him that the Third Regiment had moved to southwestern France, teasing Massar about how hard it was guarding the French Boudreaux fields and all the wine he was missing. He hadn't heard from Oberst Boxberg since the Regiment's transfer to the east front last October, understandably since he was now "back in the war."

The war in the east. It could have been him fighting there with the Second Panzer Division against the Ruskies had not fate intervened in the form of the field marshal. As fate would have it, when the Balkan Campaign was finished in May, the Second Panzer Division was ordered to the Greek port of Piraeus near Athens where it uploaded its tanks and tracked vehicles for shipment to Marseilles and back home to Germany for rebuilding. As bad luck would have it, a British U-Boat sank the very two ships that carried his precious tanks, sending them to the bottom of the Mediterranean.

What is a forty-year-old Quartermeister Staff Officer of a Panzer Regiment without tanks to do? But luck can be a two-edged sword: whereas bad luck lost him an assignment, good luck brought him home on leave in June to Gottingen where he happen to run into the field marshal visiting his mother. With some strings pulled, he was now Field Marshal Keitel's aide-de-camp and on the general staff. He felt melancholy at the question poised by the field marshal about combat, yet he also felt incredibly lucky at this new posting.

The field marshal interrupted Pierre's thoughts: "Massar, do you have the latest logistical and supply information for the Eastern Front, particularly Army Group Center? The Fuehrer usually isn't interested, but just in case..." As soon as Keitel finished, Massar snapped off a quick *"Ja-wohl, Herr Feld Marshal."*

"Good man. As an ole' Quartermeister, I knew you'd have it."

Slowly and with the sounds of braking, the black Mercedes came to a stop near the corner of Voßstraße 4 and Wilhelmstraße 77, pulling into the courtyard of Hitler's Reich Chancellery. Hustling aides and NCO chauffeurs escorted the cream of the German general staff were escorted out of their staff cars, all heading for the same situational briefing with Hitler as his field marshal.

Despite the several visits Massar had taken with Keitel to brief the Fuehrer within the last few months, he was always taken in awe driving through the great gates into the impressive Court of Honour or *"Ehrenhof."* Quickly, the generals, staff officers, and aides formed on Keitel, who took the lead of this impromptu general-officer "platoon" through the courtyard to the chancellery main entrance. From here, the party again viewed the two bronze statues flanking the doors, "Wehrmacht" and "Partei" ("Armed Forces" and "Party"), then entered the main entrance. Once inside, the reluctant Massar, as part of the staff delegation, entered an outside staircase that ascended into a medium-sized reception room where they were greeted with impressive Bavarian oak double doors almost seventeen feet high, which open into a large hall clad in mosaic that he remembered all to well.

Hitler's Reich Chancellery Entrance

The delegation continued on, ascending several more steps, with each one echoing the sounds of jack boots on polished marble, passing through a round room with a domed ceiling. Pierre was in awe at how much the

Nazis loved marble—everywhere as far as the eye could see. Continuing before them lie an immense gallery 480 feet long, twice as long as the Hall of Mirrors where the infamous Treaty of Versailles was signed in 1919.

The marble hallway towards Hitler's office

Massar couldn't help but feel dumbfounded. He had made his first visit last September, noting the many works of art hanging prominently throughout the gallery. On this visit, while still impressed at the vastness of the hall, he was equally surprised at the new pieces of art on display: Goya, Matisse, Van Gough, and other works of treasure "acquired" from throughout the Third Reich and no doubt donated by the many Nazi party and Wehrmacht generals to Hitler as "gifts." Throughout this seemingly endless staff parade, the watchful eyes of the dreaded SS guards were ever present and never far off.

Continuing on, the delegation arrived at a series of rooms comprising the approach to Hitler's reception gallery, decorated with a rich variety of materials and colors, totaling 725 feet in length. The gallery itself was 480 feet (145 meters) long. Hitler's own office was 400 square meters in size. To make the 0930 staff briefing, the general staff officer delegation needed approximately twenty minutes from leaving the Court of Honour to arriving at the chancellery situation room, a fast clip for these old soldiers, all of which were meant to engage and overwhelm visitors—civilian and military alike! It worked, for Massar could feel his confidence sputter with every step taken.

Once in the outer office, Hitler's Wehrmacht Adjutant Colonel Rudolf Schmundt met Keitel and the remaining generals. Schmundt, forty-five with graying hair, brought about no doubt by the incredible pressures one would find working for Hitler, came to become the Fuehrer's personal adjutant in 1939 on loan from the Wehrmacht. For him, to see the familiar faces came as a relief from the numerous Nazi party political meetings and foreign leader diplomatic visitations.

Schmundt quickly came from behind his desk and smartly extended his right arm in the all-too-familiar ritual that all too many a senior German officer found personally offensive. "Heil, Hitler," he called out to Keitel, the senior officer present.

Keitel replied almost robotically, and then extended his hand out to shake Schmundt's. "Rudolf, good to see you again. What sort of mood is Der Fuehrer in today?" Keitel inquired.

Schmundt responded, "Excellent mood, as you all will see for yourself in a few moments. Ever since the Japanese bombed the American Naval Base in Pearl Harbor, bringing the United States into the war, he's been ecstatic. I even heard a rumor the boys over at Goring's Luftwaffe HQ had to look on a map to find where Pearl Harbor is. You know, we've been close to war with the Kriegsmarine and the American Navy jousting in the Atlantic for the past eighteen months. Maybe now, the Americans will have someone else to worry about. As for the east, he's not doing so well, so hopefully you will have some good news here."

Keitel cleared his throat, "Well, the situation——." Before he could finish, the massive red marble doors to Hitler's office suddenly opened to the presence of a black uniformed SS officer who quickly stepped forward and then off to the side. Two highly decorated SS generals, glittering with gold and silver braids and medals, strode through the doorway and contemptuously waved a quick "Heil, Hitler" salute at Keitel, and the general staff officers assembled. Keitel, with great curiosity, asked, "What were Reich Fuehrer Himmler and General Reinhard Heydrich doing here? Don't tell me they found Jews working within the Fuehrer's office?"

Schmundt, quickly replied, "They were here meeting with the Fuehrer to get his approval on moving the postponed December 9 conference on the *Jewish question* to January 20, and they would like to hold it over at Heydrich's retreat in Wannsee."

"The Jewish question or, more likely, a conference to determine the final solution to the Jews?" Keitel retorted.

At that moment, the SS officer returned to the doorway and announced, "Gentlemen, the Fuehrer will see you now for the morning situation brief." The briefing party quickly entered Hitler's office only to become swallowed up in its immensity. It was perhaps the world's largest personal office, just over 400 square meters in size and tastefully decorated in beautiful oak. Since Hitler neither smoked, nor tolerate those who did in his presence, the wood paneling displayed prominently throughout the office gave off the fragrance of being inside a woodcarver's shop. If one was to close his eyes, he might imagine himself in the *Schwartzwald* or "Black Forest." Above the doorway was a seven-foot-wide German War Eagle sitting on top of the very symbol of Nazi power, the swastika, identical to the cloth badge they wore on their uniforms. Massar thought he could feel the very eyes of the eagle were watching every move the general staff officers made.

Hitler's Office

Upon entering, the general staff officers were drawn to the massive, marble-topped table laid out with maps of Russia and North Africa, orbited by aides laying out units, status reports, and other items that the generals would need to reference should Hitler desire to pursue a particular item of interest or topic further. Experience with the many prior briefings made an excellent teacher. Hitler was already at the map board along with Field Marshal Herman Goring, grinning, looking briefly at Goring, then back to the map—studying it as if he would try and stump the generals by telling them something they didn't know.

The black-uniformed SS officer directed the OKW and Oberkommando des Heeres (OKH) general staff officers across the room toward the marble table, where they took their respective positions surrounding it. The chatter associated with the pre-brief quickly died down to silence; who would speak first?

Hitler didn't waste any time. "Well, Keitel, what have you for today? Tell me how Operation 'Typhoon' is going?"[7] he smiled. Keitel had read the Eastern Front situation reports the night before and knew the news was not good. His

7   *Operation Typhoon* (Taifun) is the code name for the final offensive as called for in Fuehrer Directive 34, issued 12 August 1941, identifying Moscow as the future priority objective. The final offensive was scheduled to commence 30 September 1941, but due to logistical issues, was delayed until 2 October 1941.

aide, Major Massar, quickly handed him the prepared OKW staff briefs, which he briefly glanced at again to refresh his memory, then looked up.

"Mein Fuehrer, the situation in the east continues to deteriorate. Since December 6, the Russians continue a massive counter-offensive against Army Groups Center and South. As you recall, on the evening of the eighth, I called Field Marshal Von Bock of Army Group Center by telephone to informed him of your suggestion he take extended leave to restore his health.

"Per your instructions, I replaced him with Field Martial Guenther von Kluge the next day. Von Kluge is currently withdrawing back to preserve the army."

Everyone around the table could not help but notice Hitler's fists begin to clench and his neck tighten. Keitel continued. "The assessment is that if Army Group Center is allowed to conduct a limited withdrawal, we cannot only avoid the Army Groups encirclement but also slow down if not stop the Russian counterattack." Upon hearing the word "withdrawal," Hitler began to get red in the face, causing him to interrupt Keitel.

"Keitel, where a German soldier stands, he will defend. He will not retreat!!" Hitler blasted, smashing his right fist on the map board. "I don't want to hear any more about retreats. All I've heard of for the past week is retreating in the east. The Russians are almost finished!! I want you to make sure that Army units form strongpoint's around here, here, and here as per my Directive number 39,[8] which I signed last week!!" Hitler said as he circled selected areas with grease pencil on the Eastern Front map before throwing the pencil at Keitel.

"Brauchitsch and Halder," Hitler bellowed to Field Marshal Walther von Brauchitsch, Commander-in-Chief of the Army, and Colonel General Franz Halder, Chief of Staff of OKH, the Germany Army High Command, which was subordinate to OKW.

"Coordinate with Keitel and Jodl to ensure these orders are carried out immediately. I don't want any excuses. Continue, Keitel!!" The surrounding

---

8   Fuehrer Directive 39, signed 5 Dec 1941, allowed for the Wehrmacht to assume a defensive stance along the Eastern Front. Unfortunately, it did not allow for tactical retreats in order to occupy better defensive positions.

general staff officer group watched in astonished disbelief at this action, which for a few, was occurring with increasing frequency.

"Operationally, the Soviet Fiftieth Army recently counterattacked southeasterly out of Tula, trying to link up with the Soviet Tenth Army here in order to cut off the Twenty-Fourth Panzer Corps and Fifty-Second Corps." Keitel pointed to the map near Tula, nearly 100 miles southeast of Moscow. "It was only through General Guderian's frantic efforts with the Second Panzer Group that these forces were able to escape encirclement. Directly in front of Moscow, the Soviet Sixteenth Army smashed headlong into the Third Panzer Group's right wing, seizing Istra today and appearing to split the seam between the Third and Fourth Panzer Groups despite the best efforts of the Fifth, Tenth, and Eleventh Panzer Divisions—."

Hitler interrupted, "What is the Das Reich SS Division doing since they are in the area? Have them counterattack immediately!"

Halder quickly responded: "They have, Mein Fuehrer, along with the Thirty-Fifth Infantry Division, only to be repulsed with heavy losses."

Hitler became even more infuriated, but he said nothing. Massar was quietly stunned at the incredible level of micromanagement Hitler was displaying in this particular brief.

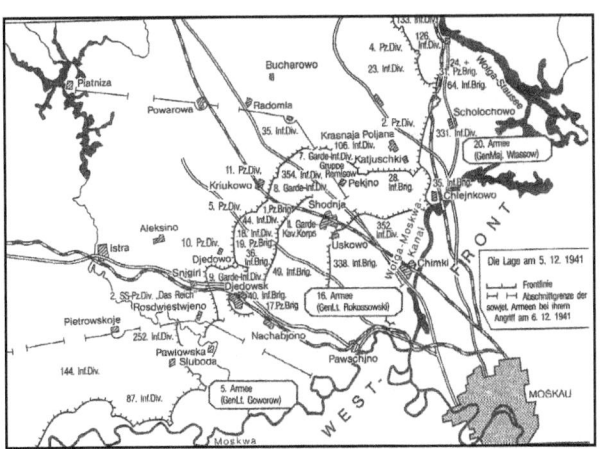

Front line and advance positions of Wehrmacht units in front of Moscow

"We expect the Soviet Thirtieth Army and First Shock Army to move on Klin, approximately 80 kilometers northwest of Moscow, and push the Third Panzer Group back to here," Keitel said, pointing to the map, "in order to set up defensive positions approximately 60 kilometers northeast of Volokolamsk. That should stem the red tide. I have directed the Third Panzer Group and Panzer Group Four to consolidate their four-panzer and one-panzer grenadier divisions within the Klin area. I believe they will be strong enough to hold these two Red armies until we can stabilize the front and redirect reinforcements to them."

Hitler raised his hand to pause Keitel as if to absorb what the Keitel had just told him. Still red in the face, he turned to Keitel and asked him to continue. Pierre could not help but notice beads of sweat building on the field marshal's head. Even the seasoned staff officers present sensed Hitler was in a mood few if any had ever seen before.

"Mein Fuehrer, the situation is some what better in Army Group South," Keitel stated while adjusting his collar. "Since November 20, we had taken Rostov, as you know, but in early November, Rundstedt had a heart attack. However, he refused to be hospitalized and continued his advance, but a Red Army counterattack against Army Group South forced him back.

"Field Marshall Von Rundstedt did not believe he could hold it and had requested permission to abandon the city and pull back to better defensive positions, which he went ahead and did on his own accord. Per your instructions, he was relieved and replaced with General Walther von Reichenau from the Sixth Army. As of this date, per your guidance, Army Group South has pulled back to these defensive positions west of the Mius River," he said, pointing on the map to the major river system just to the west of the city of Rostov.

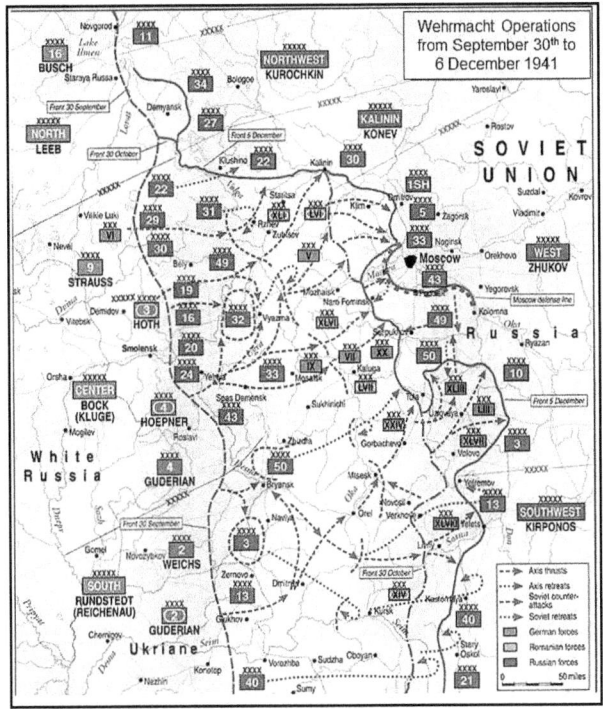

Hitler smirked. "Reichenau is an excellent choice and a good man. He follows orders unlike many of my other so-called generals. Who have you recommended to replace him at Sixth Army?"

At this time, General Halder stepped up. "Mein Fuehrer, General Reichenau will be replaced by his deputy commander, General Frederick Von Paulus."

Hitler seemed pleased. "I know this man. Wasn't he in charge of the team that initially developed Case Barbarossa?"[9] Several general staff officers in addition to Generals Keitel, Jodl, and Halder simultaneously, as if part of a school choir, rang out, "Ja-wohl."

---

9   Case Barbarossa (Fall Barbarossa) or Fuehrer Directive 21, named after the Holy Roman Emperor Friedrich Barbarossa, was the invasion plan of the Soviet Union, issued 5 December 1940, and commenced launched 22 June 1941.

Hitler stood, silently looking at the map. "Keitel, I am still not clear as to why Guderian and his Second Panzer Group still have not taken Tula?"

Keitel stood his ground, putting his briefing papers down on the map top. "Mein Fuehrer, you must take into account the daily temperature there is approximately 20 to 50 degrees Celsius below zero, freezing troops and equipment, which was not designed to operate at that temperature. Major Massar, how many frostbite cases in the last month?"

Massar replied, "Approximately 130,000 in the past three weeks, Herr Feld Marshall."

Hitler was unimpressed. "don't you think the Russians are suffering frostbite casualties as well?" Keitel continued.

"You must also take into account his troop loss situation. Guderian has lost approximately 55,000 soldiers since the 22 November Fuehrer staff brief, but to date has only received a little fewer than 30,000 troops from the *Replacement Army*. As for armor, he has received only one panzer for every eight lost in combat!"

Again, Hitler was unmoved, retorting, "Keitel, I authorized OKH to release from reserve stocks to Army Group Center 307 panzers last September as well as committed the Second Panzer Division from duty in France. I am losing my patience, Keitel!"

Keitel knew whatever argument he employed with Der Fuehrer, Hitler wouldn't accept. He still had one last case to make.

"Fuehrer, you cannot discount the deteriorating resupply situation our armies have had to experience over the past few months. It cannot be ignored!"

Hitler, staring at Keitel, demanded, "Please explain!!"

"Fuehrer, my aide-de-camp was the supply officer within the Second Panzer Division while it was in the Balkans last spring." Massar knew from that intro that within seconds, he would soon be talking directly to the supreme commander of all Germany. His stomach began to feel as though it weighed several tons.

"He has been tracking the supply situation along the Eastern Front and is prepared to brief you." Keitel lied: the field marshall was to brief the Fuehrer, not him. But in this case, Keitel needed a break, and what was an aide-de-camp if he wasn't able to pitch in for his boss when the time counted?

Keitel turned, then pointed to Pierre. "Major Massar, inform the Fuehrer of the logistical situation OKH East is experiencing." With that intro, Pierre felt a thousand eyes staring at him as if he were the opening act at a downtown Berlin cabaret The most important set of eyes in the audience, however, were those of one man: Adolph Hitler.

"Mein Fuehrer..." his voice, quite hoarse and scratchy, made him almost inaudible. He quickly coughed, swallowed, and then spoke. "Mein Fuehrer...." But before he could continue, Hitler beat him to the punch. "Yes, Major: go on! What is it?" Massar was now rattled, but quickly recovered.

"Mein Fuehrer, the situation in the east boils down to three items: insufficient rail heads, insufficient truck transport from the rail heads to the front lines, and insufficient fuel for the Panzers."

"Go on," Hitler responded. Pierre was momentarily relieved. He didn't have his head handed to him, but then again, the brief was far from over.

"For starters, Mein Fuehrer, Army Group Center has only two *Eisenbahn* (railroad) repair regiments available to them to covert Soviet gauge track, which is bigger than European gauge. At best, they can only do approximately twenty kilometers per day."

"So what is the problem, Major?" Hitler retorted as he did with Keitel.

"Sir, the problem is, in addition to converting rail, they also have to fix or rebuild damaged bridges and rail facilities—something they are not manned to do."

Hitler placed his hand on his chin, with everyone close by hearing a, "humm. Go on."

"The rail repair situation is only part of it. Army Group Center requires thirty trains with each train delivering approximately 450 tons of supply per day, but at present they are only receiving twelve to twenty trains per day, delivering to four railheads located here at Nevel, Smolensk, Rosval, and Gomel," using the pointer Keitel handed him to point out on the map, "so, whatever is placed in the supply channels is simply not getting there."

Hitler's face changed from anger to curiosity, muttering, "very interesting. Please continue."

"As I mentioned, Sir, the next issue is insufficient truck transport. As you can see each of these railheads is more than 100 kilometers from the front. To get supplies from the railhead to the frontline troops requires lots of trucks and there is only one Grosstransportraum[10] Regiment available to Army Group Center. This is clearly insufficient to bring supplies from the railhead to the various Army Corps. Basically, Army Group Center requires 13,000 tons of supply per day, but only has the truck transport to move 65 percent of this requirement."

"What about Luftwaffe support? Goring, what are you doing to assist with the Luftwaffe?" Hitler asked.

For the moment, both Massar and Keitel were relived that Hitler's focus was on the rotund Luftwaffe field marshal, standing half-asleep beside Hitler.

Goring, relaxed, as if he already had a couple of schnapps, quipped, "Mein Fuehrer, I have Luftwaffe 2 make available her three transport groups, capable of carrying a total of 200 tons if needed."

General Alfred Jodl, Chief of Operations for OKW, silent up to this point, could not resist the opportunity to take a shot at Goring: "That is, Mein Fuehrer, once the weather clears up. The weather has been poor for air–ground operations for the past two weeks. I must also remind you last

---

10   Motor Transport Regiment, consisting of 1,500 vehicles capable delivering 6,500 tons. Typically, one regiment was assigned to each Army Group though all were not up to full strength and many employed trucks acquired from throughout the Third Reich

October, Guderian requested the Luftwaffe to deliver 500m^3 of fuel[11] to his Fourth Panzer Division at Orel, but Soviet fighters were too numerous at that time, so he had to spend two critical clear weather days because of no fuel."

Hitler looked at Goring. "I want full Luftwaffe support in these operations. I know you will not let me down. Go ahead, Major: continue your brief."

Massar could see both Keitel and Jodl momentarily sigh, knowing full well Goring would continue to operate to his own show irrespective of OKW's plight at the moment. They may have won a battle, but Goring won the war.

"Mein Fuehrer, since General Jodl mentioned fuel, this is the last supply item I need to comment on. Ever since I was an Ib[12] with the Second Panzer Division, I can tell you from firsthand experience the basic fuel load or *Verbrauchssatz* or what we call a "V.S." for a Panzer Division to move every vehicle 100 kilometers was 125m^3 (33,000 gal). Wehrmacht doctrine calls for the division to carry four V.S. if involved in offensive operations. Because of the supply and railhead breakdown, a typical Panzer Division slightly less than two V.S., resulting in similar situations that General Jodl mentioned. Since fuel is part of the overall supply distribution, without sufficient transport, Second Panzer Group's chances of success are pretty poor. Quite frankly, Mein Fuehrer, it is amazing Guderian got as far as he did." Massar felt good making a "plug" for his old Panzer boss, Heinz Guderian, with Der Fuehrer.

---

11   Im^3 equals 1,000 liters (264 gal) of fuel, so 500m^3 equals 500,000 liters or 132,100 gallons

12   The Ib is the staff officer responsible for the supply of an entire Division and all matters of supply, movement of supplies, rations, ammo, etc, and the movement of wounded and prisoners. The Ib also was in charge of the movement of supply trains, deployment of construction facilities, traffic regulation, and air-raid protection in the areas of the back-line services of a Division.

Hitler stood straight up as if he had finally gotten a clear picture of what the problem really was, but he still looked like he had to make the final comment in this discussion.

"Major Massar, with the severe cold weather we are experiencing, where is the winter clothing I authorized for the soldiers?" Hitler asked.

Pierre knew the answer to this question and, from what he had observed from Hitler, knew he would not like the answer. Suddenly, Keitel inserted himself into the discussion, whether it was because Massar was getting too much "exposure" with Hitler, or to spare his aide the grief that came with delivering bad news.

"Mein Fuehrer, excuse me, but because of the limited rail capacity Major Massar had mentioned, someone assigned winter clothing a lower transport priority. As such, it is in storage within depots in Poland awaiting transport." Keitel had thrown himself on the proverbial "hand grenade" in order to protect is aide, but for one, fleeting moment, Major Massar felt honored that eyes and attention of the Reich Chancellor, Adolph Hitler, were on him and that he was listening.

As much as he felt pleased with himself, it was quite apparent Hitler was not happy with Keitel. As the field marshal picked up his briefing papers, cleared his throat, and began to discuss the situation in Army Group North and with Rommel in North Africa, Hitler raised his hand and stopped him cold.

"I've heard enough!" he screamed, his actions vaguely resembling that of a spoiled child who could not have his way, Massar thought. "I was going to wait until the conclusion of this brief to inform you of my plans for next year, but you and the other incompetent generals here have made such a mess of the Eastern Front that drastic measures will need to be taken."

Hitler continued to scream at the assembled audience, generating spittle onto the maps and the unfortunate staff officers within close proximity, while pounding his fist down on the table in the process. "I had hoped that we could wrap up this affair so that I can then concentrate on finishing the British and declare war on the Americans. For now, all our efforts will be focused on defeating the Russians as quickly as possible. Many of you thought I was going to declare war on Roosevelt and his Jewish conspiracy running America during last night's speech. I am not about to get involved in another debacle and whined up in a two-front war. I want the Soviet Union destroyed! Once that is accomplished, we will then shift our efforts to either negotiating diplomatically with the British or smashing them, as we did their incompetent French allies. From what I have read, it will take the American's at least two years as it did in the First World War to raise and train an army. Since they are now tied down in the Pacific, I don't think we will need to worry about them for a while."

Halder looked at Hitler incredulously, as if he couldn't believe what he was hearing. "Mein Fuehrer," Halder stammered, "you cannot ignore the American industrial base..."

Hitler looked straight at Halder and spoke. "Halder, the American industry is highly overestimated. Can you tell me of one American car, *just one car*, which ever won an international tournament? How about their airplanes? They look fine, but their engines are worthless. Even the tanks they send the British in the desert end up becoming scrap iron to our 88s. I tell you, even if the Americans get into a war with us, their industry is highly overrated. The only things America is capable of making are chewing gum, razor blades, and Hollywood starlets!"

He then stood up, pulled his tunic down and, with his right hand, waved it over his face in the process straightening his hair, which had cascaded down on his face while pounding the map board. In a more calm voice he said, "Doenitz," as he called to his naval representative from the Oberkommando der Marine (OKM),.

"You will continue to keep the pressure on the Americans with your U-Boat fleet in the Atlantic, intercepting and sinking all cargo that enters the "exclusion zone" around England. The Americans will not be so interested in chasing you down with their Navy; that they will not have many ships left over once they send what few they have over to the Pacific to replace the fleet sunk by the Japanese. If the Americans wish to risk a two-front war in order to supply the British and ignore their supposed neutrality, then so be it!"

Hitler stared straight at Doenitz, ensuring he clearly understood. Doenitz stood straight up, raised his right hand in the all-too-typical Nazi salute, and boomed, "Ja-whol, *Mein Fuehrer!* It shall be done!" Hitler had given the commander of the German U-Boat fleet an early Christmas present.

Hitler then turned from Doenitz to the OKH commander, Field Marshal Walther von Brauchitsch. "Field Marshal von Brauchitsch, for reasons of ill health, I am relieving you of command of OKH effective immediately."

Brauchitsch stood there along with the rest of the general staff in utterly stunned disbelief. Massar had never seen a general or field marshal "fired" before, must less the commander of the German Army, but with the news from the Eastern Front and the Wehrmacht failing to kill once and for all its hapless Russian victim, made for extraordinary times.

General Jodl broke this awkward moment by stepping forward and in a semi-defiant stance asked, "Mein Fuehrer, if this is truly what you desire to do, who will you replace General Brauchitsch with?"

Hitler quickly looked at Jodl, staring him down as he had done with Doenitz, and replied, "It is my desire to replace him for the failure of the eastern campaign. You have always heard me call out 'heads will roll' time and time again. This time I need to teach you incompetent generals that you cannot fail the German people and simply walk away. I intent to replace Brauchitsch with myself as commander of the German Army, and as commander I can assure you that more heads will roll within the next few days for your failures.

"Halder, I want you to begin developing a plan for next year's campaign in Russia as soon as I develop and give you the operational and strategic planning guidance. Keitel, Jodl: coordinate with Halder to ensure full compliance within OKW, while ensuring General Rommel's Panzer Armee Africa[13] is also provided with adequate resources."

Keitel, Jodl, Halder, and those general staff officers close to Hitler rang out, as if part of a school choir a tired "*Ja-wohl!*"

Hitler contemptuously returned their salute, announcing "This staff conference is concluded. You're dismissed." The generals, each with dour faces, as if participating in Napoleon's great retreat from Moscow, turned and headed for the door. In many respects, like the famous French Emperor of 130 years prior, they were retreating from the disaster of Moscow as well as the disaster of a Nazi Chancellor.

While the German general staff fell back to their respective HQs to lick their wounds from a disastrous staff briefing, the mood at the British Imperial general staff headquarters in White Hall, London, was not much better. Churchill was very much cognizant of the German predicament in Russia, having been briefed by dispatches from the British staff liaison in Moscow as well as receiving the top-secret Ultra transcripts of German message traffic received and decoded from their Enigma machines. Now as he was meeting with his war staff to discuss the situation in the Pacific, he was handed a note by Clement Attlee, his Lord Privy Seal.[14] Churchill looked at the note, took his glasses off, and sighed.

---

13   Otherwise known as the "Afrika Korps"

14   The Lord Privy Seal or Lord Keeper of the Privy Seal is the fifth of the Great Officers of State in the United Kingdom, ranking beneath the Lord President of the Council and above the Lord Great Chamberlain. The office is one of the traditional sinecure offices of state. Originally, its holder was responsible for the monarch's personal ("privy") seal (as opposed to the Great Seal of State, which is in the care of the Lord Chancellor). Today, the holder of the office is invariably given a seat in the Cabinet.

"What is it, Prime Minister?" General Sir John Dill, the Chief of the Imperial General Staff, inquired.

"This is from the American Secretary of State, Mr. Cordell Hull. In this, he is speaking for President Roosevelt, graciously 'declining' a formal meeting between the President and myself, on the grounds that it might be inappropriate in light of the Japanese attack at Pearl Harbor and our *Europe First* policy." Churchill looked ever so disappointed; he could barely hold the note up.

"So what does this mean?" Admiral Pound, the ever-present First Sea Lord asked. Does this mean Lend-Lease comes to an end? What about American escorts to Iceland?

Churchill collected himself. He had been in similar dismal positions before; he just need to collect his strength. He cleared his throat.

"Gentleman, it appears that the American president would like to have a small staff contingent come to the United States for the purpose of coordinating actions against the Japanese—nothing more! It appears there will be no American engagement against Germany for the time being." The assembled group was stunned, but surprised. They had thought for certain the Americans would jump into the war against fascism.

The silence was broken by Churchill, continuing to regain his composure. "What is the current situation in the Pacific?"

The first to speak was General Dill. "Sir, we've received reports that the Japanese have crossed the frontier into Thailand and Malaysia from Indochina along three points. It is reported yesterday that General Yamashita's Fifteenth Army, with tanks, rumbled down the Malayan Peninsula and blew through the Eleventh Indian Division, which was supposed to stop him. It looks like he could be approaching Singapore from the north. Hong Kong continues to be under direct air attack ...."

Churchill interrupted. "How about Japanese operations against the Americans?"

Dill continued. "We hear from Washington that strong, Japanese forces have landed on the island of Guam and Lieutenant General Homma's Fourteenth Army has landed forces off northern Luzon Island in the Philippines. We don't know if they can hold them off."

Everyone present looked grim. The future of the British Empire was hanging in the balance as the Japanese empire was running rampant all over East Asia. "General Dill, there are two things I want to happen. First, I want to get a *communiqué* to General Sir Archibald Wavell, informing him I'm extending his command to include Burma. I want you to warn him that *he must look east. I am placing Burma under your command and you need to resist the Japanese advance towards Burma and India, whilst trying to cut their communications down the Malay Peninsula.* Do I need to repeat anything, Dill?" Churchill finished.

"No, Prime Minister: it seems clear enough. And what is the second item you requested?"

Churchill again cleared his throat. "Dill, I want you to head up the delegation that will meet with the Americans at their request: you are my personal representative. Admiral Pound and Chief of the Air Staff Portal will accompany you along with some civilian experts from my office. Replacing you as the Chief of the Imperial General Staff is General Alan Brooke. I believe this is in the best interest of the Empire."

All Dill could muster at this point was a solemn "Yes, Prime Minister" while displaying that all-too-typical stiff, upper lip. Churchill continued. "I want you all to make arrangements as soon as possible. The battleship *Duke of York* is at your service and sails tomorrow. I trust you will all be on it."

With Dill's relief of command and exile to Washington, clearly the British war effort in the Pacific had claimed another casualty.

Chapter 7

A Meeting with a Wall Street Lawyer

Fact: On November 9, 1939, two British SIS agents were kidnapped in a Gestapo-engineered operation near the Dutch town of Venlo. Among one of the captured agents was a list of all SIS officers and British agents within occupied Europe, causing a severe setback for British Intelligence or MI-6. This action occurred shortly after an assassination attempt on Adolph Hitler as he made his annual speech at the Munich Beer hall in honor of his staged 1923 coup attempt. The Gestapo was never able to make a connection between the assassination attempt and MI-6.

Outside the International Building
Rockefeller Center
New York, New York
1000 hrs, 14 December 1941

C hristmas brings out the best in Americans. Everyone is in a festive mood, green garland is abounding, and the fragrances of the holiday season are all around. Nowhere was this more evident than a stroll down East Fiftieth Street and Park Ave in New York. Storefronts had there best holiday wares on display, surrounded by the twinkle of little red and green Christmas lights, partly as a decoration, but mostly as a means to get the attention of passersby. If there were a war going on, one wouldn't know if from the many colorful displays.

But Jerry Curry, while admiring the beautiful holiday displays, was on his way for a meeting that FDR, Harry Hopkins, and he discussed two days ago in the Oval Office. A meeting with the newly commissioned Coordinator of Information: none other than General William *"Wild Bill"* Donovan at his office within the International Building at the Rockefeller Center.

As Curry made his way across Madison Avenue and watched the hot dog venders, each one ensconced in a steamy cloud plume due to the morning's cold air, selling their footlong "tube steaks,"   a nickname they used to refer to the busy New Yorkers out doing their Christmas shopping, he was reflecting on his telephone conversation with Wild Bill the night before after he settled in at the Waldorf Astoria Hotel, a mere three quarters of a mile from Donovan's office. Jerry wanted to make sure the general knew he made it into the city from Washington and that he was passing the president's regards to him.

There was so much to discuss, especially after Jerry read the short biography Hopkins provided him as he boarded the plane at Washington's National Airport. What a guy: a successful Wall Street lawyer who became a self-made millionaire, a 1933 Republican candidate for Governor of New York, a colonel in the famous Fighting Irish Sixty-Ninth Infantry Regiment during the First World War, where he won the Congressional Medal of Honor for his conspicuous valor and leadership in battle, as well as receiving wounds to the leg from a very nasty German machine gun. Such a hero in France was only bound to receive the nickname *"Wild Bill"* for his audacious exploits.

At last, Jerry arrived outside the thiry-eight-story International Building, unmistakable with the adornment of a bas-relief outside the entrance known as *Construction*, depicting two workers riding a steal beam as it is lifted toward its ultimate destination. Jerry had also finally reached his destination.

Immediately outside the International Building, Rockefeller Center, New York

A short elevator ride to the thirty-sixth floor, Jerry stepped out to consult a directory to find Room #3663. Down the bustling corridor of the various businesses headquartered in New York, he finally came across a very innocuous office with no identifiable business label or the identity of its occupant. Only the number "3663" on the door confirmed to him he was at the appointed place, yet he still reached into his pocket to check again to be sure. Checking the card that Hopkins handed him, it read *International Building, 45 Rockefeller Plaza, Rockefeller Center, Room 3668*. Like it or not, this had to be the place.

Jerry knocked first, and then turned the door handle, deciding to let himself in. A secretary sat behind a medium-sized oak desk loaded with papers, files, stacks of books, what have you. As a non-descript office on the outside, it had a pretty snazzy décor inside.

Before Jerry could announce himself, a middle-aged secretary, petite with medium-length hair and glasses stood. "Mr. Curry, I presume? General Donovan has been expecting you. Please go through that door over there." She pointed to the door immediately to Curry's left side.

Jerry opened the door. There immediately in front of him, bigger than life, and sitting on a large, burgundy, leather couch, was the legend himself: Wild Bill Donovan.

Jerry immediately sized General Donovan up. At fifty-eight, this short, pugnacious little man looked ten years younger despite his cropped gray hair.

"Mr Curry… Jerry, isn't it?" said Donovan, loaded with his legendary Irish charm. He bounded across the office like a used car salesman finding an unlucky victim. "How do you do? Here, please take a seat right here," he said as he point to the left side of the massive burgundy couch. "Hope all this so-called cloak and dagger stuff doesn't have you spooked. Can I get you anything - coffee, water?"

General William "Wild Bill" Donovan

"No, I'm fine, Sir, Thank you. Harry's directions here were impeccable. Now General, what exactly is the Office of the Coordinator of Information and how can I help you?"

"Well, you get right to the point, Jerry. Let me give you some background to help clear up what you might be thinking.

"FDR needed an intelligence service that operates much like what the British have within their Naval intelligence, specifically with the mission of collecting and coordinating all the information and intelligence that all the other agencies like our own Office of Naval Intelligence, Army Intelligence, and the FBI, do." At that point, Donovan reached into his breast pocket and pulled out a small three by five card.

"Per my mission here on this card given to me by FDR, I collect and analyze all information and data which bears on national security…to correlate such information and data and to make it available to the President, and to such departments and officials of the government as the President may determine." After reading the card, Donovan put it back into his breast pocket, adding, "In short, we make intelligence for Roosevelt."

"How long has this been going on?" Curry asked, somewhat stunned, overwhelmed, yet bemused.

"The President stood us up last July…the eleventh as I recall. We are funded for up to 600 people with a budget of just over $10 million. Hell, we've even picked up the undercover branch of Naval Intelligence," Donovan smirked. "You might even think of us as the contemporary version of Riley, Ace of Spies," a metaphor of a popular secret agent who operated in the 1920s within the newly formed Soviet Union.

"Very impressive, General, but why is it so important that FDR asked me to fly all the way up to New York to meet with you? I'm just a businessman who's been overseas a few times."

Donovan appeared mildly stunned at the question, but quickly responded. "Jerry, like me, we both have conducted extensive travel all over the world and, because of this, we have established a number of contacts with folks—important folks who can provide us with information... information we need and can use to our advantage when it comes to making key decisions or take executive action, if required."

Jerry sat up intrigued. If he didn't know any better, he'd think he was being seduced into becoming a spy for the government. Donovan continued.

"Jerry, do you recall when Mussolini went into Ethiopia back in '36? Who do you think was there and helped the King Haili Selassie out of his mountain hideout and off to England and exile? I never thought I could despise fascism as much as I did when I witnessed Italian troops conducting chemical gas attacks against the brave Ethiopian troops. In 1940, I spent some time in the Middle East and saw firsthand how things worked over there between the Brits, the Italians, and the Vichy French. Quite the odd combination. Despite all that, I made some high-level contacts within the Italian army that are not exactly keen on seeing Mussolini stay in power."

"Is it true you were in Spain during the civil war?" Jerry inquired.

"Yes and, believe it or not, I operated on Franco's Spanish right-wing Republican side and saw up close and personal how the German *volunteers*, otherwise known to the world as the *Condor Legion*, operated. Brutal, yet well trained and very professional in every sense of the word. The German Army will be a tough nut to crack in the upcoming war."

"Well, that army is one we won't have to face for now," Jerry inserted.

"I wouldn't be too sure, Jerry," Wild Bill retorted. "Ya gotta know I completely agree with FDR that the Germans are the real threat; but, for now, all we can do is just stare back at 'em and hope that the Russians and the Brits hold 'em until we lick the Japs. But that's going to take time, maybe up to two years to build the army up to take them on. Until that time, I advised the President we will need to take an unconventional approach toward dealing with the Germans."

Unconventional? What on earth does that mean? Jerry suddenly felt uncomfortable, like finding his place on the couch suddenly didn't have any cushion.

"General, what do you mean by taking an unconventional approach? We're not at war with the Germans," Jerry asked. "Are you saying we need to provoke them into making the first move?"

"The hell we're not; it's just not a hot one," Donovan quipped. "Read the damn papers. Every other day an American ship of some sort bumps into a Nazi U-Boat with the Americans usually on the losing end of that collision. How long do you think we can avoid tangling with Hitler? Once Russia's gone, he's going to come back against Brits with everything he's got. I believe we need to study the enemy and find a weak spot. A weak spot we can use when the time is right; that's where you come in."

"Go on, Sir," Jerry said. "You have my full, undivided attention."

"Jerry, you have contacts in Europe in general and in Germany specifically that we don't have. Contacts connected right up to the very hierarchy of the Nazi government. These contacts can give us information as to Hitler's moves for such a time and place. We can assist those elements within the German government who seek to, shall we say, remove him..."

"You mean assassination," Jerry interrupted.

"Call it what you may," Donovan responded. "Cut off the head of the snake and the whole body dies with it. We need you to meet with your contacts at your earliest convenience and report back to us any and all information about the German resistance and plots to assassinate Hitler. We have tentatively assigned this operation with the code name 'Blotter.'"

The tension of this astonishing moment, discussing the assassination, no matter how despised, was interrupted by a short knock at the general's outer door. "Yes, what is it?" Donovan responded.

The outer door opened. Alice, Donovan's secretary meekly poked her head in. "General Donovan, your next appointment is here. Do you wish to see him now?"

"Why yes, in fact; send him immediately. Jerry, let me introduce you to your primary point of contact with me in Europe."

A small, slight, bespeckled man with thin, white hair walked in and shut the door behind him. At first glace, Jerry's first thought he was back in high school and was viewing the return of his old mathematics teacher. A shudder went down his back as if he was about to be scolded for forgetting his homework.

"Jerry Curry, let me introduce you to my primary operative and your number-one contact to the COI in Europe: Allen Welsh Dulles. He will be operating out of Nazi Germany's next door neighbor in Berne, Switzerland."

"Please to meet you, Mr. Curry. I've heard so much about you from General Donovan as well as Harry Hopkins. I'm sure you'll make a splendid addition to the company."

Jerry stood up and shook his hand. "Likewise, I'm sure." He had a firm handshake—not at all like the Harvard-generated desk jockey he initially thought he was.

"Allen, why not tell Jerry here what I have in store for you once you get to Switzerland?"

"Yes, General Donovan. You see, Jerry, my principle mission is to penetrate the German Reich and discover how extensive and well-organized German opposition to Hitler is. I am to establish contact and provide resources and assistance where possible. From what we hear in Lisbon and Madrid, as well as the other neutral countries, it seems a resistance is building, especially after the mess they have now since the invasion of the Soviet Union last summer. In short, this is what the General here has coined Operation 'Blotter.'"

Donovan added, "Jerry, we're not going to kill Hitler—just give a healthy assistance to those who would more than gladly do the job for us; you are one of the keys to this, since you have contacts that we can capitalize on to make this happen."

Jerry was flattered, but also puzzled. "Well, Sir, I'll help where I can. I told the President last week I'll do whatever is needed. But, where are the British in all this? After all, they have been at war with the Nazis for the better part of two years. I would have thought they'd been after this sort of thing from the get-go?"

Both Donovan and Dulles looked at each other to quickly determine who would be the first to answer. Donovan cocked his head and rubbed his chin: he would respond.

"Well, Jerry, the British really don't have a lot of faith in the way we do things. They think we're amateurs and should let our more-seasoned and experienced English cousins run the intelligence show over in Europe. Let's start with our operation in Switzerland itself. Our British counterpart is a short-tempered, anti-American, old-fogey colonel by the name Claud Dansey. They have let it known that no amateur death-or-glory boy from the United States is going to get their hand near their network. Colonel Dansey has made it clear he is only going to pay lip service to any Anglo-American cooperation, but as far as share any contact information they've developed… forget it! Anything you can provide to Allen and his mission will go a long way. Besides that, when it comes to amateur hour, the Brits could well take the grand prize!"

"Really! Why do you say that?" Curry quipped. "From what I've heard, they've had quite a history of successful operations."

Donovan motioned for Allen to check the door to ensure there were no prying ears. When Dulles nodded it was safe, Wild Bill, ever the storyteller, continued.

"Jerry, I want you to think back to November 1939. Do you know where you were then?" Wild Bill asked.

"Germany, I believe." Curry leaned back and scratched his chin. "November 1939...humm, yes, I believe I was at an industrial trade show in Frankfurt, Germany."

"Go on. Anything particular happen then during that time?"

"Not really. Let me think..." Jerry wondered what was going on in Germany at that time. Suddenly it came to him.

"Nothing I recall happened in Frankfurt, but down in Munich, there was an attempt to kill Hitler with a bomb. I remember he appeared to give his annual speech at the Beer Hall, the *Burgerbraukeller*, where he staged his screwed-up 1923 Putsch.[15] He left early, immediately after his speech and boom, no more Beer Hall. I suppose had he stayed, there would be no more Hitler. I heard they caught the poor chap a couple of days later trying to flee into Switzerland."

Donovan smiled. "You've a very good memory. What I'm going to tell you stays in this room. That chap you referred to is Georg Elser. A basic German nobody who was nothing more than a part-time, working-Joe Communist. Himmler's Gestapo was very interested in Elser after they caught him trying to cross into Switzerland, wondering whether he was part of a British assassination conspiracy. Since Elser didn't name any names, the Gestapo would name some for him. To do this they laid an elaborate trap for the British. Sometime around the ninth or tenth of November, an undercover SS Sturmbannfuhrer[16] by the name of Alfred Naujocks arranged to meet with two British agents, a Captain S. Payne Best and Major Richard Stevens at a café in the town of Venlo, Holland. Naujocks lured these men to a meeting by giving them the impression he and others were part of the anti-Hitler

---

15 A *Putsch* is also known as a **coup d'état** (also **coup**); is the sudden, illegal overthrowing of a government by a part of the state establishment (usually the military) to replace the branch of the stricken government, either with another civil government or with a military government.

16 A *Stumbannfuhrer* is a Nazi Party designation or rank. Sturmbannführer was considered equivalent to a Major in the German Wehrmacht.

underground and needed their help in masterminding a coup against the Nazis once Hitler was declared dead. Both officers had extensive experience within the British MI-6 and Stevens was the head of British Intelligence within Holland.

"Naujocks arranged for them to meet with a disgruntled Wehrmacht officer, a Captain Scheammel, who was a well-placed official within the conspiracy. The British were promised they were to meet the general who was the leader of the conspiracy and Best and Stevens took with them Dutch intelligence officer Dirk Klop. When Best and the others arrived, the German kidnap team stopped their car with machine-gun fire, killed Klop, and forcibly dragged the British along with Klop's body over the border to Germany."

"What did the Germans expect to gain by this?" Jerry asked. "Were they trying to make a connection between Elser and the British?"

Donovan continued. "Initially, yes. It was very difficuly for them to make the case that an actual German would try to kill Hitler. Initially, they tried to make it seem like Elser worked for the Brits, but for the British, there was far more damage than being tied to a conspiracy connection. Stevens had a list of British agents on him when they were captured. Once in Germany, the agents were forced to reveal more under interrogation in Düsseldorf. With this information, the Gestapo was able to arrest British agents all over the occupied territories, especially Czechoslovakia. They also obtained information about the SIS organization and collected a list of SIS officers to be arrested if and when Britain was invaded. In short, their capture fatally compromised British intelligence and showed everyone how bungling these *experts at the trade* can be."

"It turns out that Scheammel was none other than SS Major Walter Schellenberg, the Gestapo's chief of counterintelligence," Dulles added.

"Let that be a lesson, Jerry. The Brits aren't as clever as they pretend to be, while the Germans are full of all sorts of nasty surprises," Donovan quipped, his Irish side smiling at his British cousins' embarrassments. "So,

Curry, we can't work with the British, and they're not crazy about working with us.

"How did you find out about all this?" Jerry asked. "This is top-level stuff that you never read about in the papers."

"All I can tell you is we had a highly placed contact within the Reich before he went silent last spring. We think he may have been compromised, but we can't be sure," Wild Bill responded.

At that point, both Allen and Jerry seemed satisfied with what the COI was all about. Simple enough: go back to Europe, talk with his contacts, especially General Beck, and pursue them to see how far they are willing to go to rid Germany of Hitler.

Dulles looked at Donovan and remarked, "Since we're talking about actions against Hitler and the Third Reich, have you told Curry about the operation code named 'Paper Clip?'"

"Operation 'Paper Clip?'" Jerry asked. "Where do you guys come up with these exotic names? So what is this cloak-and-dagger adventure all about?"

This time, Dulles beat Donovan to the punch. "Sir, with your permission, Operation 'Paper Clip' is the code name for an operation where we 'obtain' those scientists working for the Nazis in the development of a uranium bomb, or what you might have heard referred to as an 'atomic' bomb.

"Back in 1939, the noted German physicist, Albert Einstein, started writing a series of letters to President Roosevelt outlining the Nazis extensive research and development to make such a bomb. We believe the Nazis have a number of prominent scientists capable of making such a weapon and then using it against the Allies. Our mission is to 'persuade' them to either work for us or, well...not work any further."

"The fact is," Donovan interjected, "we can't let them get the bomb at all, or at least until we get it first. It's as simple as that."

Curry was rapidly getting overwhelmed. "You mean, we're working on such a bomb ourselves?" he asked.

"Of course, we soon will be, just like the British; they, too, are working on their version of an atomic bomb—to use that term. I believe in a week. The decision will be made by FDR to start what is called the S-I project and it will be operated out of the Manhattan Corps of Engineering District, believe it or not—right out of New York City. If I were you, I wouldn't mention that term to anybody, not even your wife."

"Well, I'm not married and too busy for a girlfriend, so your S-I secret, as well as those two operations, are safe with me. Otherwise, I don't think FDR would have sent me here, much less mentioned any of this when I last saw him."

"Jerry, there's one other thing we need to discuss with you, especially since you will be heading to Europe soon. I needn't remind you about the German Abwehr, which is their version of Army Intelligence, but more importantly, the Gestapo. We pretty much have a handle on Abwehr activities in the States, and we know who they are. But once you're over in Europe, be especially careful who you are dealing with. The Gestapo is everywhere and they have the most notorious methods of extracting information—maybe not from you, if your diplomatic immunity holds up, but your contacts are at great risk if they are caught.

"Again, this is why I mentioned the Venlo incident to you. One last thing: don't trust anybody outside this office, not even the G-Men of the FBI. Believe it or not, on the floor up directly above us is a British Import/Export office. We know that it's the center for all British intelligence wiretapping of suspected Nazis within the United States, all approved by FDR. Isn't it somewhat coincidental that it's directly above this office?

"More important, though...we've got word that J. Edgar Hoover is not too keen on this organization and has been against it from the very start. It wouldn't surprise me if almost everyone I've come into contact with is being watched by them, and we've found listening devices in some of our offices from time to time. Rumor has it that it appears we have a turf battle here as to who can conduct espionage for the U.S. government, with Hoover believing he should own it all.

"I personally believe that ole' J. Edgar has a huge case of the ass against me and is holding a grudge going back fifteen years. You see, then-President Coolidge appointed me as the assistant attorney general within the Department of Justice. While I was there, I found out that Hoover was conducting illegal wiretapping of various politicians for political gain, and as such turned him in to my boss, Attorney General Stone. Hoover got in so much trouble he was nearly fired over the incident and never forgot who it was that nearly got him canned.

"Strangely enough, Hoover, over the past five to seven years, seemed more interested in spying on the British and chasing suspected Communists operating here than looking for the Nazis. He especially hates the Russians and, since the President is currently supporting them, I believe he doesn't have too high an opinion of him as well.

"Likewise, the Brits don't trust him, since they suspect he's a Nazi sympathizer and it's not hard to scratch the surface to come up with that finding. High FBI officials I know tell me that Hoover apparently sees nothing wrong with the Nazis either politically or morally. Additionally, three days before the Japs bombed Pearl Harbor, on December 4, Hoover finally broke relations with Interpol, an agency suspected of being controlled by the Nazis and only then he did it at the urging of other top FBI executives."

"Hoover has that much power?" Curry asked, astonished. "Why doesn't the Department of Justice or Congress put pressure on him to get in line with the program?"

Donovan and Dulles again looked at each other and grinned, which quickly turned into a muted grimace.

"I don't think that any attempt will be made by Attorney General Francis Biddle or anyone else from the Department of Justice to muzzle Hoover. His predilection for maintaining files on his congressional enemies and throughout the entire federal bureaucracy was well known in Washington. It seems certain that Hoover is still taping his enemies and potential enemies to a far greater extent than is known. I have it on good authority that he accumulated a file on Justice Frank Murphy over a ten-year period that contained derogatory items from his private life, even after Murphy was appointed attorney general by FDR in 1938 and to the Supreme Court a year later," Donovan cautioned.

Dulles added, "Just listen to his speeches on the radio and in public. All he talks about is the dangers of Communism and, if you listen closely, you can hear his contempt for the Department of Justice and the President. I think if he had his way, he'd turn the FBI into America's version of the Gestapo."

"Trust me when I say the German Abwehr gets better treatment from the FBI than we do. Now, Mr. Curry, if there aren't any more questions, you must excuse us. Allen and I have much to discuss before he departs to Switzerland in a couple of days," Donovan said, looking at his watch and seeing where the morning had gone. No wonder his stomach was growling: it was well past 1300.

"Well, I thank you, Sir, for all the interesting information and advice," Jerry said as he, along with Dulles and Donovan, all stood up as if in unison. "Not at all Jerry. If you have any questions, any at all, please feel free to call me at this number," Wild Bill said as he reached into his suite vest pocket and pulled out a simple white business card and scrawled a phone number on it. "Allen will be on station at the American consult in Berne after the first of the year. He'll help you any way he can."

"Absolutely, Mr. Curry…and may I say it was a pleasure to meet you," Dulles added, reaching out to shake Curry's hand. "I look forward to our next get-together in Switzerland."

Jerry exited Donovan's office and stood for a moment in the secretary's outer administrative area. It felt good to be on his feet and relived that his visit, though intriguing, was finally over. Behind the desk Donovan's secretary,

Alice, appeared tired, filing reports, shuffling notes, and basically trying to ride the herd on the paperwork generated by the general's secret bureau.

"Are there any good places to eat around here?" Jerry asked.

"It depends what you're in the mood for," Alice shot back. "We have hamburgers, steak, Italian, Chinese, whatever. This is Rockefeller Plaza! We've got it all!"

"Well, how about a hamburger and some pleasant company to dine with?" Jerry retorted as if to make it sound cute.

"Why not. The General will be with Mr. Dulles for the rest of the afternoon and I really could use a bite." And with that, Alice walked to the general's door, knocked, and in almost a commanding voice informed him she was going out to lunch with Mr. Curry.

"Can I bring you back anything, Sir? Lunch for the both of you?" she asked.

"Just the usual from Goldstein's Deli on West Forty-Ninth, along with a couple cups of coffee," Donovan replied. "And thanks, Alice."

"See ya in an hour," she said as she closed the door closed behind her. Espionage hates an empty stomach.

Chapter 8

Not a Good Week for Visitors

The Presidential Oval Office
The White House, Washington, D.C.
1500 hrs, 18 December 1941

Early on in the day, President Roosevelt had received coordination instructions as well as advanced military coordination's radioed to him from Churchill's representatives aboard the British Battleship *Duke of York*, steaming through heavy seas from the Chesapeake Bay for four days. Looking over the military, his British friends were kind enough to have provided him with the fundamentals of joint strategy in the Pacific, long-term programs for the defeat of the Japanese Empire, and the force structure to be raised, equipped and fielded.

At FDR's behest, a call was placed for his top advisors from the War and Navy departments for a 3:00 p.m. contingency meeting in the President's Oval Office to review this new material and come up with America's response to the British on how to deal with the Japanese onslaught in the Pacific. What Roosevelt did not share with either department was Churchill's plans for American participation in a European war should the opportunity present itself.

"I think this best be left for much later," Roosevelt mussed as he handed the file to his trusted aide, Harry Hopkins. "You best keep this one under your hat for now, Harry!" Roosevelt added as he turned back to his ever-cluttered desk.

Once Harry returned from locking up the file in his office, the two old friends began to reminisce about the good ole' days when FDR was governor of New York; Alonzo Fields entered the Oval Office to inform the president he had an important call from a senator.

"Which senator are you referring to, Alonzo?" Roosevelt shot back. "We got ninety-eight of them just over the hill!"

"He said you would know who: he's a close friend of Colonel McCormick." Both Roosevelt and Hopkins knew exactly who he was referring to. "Kindly go ahead and put the call through, Mr. Fields, then you are dismissed. And please see to it we are not disturbed."

Alonzo quickly uttered a "Yes, Sir," and left.

"Looks like our man is persistent and well informed," Hopkins said. "Let's hope he's not too well informed about the Brits and any secret agenda they might try and discuss," replied Roosevelt as his phone immediately began to ring as if announcing school was in session with a class neither man wanted to attend.

Always in his grand style, FDR picked up the phone and in his Hyde Park political accent twanged, "This is the President. How may I be of service to you?"

"You seem to be in good holiday spirits, Mr. President," the voice replied back in an almost mocking manner. "Did Santa leave you the *war* you wanted in your Christmas stocking?"

"That's quite amusing, Senator. Now if you don't mind, can we get down to the business as to why I need to interrupt my afternoon to listen to you," Roosevelt snapped back.

"Well, Mr. President, I hear that Mr. Churchill is sending a few of his friends over the Atlantic to have a little visit with you and the War Department to coordinate strategy against the Japanese. I hope you haven't forgotten it's only the Japanese we are at war with. I would hate to have all this—shall we say—correspondence between you and Churchill for the past two years fall into the wrong hands. We haven't had a president impeached in, say over seventy years. I don't have to tell you there's plenty of politicians and businessmen—Republican businessmen—who would pay dearly for these unique letters of yours," the senator chided.

FDR was not amused. "If I ever get the chance, I'll see you in a nice federal penitentiary. Now you see here, Senator, you can't blackmail the President of the United States. I'll have you ..."

"What are you going to do, Franklin?" the senator taunted. "Are you going to call the FBI? I can just image what ole' J. Edgar would do with these if he got his hands on them. He's more pro-Nazi than I am. Just consider this a warning and a reminder when you visit with our esteemed British cousins. The Japanese are our one and only enemy. Remember that!" Suddenly the phone line was dead. Roosevelt replaced the receiver back on the cradle, then sat back disheartened. He tried not to show it, but he was visibly shaken.

"I take it that was our friend again?" Harry asked softly. "What did he have to say this time? Anything new to add?"

"Just a friendly reminder that when the British come a-callin' in a few days, that we need to keep the agenda focused on our war with the Japanese and to keep Germany out of it. Absolutely remarkable, Harry! How does he know so much about what's going on here and over at the War Department?" Roosevelt wondered out loud.

"Obviously the Senator has a well-placed source within either the War or Navy departments. My guess is the War Department. How else could a copy of the 'Rainbow Five' war plan get over to Colonel McCormick's *Tribune* for publication?"

"Speaking of that, what the latest on who the leaker was, Harry?" Roosevelt asked.

Harry tilted his head to the right and rubbed his jaw. "Well, from what I've gathered, Hoover's been over to see Navy Secretary Frank Knox and open an investigation, interviewing several senior officials over there.

After interviewing or, more correctly, interrogating Admiral Stark and Rear Admiral Turner, I guess Admiral Turner has given him a lot of grief telling him that all Navy officers associated with the plan considered it an "Army" plan that was—how shall I say it—impractical of consummation and highly ill advised. Hoover concluded the Navy was itching to kill Japanese and not get involved with the Germans."

"What about the author of the war plan, this Wedemeyer character? What's the story here? What have you found out so far?" Roosevelt asked.

"He's been interrogated by the Assistant Secretary of War John McCloy. Word over there was the interrogation was conducted with Wedemeyer standing at attention. Later on, two FBI men examined his office and the safe where he kept copies of the plans. What they found was a copy of the warplan with everything that appeared in the *Tribune* and *Washington Times Herald* underlined."

"Harry, do you think he's the one?" FDR inquired. "Is it possible?"

Hopkins continued. "Well, the FBI investigated his bank records and found out he recently deposited several thousand dollars in the Riggs National Bank, down on Nineteenth and G. He claims he received it as an inheritance from a relative. If that's not enough, he's admitted to personally knowing most if not all the key leaders of the America First committee—you know, General Robert Woods and Charles Lindbergh—as well as having attended several of their meetings. The FBI also interviewed a few of the Army staff boys over at the War Department, and the popular opinion is he's the leaker. All in all, it looks pretty bad for him."

"Well, have the FBI continue to investigate and it might help to keep a tail on Wedemeyer to see who he meets in the future," FDR directed. "Harry, I don't know about you, but I'm ready for a little lunch. How about joining me?"

FDR hit a special buzzer and immediately Alonzo popped into the Oval Office. "Yes, Mr. President," Alonzo chimed.

"Alonzo, how about bringing up two lunches from the kitchen along with some coffee. I believe we might be in for a long evening ahead with our esteemed guests from the War and Navy departments." He had completely his request to Alice for some deli.

"Right away, Mr. President," and in a flash Roosevelt's trusted aide was off to the kitchen.

By 3:00 p.m., Alonzo Fields escorted in the last attendee to arrive, General George C. Marshall, into the Oval Office. Assembled were Roosevelt's most trusted advisors—the very team that would chart America's course through its war with Japan to its conclusion. In addition to the newly arrived Marshall were Admirals King and Stark, Secretary of War Stimson, Secretary of the Navy Knox, Colonel Reynolds representing Brigadier General Eisenhower and the War Planning Board, and a newcomer, Admiral Chester Nimitz, the newly appointed Commander of the Pacific Fleet. Knox and Stark had the unfortunate duty of relieving Admiral Husband Kimmel, Commander of the Pacific Fleet the day the Japanese attacked Pearl Harbor. Sitting off to the President's side as usual was Harry Hopkins.

Once seated, Roosevelt briefed the assembled audience with the recently received British proposals for their recommendation as to how to fight the Pacific War. Admiral King, ever the Anglophobe, looked uncomfortable in his seat as he listened to Roosevelt discussing the British versions of the fundamentals of joint strategy. *Hogwash*, he thought. *Damn Brits want to use us to shore up their crumbling empire and use American boys to maintain the status quo. This should be an American war, fought by American means, to an American finish.* While he only thought this, King knew many present within the room felt the same way.

When FDR finished, he turned the meeting over to General Marshal. After some short administrative comments, Marshall turned to Nimitz and congratulated him on his new command and wished it could have taken place under better circumstances. Most of his Pacific fleet at that very moment rested quietly at the bottom of Pearl Harbor save the three aircraft carriers that for the luck of God escaped the Japanese onslaught. On the positive side, Nimitz's repair dry docks, fuel storage, and the American repair crews remained remarkably intact. Once the pleasantries were done, Marshall's facial expression turned serious.

"Mr. President, before we continue with strategy, I've asked Colonel Reynolds here to brief us on the current situation in the Pacific."

That was John's cue. As he stood, two enlisted soldiers hidden behind the wall of senior officers stepped forward carrying a large five-by-six-foot map of the Pacific Ocean. Wax paper overlays hung over the map like an opaque curtain, each one with pictures of map symbols, lines, and shaded areas. One could barely make out many of the map features through all the wax paper.

Like the many briefings he had done in the war college and at the War Plans Department, he felt confident, yet here he was with the president's top men. *One more brief*, he thought to himself, feeling anxious. *You can never practice enough.*

"Mr. President, Mr. Hopkins, Secretaries Knox and Stimson, General Marshall, Admirals King and Stark. Before you I have depicted the latest on Japanese advances within the Pacific area over the past four days as picked up by our intelligence services and through deciphering Japanese Purple Code intercepts. Yesterday, Japanese forces landed off the north coast of British North Borneo," using his pointer to show the president where this exotic place was located. Looking over his audience, most of the dignitaries present looked puzzled at these exotic names. John quickly thought to himself, *imagine, a year ago, almost everyone present had never heard of it much less known where on earth it was located.* "We have identified elements of the 124th Infantry Regiment landing here, here, and here."

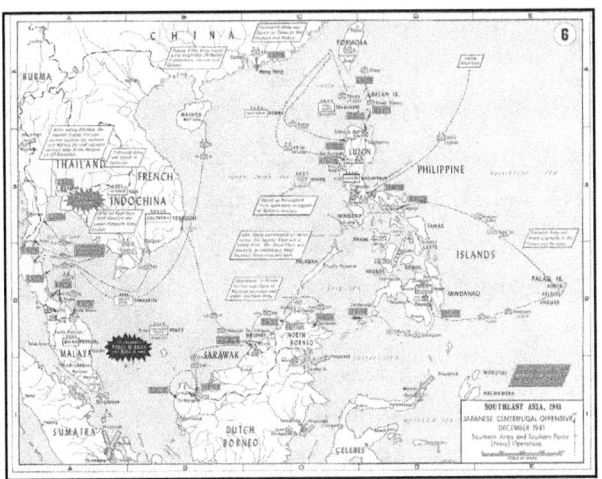

Situation off the Philippines and Borneo, December 18, 1941

Reynolds continued. "Of immediate concern is the strong Japanese force landing on the Philippine island of Luzon. Early on the morning of December 12, the Japanese landed 2,500 men of the Sixteenth Division at Legaspi on southern Luzon, 150 miles from the nearest American and Philippine forces. General Parker sent only token forces from the Philippine Army Forty-First and the Fifty-First Divisions to meet the invaders. A few U.S. fighters and bombers harried the enemy. Naval Intelligence believes the long-awaited main attack will began between the twenty-second or twenty-third of December as the 43,000 men of General Homma's Fourteenth Army enter Luzon's Lingayen Gulf. General MacArthur thinks the Japanese Forty-Eight Division and elements of the Sixteenth Division will land at three points along the east coast of the gulf. A few B-17s flying from Australia attacked the invasion fleet, and U.S. submarines harassed it from the adjacent waters but with little effect. General Wainwright's poorly trained and poorly equipped Eleventh and Seventy-First Philippine Army divisions are capable neither of repelling the anticipated landings nor pinning the enemy on the beaches as outlined in the United States Armed Forces Far East (USAFFE) defense plan. Macarthur's G-2 thinks the remaining Japanese units of the Forty-Eighth and Sixteenth divisions will land farther south along the gulf and link up with the other Japanese forces for the march south. The Philippine Scouts' Twenty-Sixth Cavalry, his only real tactical reserve, will move forward to block them, with a fight expected at the town of Rosario."

As Reynolds canvassed his audience, all he could see were ashen, stunned faces. All of this being most humbling, Roosevelt raised his hand.

"Colonel Reynolds, does Douglas have a chance of stopping them?" he asked. Roosevelt had a fond remembrance of General MacArthur. After all, he was the Army Chief of Staff when FDR was inaugurated in 1933. However, MacArthur's support for a strong military and his public criticism of pacifism and isolationism made him unpopular with the Roosevelt administration. Following MacArthur's retirement in December 1937, he reverted to his permanent grade of major general and accepted an offer from the president of Philippines to supervise the creation of a Philippine Army and in the process become its first and only *Field Marshall*. MacArthur elected not to retire but to remain on the active list as a major general, and with President Roosevelt's approval he accepted the assignment.

"Mr. President, I can only give you an estimate based on what I presently know. Since the Japanese destroyed General MacArthur's Army Air Force within the first two days of the campaign, they have uncontested air supremacy. Because of this, the U.S. Asiatic Fleet is all but doomed without American air cover and, if it isn't destroyed by now, it will have no choice but to withdrawal from Philippine waters. USAFFE is now forced to fight a ground war without air or naval forces which they had not envisioned when they developed their 'Plan Orange'."

Harry Hopkins seemed puzzled. "I thought we did away with the color-coded war plans when we adapted the 'Rainbow' series a few years ago?" he quizzed.

John responded, "we did as far as national defense plans, but MacArthur and his then chief of staff retained them for the defense of the Philippine Islands against the Japanese."

Roosevelt looked at Marshall, then back at Reynolds, asking the question, "What exactly is MacArthur's strategy and this 'Plan Orange'? What is he trying to do?"

"Basically, 'Plan Orange' calls for USAFFE along with the Philippine government to withdraw to the heavily fortified island of Corregidor located here within the western side of Manila Bay," Colonel Reynolds said as he pointed to the map of the Philippines. "As of two weeks ago, MacArthur had approximately 90,000 soldiers under his command. Those forces on Luzon that are capable will retreat back to the Bataan peninsula, located here, just north of Corregidor and hold out until relief by the Navy. That assuming the Navy has the forces capable of doing just that."

Marshall interjected. "The Navy will do its part when it's capable. Colonel Reynolds, do you know if Corregidor is fortified enough to hold out until help arrives?"

Reynolds looked the chief of staff in the eye and told him he didn't know, but there was one man available who knew "Plan Orange" to infinite detail.

"And who is this man?" FDR asked. "Sir, the man who co-wrote *Plan Orange* is none other then Brigadier General Eisenhower. He was MacArthur's Chief of Staff in the Philippines for almost four years before returning back to the States in 1939. As a matter of fact, he recently told me when I asked him how well he knew MacArthur, General Eisenhower replied, 'Know him? I studied dramatics under him for seven years!'"

The assembled audience gave a slight but well-received chuckle that was much needed to break up dreadfully bad news.

Roosevelt picked up a message, holding it up; he first looked at Hopkins, then General Marshall. "I guess that would explain why I received this message from Douglas about sending him General Eisenhower back. General Marshall, I'd like for you to make arrangements for Brigadier General Eisenhower to brief me separately about the Philippine defense plans and look into whether we can spare him to help Douglas out of his terrible predicament."

Marshall nodded and acknowledged with a customary "Yes, Sir."

The president then looked at John: "Please proceed with your brief, Colonel Reynolds. Tell me about the British situation in Burma and Malaya. I want to know just what kind of a jam they're in when they come for help in a few days."

John was relieved to get off the appalling subject of the Philippines and on to someone else's headache. "Sir, as you can see here, strong Japanese forces belonging to the 143rd Infantry Regiment and Fifth Infantry Division have landed all along the Kra peninsula in effect cutting Burma off from British Malaya. Since the Thai capitulation last week on December 11, the Japanese Fifteenth Army is free to move its remaining forces at will either north into Burma or south down into Malaya. Of course, the most devastating of all to the British was the loss of their two most prized ships on December 12: the battleship *Prince of Wales* and the battle cruiser *Repulse* to Japanese naval aircraft approximately 200 miles off the town of Kuantan, located here along the Malaya coast in the South China Sea."

Roosevelt's cigarette holder, which until this point was in the up position indicating reception to whomever was speaking, noticeably dropped like a railroad flagman indicating "Stop!"

"I was just on that ship last August, off Newfoundland with Churchill," a stunned FDR commented. "And now, the pride of the British fleet, the victor over the German battle cruiser *Bismarck*, has gone to her grave."

After a moment of silence at the British loss, Reynolds asked if he should continue.

"No, Colonel Reynolds, I believe we've all heard enough for now. Both Mr. Hopkins and I will read your report if we need further details." Turning to the assembled audience of military and civilian advisors, Roosevelt spoke. "Gentleman, as I mentioned earlier, in a few short days our esteemed British allies will be meeting with us to formulate a cohesive strategy. I do not want to get side swiped by them into adapting their plan for lack of one of our own, so gentleman; I want to ensure we brief them on our equivalent strategy and plan. General Marshall, your team from the War Plans Division just recently briefed me on our new plan, 'Rainbow Two,' if memory serves me correctly. My guidance to you and admirals King and Stark, is that we will give any and all aid possible to help the British in Asia, but under no circumstances will we provide any additional aid to the British under Lend-Lease if it means co-opting our boys. Building the American army to fight the Japs is our number one priority."

Admiral King sat and grinned like the Cheshire cat from Alice in Wonderland. "Thank you, Mr. President. While I'm sure General Marshall is thinking the same thing about the Army, the U.S. Navy will not let you down," he said.

Roosevelt continued, "I know you and Marshall won't, but let me also add that I don't want to provoke the Germans any more than what happened last fall. American ships reserve the right to defend themselves on the high seas, but I don't want to go looking for trouble at the very time we can ill afford it. From now on, the British can pick up their Lend-Lease from our forward base in Iceland. I don't want Mr. Hitler to start a U-Boat frenzy and sink our shipping when we need all we can get our hands on. For the time being, as far as American strategy is pertaining to Europe and the Germany First policy Mr. Churchill and I discussed last August, it's off the table for obvious reasons. You'll just have to explain to our British allies that *they're simply on their own* for the time being. In short, gentleman, I will not be bulldozed by them like they did to me at Argentia last August. They can either play with us in the Pacific, or they can play alone. Mr. Stimson, I want you to head this team up. Do you have any questions?"

Secretary Stimson raised his hand. "Mr. President, since we're trying to tie the British in with our 'Rainbow Two' war plan, I think it would be a good idea if Colonel Reynolds attended the strategy session in addition to the Chief of the War Plans Division General Gerow and his deputy Brigadier

General Eisenhower since John's the author and the most knowledgeable one about this particular plan."

The president nodded, "Agreed. Take Colonel Reynolds and, I may suggest, I would like General Hap Arnold to go along as well. I want to make sure that our top expert in air warfare is present as well."

Stimson looked at his staff, "Gentlemen, let's reconvene at my office after dinner. Say 1900 hours?"

From his seat in the rear of the audience, John sighed. He had only been to Washington for less than ten days and still did not have the chance to find a place to stay outside his bachelor quarters at Fort McNair. From the sound of things, it didn't look like he would have a chance until probably the middle of January. The Union Civil War General William Tecumseh Sherman was right: "War is Hell!"

Within forty-eight hours, Stimson and his team had finished the American response to the British agenda and were well prepared. He knew there would be some initial friction between the two fraternal allies from the First World War: how much aid could the Americans continue to give the British at the expense of her own forces, when and where to strike back at the Japanese in the Pacific, and what would be the American response to the Germans in the future. After all, the Japanese were running rampant across Asia, killing American and Commonwealth forces in large numbers, while Europe was a veritable stalemate with the British and Germans staring at each other across the English Channel. The threat of an invasion of British Isles had largely disappeared since the Wehrmacht's invasion of the Soviet Union. From the looks of it they were going to be in Russia for the foreseeable future. Britain's only major action at this point was a see-saw war in the North African desert, launching their latest offensive, Operation *Crusader*, against the famed German Afrika Korps in November, succeeding in relieving their garrison at Tobruk as well as eliminating the German threat to seizing the Suez Canal. For the time being, the Germans were right back where they started their desert campaign in March 1941.

On December 23, the British delegation arrived in Washington to unseasonably warm fifty-degree weather with gentle winds, coming as a relief after ten stormy cold days at sea. After settling in at the Hotel Washington, the two combined staff assembled at 1000 hours the following day at the board room of the Federal Reserve Building, a short one-mile walk from the hotel with the White House in full view all along the way.

General Marshall opened the meeting greeting his British contemporaries for maintaining their brave fight against the Germans in North Africa while concurrently fighting the Japanese in Malaysia thousands of miles away. General Sir John Dill, heading up the British delegation, was equally complimentary of the American resolve in the face of the Pearl Harbor disaster, and that he was confident the two allies would be ultimately victorious against the Japanese and hopefully Germany. Many on the American side grimaced when they hear "Germany" for their inclinations were about to come true—somehow the British were intent on getting the Americans into a European war "by rook or by crook."

At this point under the direction of Marshall, General Hap Arnold, Chief of Staff of the newly created U.S. Army Air Forces, was chosen to lead off talks with his counterpart, Air Chief Marshall Sir Charles Portal. This was part of Marshall's strategy in introducing the now newly promoted Lieutenant General to the assembled group as a full speaking partner of the American team. They began with a presentation of the U.S. War Department agenda that was hammered out with Secretary Stimson a fortnight before. Portal, speaking for the British, fundamentally accepted the agenda, but made a few offhand snide comments about how the British had bore the brunt of the fighting to that date and had believed they had a better hand on the overall strategy. The Americans, for the most part, shrugged off the comments, but they left their mark.

As the meeting drew on, Colonel Reynolds, sitting in the back, couldn't help but notice that it was becoming rapidly evident that vast differences in both attitude and outlook existed between the two delegations. Reynolds became acutely aware of Portal's "air of superiority" in strongly hinting America's need to provide bombers to England to "help out the British bombing effort."

Arnold was aghast. "The United States needs all its bombers at her disposal in order to carry the war all the way to Japan!" he responded. The first clash between the two "bomber barons" had begun.

Portal smugly suggested, "I would think you would have the American Navy order its surviving three aircraft carriers to rapidly steal up to Tokyo and carry out an American-style Pearl Harbor. That should free up a few bombers that might be better used elsewhere."

Reynolds, along with the American delegation was stunned at this incredible statement. Was the Chief Air Marshall serious? His statement was "wishful thinking" at its best, insanity at its worst. No doubt, the British would stoop to any lengths to get their hands on any heavy American bombers, especially the B-17s that they had had great success with, having received their first twenty that past summer.

By 1600 hours, both sides adjourned for the day with the announcement that talks would resume at 1000 on December 26. Once the British had cleared the room and started returning back to the Hotel Washington, Marshall surveyed the American team. A few looking tired, many frustrated, all ready to head home for Christmas Eve festivities. The first official staff contact between the Americans and British in regards to coordinating the Pacific war ended with suspicion and acrimony. Marshall asked the first question to the assembled group, inquiring how they thought it went.

Admiral King, a salty seaman if ever there was one began, "Well, General Marshall, I don't know about you or the other gentleman present, but from Portal's initial statement about bearing the war brunt, as well as other comments from our distinguished British cousins, they come across like a bunch of arrogant *know-it-alls*. I'm convinced they came less to coordinate the Pacific war effort and more to present a shopping list of military hardware and equipment they can get their hands on to fight the Germans."

General Arnold, who bore the weight of Portal's earlier comments agreed, "Sir, if I didn't know any better, I'd think they believe we should back burner the Pacific effort and provide the fullest support to their European war. We need our long-range bombers in the Pacific, not provide spare planes to the RAF. Of the twenty we provided them last summer, they've already lost eight. Hell, since the Germans handed their asses to them over France, they've switched to nighttime bombing. Clearly, when it comes to the art of war, they have a bit of learning to do themselves."

Marshall rubbing his chin, looked forlorn, but agreed, "It's sad, but I get the distinct impression they think we are still in nursery school. All right, let's learn from this while you celebrate Christmas with your loved ones and families."

Later on that evening across town, the White House and decoratively lit Christmas tree brilliantly stood out, announcing to the world the birthday of 'our savior' was upon the world; Christmas had arrived. Looking out from the Hotel Washington's lobby window, staring in disbelief at this display in wartime Washington, the British delegation, grouped together in the lobby for a cocktail before dinner, had their own misgivings about the day's meeting with their American counterparts.

General Dill observed over his gin and tonic, shaking his head in the process. Gentlemen, please take note of the display across the street. Ironic isn't it? The Americans are now at war but really don't grasp the situation they're in, or the realities of what war really means. They think its business as usual."

Admiral Pound, quiet for most of the day's proceedings, agreed, "I think its truly tragic how disorganized they are after all these years. How do they expect to unite together as an armed force, especially one to be considered seriously, with all its bureaucratic problems and the inter-service rivalries?"

"Agreed," Dill responded. "I think since we've been fighting Jerry[17] now for over two years, you'd think we've learned a thing or two to pass on to them. All the Americans are facing is the Japanese. We've got the Germans and now the Japanese to deal with, so you would think they'd be a little more sympathetic to our situation."

It was at that moment a bell boy handed a cable to Sir John Dill. Putting down his drink, the delegation closed in around him as he opened the message.

"It's from Churchill," he commented. "He's wishing all of us a Merry Christmas and holds the hopes and prayers of the Empire on our success in working out an agreement with the Yanks. Please pass on my sincerest and warmest regards to President Roosevelt and the American chiefs of staff."

"Bloody right; does he have a sense of humor or what?" Air Chief Portal murmured.

Dill promptly folded the cable and put in into his breast pocket. "Well, let's go ahead and enjoy the holiday here with our American cousins and hope that Friday's meeting is more productive than today's. Otherwise, I believe I'll need to advise the prime minister there's no point in overstaying our welcome."

As the British mission began moving into the dining room, a clerk came up to Dill, informing him he had a phone call from none other than General Marshall. Excusing himself, he followed the clerk to the phone.

"General Dill here, Sir," he responded in the utmost of stiff British accents. "Sir Dill," Marshall replied, "On behalf of the President of the United States and the American Armed Forces, I wish to invite you and your colleagues for a little Christmas holiday reception tomorrow over that the

---

17   British nick name when referring to the Germans

Fort McNair Officers Club, say 1500 hrs? It will be a chance to start this proceeding on a cheerier note. I'll send you a car as well."

"Jolly good show, Sir. We'll be delighted to attend your party, General Marshall. By the way, Mr. Churchill sends you his regards, wishing you and yours a Merry Christmas." It was a lie of course, but in the world of diplomacy, a little white lie can sometimes work wonders and soothe bruised egos. "We'll see you tomorrow and we look forward to it," and with that, Dill hung up. He returned back to his party, now feasting on a wealth of Maryland crab legs and bountiful California wine, informing them of their change in plans for Christmas Day.

At 1445, just as Marshall had promised, Colonel John Reynolds stepped out of the first of a two army green staff cars in the "convoy" and introduced himself to Sir Dill who as the Chief of the British Joint Staff Mission was just exiting the hotel. After an exchange of pleasantries, the party departed down Fifteenth Street for the short three-mile excursion to Fort McNair. Along the way, both Dill and Portal commented to Reynolds about the unseasonably warm December weather.

"The last time I visited Washington," Portal commented, "it was frightfully cold in the winter and terribly hot in the summer. So hot we almost consider this a *tropical assignment!*"

"I don't know about that," Reynolds chuckled "but it does get damn hot and humid here. That's why most of the Congress and legislature goes into recess in July and August, to go home and escape the heat."

After a few minutes of silence while waiting for the traffic light at the corner of Fifteenth Street and Maine Avenue to change, Dill asked Reynolds, "On a personal note, Colonel, do you think the Americans will ever go to war with Germany?"

Reynolds was surprised at Dill's question. "Sir, I'm a soldier, not a politician. Anything I say doesn't count for anything."

Dill was not satisfied and continued to press. "Colonel Reynolds— John, if I may? I know you were posted as the American military attaché in Germany for a little under two years. Certainly you of all people understand our need to form a united front in order to stop Hitler and the Nazis?"

"I completely understand the need to stop the Germans, but they didn't launch a surprise attack against us; the Japanese did. We have to think about Hawaii and the defense of the West Coast, the Panama Canal, as well as how we are going to save the Philippines. Also, Hitler doesn't have any territorial ambitions against us," John replied.

"The hell he doesn't," Portal chimed in. "It's only a matter of time before his saying 'Today Germany, tomorrow the world' comes true."

Reynolds responded, "You British don't give yourselves enough credit. Look at what you've done in North Africa against Rommel. And if that's not enough, one look at his situation in Russia is enough to convince me he and the whole German army will be there for some time to come."

"Perhaps, but remember your history, Colonel," said Dill. "Eventually the Kaiser beat the Russians with our combined armies on the Western Front back in 1917."

John couldn't let it end there with Dill's arrogant comment. "But if you must know what I really think, here are two things to consider about any American involvement in a European war. First, of all the time I spent in Germany and talking to her people, I am convinced they don't want a war with us any more than we do with them. The average German today who was around during the First World War knows or believes they whipped both you and the French fair and square in 1918 and the only reason they lost the war was our entry that year. I don't think they want to go through that again."

Both British officers drew a deep breath in anguish and disbelief, but Reynolds went on. "The only reason Hitler is there in charge in the first place is the wonderful piece of diplomatic work the French and you cooked up at the Versailles Treaty. Your countries could not have put the Germans in a worse predicament to set the stage for Hitler to walk right in. Most of us Americans haven't forgotten the screw job we got bailing you out, then given the bum's rush when the treaty was being put together in 1919. I'm not a Nazi, but I don't think the average American Joe here has forgotten that sucker job. And if I may be blunt, here's another historical cliché that seems to identify your situation in Europe today: 'Those who don't learn from the past are doomed to repeat it.' In other words, I think we have a *deja-vu* here, gentlemen."

The conversation, like the Western Front of World War I fame, came to a stalemate and none too soon, for they had just pulled up to the front security gate of the Fort McNair installation. Reynolds flashed his identity badge and vouched for the British guests loaded within the two olive and drab-green Army staff cars. Within a minute, they passed the parade field and arrived at the club. In front was an awaiting squad of white-coated assistants and the master of ceremonies himself, General George Marshall. John looked at his watch: 1449 hrs. The Army Chief of Staff would not be disappointed.

Fort McNair Officers' Club

The general warmly greeted the civilian-clad British guests as they quickly assembled out of the Army staff cars in front of the splendidly built Virginia club. Dill marveled at its plantation-style architecture, commenting to Marshall it reminded him of the splendid manors he lived in while stationed in India a decade prior. Admiral Pound and the rest of the delegation could not help but notice the vast amount of naval ships passing through the Washington shipping channel to their right as they entered the club, decorated in festive Christmas flair.

Pound thought how one German U-Boat slipping into the channel would have a bloody field day with all those ships. After all, it was under his watch shortly after his appointment as First Sea Lord in 1939, a U-Boat penetrated the massive British Naval base at Scapa Flow and sank the battleship HMS *Royal Oak* anchored there while a second torpedo attack blew a thirty-foot hole in the *Royal Oak*. It immediately flooded and capsized, killing 833 of her 1,400-man crew. To add insult to injury, three days after this submarine attack, four Luftwaffe Junkers Ju 88 bombers raided the same base and badly damaged the former battleship HMS *Iron Duke*. "What a pity," he said sadly, "if that should happen to the Americans here as it happened to us."

John was none too glad to shed his escort duty as he followed Marshall and his British guests into the club. There a world brightly lit in various shades of the holiday, decorated in red and green garland, mistletoe, and all things festive—as far removed from the ravages of war—awaited all who entered. Many of his colleagues had been there for some time along with their wives or sweethearts and were far along in getting into the Christmas spirit. In the background, a band from the nearby Fort Myer Army Music School was playing the latest Tommy Dorsey and Glen Miller tunes with a dozen or so officers and gals on the dance floor "cutting the rug" and doing either the swing or the jitterbug.

Saddling up to the bar, Reynolds finally felt he could relax, if only for brief time, and ordered a whiskey and rye. To his left, he noticed the Brits settling in and singing holiday songs from England. A touch on his right elbow, he turned to be greeted by Eisenhower and his wife Mamie.

"We haven't seen you over the house much these past days," Mamie said. "Dwight tells me you've been working like there's no tomorrow." Eisenhower tilted his head slightly to the left and winked, indicating he knew full well Reynolds impending workload.

"Your husband, the General, sets high standards, Mrs. Eisenhower," John said.

"Please, call me Mamie. I know Dwight wouldn't mind. After all, you're the best officer on his staff until he ships out."

Slightly embarrassed at the comment, he looked at Brigadier General Eisenhower standing nearby and decided he couldn't resist asking the question. "Sir, since you'll be leaving us soon for the Philippines to bail out your old boss, who's your replacement?"

Eisenhower took a sip of his drink and reached out and padded Reynolds on the shoulder. "John, from what I've seen of your work and what both the President and Marshall have to say, I'd say you'll find out soon enough. A good man has the right to know who his boss is."

At that point, Mamie reached over and kissed John on the check. "Merry Christmas, John. May God bless you this year. Now, if you don't mind, I must have a few dances with this gentleman before the night is out. If you like, we still have an extra bed if you don't feel like heading to your hotel." She then turned, wound her arm in the general's, and headed toward the music and the dance floor.

All through the evening, both American and British staff began to forget their differences of the day prior, laughing, telling stories, and singing military songs of the First World War. Around ten o'clock, the mood was suddenly broken by Portal as he asked for quiet while turning up the volume of the club's four-foot-high Zenith console radio.

We repeat . . . British Imperial Forces in Hong Kong have surrendered. Cut off from power stations and with no water, the Commanding Officer, Major General C.M.

Maltby, along with the Governor, Sir Mark Young, surrendered the city to forces of the Japanese Twenty-Third Army under the command of Lieutenant General Saki, leaving approximately 1,500 Commonwealth soldiers dead.

Meanwhile, in the Philippine Islands, General MacArthur's efforts to stop the Japanese on Luzon have failed, resulting in his withdrawal from the capital city of Manila to defensive positions on the Bataan peninsula. In the Pacific, strong Japanese forces captured the Wake Island after two weeks of fierce combat action...

A voice from somewhere in the assembled crowd yelled, "Turn it off." Portal, grief-stricken, reached over to the switch and complied. Many of the British Joint Staff mission present bowed their heads, with a few wiping the tears from their eyes.

Pound was the first from the delegation to speak, being one of the few quieting weeping at the stunning news. "Astonishing, simply astonishing. I must speak with the Prime Minister as soon as possible."

Bowing his head as if in shame, Dill commented, "This is the first time a Royal Crown Colony has been lost to the enemy. I can't believe Maltby would've surrendered. I served with him, you know, in India. I would have thought better of him."

Admiral King was equally stunned by the news. For a little over two weeks, his Navy and Marines had stood up to the Japanese invaders at Wake Island, repelling the few attempts they made to take the island by storm. But just as the luck for the British in Asia began to turn for the worse, it had also turned for the few Marine and Navy personnel fighting for their lives on that tiny piece of coral real estate, slightly smaller than three square miles. He was still miffed at the call back of a projected U.S. relief attempt by Admiral Wilson Brown's Task Force 14 (TF-14) and Admiral Frank Fletcher's Task Force 11 (TF-11) consisting of fleet carriers *USS Lexington* and *Saratoga*, along with the cruisers *USS Astoria, Minneapolis, San Francisco,* and ten destroyers—quite a sizable force in the Pacific considering what was left over from the Pearl Harbor debacle. Within this relief effort, King directed the dispatch of the Fourth Marine Coastal Defense Battalion, and a VMF[18] fighter squadron equipped with F2A "Brewster Buffalo" fighters. Since the garrison had been under attack since December 7, an ammo resupply of large caliber artillery and small arms ammunition was also sent.

Unfortunately, late on December 22, the task force received a controversial orders signed by Vice Admiral William S. Pye, the Acting Commander in Chief of the U.S. Pacific Fleet (since Nimitz had not arrived yet from Washington), to return to Pearl Harbor for fear of losses, so no naval battle or relief of Wake took place. King made a mental note that this admiral would never command forces in battle again. Like his guests in attendance, the sting of loss in battle was not a uniquely British experience.

Whatever Christmas cheer that was present a few moments ago had evaporated into despair and grief. Both sides coalesced into their separate groups at opposite ends of the bar. After a few moments, Sir Dill approached Marshall.

"It's not too late to divert your reinforcements destined to the Philippines over to the defense of Malaya."

Marshall quickly retorted "That, Sir, is completely out of the question. I believe in speaking for the President, those forces are needed for the defense of the Philippines. Maybe we should discuss tomorrow the need to establish a unified command of some sort within the Pacific area."

Dill winced at the idea at the notion of appointing a Supreme Allied Commander, noting the other British officers present also nodding in agreement. "I still think your reinforcements will assist our defense of Malaysia and Singapore and I intend to discuss this with Mr. Churchill. As for a unified command in the Pacific, I can't make that decision," he said. "That will have to be decided by Mr. Churchill."

---

18   VMF – Volunteer Marine Flyers. USMC aviators.

"Well then," Marshall responded, "Shall we call it a night and reconvene at 1000 hours tomorrow morning? I'll send for your cars immediately." He waved over to Colonel Reynolds, who was sitting off to the side carrying on a conversation with the bartender. Reynolds recognized Marshall's gestures and concluded the evening would soon be over.

"Colonel Reynolds will see to your return back to the Hotel Washington." Looking at the grouped but dispirited joint mission, Marshall wished them all a Merry Christmas and a good evening.

As John signaled for the staff duty drivers to fall in on him, Eisenhower approached him from behind and squeezed his left elbow, "Ya know the offer to stay over after all this still stands. I could use the company driving over to the conference tomorrow."

John, tired, nodded in agreement. As he turned and departed outside to the awaiting guests and cars, he looked at his watch. *Twelve- thirty in the morning,* he thought. "Tomorrow is already here."

Chapter 9

In the Shadow of Napoleon

Ten kilometers west of Radomia, Russia
1300 hrs, 26 Dec 1941

Christmas, 1941. For many Germans, the day after Christmas Day is spent with family and close friends. It is also a day to recover from the celebration and holiday cheer of the previous two days; from a warm Nürnberger *glühwein*—a traditional hot spiced wine with an incalculable amount of sugar in it—to the traditional eggnog laced with rum. If all else fails, a good ole' fashioned *hefeweizen*[19] would suffice. For the soldiers of First Kompanie, Thirty-Eighth Pioneer Battalion, this Christmas would be very different. While there was an acute shortage of German wines and beer, much less a warm Nürnberger *glühwein*, there was no shortage of alcohol for consumption. Over the past months, the German pioneers had accumulated a large stock of Russian vodka; if all else failed, vodka would do the trick. At first, many of the company soldiers hesitated to drink this potent Russian liquor, but as the nights became long and cold, that hesitancy soon disappeared. Many German soldiers by this point in the eastern campaign had come to enjoy drinking this Russian "anti-freeze."

Yet, the holiday season wasn't the only reason for libation. For many an officer and soldiers alike, the situation in Russia over the past month had taken a grim turn for the worse. With the advent of the recent Soviet offensive across the front, German troops, from the generals down to lowly

---

19   Hefeweizen – wheat beer popular in southern Germany

privates, were now confronted with a new paradigm: this campaign would be very different from the past victorious actions in France, the Balkans, and Poland—different in that final victory had eluded them for the moment and they would not be going home to Germany in the foreseeable future. Thank God for vodka …

Lieutenant Menter's mounted infantry unit pulled up next to a large gathering of Wehrmacht vehicles and tentage, group around a medium-sized building. Looking for fuel, he figured someone in this mass of gray and winter white could help him locate the fuel point. Getting out of his *kubelwagen*, he was quickly joined by Hauptman Lampon, who more than any thing else needed the break to stretch his legs from the four-hour road march.

Wehrmacht infantry pulling back to the Third Panzer Regiment Command Post

They both walked over to what appeared as a command post due to the number of antennas protruding from the roof. A guard standing near the checkpoint saluted and then asked for their identity papers. Eric made a quick joke with the sentry present, telling him, "It's Ivan and Boris Stalin wishing to infiltrate your headquarters…." The sentry only slightly smiled at the attempt at humor, handed their identity cards back to them, and motioned them through the door.

As the two entered, both were taken aback by the chaos ensuing throughout the command post. Radio operators were yelling into their hand mikes, as if the operator on the other end could hear them better. Vast cartons of boxes were stacked on tables with staff officers and NCOs ruffling through them looking for key documents. Maps hung haphazardly on the walls in various worn states, giving the appearance of cheap wallpaper hung by a drunk. And everywhere within the room, the smell of filthy men, stale urine, excrement, suppurating wounds, and the not-unpleasant smell of Kascha, a sort of buck-wheat porridge, mixed with a cloud of acrid Russian cigarette smoke as if a fog bank had moved in.

"Welcome to the Third Panzer Regiment Command Post," an NCO announced as he greeted the two strangers. "I am Sergeant Dietz. May I be of service to you?"

"Third Panzer Regiment? Ah, yes, Oberst Bernatz' outfit," Eric responded. "Yes, there is something you can do for us. First, we need fuel. Can you tell us where the nearest fuel point is?

"*Ja-wohl*, Herr Hauptman. The fuel point is located approximately 150 meters outside near the remains of the red barn over there. You can't miss it. There are two tanks nearby in the regiment repair shop and two still loaded on lorries," as he pulled back the window covers and pointed out. "You'd better hurry, though; I don't think it will be there long. We'll be pulling out of here within the hour and moving west."

"That would explain the chaos here," Eric commented to both the NCO and Menter.

"Your second request Herr Hauptman?" a now impatient Sergeant Dietz asked, anxious to get on with movement preparation.

"Ya, where is your commanding officer, Oberst Bernatz. If I'm in his CP, I wish to express my regards to him, since he paid me a visit a few days ago."

"Sirs, if you would, please come this way," Sergeant Dietz replied, changing his attitude in light of Lampon's recent acquaintance of his commander.

No sense having this Hauptman put in a bad word about him. After all, there are worse places to be assigned than a warm CP in the middle of Russia.

As Dietz turned, Eric told Menter to take what men he needed and head for the fuel point. "One of us has to see that we get refueled before it un-assess the area," he told Menter.

"*Ja-wohl*," Hans quickly acknowledged and left the CP.

Eric followed Dietz to the back room of what appeared to be a rundown Russian inn. There, they found the black-clad warrior sitting at his make-shift desk, crest fallen, holding what appeared to be orders in his hand.

"Herr Oberst," Dietz said as he knocked on the door.

"Ya, what is it, Dietz?" Bernatz snapped, still looking at a piece of paper.

"There's a Hauptman Lampon from the Thirty-Eighth Pioneer Battalion here to see you."

Bernatz looked up. "Lampon? Thirty-Eighth Pioneers?" Looking up and over at Dietz, Bernatz immediately addressed Lampon.

Upon Bernatz's recognition, Lampon immediately snapped to attention and saluted.

"Greetings, Herr Oberst," said Eric. "I was in the neighborhood and thought I'd stop by and pass on my compliments."

"Herr Hauptman, I hope you don't think me a bad host, but I don't think you'll be staying long in this neighborhood. What on earth brings you here to my happy CP?"

"We've been ordered back as part of the division's retreat to a place here, a town called Karmanowo, then on to Rzhev," Eric pointed on Bernatz's map. "It may not be heaven, but we'll call it home for now."

Bernatz finally broke a smile, a break from whatever bad news he just received. "Dietz, how about two cups of coffee for my guest and me? Can you stay a bit, Hauptman? It's the least I can do to repay your hospitality. Here, have a seat," as Bernatz cleared a pile of equipment and files from an old wooden chair.

"Certainly, Herr Oberst," as Eric sat down. "What's going on with the regiment and the division?"

"This," Bernatz said as he held up the piece of paper, apparently written on Wehrmacht stationary. "You can read it for yourself ….."

Oberkommando der Wehrmacht [German High Command]

Fuehrer HQs   *No. 442277/41 g.K.Ch. WFSt/op.(h)*

Classified — Top Secret! Only via Officers

The Fuehrer has issued this directive for combat operations:

1. On the defense, every foot of ground is to be fought for to the last. Only by this means can we inflict heavy and bloody losses on the enemy, weaken his morale, and uphold the unbroken superiority of the German soldier.

2. Relinquishing even makeshift positions without a fight leads under present weather conditions to irreplaceable losses in material and ammunition and thus reduces our own fighting capacity, giving the enemy greater freedom of action.

3. Defensive capacity must be increased in particular by turning all villages and farms into strong points and by the greatest possible distribution in depth. Each troop unit, regardless of branch, including supply troops, has the duty to hold prepared shelters to the last. This way, the enemy is denied entrance to the villages and will be forces to expose themselves to the cold of the open. They will be cut off from the roads and thereby from supplies and by this means succumb sooner.

The Chief of the Wehrmacht High Command

sig. Keitel   *Ack F.d. R. Hauptman*

Eric finished reading with his face expressing astonishment.

"He can't be serious?" Lampon asked. "Does OKW have any idea what is going on out here? Where and how are we supposed to find these 'strong points' out here? Hell, it's so cold you need to explode an artillery shell to crack enough earth open for a small foxhole, much less a strong point! What happened? Did the lunatics take over the asylum over at High Command?"

The comment surprised Bernatz, but he continued.

"Lampon, you don't know the half of it. From what I've heard, Hitler's fired quite a few generals as an attempt to kick some ass of out them here."

"Who did he fire?" asked the Hauptman.

"Well for starters, two of the Army Group Commanders, the Grand Field Marshals, Rundstedt down south and our own Von Bock up at Army Group Center, both got sacked."

Eric was absolutely transfixed, dropping the OKW Directive he had just read to the ground.

"I found out about Bock from his nephew, Colonel Henning von Tresckow, whom I attended the Kriegs Academie with and is an old friend. Last I heard, he was a senior staff officer up at Army Group Center and occasionally fills me in on all the madness going on up there. Shall I continue? Colonel General Hoepner of the Fourth Panzer Group and to our north, General Strauss of the Ninth Army—both for pulling their troops back to better defensive positions contrary to this ridiculous order. I heard Hitler was extremely pissed at Strauss for pulling out of Kalinin. I saved the best for last and it's a good thing you're sitting down. Yesterday as a Christmas present, Hitler relieved Heinz Guderian from the Second Panzer Group and sent him home packing, and last week, he fired the OKH Army Commander Brauchitsch and took over the job himself!"

"God help us," was all Eric could muster. "What about the division and the Panzer regiment?"

"What about them? I have a handful of tanks—maybe twenty—to defend this worthless area. Fortunately, most are the newer Mk III "Js" with the long 50-mm cannon. I just received two more yesterday and they're still on the transporter near the ammo point and our repair shop. Haven't had the time or the crews to off load 'em and get 'em to one of the battalions. Fortunately, in all this chaos, Division is ordering me back near where you're going. Seems Ivan is running a little low on steam himself."

A knock at the door brought a welcome change in the subject. Feldwebel Dietz had arrived with two cups of hot coffee.

"Excuse me, Herr Oberst. Sorry for the delay. Gentlemen, your coffee." As he handed each officer a shoddy looking cup with a brown-black steaming fluid in it.

"*Danke*, Dietz" Bernatz responded, then turning to Lampon, raised his cup and smiled "To your health, Hauptman. Germany needs all she can get her hands on now."

Outside, Menter returned to the five Opal Blitz troop transports carrying the remains of his infantry company.

"Sergeant Kopas, have the men dismount, then have a detail take these trucks over to the fuel point near the red barn," yelled Hans over the din of truck and troop transport passing by.

The soldiers welcomed the chance to offload and stretch their legs. Many were in need of relieving themselves and made for the nearest field latrines or what ever tree or bush was closest pending on the need of urgency. Once the trucks started moving, Kopas joined the tired lieutenant as they walked over to the fuel point.

"So, what is the word, Herr Lieutanant? What's going on here?" asked Kopas.

"Seems we've stopped by the Third Panzer Regiment's command post and since we're here, paid our respects to their commander, Oberst Bernatz.

You remember him from a few days ago. He's the commander who dropped by 'cause he misplaced his CP."

Kopas chuckled. "There's been so many lately, Herr Lieutenant, I've lost count."

"Well, we can't misplace you, Kopas; I don't know how we'd survive without your skills. Seasoned *feldwebels* are a rare breed."

Kopas enjoyed the compliment, but couldn't acknowledge it; it just wasn't the professional German Army NCO's way.

The two unit leaders reached the fuel point, which consisted of three trucks each loaded with twenty-five 210-liter[20] barrels. A soldier would sign for a barrel, push it off the fuel truck, then roll it on its side over to the troop lorry. Another soldier would then open a small lid on the top and insert what they nicknamed "an Italian pump" – a 3-cm siphon hose in which some poor unfortunate chap would end up with a mouth full of benzene. All in all, a long, laborious process not made any easier by the ice and snow present.

After about thirty minutes, the last of the infantry company's trucks pulled up to receive its fuel. As the already familiar process was undergoing its fifth and final run, Kopas heard a rumble of a large object crashing through the woods.

"Do you hear that, Herr Lieutenant?" Kopas asked, unslinging his rifle.

"Ya, it's coming from over there, about twenty meters in the woods," Menter replied pointing toward the north as he unsnapped and opened his pistol holster. The soldiers conducting the refueling briefly looked up, then seeing nothing, went back to the business at hand.

Suddenly, breaking out of the wood line was a tank of green with a mottled white color—a Russian tank!

"Holy shit—tank!!" yelled Kopas. "Get under cover…" but before he could finish, a round from the tank's cannon fire scored a hit on the first troop truck, bursting into a thousand pieces of flaming metal and debris.

---

20   One barrel contains 40 gallons of fuel

"Get down!" Menter yelled. "Shit, now what?"

Kopas looked around. "Sir, if I can get a couple of anti-tank mines from the ammo point over there, we can sneak up from behind and place them on the tracks."

Boom! Another tank round found its home hitting the second truck. Debris rained down all over the area. Looking up from behind cover, both Kopas and Menter could see five soldiers on the ground, most likely killed when both trucks blew up.

"Krauss, Krawkow, Schmitt, come with me," Kopas called out, moving at a crouch as low as possible in order to keep moving.

The sound of the tanks diesel engine revving gave notice it was on the move, slowly scanning its newfound killing field, much like a lion having found a feast. Within seconds, the tanks coaxial machine gun began tearing into the fleeing German troops, cutting down those unfortunate enough to not have moved quickly enough to find cover.

While Kopas and his three aides moved toward the ammo point, Menter was able to get a better look at the tank, having moved closer to his position.

"A Goddamned T 34—shit!" he thought. No ordinary piece of Russian junk. These tanks, when they showed up, were a pain in the ass to kill and oftentimes resulted in wholesale panic among German troops. This was the closest Menter thought he'd be toward meeting his maker.

Russian T-34 Tanks on the move

Meanwhile in the command post, both Lampon and Bernatz jumped to their feet upon hearing the two booms followed by the banging of metal on metal. Tank alarm! There were Russian tanks in the immediate area.

Bernatz grabbed his sidearm and raced outside the CP. He had no trouble pinpointing where the action was; the telltale plume of smoke and flames near the fuel point drew his initial attention. The familiar staccato of the Russian 7.62-mm machinegun in the same area told him immediately he had trouble—big trouble!

Lampon was right behind him. "What are you going to do, Oberst?" Eric asked, half joking, half terrified.

Bernatz yelled over to Dietz, "Have First Panzer Battalion dispatch one company here immediately if we would have a CP by nightfall! Move your ass!"

"Don't you have an anti-tank section set up somewhere?" Lampon asked.

"Don't make me laugh," Bernatz replied. "Those 37-mm doorknockers wouldn't scratch the paint off one of those tanks much less take one out. Only thing they're good for is killing trucks and light stuff. I've got to get over there—you coming?" And with that, Bernatz was fast on his heels heading toward the red barn. Lampon, realizing his infantry company and engineers were already there, followed closely behind.

Kopas along with his three soldiers reached the ammo point, quickly finding the boxes marked "Meiniger Erzähler" or "Teller mine." Each soldier grabbed two of the one-foot-diameter dinner-plate-sized explosives and headed back to the fuel point closely following Kopas. Moving quickly to reach the left side of the tank, the soldiers neglected to take cover—a quick burst from the tank's machine gun caught Schmitt, cutting him down while Kopas and Krauss ducked down into a ditch. The tank, thinking it killed all its intended victims, continued slowly toward the regiment's command post.

Bernatz and Lampon quickly reached Menter's position, aghast at all the destruction this one tank has already caused.

"Report. What's going on?" asked an exhausted Bernatz. Hans relayed what had transpired, pointing out where Kopas and Krauss were and what they intended to do.

Keeping low and directly behind the turret, the two soldiers made their way to the T-34's left side, quickly depositing two Teller mines on the tracks, then immediately ran back to the ditch they had just occupied. As the tank moved forward, within seconds, the mines dropped off in front of the tank erupting in an immense explosion. The sounds of cheers immediately burst out from the remaining soldiers. There for all to see was one Russian tank with its left side of track completely destroyed. The lion had lost its life.

When Kopas reached the officer position, Bernatz offered him a hearty congratulations and his appreciation at completing the task at hand. Kopas saluted and turned to Menter for further instructions.

"Hans, take a squad down there and see if you can find anything of interest, anything that Staff Intelligence might be able to use once we get the wounded policed up," Lieutenant Menter instructed his *feldwebel*.

After a quick "*Ya-wohl*," he was on his way, instructing Krauss to grab a few men, then he headed over to the iron beast to inspect his kill.

Medics from Bernatz's regimental aid station were soon at the scene, carrying off the company's wounded over to the regiment's makeshift hospital near the command post. Lampon and Menter were surveying the damage to their trucks—two destroyed, one shot up but still drivable albeit without windows. Not a good thing for drivers when its -25 F at night, but it will have to do for now. But a far-grimed truth were his casualties: ten dead, ten wounded, reducing his pitiful company down by a third.

After about five to ten minutes, life appeared to be returning to the normal chaos of war, or at least as normal as a Panzer regiment about to move out could get. Menter and Lampon stood next to the tank and marveled at its engineering—so clean, so simple, yet so deadly. Shaking their heads, they suddenly heard voices, Russian voices. Within seconds, the turret of the supposedly dead beast began to traverse.

"Take cover!" yelled a German soldier. The scramble to find protection was back on.

Nearby, Oberst Bernatz was standing next to his two Panzer Mk. IIIs in the makeshift regimental repair shop, asking his "Workshop[21]" chief how much longer his tanks would take before becoming ready for release.

"About three days, Herr Oberst. Fire control works, but automotive, I need a couple of fan belts," replied the seasoned but overworked Lieutenant Myer.

Bernatz dreaded the thought of dragging this "pig iron" to the next position when he again heard the clanging of metal on metal. "Another tank!" he thought?

A soldier ran by and John grabbed him.

"What's going on?" he asked. "That tank's come back alive..," he said and ran off.

Seeing the wounded tank from where he was standing, the Oberst quickly hopped onto the disabled Mk III, sitting himself into the gunner's seat.

"Myer!" Bernatz yelled out from inside the tank. "Get your ass in here—now!"

Myer's hopped into the tank and stated, "I'm here, but this tank isn't going anywhere as I told you."

"Load one round of hype-shot," Bernatz commanded, while manually traversing the turret.

The lieutenant immediately grabbed a round and slammed it into the breach, snapping shut with a clang. Within a minute, John had his gunner's reticle on the T-34 and snapped the trigger.

---

21   Equivalent in Western Armies to a Regimental Maintenance Officer. Usually a First Lieutenant

"Boom!!" Within seconds, the turret was filled with smoke and dust from the fired 50-mm round, while both officers became disoriented and deafen by the noise. John looked thought the scope, but the cheering he heard from Lieutenant Myer who quickly went "top side" on the Mk III told him he hit his mark. There, burning brightly for all to see was their "Christmas star"—a burning Russian tank, and this time, it wouldn't bother them again.

Bernatz hopped down from the turret, smug but glad it was all over—at least for the moment. The sun was just setting, but the light from the burning T-34 would illuminate the command post area in getting ready to move out. Heading over to his CP, he informed the adjutant, "Let's get the hell out of here."

Meanwhile, 5,000 miles away, Colonel John Reynolds awoke from what little sleep he received the night before as part of General Marshall's Christmas celebration entertaining the joint British delegation. It had been quite a night that unfortunately ended on a tragic note with the fall of Wake Island and the loss of the Royal Crown colony of Hong Kong. Clearly the British would try even harder to get the Americans involved in their fight with the Axis Powers.

"Morning, John," chirped Eisenhower, all dressed up in his Class A uniform, sitting at the breakfast table sipping his morning coffee. "Cups are in the cabinet and coffee's on the counter."

Reynolds was surprised. Yes, the second day of the conference would continue where they left off two days before, but why the Class A uniform? As he reached for the cups, Dwight reminded him they had to be at the Treasury building a little bit early before the "festivities" of the day would commence.

"You don't have much time to get into your A's. We've got to be there by 0930 hours, so you might want to make that cup to go!"

"I'm sorry, Dwight, but what's the occasion? Class A's? I thought this was a staff working session," responded Reynolds.

Eisenhower smiled. "All I know is I have my orders. We are to report in and we're supposed to be in this uniform. Now as you're departing boss, get a move on, Mister!"

With equal parody, John snapped a quick salute and belted out a "Yes, Sir, right ah-way, Sir, I'm coming, Sir," executed a quick 180 and entered the spare bedroom, emerging fifteen minutes late in his "war suite" complete with colorful ribbons and the polished brass of an infantry officer. "Ready for inspection, Sir," John chimed as the two of them grabbed their hats and departed the quarters and into Eisenhower's Army staff car and his driver.

Twenty minutes later, the car pulled up on Fifteenth Street in front of the Treasury building. As the two officers got out of the car, they couldn't help but notice the British delegation, lead by General Dill, walking across Fifteenth Street toward them from the nearby Hotel Washington.

"Good morning, Sir Dill," Eisenhower started, taking the initiative, saluting the senior general, then extending his right hand. Reynolds saluted as well, thankful that Dwight would do the first round of "glad handing," which was something he had a natural talent for. "And how is England's finest this day-after-Christmas morning?"

"Very good, General," Dill responded. "I trust we have a more productive day than last Wednesday. As a token of our appreciation as well as to help your President understand the gravity of this situation we now find ourselves in, we have been allowed by Mr. Churchill to share, shall I say, sensitive information with your senior officers."

With that, the senior officers headed over to the Treasury building entry checkpoint. As they approached the checkpoint, John immediately recognized the soldiers of the IIIth Field Artillery Regiment, Twenty-Ninth Infantry Division, and their burly commander, Lieutenant Colonel Kenny Smith.

"Gooood morn-nan, Sirs." Smith greeted the Brits with his customarily "thicker than molasses" southern accent. "Please have ya papers out for my NCOs to check and we'll have y'all in in no time a-tall."

Reynolds quickly smirked once at Smith as he approached and handed his identity card over to him.

"Colonel Reynolds, Sir! Isn't this a nice reunion? How y'all, been Sir? Did ya have a nice Christmas? Did ole' Santa leave you somethin' special?" Smith quipped as he handed John his card back and rendered a quick salute.

John smiled and returned Smith's customary salute. "Colonel, all I wanted for Christmas was two weeks leave to find a place. I guess Santa's got more pressing requisitions to fill at the moment."

Smith smiled and said "Maybe y'all get lucky in the next few days. I hear all sorts of units and staff officers are moving out soon. After that, they'll be plenty of space left over. You, Sir, have a nice day!" At that point, the Virginia colonel turned and resumed greeting one of the British officers still outside the checkpoint waiting to get into the building.

Eisenhower and Reynolds were immediately taken by the number of personnel present—not only military, but a number of civilians were also in attendance, each carrying notebooks or briefcases or both. As the two headed over to the small room adjacent to the main conference room where the two combined staff were scheduled to assemble shortly, Reynolds spied Colonel Robert "Butch" Watts posted immediately outside, also in his Class A uniform.

"Watts, so what's Marshall's SGS doing here? Something big going down or what?" Reynolds asked.

Butch looked down at the ground, then up at the inquisitive colonel. "You'll find out in about five minutes, as soon as General Marshall finishes his call with the President," he said as he pointed out the chief of staff on the telephone within the small anteroom. "You might as well wait here with me 'cause I think he wants to talk with you."

Reynolds became immediately red-faced. *Did I do or say something inappropriate at the Fort McNair Officers' Club the night before?* he wondered.

As soon as the General finished his phone call and hung up, he signaled Watts, who in turn as if rehearsed signaled a number of other staff officers, all of which immediately converged within the small anteroom. Suddenly, Eisenhower was present, standing alongside General Marshall.

"As you know, General Douglas MacArthur has requested and it was granted that Brigadier General Eisenhower return to the Philippines as his chief of staff. If anybody can help MacArthur, Eisenhower can. We're going to miss him. On his recommendation I hereby take this opportunity and pleasure to announce his replacement as Colonel John Reynolds. Colonel Reynolds, front and center if you may." John stepped forward toward General Marshall, slightly embarrassed at all the attention now thrust upon him.

"Turn around, Reynolds, so everyone can get a look at you. Gentlemen, before Colonel Reynolds is given this assignment, the following administrative action needs to be taken." And with that, Marshall signaled Watts.

Watts stepped forward while opening a manila folder and in a clear, loud voice announced "Attention to orders..." Suddenly, without thinking, everyone present within the room snapped to attention.

Watts continued. "The President of the United States having expressed trust and confidence in this individual hereby promotes John Reynolds to the temporary rank of Brigadier General, effective 23 December 1941, with all the rights and privileges afforded..."

John's head began to spin around. "Brigadier General.... holy shit!" he might have tumbled over had he not felt Marshall's hand sliding under his left shoulder epaulette, removing his colonel's "eagle" and replacing it with the single, bright, shiny, five-pointed star of a newly minted brigadier. Within what appeared to be seconds, his right side was newly pinned as well.

"Congratulations, Brigadier General Reynolds," the chief remarked. Marshall held out his left hand, dropping the now homeless eagles into John's left hand while simultaneous extending his right hand to shake in congratulations. "I know you'll do a great job in War Plans. I'd have you make a speech, but we have a conference to get started. We can celebrate at the McNair O-Club later on. Gentlemen, so if you may, let's move over to the main conference room. We can't keep our distinguished British colleagues waiting. They have their war and we have ours." Then Marshall directed him toward the main conference room.

As the small promotion party entered, John was immediately taken by the number of attendees—this time the room was not only filled with the usual Army- Navy brass, but those same civilians with bulging briefcases he saw outside were prominently seated in the area immediately near the two key luminaries of Marshall and Dill. Apparently, this conference was taking a different course than before.

"Gentlemen, if we can all take our seats, we can get this meeting started," said General Marshall, clearly letting all present know this it was his conference. "Before we commence with today's agenda, there are two things I wish to announce before we get started. First, I apologize to our esteemed British colleagues for our tardiness. This morning, Brigadier General John Reynolds became our newest general officer and will be taking over from Brigadier General Eisenhower, who will be departing very soon to help General MacArthur with our defense in the Philippines. So, if you get the chance, please extend your congratulations to both of these fine officers during the conference breaks."

Reynolds could feel the eyes of the various attendees descend momentarily upon him—some saluting, some giving the thumbs up, others glancing at what a newly minted U.S. Army brigadier looked like. Fifteen minutes of fame can feel like an eternity if one isn't used to the undue attention. Marshall continued with his raspy voice immediately snapping Reynolds back to the present.

"The second item to point out is on December 18 the President authorized the formation of a scientific work group to begin development of an atomic weapon. This group is called the 'S-1' project and we have present a visitor, a Mr. Bill Armstrong available from New York, to begin initial coordination with our British friends in order to prevent duplication of effort and to share ideas and techniques. Mr Armstrong, it you may, please stand and let everyone present see who you are."

A slight, thin, black-haired gentleman with black horned-rim glasses slowly rose, then held his arm up as if called upon to give the answer to some college math problem, all the while still clutching his brown briefcase. John immediately noticed the handcuff and chain from the case to Armstrong's right wrist. "Obviously, Armstrong came prepared with a few atomic secrets to share should the right time and required British contact come along," Reynolds thought.

Armstrong let everyone know he would be available for the duration of the conference, but could only provide the slimmest, vaguest details of his mission. As he sat down, Marshall continued.

"The S-1 project is the responsibility of the U.S. Army Corps of Engineers and is presently headquartered in the Manhattan borough of New York City. Unless you have the right top secret credentials, that's about all we can say about this for the time being. Now, gentlemen, if there isn't anything further, I suggest we entertain the first item on the agenda: the sharing of intelligence collection for mutual use between our two governments. Colonel Butch Watts, newly assigned to the Far East Section of my G-2 Intelligence Division replacing Colonel Rufus S. Bratton, will now brief."

Watts rose and began announcing that in conjunction with the Navy, the Intelligence Division was in possession of the Japanese diplomatic code and had access to their decipher machine, reading their traffic faster than the Japanese were able to.

"In the late 1930s the U.S. Army's SIS broke into the highest-level Japanese diplomatic cipher which we codenamed 'Purple'. From here, we ran all our intercepts through a code via our little crypto-machine and the product was codenamed 'Magic'," Watts said proudly.

"Through the various signals and listening stations we have positioned throughout the Pacific, we had a fairly good idea where and when the Japanese would strike. Monitoring stations such as Station HYPO in Hawaii logged 129 radio messages from the Japanese fleet between November 15 and December 6. So powerful were the Japanese fleet transmitters that a radioman on the passenger ship SS *Lurline*, listening to Japanese transmissions to the fleet, was able to pick up the fleet's replies and plot the fleet's position. Upon arrival in Honolulu his logbook and map of the Japanese fleet's progress across the Pacific was quickly delivered to the Office of Naval Intelligence. Yet, for some reason unknown to us, this information never got to Admiral Kimmel quickly enough for him to take action."

Reynolds as well as half a dozen Army officers sat up clearly astonished. All that technology and clearly knowing the Japs were going to strike and yet, they got completely through and virtually destroyed the U.S. Pacific Fleet in a matter of two hours.

Watts continued with his now attentive audience. "At this time, all four of the Imperial Japanese Navy code systems used by Admiral Yamamoto were broken in the fall of 1941 and were used by Station HYPO located at Pearl Harbor. We now know them to be increasing in the use of the new JN-25 code. This code is the current one in use by the Jap Navy for their high-level operations—movement and planning commands, for instance. It is a super-encrypted code and it was until recently state of the art. Our cryptanalytic progress is slow, but we are making fairly good progress in cracking this. At present, we have increased IJN naval traffic decryption from around 10 percent to roughly 20 percent at this time, so as long as our stations in Cavite Bay in the Philippines, and Guam, as well as our allied brethren listening stations in Batavia and Frumel, Australia, hold up and collect Japanese naval traffic, we will eventually decipher it."

Watts felt satisfied that his brief to the conference attendees went over well, but noticed the British delegation did not appear as surprised as his American colleagues; in fact, they appeared quite bored. The ever-vigilant Marshall picked up on the attitude as well.

"Is there a problem, Sir Dill," Marshall inquired? "In the spirit of cooperation in dealing with the present war against the Japanese, President Roosevelt felt we should pool our intelligence assets accordingly."

Dill looked quickly at his delegation, and then in a slightly embarrassed manner asked Marshall, "You mean you don't know, Sir? Your President never told you ...?"

"Told us what, Sir?" Admiral King interrupted. "What in blue blazes are you talking about?"

Marshall quickly gave the crusty ole' Admiral his "shut up, I've got it handled" look. "General Dill, what exactly are you talking about in regards to your statement about the President?"

Dill rose to his feet and cleared his voice. "Gentleman, I am deeply embarrassed to have to tell you that we've known this for quite some time. You see, our code-breaking boys in Bletchley Park have cracked the German code and obtained one of their code machines which we call 'Ultra,' but we have also cracked your own State Department ciphers as well, so as you received traffic from the Japanese pertaining to their naval chicanery, we were reading it as well. Mr. Churchill supposedly informed your President of this shortly after the attack on Pearl Harbor, or so I was informed."

There was a hushed silence across the room as Dill returned to his seat. Suddenly, reading someone else's mail, even if it was a close neighbor, wasn't exactly as the British say cricket. Above all else, Roosevelt knew of this indiscretion by a supposed "ally," but didn't tell his own delegation.

Most shocked of all was King. Always the consummate Anglophobe, he leaned over to General Hap Arnold, sitting immediately next to King, and whispered in his ear. "I told you we can't trust these bastards. They've been playing us for fools all along…"

From that point on, the conference began its slow descent into a bickering contest covered in an overhang of mistrust between the two most foremost world powers. Throughout the day, the British constantly harangued the Americans to divert their forces earmarked for the Philippines to areas the British deemed more critical—Malaysia and the defense of their Gibraltar of the Pacific, Singapore. Above all else, Dill's delegation repeatedly asked to the point of demanding the United States provide more equipment in dealing with the Germans in Africa—tanks, planes and, above all, heavy bombers such as the cherished Boeing B-17 *Flying Fortress* now rolling off American assembly plants across the country.

Marshall had his instructions as well. The Army's vaunted Chief of Staff and company tried numerous times to keep the conference on agenda—how to deal with the Japanese onslaught in the Pacific and coordinate both nations' actions as one—but it was still clear to the American delegation that the British were only interested in poaching as much of their military hardware as possible and eventually troops as they could get away with without any U.S. participation in the decisions. In short, the United States was to assist the United Kingdom is maintaining its imperial "status quo" and advancing its own narrow self-interests.

By late afternoon, the only real accomplishment between the two delegations was the establishment of a single theater command in the Pacific called "ABDA" an acronym for "American-British-Dutch-Australian" in essence, an ad hoc collection of forces and warships from the various shattered colonies within a 9,000-square-mile region lumped together under a "British" command: one General Archibald Wavell, hero of the Middle East, with an American to be named later as his deputy. Reynolds noted that the Dutch and Australians would not be happy serving under a British command and Wavell would be a hard sell, even though he was recommend by FDR himself. Through all the discussion, General Douglas MacArthur was never mention at all as a possible contender.

Just as the delegations had reached their zenith and everyone was ready to conclude for the day, Harry Hopkins popped in at the behest of Roosevelt to see how the conference was proceeding. While both Dill and Marshall exchanged pleasantries that much had been discussed and coordination begun, it was clear even to the overly optimistic Hopkins there was far too much distance on coordinating an overall strategy in the Pacific as well as distrust toward British overall motives about working in tandem with their American allies.

As Marshall recapped the day's events, Hopkins noted that the Soviet Union in its war with the Germans wasn't hampered in having a non-aggression pact with their East Asian adversaries, the Japanese. In fact, it was their recent transfer of their Siberian reserves from the east that saved Moscow from the German onslaught and spearheaded their current counterattack.

"Maybe having a non-aggressive relationship toward the Germans might play to our advantage," Hopkins quipped to Marshall. That would allow us to focus in defeating the Japanese as quickly as possible. Then, when the time is right, maybe presenting the possibility of a United States commitment toward supporting the British against them might knock some sense into Hitler. That's the sort of options I can present to FDR if this conference works out to his satisfaction."

Marshall shook after hearing Hopkins's comments. He motioned for BG Reynolds, who quickly disengaged from his conversation with Colonel Watts and responded to the Chief's inquiry.

After Harry Hopkins briefed Reynolds on a recap of what he had just discussed with Marshall, he pointedly asked what he thought would happen in Europe without the United States.

"Well, Sir, Churchill is a truly a student of the periphery strategy, that is to hit Hitler from any points outside the direct approach—crossing the channel and marching across France. If I were a guessing man and needed to make a calculated guess, they'll continue to dance across North Africa with as much aid as we can give them. If the Germans pull out, Mr. Churchill will look at trying to knock Italy out, or land in the Balkans. Or try for Sicily or Corsica for a future jumping off point into invading the southern part of the continent. Remember, Churchill served as an infantry battalion commander in the trenches of the Somme after he resigned from the Naval Ministry in 1916 due to his debacle in the ill-fated Gallipoli campaign. He's keenly aware of the losses incurred on the British Army in trying the direct approach across no-mans land during the First World War and continue trying to defeat the Germans."

Marshall in turn responded. "This is the sort of strategy—hit here, hit there—that will cost more lives in the long run. If you've got a job to do, you get in there and finish it as quickly as possible. This is why we need to nail the Japs first, while the Nazis are tied up in Russia. Do you think they're just going to sit around and wait for us to come get them? Hell no, they're digging in as quickly and deeply as possible."

"What about the Soviets?" Hopkins asked. "Do you think they can hold out? Aren't they allies, too?"

"Well, Sir," said Reynolds, "two months ago I didn't think they had a chance, and now they seem to have thrown the Germans back from the very gates of Moscow, according to our embassy there. They have virtually unlimited manpower but it could go either way. As long as the Russians are still in the fight, that's where the bulk of the Wehrmacht will be found. It's simply a matter of the Russians not running out of troops against German panzers and firepower. As the Russians re-gather their strength, the Germans will inevitably hit them again until the campaign is finally concluded. I don't think this will be a complete replay of the Napoleonic nightmare winter retreat of 1812 where he just left the country after taking Moscow. I think the Germans are committed to operations in Russia for some time to come.

At least they're not swimming across the English Channel and that should be of some comfort to our British cousins."

"So, basically, we have a sort of horse race in that we have to defeat the Japanese before the Nazis eventually defeat the Russians," replied Hopkins. "That should keep any mention of a Red menace at bay for some time to come and definitely make J. Edgar Hoover's day at the FBI.

Hopkins turned toward Marshall and gave him final instructions.

"General Marshall, proceed per the agenda the Secretary of War and your staff hammered out last week. If this doesn't seem to gel with the Brits by the twenty-eighth, then you are instructed to contact me, and I'll have the President suspend any further meetings. Meanwhile, I'll discuss what we just talked about with him and formulate a new approach."

With that, the general saluted Hopkins and asked Reynolds to follow him. As Hopkins immediately lit his ever-present cigarette and left safely out of earshot, the chief of staff commented to Reynolds that by year's end, his "Rainbow Two" war plan was a solid go—with or without the support of the British Commonwealth. As for Admiral Ernest King, the newly ordained U.S. Navy Commander-In-Chief (referred to in naval lexicon as COMINCH), his Christmas dream of a one-on-one naval war with the dreaded Imperial Japanese was about to come true.

Chapter 10

Red Sun Rising

"If you insist on my going ahead (with the bombing of Pearl Harbor), I can promise to give the Americans hell for a year or a year and a half, but I can guarantee nothing as to what will happen after that. . ."

- Admiral Isoroku Yamamoto,
Commander-in-Chief, Combined Fleet, Nov. 1941

100 kilometers west of Yokohama Naval Base, Japan
1000 hrs, 4 Jan 1942

The Mitsubishi G4M bomber slowly banked to the left then began its slow decline as it approached Japanese airspace and the Port City of Yokohama, home of the Imperial Japanese Fleet. Normally a routine flight, this particular one carried an escort of three A6M "Zero" fighters due to the special cargo onboard. It was cargo in the form of the Commander in Chief of the Imperial Japanese Navy Combined Fleet, the distinguished, fifty-seven-year-old Admiral Isoroku Yamamoto, mastermind of the recent Japanese Navy strike on Pearl Harbor.

For the past two weeks as he conducted his inspection tour of Japanese Navy facilities and installations throughout the Marshall Islands, he had been bombarded with congratulations from various army and naval officers, but today, as he suddenly woke up from his long and exhausting travels, a long-overdue sense of dread began to descend on him, much like the bomber he was on descending in altitude. Within a couple of days, he would be in attendance at the Imperial General Headquarters in Tokyo to discuss future options with the general staff, now that they were in a war with the Americans as well as the Europeans—in particular, the British and Dutch. While the others forces were insignificant to the Japanese, the Americans were a force to be reckoned with.

Yamamoto relished his short but refreshing in-flight nap. Since December 7, his days became longer and longer, as Japanese Navy and Army forces surged across the wide expanses of the Pacific and South China Sea. Everything on the surface appeared to be going according to plan. Even the Imperial Army Forces, reluctant to share any credit with him, also seemed pleased that his strategic approach, the *Nanshin* ("Go south") strategy which had been adapted by the Imperial High Command. This was in spite of the Army's reluctance to support the Navy's plan in lieu of their own desires to pursue the *Hokushin* ("Go north") option to take on the Soviet Union one more time in revenge for their humiliation at their loss in November 1939. There, at a little-known place in the Mongolian desert named Nomonhan, the Japanese Sixth Army, the pride of the Kwangtung Army of China, was defeated by the Soviets in a border incident; they suffered approximately 21,000 casualties, including 8,600 dead.

It was no small wonder that General Hideki Tojo, the Imperial War Minister and now Prime Minister, referred to this place as "the graveyard of reputations." Much to the dismay of their German allies fighting in Russia, Japan opted to take the war south into the resource-rich Southeast Asia, where British tin from Burma, French rubber from Indochina, and Dutch oil from Indonesia would fuel Japan's future ambitions wherever that would take them. Only one nation stood in her way: the United States.

In Yamamoto's mind, to stop the Americans with her bastion in Asia, the Philippine Islands, would need to be conquered. This in turn would bring in the American Navy, second to none now that the British were fighting without the French by their sides in Europe. The old strategy called for a titanic naval battle in the middle of the Pacific between the two opposing forces, until one fleet would eventually succeed. For two decades, in keeping with the doctrine of the famous naval strategist Captain Alfred T. Mahan, the Japanese Naval general staff had planned in terms of Japanese light-surface forces, submarines and land-based air units whittling down the American fleet as it advanced across the Pacific until the Imperial Japanese Navy (IJN) engaged it in a climactic "decisive battle" in the central Pacific. This would be a meeting in the traditional exchange between battle lines much as in the days of sailing that past century. It was no surprise to anyone that both sides had planned and rehearsed for such an event over the past thirty-something years. No, there had to be a better way, and that prior January he would have his way proposing a radical revision to this antiquated strategy.

Correctly pointing out to the Imperial General Staff that this plan had never worked even in their war games, and painfully aware of American strategic advantages in military productive capacity[22], he proposed instead to seek a decision with the Americans by first reducing their forces with a pre-emptive strike, and following it with a "decisive battle" fought offensively, rather than defensively. Yamamoto hoped, but did not believe deep down, that if the Americans could be dealt such terrific blows early in the war, they might be willing to negotiate an end to the conflict.

"Yes, take out the American Navy at Pearl Harbor and they would have no choice but to eventually accede to Japan's terms," he said when the completed plan was briefed to the War Ministry that past year. In everyone's mind, such a crushing defeat might cause America's fragile morale to crumble much like it had with the Russians a fortnight before under similar conditions, thirty-seven years prior. There, in a surprise move, a Japanese naval force smashed the Russian fleet outside Port Arthur ushering in the Russo-Japanese War. In fact, the very naval ensign flown by the great Admiral Tojo

---

22   Admiral Yamamoto studied at Harvard University from 1919–1921, then served two posting as the Japanese Naval attaché in Washington, D.C. This tenure in the United States gave Yamamoto an excellent understanding of American lifestyles as well as her potential industrial capability.

back in 1905 was flown again over the Pacific carrier *Strike Force* as a measure of good luck. *Such is the plan,* Yamamoto thought, *such is the plan* ...

But like all great plans, none ever survived contact with the enemy, least of all his cherished attack against the vaunted U.S. Pacific Fleet, and he soon realized it had miscarried.

In reading the initial and follow-up dispatches sent by the First Air Fleet Commander Vice Admiral Chuichi Nagumo, Japanese losses amounted to losing only twenty-nine aircraft, but they suffered damage to more than III planes. The damaged aircraft were disproportionately dive- and torpedo-bombers, thus seriously impacting available firepower to exploit the success of the first two waves. As such, Nagumo decided to withdraw.

Upon reading this dispatch a day later, a disappointed Yamamoto berated Nagumo for failure to seize the initiative to seek out and destroy the American carriers missing from Pearl Harbor. Worse, now neither Yamamoto nor Nagumo had absolutely any idea where the American carriers might be. Remaining on station while his forces cast about looking for them, he ran the risk of his own force being found first and attacked while his aircraft were out searching. Yamamoto began to realize Nagumo's aircraft also lacked appropriate ordnance for attacking the machine tools and dry docks of the shipyard, or even the massive naval fuel tank farms, whose destruction could have resulted in more serious losses than the fighting ships themselves. In any case, insufficient daylight remained after recovering the aircraft from the first two waves for the carriers to launch and recover a third before dark. Additionally, Nagumo's escorting destroyers lacked the fuel capacity for him to loiter long. Such was Yamamoto's hindsight and wishful thinking, and for that, he decided not punish Nagumo in any way for his withdrawal, which was, after all, according to plan. But that was not the worst of it.

What really made Yamamoto upset were the bungling diplomats in Washington and their failure to deliver Japan's declaration of war in a timely manner prior to the attack. On the political level, the attack was a disaster for Japan. Having spent a few years in the United States, Yamamoto knew the attack without a declaration of war would arouse American passions for revenge due to it being considered a "sneak attack." The shock of the attack coming in an unexpected place, with such devastating results and without the expected "fair play" of a war declaration would galvanize the American public's determination to avenge the attack. Now rather than a cowed enemy the Imperial General Staff had planned on, the Americans would come after them with everything they had, thirsty for revenge.

"Are you all right? Sir?" Commander Kamei, his aide-de-camp asked. "You seemed to be in a trance. Can I get you some water from the plane's galley?"

Yamamoto slowly turned to the aide and smiled. "Kamei, we have so much to do and so little time to do it. Even as we speak, the Americans are gathering their strength and will be upon us very shortly. Their industrial capacity is immense, beyond anything we could possibly imagine. It would be different if our so-called allies, the Germans, had decided this was the time to declare war on the Americans, but this is not to be the case."

"But, Admiral, I don't understand. We are winning against the western imperialist forces. Our fleets and armies are advancing everywhere, inflicting crushing defeat upon defeat on them where we meet in battle," replied Kamei, somewhat stunned by the Admiral's questionable prognosis.

Before Yamamoto could answer his young aide, a voice came over the aircraft intercom.

"Sir, we are beginning our approach to Yokohama Naval Air Base. I ask that you and your aide please fasten your seatbelts until we have landed, which should be in approximately ten minutes."

From the open door of the forward cockpit, Yamamoto waved to the co-pilot acknowledging he heard and understood his instructions. As the plane banked to the left, the Admiral couldn't resist looking out the aircraft window at the blue Japanese sea and the approaching port, filled with shipping of all shapes and sizes. One particular ship immediately drew his attention, dwarfing all other ships within the bay. He signaled Commander Kamei to look outside.

"There she is, Kamei, the Battleship *Yamato*, the world's largest battleship," said the admiral, almost like a father showing off his newest son.

Yamato on trials

This was clearly no ordinary battleship. Even from an altitude of 5,000 feet she was immense, making all other ships nearby look like bathtub toys. At 862 feet in length, she was almost one third the height of New York's Empire State Building, while displacing some 72,000 tons of water. One would never forget viewing this massive ship for the rest of one's life.

"I understand soon she will be your new flagship and that you will be transferring your colors from the *Nagato*. What is she doing down there?"

"She's undergoing sea trials since her commissioning on December 16, sailing up from the Kure Navy Yard. Once her trials are completed sometime in February, she'll be our new home," said the admiral. "Her sister ship, the *Musashi*, is also at Kure under construction, but will not be available until this summer."

"That's what we need, Sir, more ships like her for the glory of the Imperial Navy," the proud commander replied. "Hopefully, I will be in command of one of these ships before the war ends!"

Yamamoto leaned back from the window and smiled at his young aide. "You have much to learn, Kamei, so much to learn. Would you be surprised if I told you I was against building these type ships from the very start? In the day and age of naval aviation and aircraft carriers, these 'dinosaurs' are truly an unwise investment of our precious resources. Do you know what we need more than this type of super-battleships?"

Commander Kamei, stunned at hearing this form of naval blasphemy from the very Commander in Chief he faithfully served, just shook his head. Yamamoto was never known for pulling his punches.

"More important than all the super-battleships we can construct is the need to have a strategic plan! Imagine, Kamei, here we are at war with the West, and we do not have a master plan to follow to obtain victory."

"How can that be, Sir?" an incredulous Kamei responded. "We are winning!"

"It's an illusion," said the Admiral. "We have masqueraded strategy as a campaign plan. What should be called a campaign plan we have substituted as a battle doctrine. In other words, our plan, as you would call it, was to fight and win one decisive battle. There was no thought for a contingency for anything else than total victory. We basically put all our eggs in one basket. Let me put it another way. Have you ever been to Europe—say, Italy?"

Commander Kamei again nodded his head. "No, Sir, I've never had the opportunity."

The admiral continued. "A few years ago, I was visiting a museum in Italy and happened to view an astronomical clock created by a famous fourteenth-century clockmaker, Giovanni de Dondi. This man assembled a majestic planetary clock of dials and wheels within wheels, representing the then worldview of the universe: beautiful, imaginative, ingenious, carefully crafted, but hopelessly misdirected and obsolete even as it reached its pinnacle of achievement. We, the Imperial Japanese Navy, Commander Kamei, are the modern day equivalent of de Dondi's timepiece. All we can do is buy time until we can formulate a strategy to deal with the Americans. Hence, now you know my mission for traveling to the Imperial General Staff Headquarters. They know it as well, but won't admit as much."

All Commander Kamei could do at this point was to sit back in the web seat and ponder what his boss has just informed him of. *We are winning, but we will not win the war; how was this possible in light of what the Imperial General Staff had been telling us all along?* he thought to himself over and over.

The now uncomfortable quiet between the two Japanese Naval officers was shortly interrupted by the sudden "thump" of the aircrafts tires hitting the concrete airstrip of the Yokohama Naval Base. Kamei looked out the window in order to spot the general's reception party. Within five minutes, the Mitsubishi taxied up to a large hanger where three very official cars were parked, surrounded by a squad of blue uniformed naval personnel.

As the plane gently came to a halt, Yamamoto, tired of having sat for so many long hours over the Pacific, quickly removed his seatbelt and made his way forward to the cockpit, when it opened with a jolt and the face of a young naval lieutenant appeared:

"Sir, I am so sorry for that hard landing. I will never do that again," the lieutenant said, but before he could finish, the admiral smiled at him, nodded his head and like a father counseling his son for going over a bump in his car too hard, reassured the young officer.

"I was a pilot once many years ago and, let me tell you, any landing you walk away from is a good landing. Thank you for your service to the Emperor." And with that, he shook his hand, and quickly left the plane, Commander Kamei closely in tow.

As they emerged, a blast of winter air off the bay made both quickly realize they were no longer in the tropics. Heavy jackets would need to be broken out from their baggage immediately.

The honor guard quickly snapped to attention, under the watchful eye the more seasoned Imperial Japanese Navy Lieutenant Kendo. Kendo began to signal the accompanying band to render honors to the visiting Commander in Chief, but Yamamoto was too quick for him, nodding his head from left to right that music was not the order of the day.

"Lieutenant, we don't have time for all these pleasantries. Just get me and my staff to the Yokohama rail station where my train awaits as soon as we get our jackets out of our baggage."

"Yes, Sir," Kendo barked, disappointed at his first and largely unimpressive meeting with the admiral. He quickly yelled instructions and just as quickly, the admiral's baggage was loaded into the cars and was immediately on its way.

As the three-car procession left the base, Yamamoto looked at his watch. "Humm, 1110 hours, Kamei. We'll reach the station within twenty minutes. If the Gods are with us, we'll be underway to Tokyo by noon and should be within the city in –forty-five to sixty minutes. Once we arrive at the train station, I want you to send a signal the Naval Ministry of our arrival there this afternoon and that we'll be in attendance at the Imperial General Headquarters strategy session if it is still set for 1000 hours tomorrow."

Kamei quickly copied the admiral's information down as only a proud and capable aide-de-camp could. Sure enough, as if the admiral had looked into a crystal ball, they arrived and occupied Yamamoto's special car, pulling out of the station at precisely 1201 hours. Kamei barely had time to get his signal off before seeing the train brakeman signaling they were ready to depart.

As they felt the warmth of the car's heater, both naval professionals had forgotten that winter in Tokyo is almost as cold as Berlin. Just twenty-four hours prior, both enjoyed the warm weather of the Marshall Islands. There, the war seemed so far away…

Commander Kamei stared out into the snowy countryside as the train zoomed past the countless small villages and hamlets enroute to Tokyo. His silence began to become unnerving to Yamamoto, and he began to wonder whether he may have said too much to his young aide.

"Commander, what are your thoughts? Are you disturbed by what I told you earlier?" the admiral inquired.

As if snapped out of a trance, Kamei immediately gave his admiral his full attention. "Sir, with your permission, may I speak freely?"

"Please," Yamamoto responded, "you know I appreciate your candor. Tell me what's on your mind. I cannot go to a major strategy session with the Army with my best aide distracted."

"Admiral, please let me be blunt. If what you say is true, is winning this great war possible?" Kamei asked. "Certainly the other generals and admirals in attendance know this as well. What about the Emperor?"

Yamamoto leaned back in his seat. With his left hand, he reached up to scratch his head, searching for the right words to inform his naïve aide what the situation was.

"Kamei, Japan is a military dictatorship. In case you haven't guessed, it's the Army under General Hideki Tojo that dominates our entire nation's decision making and there's nobody strong enough to rein them in. Think about it: why is it both the Army and Navy have their own air force, marines, even ships? Each service pursues its own independent war polices with no one great enough in the government to decide which course is the best. Like two kids, each one pursuing their own selfish goals regardless of how it works for the greater good. Relations between the Army and Navy general staffs are never cordial, and as you will soon see, marked by deep hostility. The Army sees the Soviet Union as Japan's greatest threat. We on the other hand look across the Pacific and see the United States as the greatest threat. Hence, the purpose of this conference is to try and reach agreement between the Army and Navy on strategic planning—a most difficult task."

Yamamoto glanced out the window at the white countryside. "As long as the conflict stayed in China, the rivalry between the Army and Navy was manageable. But when Tojo became Prime Minister last fall while retaining his status as the Army Minister, we all knew war with the West was inevitable."

"If it was inevitable. Why did the Emperor allow it to continue if we didn't have a chance?" Kamei asked.

Yamamoto continued. "After over four years of war in China, it became apparent to all but the blind that China with all her vast resources could not be defeated by our Imperial Japanese Army. This war, Kamei, is costing us a staggering 22 million yen[23] a day and is warping our trade balance, which is massively compounded by last year's crippling American trade embargo. We simply cannot let this go on without going down into financial ruin.

"No, for us to win we would need to quickly surround China and to do that would entail our going into Indochina and Burma. Such an action would ultimately involve going to war with the great colonial powers of Great Britain and France. To seize British Burma, we would have to destroy them in Malaya and in turn destroy their naval bastion at Singapore. Following this train of thought inevitably it would bring the Americans in since we could not afford to leave our flanks open to an American presence in the Philippines. To remedy this, we took the initiative to destroy their fleet at Pearl Harbor hoping it would once and for all give the Americans time to pause and perhaps reconsider their position and leave us in peace. Ultimately, for this scenario to have work to the benefit of the Empire, our leaders fecklessly gambled on two major assumptions."

Kamei sat staring incredulously at the admiral. "What were they, if I may ask?"

---

23   Five million dollars at the 1940 currency exchange rate

"The first assumption they made was the Germany would triumph in Europe and would win its war against the dreaded Communists in the east. With the great colonial powers gone, occupying Southeast Asia would not be a problem. I think it is the most apparent the Germans have failed, but it's far from over."

The aide-de-camp took a deep breath. "But everyone can see we are winning against the British and Dutch. Their forces fall before us like sheep and once the Germans conquer the Soviet Union, our Army will once again walk in victory against what Russians are left in the Far East, just like we did in 1920."

Yamamoto could see he wasn't getting through to his idealistic young aide. "Kamei, you must ask yourself, are these *victories* against the colonial powers a real display of our energy and prowess, or simple reflection of local weakness of the vanquished?"

Kamei thought silently for the moment, pondering Yamamoto's question. When it was apparent he could not come up with a suitable rebuttal, he again took the offense.

"And what, Sir, was the second assumption the Imperial General Staff made?" Commander Kamei asked.

The Admiral turned from the window and stared ahead, ashen-faced as he responded. "We gambled that the United States would not have the stomach for a long conflict. Now, because of the circumstances our bungling diplomats in Washington have created, they will come at us with everything they have and that, my friend, is what this conference is about. How do we fight and win a modern war against the Americans when 40 percent of our population is predominantly rural, working off the land?"

"You mean to tell me, Sir, that we cannot possibly defeat the Americans?" Kamei inquired.

Yamamoto signed, drawn down as he prepared for the statement he dreaded to say, but had to.

"Kamei, what I have to say must remain here in this car. It is a poor secret among the senior admirals, but as a rule of thumb, we have known that deep down we do not have the capability to defeat the Americans. We had hoped that our strike at Pearl Harbor would have been devastating and shocking enough that its success would have ultimately translated into an acceptance by the United States of our new arrangement of power on the Pacific. However, as you have become painfully aware, our government as a whole placed all its efforts into *hope* and, as you are aware, *hope* is a poor basis for a plan."

Yamamoto's aide could readily tell the admiral was in pain disclosing this surprising but true fact about their own government. Japan, a nation that reached back over a thousand years with a people who could not imagine they could ever be defeated in war, now faced that bleak prospect as present by Yamamoto.

"Kamei, we have a lot of work to do in the next days as to how we are to delay the inevitable..." Yamamoto stopped as he leaned back in his seat signaling the conversation was at an end. All the two officers could do was listen to the rhythmic vibrations of the train rolling north toward Tokyo, less than an hour away.

After a fitful and restless night in the capital, Admiral Yamamoto and Commander Kamei met up with his driver for the short trip to the Imperial General Headquarters located on the grounds of the Emperor's palace. Both naval officers could not help but marvel at the spectacular view afforded to but a rare few privileged who served the Emperor, especially for Kamei who only last year made his first visit there.

Emperor's Palace in Tokyo

As per protocol, an Army detachment functioned as the Imperial Headquarters security force, checking identities and ensuring only those with the highest clearance were allowed to enter the headquarters compound. As the admiral's car approached, the detachment commander ordered the entire detachment to file out, rendering Admiral Yamamoto a salute while crying *"Bonzi!! Bonzi!!"*

The admiral returned the salute, slightly embarrassed at this overt jester. Commander Kamei looked at Yamamoto and seeing his slight discomfort commented "Sir, you cannot blame them. You are regarded as a national hero. That alone should help your position in dealing with the Army hotheads this morning." The admiral silently nodded and waved to the soldiers as the car proceeded forward.

His driver, Seaman Masaharu drove through the security checkpoint as directed by the detachment commander to a building where a senior naval officer was standing, anxiously awaiting the arrival of the admiral himself.

"I see Commander Watanabe is right on time," commented the admiral with a smile. Yamamoto's favorite junior officer, Commander Yasuji Watanabe, was a old favorite of the admiral's and was chosen by him the year prior to work with his operations officer, Captain Kameto Kusoshima, to review and elaborate on Commander Minoru Genda's draft plan on attacking Pearl Harbor. Now he would call upon his young friend once more to help him out, especially since his old trusted Kuroshima was moving on to a new assignment.

"Yasuji will make a fine replacement for Kuroshima," Yamamoto commented to Kamei, adding, "I like the way he thinks, considering every possibility and what we're up against."

The staff car pulled up to the special parking place with Yamamoto's name placed prominently. Immediately, as if following a close action precision battle drill, Seaman Masaharu raced out of the car to grab the admiral's door, but was blocked as his door slammed into Watanabe, knocking both the seaman and commander off balance. Yamamoto calmly opened the door and stepped out bemused, as he looked at the two surprised naval personnel picking themselves off the ground.

"I am so sorry, please forgive me, honorable Sir!" Masaharu sputtered out while trying to unsuccessfully place his sailor's cap back on his head.

After recovering from his sudden car door body slam, Watanabe laughed as he picked himself up and brushed the combination of snow and dirt off his dark blue wool jacket. Yamamoto also chuckled, extending his hand to the dazed commander, helping him up onto his feet.

"Watanabe, this is no time to get yourself injured, not when I need you as my new operations officer and we have so much to do," lamented the admiral. "We have much to discuss while we stroll to the conference."

The Imperial General Staff conference room was immense, far bigger than anyone on the admiral's staff imagined, far larger than the conference room found on the admiral's flagship. Colorful paintings of cherry trees,

Mount Fujiyama, and his majesty, Emperor Hirohito, adorned the walls. Toward the back of the conference room, a platoon of female stenographers conjugated near a series of small tables filled with refreshments comprised of coffee, tea, oranges, apples, and grapes. This headquarters staff knew how to live.

Imperial General Staff Conference

On one side of the large teak, twenty-five-foot table, distinguished by their forest green tunics were the generals and senior members of the Army General Staff, many adorned with their yellow staff officer cords hanging from their right shoulder. Near the head of the table was their Imperial chief of staff, the feared General Hajime Sugiyama, an aggressive army officer believed to be descended from samurais. Since becoming the chief of the Imperial Japanese Army General Staff in September 1940, Sugiyama became one of the leading Army officers lobbying for war with the great Western powers, especially Britain and the United States. Prior to today's conference, rumors floated about that the almighty chief of staff had been severely berated by Emperor Hirohito that previous September for his having earlier predicted back in 1937 that the Imperial Army invasion of China would be completed within three months. Much to his embarrassment, the Emperor further challenged him over his confidence in a quick victory over the Western powers should war break out. Today, however, he could marginally gloat that maybe the Emperor was wrong.

On the other side of the long teak table, as if looking at a distorted negative image of the green-suited army officers, were the dark-blue–uniformed member of the Imperial Japanese Navy Staff, headed by their respective chief of staff, Admiral Osami Nagano, who also assumed his esteemed position in 1941. Yamamoto, immediately upon entering the conference room and spying the Naval Chief of Staff, made a beeline toward his old and trusted friend.

The two of them went back many years, when Yamamoto, then a young lieutenant commander, served with Nagano in Washington, D.C., while they both were military naval attachés to the United States, in which capacity they both attended the infamous Washington Naval Conference. Although he was a proponent of the *Nanshin-ron*, Nagano, like Yamamoto, was against war with the United States, for he too knew the inevitable. The Naval Chief of Staff was also a pragmatist, concluded that if Japan were able to take over British and Dutch colonies in Asia without directly attacking the United States, possibly the isolationist factions within the American government would prevent the United States from declaring war against Japan. The rest of the Imperial Naval Staff felt otherwise, thus his need to task and eventually adopt Yamamoto's plan of attack against the American fleet at Pearl Harbor that past fall. Yamamoto may have planned it, but it was Nagano who ordered the strike. Now the two old friends were united one more time against a common foe, and this time it wasn't the Western powers.

As the two admirals exchanged pleasantries. General Sugiyama spied suspiciously at these two comrades while his Army staff officers near the front of the long table were busy positioning briefing easels, each one displaying colorful maps or briefing points.

"What are these two up to?" Sugiyama wondered, feeling uncomfortable that the top talent of the Imperial Japanese Navy were in such close discussion. While the entire country was rejoicing in the fact that the mighty American fleet at Pear Harbor had been smashed by Yamamoto's plan and Nagano's carrier task force, the Army Chief of Staff, as well as the remainder of the senior army staff knew it was not the total victory they needed. No American carriers at Pearl Harbor meant they would live to fight another day.

An Army general with two bright yellow collar tabs, each with a single star designating the rank of a Major General entered the conference room. His very presence immediately brought the Army side of the table to attention. It was Major General Meji Honda, General Hideki Tojo's personal adjutant, entering to signal that the prime minister himself would be entering within the next few moments. Everyone present quickly understood this unwritten protocol and headed for their assigned seats around the table.

"Gentlemen, the Imperial Prime Minister," announced General Ishi Honda, Tojo's aide, in a loud baritone voice. In unison, dozens of senior flag officers, staff, and secretaries launched to their feet.

And there he was, a short Army officer even by Japanese standards, born of an Army general who served under the great Emperor Meiji, father of modern-day Japan. The great General Tojo entered the room, bedecked in his dozens of medals, yet presenting the somewhat "sloppy" appearance of a senior officer who was not in need of requiring anyone's approval. In spite of his rather undistinguished appearance, everyone present knew he had the meticulous reputation of a ruthless first-rate administrator and disciplinarian. He was a man to respect as well as avoid, and had gained the nickname "The Razor." He was as sharp as a razor, but also known to have a psychopathic personality.

"Please be seated," Tojo said as he, too, took his seat in the special chair identified for the prime minister at the front of the long table. "General Honda, if we are ready, please proceed."

Without hesitation, the spry fifty-five-year-old general and his two Army aides sprang to their feet.

General Hideki Tojo

"Senior officers of the Imperial Army and Navy General Staffs, the purpose of this conference is to review where we are in relation to the completion of our First Operational Phase."

Honda snapped his fingers causing an Army major to quickly uncover the first easel.

"As you can see, I will review for you our overall campaign plan. First, both Army and Navy will conduct the First Operational Phase or what we term the 'centrifugal offensive' with the first part striking throughout southeast Asia, securing French Indochina, Siam, Wake Island, Hong Kong, the Philippines, Guam, and the Gilbert Islands. This offensive is then followed up with Part II, our seizure of Singapore, Dutch East Indies, British Borneo, the Bismarck Archipelago, and the neutralization of British airpower in southern Burma."

Admiral Nagano immediately raised his hand to stop the brief dead in its tracks. "General Honda, I believe everyone present is well aware of our overall success so far, but speaking for the Navy, we should move on to the next phase!"

Honda would not back down. "Sir, I think it's important to everyone present that we illustrate how glorious our Imperial Japanese Army is performing against the weak so-called 'Great Powers'." Honda's intention was nothing more than the Army's veiled attempt to try and humiliate the Naval general staff officers present.

Tojo looked at Nagano. "The Navy will soon have its turn. Honda, please proceed."

Nagano appeared rebuffed, but quickly saw Tojo wave his hand for Honda to continue.

"As we speak, our Twenty-Fifth Army under the command of Lieutenant General Tomoyuki Yamashita is tearing through the weak British positions throughout Malaya and is preparing to advance into Burma, where he will pass operations on to Lieutenant General Iida's Fifteenth Army. We expect General Yamashita to be in the vicinity of Singapore by the end of the month," Honda said proudly as his Army assistant pointed out the Twenty-Fifth Army positions on the nearby map.

"Meanwhile, our secondary drive is against the American bastion in the Philippines by Lieutenant General Masaharu Homma's Fourteen Army, is making good progress across the island of Luzon, having completely destroyed all American airpower within the archipelago. He expects to have operations completed by the end of February." Again the Japanese Army major pointed out Homma's advance positions on the large map.

Honda could tell by the expression on the prime minister's face that he was extremely pleased if not outright proud of the Army's successes throughout Southeast Asia.

"When do we begin operations against the oil fields of the Dutch East Indies and those other island groups to the south?" an inquisitive Tojo asked.

"Sir, Lieutenant General Imamura's Sixteen Army has already started small actions within the island chain as an attempt to probe enemy resistance, but is projected to land his force along with using his paratrooper force to seize key airstrips starting on January 11."

Tojo interrupted. "General Honda, time is short. What is the Army doing to prepare for the Allied response?"

Honda gave a pre-arranged signal to his two assistants, who on cue replaced the current operations briefing maps and charts with new ones.

Within a matter of two seconds, he was ready to answer the prime minister's questions.

"Sir, our Second Operational Phase consists of a period of consolidation of our conquests to fortify our newly captured territory and to enable the resources of conquered territories to be diverted to Japan. We then conduct a rapid transition to our third and final operational phase, conducting defensive operations in order to wear down our adversaries into a negotiated peace. However, our problem at this point is this: as the Allied resistance to us is crumbling far faster than we anticipated, we will easily meet our April-May timetable for wrapping up the First Operational Phase."

After a short pause, Honda continued, "At this point, there are opportunities presenting themselves to us we have not considered."

The prime minister glanced over to the Army Chief, General Sugiyama and his Operations Chief, Major General Shin'ichi Tanaka.

"Tell me, Sugiyama, where is the Army in its planning for the Second Operational Phase?" Tojo asked, pulling off his glasses to wipe the lenses clean.

Before he could answer Tojo's question, Tanaka immediately stood up.

"Sir, at this time, we have not prepared any detailed plans for this or the final phase. First and foremost, we are regrouping our combat forces in China in order to prepare for deceive action against the Chinese. Once we have completed operations within the southern regions, we will redeploy these forces back to China with those forces left behind tasked with constructing defenses. Meanwhile, I have tasked we are in the process of contemplating a plan to take advantage of the expected German spring offensive victories in the Soviet Union in order to attack the Russians from the rear, possibly as early as the summer," said Tanaka. Sugiyama looked pleased as his operations officer returned to his seat. For the moment, the "Razor" didn't have any more questions for the Imperial Army Chief.

Tojo now leveled his gaze to the Imperial Navy Chief of Staff, signaling it was the Navy's turn to face the heat.

"Admiral Nagano, what is the Navy and the Combined Fleet doing in preparing for the Second Operational Phase? I understand that our victory at Pearl Harbor was not as complete as one was led to believe." Once again, the "Razor" made his cutting point to the assembled naval staff.

Nagano drew his breath then stood to his feet. "Sir, on 9 December 1941, Admiral Yamamoto ordered his Chief of Staff, Rear Admiral Matome Ugaki, to draw up plans for an invasion of Hawaii. If we are to win against the mighty United States, bold military action is needed in order to force the Americans to accept the wisdom of entering into peace negotiations with Japan. If we achieve the total destruction of the U.S. Pacific Fleet and seize Hawaii, we might persuade the Americans that winning the war would be too costly for the American public to stomach. Admiral Yamamoto has also instructed Ugaki to draw up alternative plans for a carrier strike into the Indian Ocean against the British Eastern Fleet and for an invasion of Ceylon. However, Hawaii has to be the priority target because only that could ensure total destruction of Japan's most feared enemy, the United States Pacific Fleet. Yamamoto was not interested in an invasion of Australia at this time because he believed that destruction of the U.S. Pacific Fleet should be Japan's top strategic priority, and he felt that an invasion of Australia would not necessarily produce this result."

When Nagano finished, Tojo looked at the Commander-in-Chief of the Combined Fleet. "Admiral Yamamoto, do you have anything to add to Nagano comments?"

Yamamoto was ready. In the brief period prior to the start of the conference, Commander Watanabe brought the revered Admiral up to speed as to what his chief of staff had drafted while he was on his inspection visit to the Marshall Islands.

"Prime Minister, in the wake of our shortcomings at Pearl Harbor, I had Rear Admiral Ugaki's staff officers weighed both options and formed the view that capture of Hawaii was an unrealistic and highly risky option while the United States Pacific Fleet aircraft carrier force was intact and because the element of surprise was no longer available. He has also looked seriously to striking south toward the northern coast of Australia. We can harass and destroy much of their airfields and port facilities, in particular the port of Darwin, but without an invasion, they will soon rebuild and launch operations against our southern flank."

General Tojo raised his hand to interject: "How many Army divisions would it take for such as invasion?" he asked.

Yamamoto quickly glancing at his notes "Admiral Ugaki projects three divisions or approximately 60,000 troops in to invade and hold," he replied.

General Tanaka immediately jumped to his feet. "Honorable Prime Minister, this is utter nonsense. In our study of this ridiculous option, we find that a successful invasion of Australia would require at least ten Army divisions, which we cannot spare at this time. Moreover, there is no possible way the Navy could not provide logistic support for ten divisions in Australia at that point of time! Shipping to re-supply ten Japanese divisions in Australia was simply not available. My staff officers have pointed to the heavy manpower and logistic strains imposed on our Army by the rapid deployment of our forces across Southeast Asia, from Burma to Rabaul and from the Philippines to Wake Island, in the central Pacific. It simply cannot be done!" Once he made his point to the prime minister's apparent satisfaction, Tojo motioned the Army operations officer to take his seat.

The "Razor" again turned his attention back to Yamamoto. "What other options have your staff considered available for the Imperial Navy and Combined Fleet?" in effect subtly dismissing the Australian invasion option.

The Admiral, after a short moment to regain his thoughts, responded. "They recommended instead an invasion of British Ceylon. The capture of Ceylon, my staff argues, would enable us to dominate the Indian Ocean and intercept oil and any military support that Great Britain might provide for Australia and to India. Additionally, we will be in a great position to link up with the Germans should they be successful in defeating the British in North Africa and seize the Suez Canal. Although I was deeply disappointed by the findings of my staff with regard to the Hawaii option, I have instructed them for now to plan for an attack on the British Fleet and for an invasion of Ceylon sometime this spring, while keeping our Hawaiian option open for the time being should the opportunity present itself. I must tell you though that the Army is firmly opposed to any proposal that required massive commitment of troops for such an operation against Ceylon."

Sugiyama immediately shot up from his seat like a rocket. "It's another foolhardy and ridiculous operation Yamamoto's staff dreamed up! It's apparent to everyone here that they are trying to divert attention from your Pearl Harbor attack shortcomings to run and hide in the Indian Ocean like cowards where the British are not capable of mounting any serious opposition against you. Besides, we simply do not have the troops available and I seriously doubt you and the Navy have the resources to support them." At this point, the volatile Army chief, red-faced and now possessing the appearance of a demon samurai, looked squarely at Yamamoto, uttering, "I should have had you killed when I had the chance …"

The comment stunned all present within the room, with an obscure remark from a army staff officer seated in back saying, "it not too late to do in the coward…"

It was Admiral Nagano's turn to stand and defend the honor of the Imperial Japanese Navy and the revered Commander-in-Chief of the Combined Fleet.

"May I remind you, Sugiyama, that had the Army defeated China years ago *as you promised the Emperor*, we would not be in the predicament? Nagano did not pull any punches. "Maybe you should be more careful when you step outside..."

Now several Army and Navy senior officers jumped to their feet, giving the appearance that a high-level barroom brawl was about to begin.

"Silence!!!" Tojo yelled, surprising all in attendance with his higher-than-normal-pitched voice, visibly upset at the adversarial relations between the two senior chiefs of staff.

"Enough of this petty arguing!! You will cease this incessant bickering between the both of you immediately!"

"Admiral Nagano," the now highly upset prime minister asked, "the Army has over 1 million troops tied down in China, with another 400,000 troops tied down conducting operations in Southeast Asia and the Philippines. How many more soldiers does your staff project are required to invade Ceylon?"

"My staff projects one to two divisions," Nagano meekly responded over the light chuckling from the chorus of Army senior officers. While the Army found the answer from the Navy's chief of staff amusing, Tojo did not.

"If the Imperial Japanese Navy feels the need to sortie out into the Indian Ocean and take Ceylon, it may by all means do so, by all means, but without Army support." Clearly the combined prime and war minister was showing his biases toward his Army brethren and was not going to bother tying down forces for what seemed a Navy diversion.

Tojo continued. "I need to remind you that the American carrier fleet still needs to be found and destroyed in order to ensure they are no longer a threat in shipping our newly secured resources back to Japan. The Army will continue their planning as presented to me today in regards to regrouping our forces throughout Asia in preparing for decisive operations against China while keeping a close eye on what our German allies do in the Soviet Union and in North Africa this spring, taking advantage on any opportunity that might present itself in seizing Siberia and the Russian port of Vladivostok or the Suez Canal should the British capitulate."

With a nod to his aide, General Honda standing in the wings, the command of attention bellowed across the conference hall, bringing both adversaries and their staff officer teams to their feet in utter silence except for the sound of chairs pushed back across the floor.

The "Razor" stood up, straightened his Army tunic, then turned right and exited the conference room, followed closely by Honda and several Army general staff officers.

Nagano moved away from the long table and safely out of earshot of the various Army generals and staff officers still in lingering within the conference room, many now heading toward the refreshments table. Within short order Yamamoto and Watanabe joined him off to the side in a form of conference after action review.

"And so you have it, my dear friend," Nagano commented to Yamamoto. "It appears we are on our own if we are going to conduct future operations. Tojo and the Army are too busy making excuses about losing in China than desiring to win this damn war fighting it as a combined effort!"

"What do you propose, Nagano? You and I know the Americans will eventually overwhelm and destroy us," responded Yamamoto.

The Navy chief looked up at the ceiling as if hoping to receive divine guidance from the God of War. After a few short seconds of silence, he turned toward the two officers.

"Admiral, until we find and destroy the American carriers, our flank to the Pacific cannot be secure. However, we committed to helping the Army in Burma, so here is what I want the Combined Fleet to plan for and accomplish. First, I want you to take a few a carriers of the First Air Fleet down to the Coral Sea to support our Dutch East Indies operations as well as attack allied airfields and port facilities in Northern Australia. If you can take out the Australian port of Darwin, do it." While Nagano was conveying his planning guidance, Commander Watanabe was busy copying everything the Navy chief was saying down on paper.

"Go ahead and look at planning your Indian Ocean operation once you have fairly well destroyed the Allies' ability to launch anything from Northern Australia. That should buy us time to secure Ceylon from any British effort from the east, and if the Germans are successful in North Africa, we are in a position to exploit that success."

"Sir, what about the Americans?" Yamamoto haphazardly asked?

"I want you to dust off and update your Hawaiian plan and prepare for operations against them in early to mid-summer. What sort of operations concept and timetable did you plan on?"

"Sir," Watanabe asked. "The plan I wrote for the Admiral calls for us to secure bases between Midway and Pearl Harbor from which we can launch land-based planes to attack Pearl Harbor. The Combined Fleet's plan for an invasion of Hawaii could be completed by the end of April 1942 if allowed and resourced. Shall I continue?"

"Go on," said Nagano.

"The timetable I envisaged was as follows: Midway and the Aleutian islands would be seized in early June 1942, triggering a decisive battle that would complete the destruction of the U.S. Pacific Fleet; Johnston and Palmyra Islands would in turn to be secured by late summer, perhaps by August; the attack on the large island of Hawaii would begin in the fall, and culminate in an assault on Oahu in March 1943."

The Navy chief seemed satisfied at this impromptu strategy session. He looked at Yamamoto for comment.

"What do you think? Is this plan possible?" Nagano asked.

"If we do nothing, we most certainly invite our eventual destruction. As you know, most of the Imperial Japanese Fleet is in the second half of its lifespan and facing obsolesce. We simply do not have the resources to conduct and win a ship-building program against the United States. If we boldly move on and capture Hawaii, we then possess a mighty bargaining chip to draw the Americans into peace talks as we discussed earlier that would force them to recognize our dominance in the western Pacific region in return for us giving up Hawaii," the Admiral added.

"In other words, if don't move decisively now—" Nagano replied,

"—we will not ever get a second chance," Watanabe finished, deliberately cutting off the Navy chief of staff.

"Precisely," commented Yamamoto. "We all know whatever the Army hotheads plan, it inevitably boils down to what we three here will do in the next six to eight months."

"Well, gentleman," said the grim-looking Navy chief of staff. "I will not keep you any longer. Have your revised plans to me for review and approval by the end of the month."

Both officers stood and saluted, leaving the conference room to their own thoughts.

Chapter 11

A Winter Vacation

Fact: In early 1942, a group of influential Germans dissidents, disgusted with the way the Nazis were leading Germany, began to meet together at the Kreisau estate of Helmuth James Graf von Moltke, creating what the Gestapo would eventual coin the *Kreisau Kries* or *Kreisau Circle*. This circle of dissidents and conspirators were committed to the overthrow of Adolph Hitler and is celebrated as one of the few instances of German resistance to the Nazi regime. They were united by their abhorrence of National Socialism and a desire to conceive a new Germany after the disposal of Hitler.[24] To assist them with their mission, the circle established contacts with the American Office of Strategic Services – 'OSS' in Switzerland…

"Espionage is not a nice thing, nor is the methods employed exemplary. Neither are demolition bombs nor poison gas… We face an enemy who believes one of his chief weapons is that none but he will employ terror. But we will turn terror against him…"

– Major General William J. Donovan,
Director, Office of Coordinator of Information
(Soon known as the OSS)

The American Legation
Jubilaumsstrasse 93, Berne, Switzerland
1300 hrs, 24 Jan 1942

---

24   Most members of the group were conservatives from the traditional aristocracy and gentry, but it did include people from a wide variety of backgrounds. There were two Jesuit priests and two Lutheran pastors, political conservatives, liberals, socialists, landowners, former trade-union leaders and diplomats. The long meetings and discussions at Kreisau developed an image of a society based on Christian values and on small communities that would avoid manipulation of the whole of society like the one Hitler had created.

A dull, tan colored Mercedes taxi, coated with the gray grit of winter slush, pulled up in front of the old long gray building, located near the end of a quiet section of central Berne. Just over 100 yards ahead the icy Aare River awaited any unfortunate traveler who, if not paying attention, would slide into the river and take a frozen bath.

"93 Jubilaum Strasse," the Turkish taxi driver uttered, looking over his shoulder at his heavy clothed and very exhausted passenger. "That will be 15 Swiss francs!"

The tired passenger stepped out of the car, partly to stretch after his short trip from the Berne train station, but mostly to reach into his wallet and extract the driver's fare. All the while the Turk was scrambling to open the taxi's trunk and secure his passenger's bags, all under the stern gaze of the two American Marines guarding the building's entrance.

"So this is where the American Legation in Switzerland is located," the passenger mumbled to himself. "Not exactly the type of building you would mistake for an embassy or consulate you typically see in Europe..."

"Fifteen francs, sir!" the driver repeated again. Obviously, he had something else to do and spending time with an unknown American tourist was not on his agenda, especially since the air was filled with the aroma of lunch being prepared across the Aare River.

The American pulled out a 20 franc note and handed it to the driver. "Keep the change...," he said. But judging by the speed the Turkish driver snatched the bank note, giving this tired passenger his change, any change, was probably the last thing on his mind. Within seconds his tan and gray colored taxi was gone in a blaze of flying slush.

Alone on the street, the American picked up his two suitcases and trudged to the main entrance of the legation. As he approached, the two Marine sentries became tense as they evaluated who had been "dumped" on their doorstep.

"Good day gentleman," the stranger offered. "I am here to see Mr. Allen Dulles."

The first Marine, a Sergeant, smiled as if he was preparing a wise crack. "Right sir, and may I ask who is asking for Mr. Dulles?"

"Tell him a Mr. Jerry Curry has just arrived from the States."

"Sir, before I ask for Mr. Dulles, I'm going to require that you show me some ID," the Non Commissioned Officer flatly stated.

Jerry dropped his bag and reached into the inside of his outer coat pocket. One thing he had learned during his past travels to Europe was you always needed your passport readily available. As he pulled it out it became apparent, based on the passport's cranberry color, that its owner was carrying identity papers equivalent to a diplomat. The Marine Sergeant stepped forward and once he verified that the picture on the passport was the man standing in front of him he motioned to his junior partner. The second Marine quickly ducked into an alcove and spoke into an intercom device. Jerry could hear the exchange between the Marine and the legation's security officer. After a couple of minutes standing in the cold, the silence of the outside world was interrupted by an annoying buzzer, followed by the click and opening sound of a large, well protected door. Out into the cold winter air walked a short, balding bespeckled legation clerk, who looked more at home at the local library than at the center of gravity of the American espionage effort against the Germans.

"Mr. Curry, greetings and welcome to Berne," said the legation official as he extended his hand upward to the towering Curry. "My name is Clark Brown. I'm Mr. Dulles's administrative assistant and I'm to escort you to him. I can tell you he has been most anxious for your arrival."

Jerry looked curiously down at the pseudo dwarf of a clerk. While Brown may have been only 5'3", compared to Curry he looked even smaller.

"Sergeant Lewis," Brown snapped at the Marine Non-Commissioned Officer hovering nearby, "Please have Mr. Curry's bags taken to room 314 upstairs."

The Marine Sergeant gestured to his assistant and within seconds Curry's bags were removed.

"Mr. Curry, if you would, please follow me and I'll take you to Mr. Dulles," said Brown.

As the two walked towards the elevator, Brown noticed how exhausted Jerry looked.

"You must be famished Mr. Curry," Brown asked. "Mr. Dulles is getting ready to have lunch with a visitor. If you're hungry, I can have the kitchen rustle you up something."

"Coffee for now would be fine and please, call me Jerry. When you address me as 'Mr. Curry' I think you're talking to my father."

"Great, then please refer to me as Clark," replied Brown.

The trip in the elevator to the third floor felt as long as Curry's trip to Europe. Both looked at the slow change of floor numbers and tried to make small talk. However Jerry was too tired to ask even the most mundane of questions.

Once out of the elevator the pair strolled a short distance to Room 314. Clark knocked and was greeted by the faint but clear voice of a woman instructing them to come in.

"Hello is anybody home?" chimed Brown in an attempt at humor as he strolled in.

"You must be Mr. Jerry Curry?" the woman asked. "I'm Allen's assistant at the legation, Mary Bancroft. Allen just stepped down the hall to order some lunch for you."

Mary was a beautiful dark haired coquettish woman of 39 years and wore a bright slash of red lipstick. She spoke beautifully accented German to a tee. As she approached Curry, he could feel her sexual energy.

"Please, have a seat right here," she directed. "I can imagine you must be exhausted. Tell me is New York still as exciting as ever?"

"You've been to New York?" Jerry asked, somewhat surprised.

"Yes, believe it or not, I was in New York City on the day I saw General Donovan march down Fifth Avenue at the head of his 69th Infantry Regiment during the Victory Day celebration. I was 15 years old, but remember it like it was yesterday. I was exhilarated that spring day, filled with pride at being an American."

Jerry tilted his head in amazement. "From your accent, I thought you were either German or Swiss-German."

"Nope, wrong on both counts," Mary countered. "Would you believe me if I told you I actually come from a very proper Boston family that wanted me to become a debutante and marry the appropriate young and rich man?"

"Based on your presence here, it appears that was not on the cards," Curry replied. "How on earth did you end up here in Berne?"

"Well, that's a long story for another time," she responded.

At that moment, Allen Dulles walked into the office, accompanied by another younger man.

"Ah Jerry, so good to see you. Please don't get up. I take it that Mary has kept you company while I was detained," said Dulles, dressed in his typical tan tweed jacket and bow tie and carrying his ever present pipe.

"Yes she has, and, I might add, a bit of a surprise," Jerry replied. "I thought you might have hired one of the locals here."

Allen looked at Mary blushing then asked her to insure that after lunch had arrived they would not be disturbed.

"Gentleman let's move over into this secure office so we can become better acquainted," said Dulles as he opened the door to a smaller conference room immediately adjacent to his.

As Jerry got up, he felt as though he weighed a ton. He dreaded leaving this comfortable stuffed chair for that of a hard conference room seat, but maybe it was for the best. Another few moments and he would have been fast asleep.

Once the three men found their seats, Dulles began.

"Jerry, since our last get together and with my arrival here in Berne, we have established some remarkable initial contacts with a few Germans that are, shall we say, disgusted with Hitler and the Nazis. It appears that the war in Russia is a recruiting boom for the German resistance."

"So it would seem, but what do you have in mind for me?" asked Jerry. "Remember, I'm just a businessman who has done a lot of work in Europe."

"And that makes you perfect for this operation," the stranger inserted in German-accented English.

"Forgive me Jerry, I would like to introduce you to a man I've known for some time going back to his father when I was here in Switzerland back in 1916. This is Dr. Gero von Schulze-Gävernitz. His family has many businesses holdings here which allows for his easy travel in and out of Germany. As for Gero, well, he's a half Jewish millionaire playboy, but don't hold that against him. He has been a great contact for me in painting the mood of what is going on within Germany today," said Dulles.

Gävernitz smiled, "You are too kind Allen. What he forgot to add is that I am also a strident anti-Nazi who is ashamed of what Hitler and his gang of thugs have done to my country."

"You see Jerry, Dr. Gävernitz is the key to meeting with the various military and civilian anti-Nazi groups located throughout Europe. He can assist us in many ways to connect together all these factions into one unit to bring Hitler down," Dulles added.

Jerry sat up in his chair in amazement. "How high placed are your connections?" he asked.

"I can not tell you that at this time, but I think you would be astonished at the level." Gävernitz replied. "As a down payment shall we say, I am going to introduce you to one such contact tomorrow night from a group recently formed a few month ago known as the *Kreisau Circle* after its leader."

"Allen, why can't you meet with this group?" Curry asked.

Dulles took a drag from his pipe and filled the room with the aroma of burning cherry tobacco. When he was finished, he put his pipe down and stood up.

"You see Jerry, in my position here at the American Legation, I am under constant observation, just like any other spymaster is here in Switzerland. Anywhere I go, they would be right on top of me. To travel to Occupied France is completely out of the question. Come here and see for yourself."

Allen led Jerry back to the other small entrance room they had recently vacated, took him over to the window and pulled back the blinds.

"See that small white van parked on the other side of the street near the lamp post?" asked Dulles.

Jerry nodded. He remembered seeing that same medium size dirty white van parked there when he arrived in his taxi an hour ago.

"Hungarian intelligence," replied Dulles as he closed the blinds again. "Any Gestapo here would stand out like a sore thumb in Switzerland, so since we are not at war with Germany, they've asked their friends the Hungarians to keep an eye out on us. I guess they have more important folks to watch like ol' Claude Dansey MI-6's spies over there at the British Embassy. More power to them! You'll need to be mindful of them if you spend any time here at the legation."

Walking into the small room, Gävernitz jumped in. "Herr Curry, don't you see; with your legitimate business dealings and contacts, you could easily travel into Vichy France and Germany without raising suspicion. After all, there are a great many American companies currently doing, or still willing to do, business with the Nazis, regardless of what they are doing in Europe. War is still a very profitable inducement for both parties."

Jerry smirked. A secret agent? The thought still intrigued him since Donovan first suggested it back in New York a fortnight prior.

A quick knock at the door brought Curry back to reality or as near to it as the current conversation allowed.

"Gentlemen, your lunch is here," said a legation employee, pushing a cart into the outer office. "Did you want to eat out here or in the conference room?" he asked.

"It's about time," Dulles sighed. "Jerry, I believe you must be absolutely famished," he said as he tapped the expended tobacco out of his pipe. "You can go ahead and bring it in here," he instructed the employee.

The aide pushed the cart into the conference room and three piping hot plates of Wiener schnitzel, complete with side orders of potato salad topped with parsley and butter, were sited squarely in front of the three hungry conferees.

"And what would each of you care to drink?" the aide inquired. "I have coffee, tea, or water."

"Jerry, we have a delightful tea we get on occasion from the British. It's probably the only worthwhile thing we get from them here in Berne other than bad advice. I highly recommend it," Allen bragged.

"Ya, it's better than anything you'll find in the gasthaus' in the city," Gävernitz added.

Three cups of tea soon found their place adjacent to the rapidly disappearing schnitzel. To Jerry lunch had never tasted so good!

Across town Kamel Unakitan was sitting inside a crowed restaurant amid the cigarette smoke and lunch time noise, savoring a warm beef roulade filled with onions, bacon and pickles. He had decided after dropping off the large American at the legation, and now flush with francs, that lunch was in order. He found a nearby café and after waiting nearly 40 minutes, his prize of a warm meal was finally delivered to him.

As he finished, Unakitan felt uncomfortable, as if someone was watching him. Quickly gazing around, he noticed two middle aged gentleman in gray suits sitting nearby, slowly stirring their coffee, and occasionally taking a short sip. He tried to look away, thinking maybe their interest was in someone else. After a few moments, Unakitan would look back at the two, only to confirm in his mind he was their item of interest.

"I'm just a taxi driver, what could be of interest to them?" he thought to himself as he sipped his now lukewarm tea.

But as quickly as his anxiety came on, he felt instantly relieved when he saw the two men get up, put their hats and coats on, place their money on the table, and leave.

"I must be getting paranoid," he thought as he too decided it was time to get back to work. "Check please," he asked the nearest waitress and within a couple of minutes, Kamel was on his way to his means of employment – his dirty tan taxi.

As he rounded the street corner where his cab was parked, Unakitan suddenly came across the two men who had been observing him in the restaurant standing near his taxi.

Shocked, Kamel immediately approached the first one, the smaller of the two.

"What do you want?" he asked, half scared, half combative. "Do you need a lift somewhere?"

"Nein, we don't need a ride, but we do want something from you taxi man," the larger, older gentleman responded.

Kamel immediately noticed his accent. While he may have spoken German, his accent indicated a more eastern European tone; perhaps this gent was from either Czechoslovakia or Hungary?

"OK, what do you want? Do you want hashish? Are you looking for a girl for the night?" he asked, puzzled at what these two could possibly be interested in him.

It was now the younger man's time to speak. "About an hour ago, you delivered a large man to the American Legation over on Jubilaum Strasse. What can you tell us about him? Was he an American? Why is he here in Berne?"

"Is that all?" Kamel thought to himself. "I guess he was American. He spoke like one. Why do you want to know and who the hell are you?"

"Who we are is not important to you Turk, what we want to know is!" replied the older gentleman.

"What did he say and why is he here?" the younger impulsive gent inserted.

"All I know is he's a businessman who just arrived from America and he had some appointment with someone in the building. That's all I know," Unakitan quickly responded, feeling very uncomfortable about his situation. The two did not appear satisfied.

"The Turk's lying," the younger man challenged. "Give me five minutes with him." He pulled a device out of his back pocket that quickly opened up into a six inch switchblade.

"Jani, that's enough. Put your toy away," the older man chastised. "Let's make it worth the Turk's while."

The older man reached into his pocket and pulled out a card, quickly scribbling something on it then handed it to Kamel.

"If you happen to remember anything more, or if our American business friend happens to need a ride in town, we would be very interested to know and would, shall we say, generously reward you for your information."

Unakitan nervously took the card and briefly looked at the number before placing it into his coat pocket. He felt a little relieved when he saw Jani folding his knife; returning it to his back pocket.

"Auf Wiedersehen until we see you again – Turk," Jani said to Kamel with a wink of the eye and a grin as he and the older gent turned and walked across the street entering an awaiting black car.

Kamel headed immediately for his taxi, wondering to himself how he had gotten into this situation. Breathing heavily, almost to the point of hyperventilating, he threw the car in reverse, bumping into a car parked behind him. Uttering a Turkish curse word, he quickly slammed the stick shift forward, clipping the car immediately in front and to his right as he sped off.

"What is going on?" he thought. "Was this American a millionaire or something?"

After driving for about five minutes through downtown Berne's post lunch time traffic, Unakitan pulled over to the side of the road to get a grip on himself. He pulled the card out and looked at the phone number scribbled down. He recognized the prefix; that was over near Willadingweg Strasse, not more than a few kilometers from here.

"What was over there" he thought?

Suddenly Kamel was rudely surprised by the sound of a loud car horn blaring by his left side. Furiously, he rolled down the window, only to see it was a fellow cabby who had just pulled up along side, checking to see if he was alright.

"Hey Kamel, how are going to make any money sleeping on the job?" the Swiss cabby asked. "No tourists over here, you just taking an afternoon nap?"

Kamel immediately recognized his fellow taxi colleague Gustav. Gustav had been a taxi driver longer than Kamel had been on earth.

"Hey Gustav, ever been to Willadingweg Strasse?" Unakitan asked.

"Sure, a few times. Why do you ask?"

"What's over there?" said Kamel. "I might need to pick up a customer there in a couple of hours." Kamel hated to lie, but until he knew more about what he was into, no sense letting Gustav know too much. While they were both cabbies, he barely knew the guy.

"Willadingweg Strasse? Hmm, there's a few embassies over there," he replied.

"*Embassies?*" Kamel thought. That would make sense. Both men had a foreign accent.

"Which ones are located there?" asked Kamel.

Gustav looked inquisitively at Kamel. "Well, the largest one over there by far is the German embassy, then you have..."

But before he could finish, Kamel uttered a quick "thanks" then drove his taxi forward and off into traffic, leaving a bewildered Gustav to ponder what he had said to make the Turk drive off like a madman.

"Germans – they couldn't be, not with that accent," the Turkish driver thought to himself as he drove home to call it an early day.

Back at the legation, the aide had just finished clearing the lunch dishes from the conference room, stacking them neatly on his cart in the same, precise order he had delivered them 90 minutes prior.

"Thank you for a wonderful lunch Schmitt," said Allen. "As usual, please extend my compliments to the kitchen chief and the crew down there."

"Will here be anything else, Mr. Dulles?" asked the aide. Dulles nodded no, then closed the outer office door once Schmitt and his lunch cart were in the hallway and clear. He listened through the door to ensure he could hear the noise of the cart getting fainter as Schmitt returned his dishes and glassware back to the kitchen via the third floor elevator.

"Now gentleman," said Dulles, reaching into his pocket for his pipe lighter, "Let's talk about contacts. Gero, what have you got for us?"

Gävernitz sat upright and reached into his briefcase, pulling out a small piece of paper.

"Tomorrow night, I've arranged for a well placed contact to meet us at Allen's place sometime after midnight. I have made all the necessary preparations to sneak him in within the back seat of Allen's staff car where he'll enter my apartment building from the house directly behind Allen's."

"How will I get there?' Jerry asked. "I haven't even checked into my hotel room yet."

Dulles was ready with an answer. "Jerry my friend, you'll spend the next few nights with me at my apartment located about two kilometers across the river within the city old quarter on Herrengasse 23. Plenty of room, so I won't take no for an answer. In the future, we think we'll conduct our business there out of the prying eyes of any Gestapo or the Hungarian Intelligence."

"So what can you tell me about the guy?" Jerry asked Gero.

"He's about 38 and a senior diplomat stationed at the German Consulate in Zurich who was recently transferred to the embassy here. He's a powerful contact who has worked in the German Interior Ministry and now works within the Foreign Service. His high ranking contacts have gotten him assigned to the embassy and we need to take advantage of that," said Gävernitz. "He is our key!" he underscored.

"Okay, so he's a bigwig," Curry quipped. "What's he going to tell me — that the Germans are really pissed off at Hitler and they want him out?"

Gero was not amused and somewhat surprised at Curry's comment. "Herr Curry, I don't think you understand the gravity of the situation. Without the Americans in the war, it is only a matter of time before the Nazis subdue the Russians and turn all their energies over into two highly important areas; knocking the British out of the war once and for all and developing their special weapons program."

"Special weapons program?" Jerry inquired. "What on earth are you taking about?"

Before Gävernitz could respond, Dulles interjected.

"Jerry, your unaware the Nazis are well on the way towards developing a uranium bomb project. From our intelligence, I would say we are neck to neck with them on who will build it first. On top of that, they also have a highly developed rocket program and that's the scary part; even if we finish first, they will have the means to deliver their bomb, and you can guess what their first target will be."

Now it was Gero's turn. "We have intelligence that suggests the Nazis are building a massive secret airbase in Norway from which they can launch a strike against the United States with their uranium bomb, should the time come and the political situation is right. Right now, with the war in Russia, Hitler cannot afford to take on the Americans, but once he wins, it's only a matter of time, and so now you see why we need to, how do you say it — *take him out?*"

Jerry sat back taking it all in. "Why can't the British take out the airfield? It can't be all that difficult!"

Both Gävernitz and Dulles shook their heads.

"Not that easy Jerry," Dulles responded. "The Brits are having a rough go just bombing close targets within Northern France, much less the Reich itself. Besides, they have to find the base in the first place."

"Meet with my contact tomorrow night and listen to what he says," said Gero. "Get this information to your President and to General Donovan and see what you Americans can do to stop this madman from torching Europe for generations to come."

Dulles could tell he was losing Curry's attention due to his exhaustion.

"Come on Jerry, let's get you some rest over at my apartment. We have a long evening tomorrow night."

Five hundred miles to the north in Berlin, another meeting was about to take place. Major Massar had just finished his briefing notes for OKW Chief's daily afternoon staff meeting. As he stuffed his notes into his briefcase for the short walk over to Keitel's office, a courier popped in and handed him a note from the Field Marshal seeking his presence immediately. Thanking the courier, he quickly made his way down the command's hallway to Keitel's office where the Chief of OKW was standing in his outer office.

"Come in Massar," Keitel ordered. "I have a mission for you."

Massar immediately followed Keitel into his office. Before the Field Marshal reached his desk, he instructed his enlisted aide to close the door and not to interrupt.

"Major Massar, this will not take long, so please have a seat. As you know, our endeavor in the Soviet Union is far from complete and I am all but certain that shortly Der Fuehrer will give us guidance for the conduct of future operations. What I need is facts and information on what exactly is going on over there."

Massar looked at his boss in puzzlement. "What about all the situation reports we're receiving from OKH and the Army Groups?"

Keitel glared at his young aide for asking such a naïve question.

"Are you serious?" he responded. "Hitler's firing anyone and everyone bringing him any bad news. How many generals have been sacked over the past few weeks? Lately anyone bringing him information or knowledge about unauthorized retreats or failure to follow his explicit orders, gets fired or shot, or both; I'm not joking around. I've been directed by Hitler to dispatch from OKH 500,000 replacements for the east. Have you any idea where I'm supposed to come up with that many troops?"

"I suppose sir, you'll have to take them out of the west; say France and the Low Countries," Pierre replied, half serious, half jokingly.

"In short, I need you to fly to Field Marshal Kluge's HQs at Army Group Center and gather whatever information about the situation at hand over there. With all the craziness that's going on here, there is no possible way I could do this fact finding tour by myself, not at this time. Hell, I probably might not have a job if I were to go. Massar, I need you to do this mission for me. Consider this your winter vacation away from all of the insanity here. Do you have any questions?" Keitel finished.

"I understand Herr Field Marshal," Pierre voiced loudly, surprising himself in the process. "As for questions, well sir, not to sound stupid, but how do I get there?" he asked.

With that, Keitel opened his briefing note pad and pulled out a beige file folder.

"Major, here is a copy of your orders. You are to report to hanger 215 at Templehof Airfield tomorrow morning at 0600 hours. There, you will meet up with a small OKH staff delegation flying out on a ME-III bomber towards Smolensk. The trip itself, if you have good weather, should take about six plus hours. Spend a few days there with Kluge and his staff, collect your facts and gather as much information as possible, then get back here quickly. I have a feeling that February will be a very busy month here!" At that Keitel handed the beige file folder to his trusted aide.

As Massar received the folder he promptly saluted his boss and made an abrupt about face, tucking the folder under his arm as he started thinking about his upcoming eastern adventure. As he reached the door, Keitel offered one departing comment.

"Major, make damn sure you dress warmly. I can tell you first hand that despite all the creature comforts our illustrious Luftwaffe is used to, those planes will not have much in the way of any heat at all. Be safe and be careful!" And with that, the Chief of OKW went about resuming his daily functions of running an ever increasingly difficult war.

It was early afternoon on a clear, cloudless Sunday, January the 25th, when Jerry Curry awoke after his first restful sleep in days. Looking out Dulles' guest bedroom window, he marveled at the freshly laid snow which had fallen overnight, covering up the dinginess of the city. Putting on his robe, he followed the sounds of American jazz that grew louder as he approached what appeared to be a small kitchen. There, Allen Dulles was sitting, fully dressed in a dark suit with bow tie, alternating between puffing on his cherry scented pipe and sipping his coffee.

"Sure smells wonderful Allen, may I join you?" Jerry asked as he strolled on in.

"Help yourself, cups are in the first cabinet right over the stove and cream and sugar are on the table," said Dulles, using his pipe as a navigation pointer. "How'd you sleep? I figured you be out for a couple more hours."

"Fine," Jerry responded as if he was still trying to convince himself he really was awake.

"Say Jerry, I have to run a couple of errands this afternoon, you know, pick up a few things for tonight and stop off to see the Brits for a short while. Relax and make yourself at home. You might even enjoy the local newspaper here. It's really quite informative," and with that comment Dulles rose, grabbed his hat and departed, leaving Curry alone except for the small cup of coffee he was now using to warm his hands.

Jerry sat looking out the window over the city skyline, still trying to comprehend yesterday's initial conversation at the legation. He was having a hard time believing he was there in Switzerland not as a businessman, but as an amateur spy for Bill Donovan at the behest of the President of the United States. A President he didn't even vote for in the last election.

Relaxing, he thumbed through the local newspaper, the *Berne Zeitung*, trying to get a feel for what was happening locally. He was surprised his German reading was still fairly good. One item in the first section did catch his eye – he saw an obituary of a cabbie who appeared to have been murdered near the city center, killed with his throat slit. While the murder of a taxi driver in itself was not unusually, this one was identified as one of *Turkish* descent.

"Now that's an odd coincidence," Curry thought to himself. "I wonder if he was the same one..." but before he could finish his thought, the ringing of the phone forced him back to reality, causing his small cup of coffee to erupt all over his robe.

"Damn it..." he uttered as he stood up to grab a towel while simultaneously searching the immediate area for that phone.

Grabbing the first piece of cloth resembling a dish towel, Jerry quickly located the phone and answered it.

"Hello, Dulles' residence," he barked into the receiver. "Hello, is anybody there...?"

A German sounding male voice responded "Is Herr Dulles there?"

"No, he isn't, but he'll be back soon. May I ask who's calling?"

The voice was silent for a brief moment. "Would you tell Herr Dulles that "H" called? He'll understand." The line went dead.

Jerry replaced the receiver back on the cradle and looked down at the fresh coffee stain on Dulles' guest robe. "What the hell have I gotten myself in to?" he thought as he went back to pour a fresh cup of coffee and finished reading the paper.

That evening, both Dulles and Curry sat in the living room listening to the evening news broadcast on the BBC. Again the news was not good; in North Africa, General Rommel was on the move again beginning a counter-offensive with his famed *Afrika Korps* from El Agheila, while Japanese forces were pouring into the Dutch East Indies. Allen had enough and switched stations, finding a local radio station playing classical music.

"Might as well relax before Gero pops in," Dulles said to Jerry. "Things are tense enough already. In fact, how about a brandy Jerry? It might just loosen things up while we're waiting," he asked as he headed for the brown colored decanter sitting by the other various bottles of liquor he'd accumulated entertaining his "guests."

"Better make that three brandies," a female voice interjected appearing from the darkness of the apartment's kitchen.

"Ah Mary! Nice of you to join us. Jerry, you remember Ms. Bancroft, my assistant at the legation? I thought it would be amusing to have her listen in and get her perspective on our mystery guest. Did you have any difficulty getting here?" he asked.

"Not really, but I took the necessary precautions," she replied, receiving the brandy from Dulles as she took a seat on the stuffed chair next to Curry.

"Jerry, I typically have Mary present when I am interviewing contacts. She has a keen way of seeing things I might overlook. Sorry for forgetting to let you know in advance."

Jerry suddenly remembered the phone call from early afternoon.

"Speaking of forgetting Allen, do you happen to know someone by the name of "H"?

Both Dulles and Bancroft glared at Curry in astonishment. "Yes, I do, but how do you know this chap?"

"He called shortly after you left this afternoon. He didn't leave a message, just told me to let you know he called."

"I'll be damned," Allen exclaimed, "He's back in the country."

Before Dulles could finish, there were three loud knocks at the back door, causing everyone in the room to freeze in place. Allen went to the rear room and shut off the light, leaving darkness to mask the entry of Dr. Gävernitz and his mysterious contact.

Jerry looked at his watch; 12:01. "This man is prompt," he said to himself as Dulles and the two men returned to the living room. Curry could clearly see, even in the darkness, the contact Gero brought with him was almost a foot taller than the other two.

"Jerry Curry, let me introduce you to Hans Bernd Gisevius of the German Foreign Service. He's the German Vice Consul, but in reality he's an Abwehr[25] agent who has come all the way from Zurich to visit us," said Dulles.

---

25   The **Abwehr** was a German Intelligence organization formed in the inter-war years. The term *Abwehr* (German for *defence*) was used as a concession to Allied demands that Germany's post-World War I intelligence activities be for "defensive" purposes only. After February 4th, 1938, its name in title was Foreign Affairs/Defence Office of the Armed Forces High Command (*Amt Ausland/Abwehr im Oberkommando der Wehrmacht*).

Gisevius extended his right hand towards Jerry. "A pleasure Herr Curry," the 38 year old tall diplomat said in a polished fashion. "It's been a while since I met an American other than Herr Dulles here."

After the informal courtesies everyone took a seat in Dulles' living room with Dulles bringing in a container of Swiss coffee for all to partake.

"Herr Curry," Gero began, "Let me tell you a little about Gisevius. For starters, he started out with the Geheime Staatspolizei, what we refer to now as the *Gestapo*, a few years back before they became the thugs they are today."

"Why did you leave?" asked Curry, surprised at being this close to a Gestapo agent, even if a former one. "I thought once a Gestapo guy, always a Gestapo guy."

"Well, it's hard to advance with that type of organization when you're not a member of the Nazi Party. I started to become more critical of their brutality and corruption which in turn did not endear me with the leadership. Soon after, I left and with some well placed friends of mine within the Abwehr, I was able to secure this position within the German consulate in Zurich."

"And so being with the consulate provides the perfect cover for your travels to and from Germany," Bancroft added. "Allen, do you know what this means, what a coup this is for us?"

Curry still had a skeptical look on his face and looked over to Allen. His concern translated immediately to Gisevius and Gävernitz. If Hans Bernd was to convince Jerry of his worth, he had better provide some sort of proof – fast!

"Herr Curry, I represent a group of German people who believe Hitler and the Nazis are leading my country into total catastrophe. Herr Dulles here informs me your mission is to establish contact with such a group and determine what assistance you Americans can lend us in overthrowing Hitler and restoring order to my country."

Jerry cocked his head partly in astonishment and partly in disbelief.

"Well, as I told Allen earlier, how do I know you are the real deal and not a put up job by the Gestapo to us to smoke out the resistance?" Curry asked.

Gisevius was well prepared for that question and smiled. He reached over to his satchel, opened the buckle straps, and pulled out a manila folder.

"Herr Curry, the reason I waited so long to meet you is because I was waiting at the consulate for this document that we just received earlier today. These are the notes of a high level conference attended by the most senior Nazi officials that took place in a suburb of Berlin at a place called Wannsee. These notes contain details as to the Reich's policies in coordinating all agencies in dealing with the Jews, both in Germany and the occupied countries. In short, you might call this the blueprint for the final solution to the Jewish question."

Gisevius handed the file over to Dulles, who immediately began pouring over the various pages.

"How did you get copies of the notes of such an astonishing meeting?" Allen asked. "From what I'm seeing here, this is nothing short of an attempt by a country to legalize *genocide*[26]!"

"Herr Dulles, this is my point exactly. Not all Germans are monsters nor are we all in step with the Nazis. I received this from my contacts at the Foreign Office who are equally disgusted of what the Nazis have turned Germany into. At this time, all I can say is my contacts are at the highest level of the government and are willing to take chances in blowing their cover in order to work with you in helping us achieve not only our goal, but I believe deep down your goal too, of eliminating Hitler!"

---

26   The Wannsee Conference was a meeting of senior officials of Nazi Germany, held at the Berlin suburb of Wannsee, on January 20th, 1942. The purpose of the conference was to inform administrative heads of Departments responsible for various policies relating to Jews, that Reinhard Heydrich had been appointed as the chief executor of the *"Final Solution to the Jewish question"*, and to obtain their full support. In the course of the meeting, Heydrich presented a plan, presumably approved by Hitler, for the deportation of the Jewish population of Europe to German-occupied areas in Eastern Europe, and the use of the Jews fit for labor on projects, in the course of which they would eventually die, the surviving remnant to be annihilated after completion of the projects.

While Gisevius was talking with Dulles, Allen handed the file over to Curry for his review and comments.

As Jerry leafed through the pages of notes, he came across one that caused his mouth to drop and drained all color from his face, astonished at the contents he'd just read. Gisevius stopped talking and all looked at Jerry who looked as if he had just seen a ghost.

"What is it?" the largely silent Gävernitz asked.

Curry held up the page in question.

"This page," Jerry responded, "Has comments from a guy named Meyer[27] who is, as far as I can tell, the head of the Reich Ministry for the occupied countries. His comments here are utterly shocking as to how widespread this is."

"What does it say?" asked Dulles, surprised at Curry's shock.

"Basically it says that the German roundup of the Jews within occupied France, Hungary, and Poland are assisted largely by various peoples within these countries. If I didn't know any better, it appears to me that anti-Semitism is not a uniquely German phenomenon." Jerry closed the file and pulled out a handkerchief to wipe his forehead. He had seen enough.

Gisevius reached over and pulled the file from Jerry's hands, returning to his diplomatic satchel.

"Well gentlemen, I trust you found my credentials are in order," he said, smiling at having now proven his worth to the group.

Now Jerry, Allen, and Mary all looked at one another.

"OK, where do we go from here?" Jerry asked.

"My friends, there are two things you need to do. First, you must let the Allies and your President know what is being planned and organized here within the Reich in regards to the elimination of the Jewish people within occupied Europe. How could we, as a German people, ever look at ourselves

---

27   Gauleiter Dr Alfred Meyer, Reich Ministry for the Occupied Eastern Territories.

again as a cultured and civilized folk if all we did was just stand by and allow this to occur? Hitler must be stopped!"

"And what is the second thing we need to do?" asked Dulles, pulling out his pipe and preparing for a smoke.

"The second thing you need to do, Herr Dulles, is for Herr Curry to meet with my people. As you are undoubtedly aware, both Herr Dulles and I are usually under observation. I think it's obvious as someone who is 193 centimeters[28], I would be rather conspicuous, wouldn't you say? I will give you the contact number for someone who will serve as your liaison to our group." Gisevius pulled out a small card and quickly scribbled a name and number on it, then handed it to Jerry.

"H?" Jerry said, remembering that morning's phone message. "What is this supposed to be?"

Dulles took a drag off his pipe and blew a small cherry scented cloud into the room and smiled.

"You just talked to him today," he said, leaning back in his chair. "In fact, his calling me this morning as you said, is an indication he's in town for the next 24 hours."

Gisevius immediately chimed in. "If this is true, the sooner you meet with Herr H, the better for all of us. We cannot afford to waste any time. The longer we remain inactive, the more people will die needlessly..."

Gero looked at his watch. "Gisevius, it's time to go if you're to catch the morning train back to Zurich."

Gisevius stood up and buttoned up his coat. In all the haste of meeting with the Americans, he hadn't even taken off his coat and scarf.

"Please gentlemen. If it's true that Herr H is in town, you must make contact with him immediately!" Hans Bernd implored. "He's your contact to our group."

---

28   6 feet, 4 inches.

"Let's go Hans," Gero said as he stood up and gently grabbed Gisevius by the elbow, escorting him through the black door into the darkness of residential Berne. As they departed, Hans Bernd Gisevius could be heard uttering a faint "Auf Wiedersehen..."

Allen, Jerry and Mary sat alone in silence, contemplating what Gisevius had just said. The beginning of organized genocide coupled with an out reach from Germans at the Reich's highest levels desiring to overthrow Hitler. Another brandy was called for.

As Jerry settled back down in his chair with a fresh snifter full, swirling the brown liquor around and around, he looked at both Bancroft and Dulles, sitting side by side on the couch.

"Why us?" Jerry asked. "The Brits have been at this longer than we have; I mean they've been fighting the Germans since '39. Why come to us?"

Dulles leaned back on the couch and dragged on his pipe, letting loose another cherry scented cloud.

"Credibility my boy!" he said "Credibility. You see, ol' Colonel Dansey at MI-6 thinks he's still a Gestapo agent. They still haven't forgotten what happened to their boys at Venlo. Gisevius knows they wouldn't give him the time of day. Just as well, I think he's a Godsend for us!!"

The wall clock chimed 2 a.m. and Dulles and Curry realized sleep was in order. Dulles pulled a blanket over Mary who had long since dozed off on the couch. In silence, the two headed upstairs to rest.

Ten o'clock the following morning Jerry awoke, still groggy from the night before, wondering if all this "cloak and dagger" stuff was just a nightmare brought about from his travel fatigue. Making his way downstairs, Allen was sitting at his usual place within the small kitchen, his ever present pipe billowing out the usual flavored scent.

"Before you pour yourself a cup of coffee, I think we need to make a certain phone call," said Dulles, pulling a drag off his pipe.

"And good morning to you too…" Curry chimed back, ignoring Dulles' comment while reaching into the cabinet for a cup and saucer.

After a short review of last night's conversation with Gävernitz and his mysterious friend Hans Bernd Gisevius, both Dulles and Curry decided now was the time to contact "H."

Dulles opened his wallet and pulled out a small rumpled scrap of paper with a faded phone number written on it. Setting down his pipe, he dialed the number while Jerry sat down with his cup of coffee.

"Ya," came the answer, low but hard on the opposite line.

"The snows were late this year in Berne, but early in Zurich," responded Dulles.

"Too bad there are no tourists to take advantage of it," was the reply.

Dulles smiled at Curry, indicating they had connected to the right man.

"Herr H, I have a special man who needs to meet you right way. Are you readily available and is it safe?" asked Allen.

"I will be in Berne for 12 more hours before my train goes back to Germany. Have him meet me at the Café Zumwalt at 1300 hours. Tell him he should take a seat near the door and wear a red scarf around his neck. I won't be back here for at least two months, so it's now or never." With that, "H" hung up with a click of the phone.

Dulles replaced the receiver back on the cradle. "Looks like you have a lunch date today Jerry."

At a quarter to one, Allen pulled up about two blocks from the Café Zumwalt.

"Jerry, you see this book store here," he said pointing to the small store-front with second hand books, "When you exit the car, go into this store as if you're looking for a book. Once I've left, depart through the store's back door, then go down the alley until you come to the rear of the Zumwalt Café, where you can enter and position yourself as per "H's" instructions. I'll meet you back here at two o'clock, and Jerry, most importantly — relax and good luck!"

Jerry departed Dulles' car right into downtown Berne traffic; heavy even for a Monday afternoon.

Within 10 minutes, Jerry navigated through various precautions Dulles outlined — the book store, alley, and even the crowded front entrance where he got the last free table just inside the café's front door.

"Eine tasse von kaffee," he asked the waiter passing by. "Might as well relax as per Allen's instructions," he thought to himself.

It wasn't long before the waiter delivered Curry's coffee. As he watched the front door, he was amazed at the number of citizens strolling by, many if not all oblivious to events taking place outside their humble country. Citizens as safe and secure as the very bank accounts and vaults sprinkled throughout the country.

"And how is Herr Dulles doing today?" a voice belonging to a late 20s, medium built man with short black hair and a goatee asked the now startled day dreaming American.

"That all depends on which letter of the alphabet I'm speaking to," was Curry's short reply.

"I believe it's the one that comes before *I*," was the young man's response, grinning as if it was some sort of private joke. He pulled out the chair immediately next to Curry and sat down.

As the stranger took his seat, Jerry extended his hand as a welcome.

"Greetings, I'm Jerry Curry and I guess you're the one who talked with Allen earlier this morning setting up this little get together."

"As you have undoubtedly gathered, I am Herr H. I understand you met one of my compatriots, Hans Bernd Gisevius last night. As you might suspect, I am the primary connection to those who want to rid Germany of Adolph Hitler and his Nazi surge. What I would like to know is what can you do for us?"

Pretty straight forward and no small talk to beat around the bush, Jerry thought to himself.

"Let's just say for the moment, I represent some pretty powerful folks who sent me here to Switzerland and desire to help with your cause."

Herr H sat up straight – impressed the Americans were interested, but didn't seem quite convinced as to how much.

"Herr Curry, if I may be so bold, just how powerful are the people you represent?" asked H.

Jerry smiled. "As powerful as I need them to be. If you don't believe me, ask your friend Herr Dulles. My mission is to make informal contact and extend any and all aid the United States can provide in assisting you. Now, if you'll forgive *me* for being bold, may I ask you who you represent so that I can determine whether or not I'm wasting my time meeting here?"

Herr H's intensity suddenly shattered. Looking at the dead serious American, he didn't know he was dealing with a businessman used to hard knuckled serious business practices, especially during the depression era of 1930's America.

After nearly a minute of silent confrontation, Herr H began to grin, then rolled back in his seat with a mild laugh.

"How about that, they finally sent someone here with balls and not some Harvard schooled state department clown," he said. With that comment, the tension was gone.

Looking around to ensure no one was close enough to eavesdrop, Herr H pulled his chair closer to Curry.

"The people I represent are placed within the highest positions through the Third Reich. Through one level of contacts I can communicate with the head of the German Abwehr - Admiral Wilhelm Canaris. Through another channel I can find out all the diplomatic undertakings Germany is making towards other countries. If that's not enough to impress you, I even have access to Hitler's every move. Is this high enough for you Herr Curry?"

Jerry had to admit — he was in awe. This young chap had his finger on the pulse of the very war making community of the Third Reich.

"You cut a very impressive resume *Herr H* and I have to admit I'm impressed. Now, where do we go from here?"

H reached into his jacket pocket and pulled out a small piece of note paper, followed quickly with a pen. Scribbling down a few notes, he slid the note over to Curry.

"The first number is a post office box in Paris. If you desire to contact me in the future, send a post card to this box number one month before your planned arrival date. On the card write *the weather in Florida is much colder than it was last year.* The second number is my contact number in London where I will meet you 30 days after the date you put on the post card. My connections in Paris will relay the information to me in order to make the trip to London. Do you have any questions?"

Jerry shook his head, indicating the meeting was over. As the two men stood up to shake hands and depart, Herr H stood for a moment to ask one final question of Curry.

"Herr Curry, since I laid my credentials out on the table, who exactly do you represent besides Allen Dulles and his folks?" he asked.

Jerry smiled at his new found friend and with a grin answered "Would you believe the President of the United States himself sent me here?" and with that, he turned and left the café.

With that now behind him, Jerry felt he had accomplished his mission for Roosevelt, or at least he had a very good handle of what the President wanted him to do. He was now in contact with the very folks capable of bringing Hitler down and with luck — out!

Walking towards the used book store, two honks of a car horn alerted him that Dulles was right behind him, ready to pick him up. As he got in, Allen could readily tell that it was a mission accomplished, but before they could savor that moment, he had some important news to tell Curry.

"Jerry, before you start, a flash cable came in today for you from Washington. Rather than tell you what it says, I thought you should read it for yourself."

Curious, Curry opened the yellow colored envelope and pulled out the decoded cable.

"From the President of the United States to Mr. Jerry Curry, US Legation Switzerland..." it began, "With the sudden death of Harry Hopkins, your presence is requested immediately at the White House. Advise immediately upon receipt of this message and advise as to travel plans and arrival time."

Suddenly, the early afternoon's achievement of meeting with a key member of the German resistance seemed small compared to the notification of the death of his close friend and confidant – Harry Hopkins.

Allen didn't have to ask – he already knew the bad news from Washington shortly after he dropped Curry off. As the two quietly drove down the Berne streets towards Allen's apartment, both were unsure as to what the next step was now that Jerry needed to return back to the States. As they turned the final corner and neared Dulles' place, he looked at Jerry and informed him his staff were already making his travel arrangements and he would be leaving the next morning on the 6.30 a.m. flight to London.

Getting out of the car and walking up the stairs towards the front door, Dulles could sense the sadness in Jerry, still stunned by the news from Roosevelt. As he put his arm around his shoulder, the only thing he could muster for words of encouragement was to tell him, "At least you have good news for him about Switzerland..."

Chapter 12

A Change in Plans

Fact: On the eve of the German invasion of Poland in 1939 and the start of the Second World War, the strength of the United States Army was a mere 189,000 soldiers, ranking 16th in the world in size. By April 1942, the United States was well on her way mobilizing vast manpower resources, increasing to 2,661,000 the number in US Army uniform, with 476,000 soldiers deployed overseas. Near the close of 1942, over 5.4 million soldiers were mobilized of which more than one million soldiers were deployed overseas. The US Army reached its peak strength in March 1945 with more than eight million soldiers mobilized for war, while the US Navy achieved a strength of over four million sailors and, along with 660,000 US Marines, manned over 6,700 ships by August 1945.

Officer's Club
Presidio of San Francisco
1600 hrs, 19 April 1942

Brigadier General John Reynolds was ready for his second bourbon and branch. For the oldest officer's club in the US Army, located right in the middle of the Presidio of San Francisco, it sure seemed a pretty somber night. Maybe another bourbon and branch would be the capper to a long and weary day of observations and notes throughout the Bay Area.

In the two days he had been in the city, he was amazed at its transformation from the famed golden gateway to California and the United States, to the largest single deployment point of the nation's resources against the Japanese. The sight he viewed was simply staggering.

"I don't think General Marshall had any idea how just how many folks we can cram into one port city," he thought to himself as he got to work on his fresh drink.

As he nursed his bourbon, he reflected on what Marshall had asked him to look over and what he had seen over the past 48 hours since he flew into the Presidio's Crissy Air Field.

From the air, the city looked like it had olive drab blotches scattered throughout. Upon closer inspection on the ground, these "blotches" were in fact vast army unit bivouac sites, hundreds of them, housing within their small olive drab tents perhaps tens of thousands of troops, all awaiting the same thing; to be loaded up on to the vast armada of gray shipping either lined up at a dock or awaiting a berth. He had never in his career seen anything quite like it, even as a young officer getting off the boat in France during the last Great War.

As he circulated throughout these army "villages," his amazement grew. Not only were these Regular Army soldiers, but National Guard troops as well. He recognized the red, blue and yellow triangular patch of the 1st Armored Division, also known as "Old Ironsides", while down on the Embarcadero as soldiers scrambled to load the hundreds of M-4 "Sherman" and M3 "Grant" tanks onto the various collection of freighters assembled. In other parts of the city, he spotted soldiers of the 32nd, 37th and 41st Infantry Divisions, all National Guard units from the States or Wisconsin, Ohio, and Oregon. While at the Presidio itself, John noticed the red diamond patch of the Regular Army's 5th Infantry Division bivouac on any piece of clear ground they could find. So many soldiers present everywhere, one would think San Francisco was an occupied city.

Intermingled throughout this sea of olive drab or 'OD'green army soldiers were heavy sprinkles of thousands of folks in either blue denim or white – sailors of the US Navy - especially near the dock areas where soldiers and sailors alike worked side-by-side loading soldiers and equipment onto the dozens of ships lined up. Even from his guest quarters at the Pershing House, when the weather permitted and the fog was gone, he could not help but feel impressed at the vast conga line of gray navy shipping constantly streaming out of the bay under the magnificent view of the Golden Gate Bridge.

As Reynolds took another sip of his drink, it dawned on him that maybe this damp mood within the club had more to do with events in the Far East than anything else. With the strength of the nation mobilizing before his very eyes, the news was still bad for both the Americans and the British. He remembered the expression on his British colleague's faces, the night of his promotion in Washington last December, when they heard of the surrender of their forces in Hong Kong. Six weeks later in mid-February, their great bastion in the Orient, the fortress of Singapore, capitulated, becoming the largest surrender of British-led military personnel in history. In reports he received from the War Department's British Liaison Officer, about 80,000 Indian, Australian and British troops were now "guests" of the Japanese Empire, joining 50,000 taken by the Japanese in their recently concluded Malayan campaign. John recalled reading that Prime Minister Churchill called the ignominious fall of Singapore to the Japanese as the "worst disaster" and "largest capitulation" in British history.

"I can only imagine how they feel now," he thought, "But they sure don't have a monopoly on military disasters."

Thinking back, the Americans still hadn't had a break since Pearl Harbor. On the plus side, the remaining US Navy fleet carriers that survived the Japanese sneak attack at Pearl had recently concluded a series of raids against the various Japanese naval bases scattered throughput the central Pacific, doing enough damage to make their presence felt, but not enough to hurt the Japanese as bad as what they did to us. And that was the good news...

The bad news was as staggering as what had happened to the British. Shortly after the fall of Singapore, a motley collection of American, British,

Dutch and Australian ships, under the command of all things a Dutch Admiral, met the Japanese Navy head on in the Java Sea, which resulted in the largest surface action since the Great War's Battle of Jutland. When it was over, the more serious allied losses amounted to two heavy cruisers, three destroyers and over 2,000 sailors including the Dutch Admiral commanding, compared to the loss of only one Imperial Japanese Navy (IJN) destroyer. One could argue the IJN was unstoppable even in light of the almost comical shelling of an oil refinery by a Japanese submarine off the coast of Santa Barbara, near Ellwood, California last February. Shortly after this tragic action, Japanese forces invaded the island of Java, thus dooming the Dutch East Indies along with their precious oil reserves to the Empire.

By far the biggest mood killer within the club for the past 10 days had been the announcement of the fall of American and Filipino forces on the Bataan Peninsula; virtually guaranteeing the loss of the Philippines. All that was left, as far as John had heard, was a small combined Navy – Marine force of 12,000 men centered around the Marine 4th Infantry Regiment that were penned up within the small island fortress of Corregidor; a tadpole shaped island, located just inside Manila Bay. It was their sad duty to report the surrender of 70,000 American and Filipino troops on Bataan to the War Department on April 9th.

"How much longer can these poor bastards hang on?" he thought, now nursing his third drink. "With the entire Japanese 14th Army breathing down their necks, the end certainly isn't far off."

There was some good news to date from the Philippines though - the month prior on March 12th, Roosevelt ordered General MacArthur to turn his command over to the newly promoted Lieutenant General Jonathan Wainwright. MacArthur then immediately departed for Australia on a motor torpedo boat where he was to organize the Southwest Pacific Command. At least his good friend Dwight Eisenhower made it out as well and was safe with MacArthur in Brisbane.

To take his mind off the gloomy war news about Bataan, John looked around the bar that was studded with various photographs of San Francisco around the turn of the century; however his attention was becoming increasingly distracted by a loud group of army-navy folks gathered at the far end of the bar, huddled around the club's Victoria.

"Turn it up," said one soldier.

"Quiet, I can't hear what he just said," yelled a sailor. "Shuddap!" yelled a few others.

This group now had John's undivided attention. "It was too early for baseball, and football season was long over," he thought. "What could be so damn interesting? Did we win a battle or something?"

Reynolds grabbed his drink and moved closer to where the action had congregated in hope of hearing the Victoria. In the now sudden quiet demanded by the crowd, the radio was easy to hear.

> "... we repeat, yesterday afternoon, April 18th, US Army B-25 bombers lead by Lieutenant Colonel Jimmy Doolittle, flying from an undisclosed location hit the Japanese capital of Tokyo causing damage to the city and dock areas ..... When President Roosevelt was asked at today's press conference where these bombers came from, he announced they flew from Shangri-La... "

Suddenly, everyone in the club went wild with the news, throwing glasses, paper and almost anything readily available into the air accompanied by cheers. John had to duck to avoid being hit by a small water glass flung by a cheerful, but highly inebriated sailor.

"*Holy Shit*, can you believe it?" he thought to himself. "We finally hit the Japanese in the groin and I'll bet it's going to smart for a while."

The air was filled with the sound of pops - champagne corks unleashed and filling the air like toy artillery rounds, landing every which way. Before he knew it, a Second Lieutenant handed the General a hastily filled half glass, spilling more on the floor than into his intended target. For the first time in a long while, the United States finally had something to celebrate.

As he sipped his new drink, he sat down to think about what just happened. Hitting the Japs at this time was just what the doctor ordered, but knowing them the way he did, and about their pride, especially now that they were on a roll conquering most of Asia, they would not take this lying down.

"I hope the boys in Washington knew what they were doing when they sanctioned this mission," Reynolds mused. "It could damn well boomerang us in the long run at a time we still aren't ready for the big leagues. But now is not the time to be a wet blanket..." he said as he finished off his glass of champagne and headed back to his old bar seat.

Five thousand miles away to the east, as morning was opening up, the fires and pall of smoke that hung over the imperial capital of Japan the day before finally drifted away, abated by the numerous fire crews working throughout the night fighting the fires brought about by the wretched American bombers.

Upon hearing of the dastardly American attack on Tokyo, Commander Kamei cut short his leave to rush directly to Admiral Yamamoto's residence. There he found the Admiral safe, along with his Operations Officer Commander Yasuji Watanabe who had just arrived an hour before Kamei. Yamamoto, dressed in his dark blue kimono, was sharing tea with Watanabe, when his aide arrived. Both officers were ashen faced with disbelief such a thing could have occurred at the height of Japan's greatest success.

"I came as soon as I heard," said Kamei. "Is the Emperor alright? How much damage occurred?"

"The Emperor is unharmed," replied the Admiral. "Commander Watanabe was going over the damage to Tokyo with me when you arrived. Please, have a seat Kamei, so that Yasuji may continue."

Once seated and with his notebook out, Yamamoto signaled Watanabe to continue.

"As I mentioned Sir, the enemy came at us with 16 long range bombers low over the eastern Pacific. The aircraft began arriving over Japan about noon and bombed 10 military and industrial targets in Tokyo, two in Yokohama, and one each in Yokosuka, Nagoya, Kobe, and Osaka. I have a report that one bomb was dropped on the aircraft carrier *Ryuko*. It is unfortunate that not one bomber was shot down by army anti-aircraft fire. Of the bombers, 15 of the 16 aircraft then proceeded southwest along the southern coast of Japan then across the East China Sea, no doubt towards safe sanctuary in eastern China. The one remaining bomber appeared to be low on fuel and headed north towards the Russian port city of Vladivostok, where I believe our Soviet friends have it."

"Sixteen bombers" Yamamoto uttered. "How? From where?"

"We don't really know except they appeared to be long range bombers, possibly from Hawaii," replied Watanabe.

"How much damage did they do?" Kamei asked.

"Not too much," responded the Operations Officer. "There are about 50 reported dead and over 400 hundred injured. Aside from the fires very little military damage occurred. Apparently the only real major casualty was General Tojo's pride. You see sir, he was returning to Tokyo that morning from an inspection tour when his plane nearly collided with a twin engine bomber that they didn't recognize. Apparently he had a fit when he was told later the plane they had nearly missed was an American bomber. Other than that, we were very lucky overall."

Yamamoto grinned at Watanabe's comment about the esteemed Imperial War Minister's unfortunate encounter with the Americans, but quickly reverted back to his role as the serious Fleet Commander.

"Watanabe – luck is something we cannot rely on if this were to happen again!" stated the now serious Yamamoto. "This is the just the sort of incident I need to get my *Eastern Operation* plan approved. Since my aide has been on leave for the past two weeks, please brief him on where we are with the *Eastern Operation* plan."

"Yes, sir" replied Watananbe. "Basically, the Admiral's plan is to seize the islands of Midway as the primary objective and Attu as the diversionary objective with two aims; the first is to extend our eastern defensive perimeter to the Midway Atoll, and thereby deprive the United States of its last island outpost west of Hawaii. During the past few months, the Americans have launched numerous carrier raids on our island outposts and airfields, causing increasing damage and concern at the General Staff level. The plan's second aim is to draw these pesky aircraft carriers of the United States Pacific Fleet to a decisive battle off Midway where they could be destroyed once and for all by us, thus setting the stage for a full invasion of the Hawaiian Islands as early as this fall."

"So why haven't they approved this?" asked an inquisitive Kamei.

"I submitted the plan to the Navy General Staff on April 2nd, where it was strenuously opposed by two officers of the Plans Division; Captain Sadatoshi Tomioka and his air expert, Commander Tatsukichi Miyo. Tomioka and Miyo did not oppose action to complete the destruction of the US Pacific Fleet, but they argued that this decisive action between our fleet and American fleets should take place in the South-West Pacific where our warships could be supported by land-based aircraft, and the American ships would be operating a long way from their base at Pearl Harbor. I especially regret that I had a serious confrontation with Commander Miyo and humbly apologize for my conduct."

"What was Commander Miyo's issue with the plan that would cause the two of you to come to blows?" asked Yamamoto.

A now embarrassed Watanabe replied.

"Sir, Commander Miyo has numerous arguments mounted against an offensive directed to the capture and garrisoning of Midway Atoll as an end in itself. He has argued persuasively that the Midway Atoll was too small to be effectively defended by a Japanese garrison, it was well within the range of B-17 heavy bombers from Hawaii, logistic support to our forces would pose enormous problems, and the atoll was too far away from Pearl Harbor for Zero fighters to accompany and protect Japanese bombers aimed at Pearl Harbor. I disagree with him and failed to convince him that Midway is but a stepping stone to greater successes like the conquest of Hawaii."

"I completely understand your emotional attachment to my plan," responded the Admiral. "At least you were successful in convincing his superior, Captain Tomioka, to provide an edited version of my Combined Fleet plan before his opposite number in Army General Staff, Major General Tanaka on April 12th. Have you heard anything of his response?"

"Sir, I heard through my contacts that Tanaka had shown unrelenting opposition to any further extension of Japan's eastern defensive perimeter. With specific reference to Hawaii, Tanaka had opposed such an operation on the ground that the logistical and operational problems were insuperable, and anyway, the army could not spare the three divisions deemed necessary to capture Hawaii. It is curious that the plan submitted by Captain Tomioka to General Tanaka made no mention of any operation beyond Midway. However, Tanaka astutely recognizes that your plan all along was intended to provide a foundation for an assault on Hawaii after Midway had been captured. I also heard he told Tomioka bluntly that an attack on Hawaii would be an unwarranted extension of Japan's eastern defensive perimeter and that the army would not cooperate in any way with the Midway plan."

So much for army participation in any plan developed by the Combined Fleet. Yet Watanabe was smiling.

"In spite of the army's resistance towards supporting this plan, the gods have favored us in two ways!" said the now optimistic Fleet Operations Officer.

"First, despite Tanaka's rebuff, Captain Tomioka appears to now be on our side whole heartedly. He has prepared a report entitled *"Imperial Navy Operational Plans for Stage Two of the Greater East Asia War"* where he stated that the Pacific should be given highest strategic priority, that Midway be seized and the US Pacific Fleet destroyed, especially the carriers we missed last December, and Midway be captured this June and garrisoned by our Imperial Navy marines. Achievement of these objectives would signal the end of revised Stage Two. In Stage Three, the Johnston and Palmyra Islands would be occupied around August with the invasion of the large island of Hawaii taking place in Stage Four sometime in October.

"Where is this report now?" asked the Admiral.

"It was submitted to the Emperor for his approval by Admiral Nagano three days ago. The timing of this submission to the Emperor is the second blessing in disguise. Because of yesterday's bombing by the Americans, they would not dare turn down your plan."

"You very well might be right," said the Commander-in-Chief of the Combined Fleet, suddenly realizing Watanabe's point. The American raid could prove to be the tipping point.

Their exchange was interrupted by the ringing of the phone. Yamamoto's enlisted aide answered, with Kamei jumping up to take the receiver from the young man. As the aide, it was his job to screen for the Admiral, even with calls to his home.

As Kamei was talking, it was apparent that the person at the other line had far more horsepower on his shoulders than the Admiral's aide. Yamamoto signaled Watanabe to see what all the fuss was about.

Kamei handed the receiver to Watanabe, who immediately began writing down a message from the caller. When he was done he put the receiver down on the phone and turned and smiled at the Admiral. Obviously something had occurred to make his Operations Officer beam from ear to ear.

"Well Commander, what news do you have for me?" queried the Admiral.

"Sir that was Captain Tomioka on the line, just returning from a meeting with the General Staff discussing yesterday's American bombing. It appears the Imperial Army changed its attitude to operations in the Pacific, and against Hawaii in particular, and now wants to get on board with the plan. Major General Tanaka informed Captain Tomioka that the Imperial Army had changed its mind about expanding the Pacific perimeters and will now provide troops for the Midway and Aleutian offensives. He asked for more information about the *"Eastern Operation"*, specifically about the capture of Hawaii, and wants to make bold initiatives in the Pacific so as to end the war quickly."

"It must be divine intervention," said Kamei. "We actually have a plan where both army and navy are joined together for a common good. Looks like a large scale change of plans for them!"

Yamamoto smiled. He was too much a professional to gloat about winning over the Imperial Army, but the victory was very sweet never the less. In a short time, the disaster of yesterday's aerial bombing of Tokyo had turned into a great victory for him and his plan to win the war for Japan, while concurrently getting the army hotheads to change their minds.

"It appears the final knock out blow we have sought against the Americans is granted. Now who would like some tea...?" offered the Admiral.

Half a world away, the city of Berlin was asleep with the exception of the now omni present Luftwaffe search light units and their more sinister brother element, the 88mm flak cannons. Once considered unheard of, they had now become part of Berlin night life with the occasional but increasing visits courtesy of the RAF's Bomber Command. Many Berliner's now scoffed every time Reich Minister and Head of the German Luftwaffe "Herman Goering's" name was mentioned, jokingly referring to him as "Meyer" after his famed comment two years ago about the RAF's inability to bomb the capital of the Third Reich.

Major Massar had just finished his record keeping of the day's activities within the OKW and noticed it was nearly 0200 hours. The staff was more or less in a joyous mood – just 11 days prior, the Wehrmacht had been on a roll again with the start of an offensive against the Russians in the Crimea and had good results so far. Reading a communiqué from the Commander of the 11th Army – General Eric von Manstein - that they were finally well in charge of the situation and intended to capture the great port of Sevastopol by mid summer, if the large siege guns named *Thor* and *Dora* he had requested were still on schedule for delivery. Guns with shells as big as a Volkswagen would make short work of the Russian bastion in no time at all.

"It's refreshing to know that someone has a handle on what's going on in the east," Massar thought to himself, putting the communiqué into Keitel's briefing book for tomorrow's update. Good news was always welcomed and there never was enough of it.

Ever since he'd returned from his visit to the eastern front last January, Pierre was a changed man. Certainly from observing the chaotic way the German Army muddled through its worst set back since the First World War he had also been amazed at its ability to adapt, as if it had a life of its own. The army's ability to rebound, reorganize, and reestablish itself was as much a credit to the leadership he met during his travels – Generals and Colonels with true leadership skills that inspired soldiers to overcome the adversity of the harsh conditions they faced daily on the eastern front and rise to the challenge. Yet, he was also exposed to a dark side of this officer corps — a side one did not talk about outside the tent flaps of the command headquarters.

While traveling to Smolensk last January, Major Massar had the opportunity to travel with a fellow Panzer Division Ib[29] and OKH liaison to the east — Major Claus von Stauffenberg. To kill time during the long flight across Russia, the two officers reminisced about the thrill of being part of the new Panzer Divisions as they "blitzed" across Poland and France. As with Massar, Stauffenberg was pulled out of his 6th Panzer Division for duty with the OKH General Staff's Organization Branch. Like any skilled, talented young officer, he yearned to be back in action.

Yet unlike Massar, Stauffenberg was no stranger to the eastern front. As their flight continued, Massar queried Claus about the east and what was really going on. After awhile, Claus felt he could trust this naïve colleague and began to open up.

Like Pierre, he felt tremendous pride at being a German officer and being within a new resurgent Wehrmacht as well as a pride at having Hitler in charge. But after his second trip to the east last August, he had witnessed unspeakable atrocities from the killing of Soviet prisoners of war to the systematic round up and murder of Jewish civilians; none of which were armed combatants. When he inquired with the various commands he visited, he was curtly informed that these actions were conducted in the name of the Fuehrer. This was something no cultured German Army officer could possibly do, yet not only was it occurring, but on a large scale and with a high degree of sophistication. As a Catholic, this shook Stauffenberg to the core and Massar could tell it had impacted him greatly.

---

29   The Ib, otherwise known as the 2nd General Staff officer, was responsible for the logistics of the entire division and all matters of supply; movement of supplies, rations, ammo, etc, and the movement of the wounded and prisoners. The Ib was also in charge of the movement of supply trains, deployment of construction facilities, traffic regulation, and air-raid protection in the areas of the back-line services.

Once on the ground in Smolensk, Claus took the efforts to square Pierre away and introduce him to the various key figures running Army Group Center. Until then he had usually heard these names at the various Fuehrer briefs in a negative tone.

"Pierre, allow me the opportunity to introduce you to an officer who has kept this part of the circus from going bankrupt – Major General Henning von Tresckow, Operations Officer[30] for the whole damn Army Group!"

Tresckow extended his hand towards Massar for a quick shake, but it was apparent the introduction would be brief.

"Gentlemen, I would love to stay and chat, but I am on my way to an awards ceremony and change of command. You're welcome to join me there and we can have a chat about life here on the Russian Riviera."

Claus looked at Pierre and within seconds, the two of them were hard on the heels of Tresckow, heading over to a large wide area that also served as a landing field where what sounded like military music was coming.

Once there, Tresckow took his place among the Army Group Staff officers assembled. Out front, a number of black jump-suit uniformed soldiers milled about under the guidon of the Second Panzer Division. Stauffenberg and Massar blended into the background of dull gray-green uniforms, both remembering their days in the not to distant past wearing similar apparel.

"Actung!" yelled the Adjutant, a short Colonel who was tasked to bring this semi unruly crowd of Wehrmacht personnel to order.

"Oberst Johann Bernatz, front and center!" Suddenly, the army group band started playing the *Presentiar March*, music played only when someone high up is receiving an award or some sort of distinguished recognition.

---

30   Also known as the Ia, otherwise known as the Chief of Operations. The Ia was the 1st General Staff officer in the organization. He dealt with all areas of the command and tactical control of the units as well as areas of leadership, training, transport, housing, air-raid protection, evaluation and presentation of combat options to the Commanding General; standing in for him when the commander himself was not available.

From the side of the audience, a black unformed Panzer Colonel strode up to the Army Group Adjutant and saluted. Simultaneously, a decorated General Officer marched up to the left side of the Adjutant, exchanging salutes with both men.

"Pierre, do you know who that is? That's the Commander of the Army Group Center, Field Marshal von Kluge. Ya' know what his nickname since assuming command of the Army Group is? *Der Kluge Hans*[31]."

"So that's von Kluge," Pierre nodded in acknowledgement – he distinctly remembered a Fuehrer brief a month prior when Hitler relieved his predecessor Field Marshal von Bock and replaced him with Kluge. "I hope he's up to his reputation of being clever, enough to keep him from being relieved as was his predecessor," he thought.

In a loud, booming voice, typical of a Prussian born Staff Officer, Kluge's adjutant announced ...

"The Knight's Cross with Oak Leaves and Swords is presented to Oberst Johann Bernatz for gallantry in the face of the enemy for his action in stopping a Russian tank assault on his command post...."

"So that's what a Knight's Cross presentation looks like," Pierre commented to Claus. Both of them were wearing the Iron Cross First Class for combat action in France, but these were handed out to mid grade officers almost as an after thought following combat action. They were important, but nothing compared to a Knight's Cross.

Then the Field Marshall stood in front of the Oberst and spoke. His voice was softer than his Adjutant, largely because of his advanced age. Everyone around the two officers strained to hear his words to no avail. When they noticed the guidon bearer for the 2nd Panzer Division advance forward, everyone immediately knew that von Kluge intended to transfer

---

31   "Clever Hans." Hans was not part of his given name, but a nickname acquired early in his career in admiration of his cleverness (*klug* is German for *clever*). It is derived from a curious reference to a celebrated horse Clever Hans, reputed to have been able to do arithmetic and remember calendar dates.

command of the Second Panzer Division to his newly decorated commander. Shortly thereafter, the ceremony broke up and everyone departed back to their duty stations – after all, there was a war still on and the sound of artillery in the distance was a reminder the Russians were not intent on taking a day off to celebrate a German Panzer Divisional change of command.

Stauffenberg and Massar chatted for a few minutes before being rejoined by the more relaxed Tresckow, complete with a cigarette.

"So you work for the great Field Marshall Keitel?" quizzed Tresckow. "Does he have a plan on how the hell we're going to get out of this mess or how his beloved Fuehrer is going to save the day?"

"Mein General," Claus interrupted. "Just because Pierre works for him doesn't mean he thinks like him. I've gotten to know this chap in the short time we've been together and he's told me some astonishing things about how Hitler and the whole OKW staff functions or more correctly – malfunctions!"

"I'm sorry Massar," responded Henning. "Ever since the fall life here, as you would expect, has been a living nightmare. We have learned to live one day at a time. You never know what the hell is going to happen next. Thank God we were able to patch a collection of units together to stop the damn Ruskies or who the hell knows how far they would have gone. God damn Hitler and this cursed campaign of his…"

Suddenly, the three of them were interrupted by the just decorated and now newly promoted Panzer Division Commander, Major General Bernatz. Up close, his Knight's Cross shinned brightly against the midnight black panzer uniform - even against the dull, gray Russian sky.

"Henning, just want to stop by and thank you for recommending me for this command with the Field Marshal. I truly owe you one for this."

Tresckow shook Bernatz's hand. "Think nothing of it Johann. Think of it as payback for those times at the Kriegs Academy[32] when you bailed my sorry ass out."

---

32   Germany Army War College

"I am sorry to hear about your uncle's removal from command by Hitler last December," responded Bernatz, referring to Von Bock's recent sacking as Commander, Army Group Center due to his retreating despite *Der Fuehrer's* order to the contrary. "He was truly a great officer."

"The laugh's really on Hitler my friend," said Henning with a wide grin. "I don't know if you're aware, but the Army Group South Commander – Field Marshall Walter von Reichennau - recently died of a heart attack. You'll never guess who Hitler selected as his replacement – the old man himself *von Bock!* So you see the ol' man one way or another is still in this blasted game. By the way, as a courtesy, allow me to introduce you to Major's Claus Stauffenberg, OKH General Staff, and Pierre Massar of Field Marshall Keitel's personal staff."

Bernatz extended his hand to each of the officers. "Gentlemen, a pleasure and let me tell you that any friend of Henning's is a friend of mine. Just watch out for his politics if you know what I mean or you might get a visit from a man in a nasty looking black suit. Now, if you don't mind, I need to return back to my new command headquarters at Karmanowo. Gentlemen, Heil Hitler!"

Pierre instinctively raised his right hand and responded with the customary Nazi salute, but immediately noticed neither Tresckow nor Stauffenberg offered it back in kind.

Once Bernatz departed, Tresckow offered the two staff officers an opportunity to meet the Field Marshall before they continued with their coordination and staff observations.

Later on that evening, Claus and Pierre shared a drink and laugh within the headquarters kantine where they were joined by General Tresckow.

"Major Massar, I hope you didn't think ill of me or take offense to my failure to render the proper military courtesy when General Bernatz left," said Tresckow, in reference to that afternoon's failure to return a Nazi salute.

"You see, many of us out here don't really see eye-to-eye with what OKW is doing in general and Hitler in particular. I think you might find we're not exactly his biggest fans here in Russia."

Pierre was stunned by the General's comments. Had this been Germany and his comments overheard by the local Gestapo, he would have been immediately arrested, tried before a court martial and that would only been a formality before being shot.

Tresckow continued. "Stauffenberg here is a good judge of character otherwise I would never had said anything treasonous before you, but someone from the OKW staff needs to know the truth about what's going on here in Russia within the Wehrmacht. We get the most ridiculous lunatic orders from high command to shoot Soviet prisoners, Jews, whatever, without any shred of human dignity. As we speak, Himmler's SS Einsatzgruppen Execution Squads are roaming all throughout White Russia and the Ukraine looking for any Jewish community to eliminate. Lousy scum sucking bastards. For every one they kill, two become partisans and who do you think they go after? Our supply trains, rear echelon depots, hospitals, you name it. When we came into Russia last summer, everyone welcomed us with open arms and flowers, called us liberators. Today, you can't walk into the forest to take a shit without some partisan taking a shot at you when you least expect it. For this, we owe it all to Hitler and that bastard Himmler!" Tresckow immediately threw down his half finished cigarette, then knocked back a glass of schnapps.

"Aren't we obligated by the Geneva Convention to take care of Russian prisoners that fall into our hands, I mean is it not only that the law and the decent thing to do?" asked Massar.

Stauffenberg's eyebrow cocked when he hear Massar's naïve comment and he now jumped in to deliver a cynical response.

"Pierre, I don't think you're aware the Soviet Union was not a signatory of that treaty, so our illustrious high command is not obliged to follow its provisions, not that they would have anyway, but they think they're in their legal rights. What crap! It's terrible for those poor slobs we capture, but I can only imagine what will happen to our chaps they happen to capture. It's truly tragic!"

The three of them stood silent for a few minutes before Henning slammed his hand on the kantine's bar, getting everyone's attention within the immediate area.

"Enough of this bad mood crap!" yelled Tresckow. Motioning to the Corporal functioning as the kantine's bar tender, Henning directed a round for everyone on the house. Once the glasses were filled, he raised his in a toast.

"Gentlemen, please join me in a toast to my uncle Field Marshal von Bock. It's hard to keep a good leader down and even harder to kick a bad leader out!" A rousing *"Hear, hear!"* was heard by the assembled mess of officers before being drowned out by the swigging of beer and spirits.

Boom, boom, boom!!

Suddenly, Pierre was awakened from his flashback to the sound of a Luftwaffe 128mm flak cannon firing at something flying over the city. His desk clock read 4:00a.m.– back in his office at OKW.

"I hope they got the bastard," Pierre muttered, trying to get his bearings with his abrupt return to the present day, albeit early morning. War had a nasty way of interrupting one's sleep.

Massar decided coffee was in order and made his way down to the night operation watch officer to see if he could steal a fresh cup before all the top brass arrived to their various offices in the next couple of hours.

As he approached the operations desk, a Luftwaffe Captain was vainly trying to stay awake, even while trying to answer calls from the various districts commands coordinating damage reports, fire fighting support, anti-aircraft engagements, you name it.

Pierre made his way straight to the coffee urn, grabbing a semi clean cup in the process.

"Mind if I help myself?" Massar asked.

The Captain, still on the phone with some high ranking civil authority, waved him an OK. Pierre was going to have a cup whether the desk officer approved or not. As he finished pouring, the Luftwaffe Officer finished his call, slamming down the receiver with a loud *clang!*

"Asshole, what the hell am I supposed to do about it...?" he uttered, forgetting the presence of the Wehrmacht Major in his presence.

"Ahemm, uh Captain, is it always this peaceful at this time in the morning?"

"This assshole Nazi Party clown wants us to send a truck over to help move his family's goods to a safe place. Since when am I *a moving company?* By the way Major, would you be so kind as to pour me a cup as well?" he asked, tossing his empty coffee cup towards Massar.

Pierre, initially stunned by this act of disrespect towards a senior officer, just as quickly dismissed it – after all it could very well have been him as the night operations watch officer for the OKH instead of this unfortunate Luftwaffe guy.

"I guess Field Marshall Goering will start the *Baedeker Vergeltungsangriffe*[33] plan for England they've recently assembled within OKL. That'll teach 'em not to mess with us..." but before the Captain could finish, another phone rang, almost like a baby crying out for attention.

"Javoll, Hauptman Siegel here, Heil Hitler!" Siegel's face changed from one of annoyance to wide eyed surprise. It was apparent to Pierre that Siegel

---

33 Retaliatory raids by the German Luftwaffe on British cities in response to the bomb- ing of the erstwhile city of Lubeck during the night from 28 to 29 March, 1942. The Baedeker raids were conducted by the German Luftflotte 3 in two periods between April and June 1942. They targeted strategically relatively unimportant but picturesque cities in England. The cities were reputedly selected from the German "Baedeker" Tourist Guide to Britain, meeting the criterion of having been awarded three stars, hence the English name for the raids.

had pissed off the wrong Party official and it was coming back to him in spades.

As he finished the last swig of his now lukewarm coffee, Massar wiped the cup clean then replaced it back by the urn and turned to return back to his office. By this time, the Captain had finished receiving his telephonic "ass chewing" and sat back in his chair pondering what the remainder of his night shift might bring.

As Pierre offered him thanks for the coffee, Captain Siegel responded, "Sir, is it really that bad on the eastern front?"

Massar looked at him, quickly guessing the watch officer's now pending fate in life if he screwed up again.

"Well, let me just say, it's a nice to place to visit, but I wouldn't want my worse enemy stationed there!"

"Thank you Herr Major – by the way, don't you work for Field Marshall von Keitel?"

"Why, yes I do," Pierre responded, wondering why all of a sudden there was interest in his current assignment.

Siegel immediately reached into his inbox and pulled out a small cardboard box that contained a briefing file. He handed it over to Massar.

"I'm sorry sir, this came for you during the night and I didn't know you were working late or I'd have gotten to you sooner. It came via dispatch rider from von Keitel's quarters last night asking for your review of the Field Marshall's comments."

Massar thanked the officer and returned to his office. Sitting down, he opened the box revealing just what he suspected – an Operations Order Briefing file code named *Case Siegfried*, but with the *Siegfried* crossed out and scrawled over with the simple word "Blue", apparently in a handwriting he recognized as belonging the Hitler himself. As he opened the briefing file, a short hand written note from Keitel fell into Pierre's lap.

Major Massar,

Enclosed you will find Directive 41 — the outline for this summer's Wehrmacht's offensive in the Soviet Union. I need you to review and comment to me by Wednesday's OKW staff call on this operations plan developed personally by Der Fuehrer and General Halder at OKH. Once you start reading you'll apparently find Hitler has decided that Moscow is no longer his objective since it's capture does not necessarily mean the Soviets will quit the war, but seizing the southeastern oil fields of Russia is now the main objective in the east, if for anything to starve the Russians while providing much needed mineral resources for the Reich. As you can see, Hitler did not agree with OKH's original name (Siegfried). When Halder presented it to Hitler on April 5th, Hitler immediately recalled the last grandiosely-named offensive operation named after the mythical Teutonic hero, "Barbarossa", had fallen short of his expectations and decided to settle on the more modest name of "Blue". I think Hitler believes naming these plans after dead German heroes jinxes it. I need your eye for detail to review and comment to me prior to Wednesday - Keitel.

Pierre set the note down, leaned back in his chair and realized Wednesday was just three days away.

"Another offensive? What folly!" he thought. "Hadn't the army in general and the General Staff in particular learned anything from their predicament in the Soviet Union?"

Pierre opened his desk drawer and pulled out a note pad containing facts and observations he had collected during his January visit to Russia.

"Let's see, of the over one million casualties incurred, we're still 280,000 troops short. The Army Quartermaster still hasn't replaced the 180,000 horses much less all the motor transport lost. The good news is there were strong indications the American lend-lease material support to the Russians had pretty much dried up, owing to America's need to re-equip itself now that she was in her own war with the Japanese."

The tired OKW Staff Major opened the document binder and began to read.

"The winter battle in Russia is coming to an end and the German soldier could congratulate himself on a defensive success of great magnitude . . . Not only had enemy forces suffered serious losses in men and material, they had burned up reserves. . ."

"What crap," Pierre said to himself, quickly thumbing through Hitler's philosophical analogy of where the army was today in Russia. Massar quickly glanced over the OKH Order of Battle to see if he recognized any particular units he had worked within the past that would be participating in this latest grand adventure.

"Oh my God," he winced. Pierre noted of the 41 new divisions added to Army Group South, 21 divisions were non-German: six Italian, 10 Hungarian, and five Romanian, and the Hungarian and Romanian had a historical animosity towards each other. His stomach tightened when he thought about the poor performance of the Italian units when his beloved Sixth Panzer Division fought in the Balkans back in the spring of '41. It was a sure sign that the Wehrmacht was having an enormous problem manning a 1,700 mile front. He continued to look over all the required and highly complex movements of two Panzer Armies, four Infantry Armies, and four so called "Allied" armies of questionable competence divided between two Army Groups. So much material traveling so far, bringing to mind that the availability of fuel would once again be at the forefront of the Wehrmacht's success or failure in this upcoming campaign.

For a military establishment that constantly reminded itself of Clausewitz's comments on keeping its orders "short and sweet", the order was long and vague. He remembered an old saying his father taught him years ago when it came to operational or tactical planning; "In war, everything is very simple, yet the simplest thing is difficult. Remember, simple is hard enough!"

This plan was far from simple. Massar knew he had his work was cut out for him for the next 72 hours.

"Got to find an eastern front map," he thought as he decided to have some breakfast down in the buildings kantine first before starting his long day's work.

While Major Massar was starting his day within the OKW Headquarters, Jerry Curry was trying to wind his down half a world away in Washington, attempting to salvage what he could of his Saturday night. His friend Alice had taken the train down from New York to spend the weekend with him, But the President had other plans for him, especially since he now had assumed the late Harry Hopkins' role as FDRs unofficial/official advisor. What he found, when he returned to Washington from Switzerland last January, upon Hopkin's death astonished him beyond belief.

For starters, Roosevelt not only offered Curry Hopkin's unofficial position, he practically coerced him in a style all too typical of this crafty "*Squire of Hyde Park.*" Had Jerry known that acceptance meant working an average of 18 hour days, he might have fought harder, but Roosevelt was the President and a wartime one at that who needed everyone he could to help with the nation's war effort. To say "no" might have come across as self serving, even selfish, so he accepted. As a perk for accepting the job, FDR allowed Jerry to take up residence within the White House itself.

"Quite a first for even this Kentucky Republican," he thought once he finished moving his things into the upstairs room just down from the President's own bedroom.

Over the course of the next few months, Curry stepped into his new role with a gusto that surprised even him. He didn't know if it was the rush of working with one of the most powerful men in the world today, or his fear of failure to the man who had extended to Curry almost complete trust as to the secrets of the inner workings of the nation's capital.

As a business man, Curry had no problem reviewing industry production schedules and quotas, making modifications and passing on advice to the President as well as the nation's top two military leaders – Admiral King and General Marshall - as to the best course and practices. He frequently went over to Capital Hill and worked with Senators and Congressmen, ensuring FDR's war time agenda was heard and voted on.

Soon it became apparent his duty day would extend beyond the nine to five routine of the White House West Wing, often times leaving his desk late evening only to be greeted by a hearty tasker in the form of a note pinned to his pillow by the ol' man himself, along with a bottle of 10-year-old Scotch to soften the blow. By late March 1942 even his Saturdays had became consumed with work, leaving Sunday his only real day to rest and catch up with himself. Even here, he had to draw the line – President or not!

But this Sunday was very different for the first time in a long time in Washington D.C. Everywhere within the White House champagne was breaking out in celebration of Doolittle's raid on Tokyo. For the first time in months the United States was finally striking back at the Japanese Empire.

Curry had slept in that morning and even Roosevelt had dared not wake him with the good news for fear that Jerry would move out, but the commotion from downstairs was more than too much and soon Curry came downstairs to see what all the ruckus was about.

"We bombed Tokyo today Mr. Curry!!" said Alonzo Fields when Jerry asked what the celebration was for. "It happened last night – some army bombers flew in and blasted the Jap capital!" Fields exclaimed. "We bombed the God-damned Japs..."

"It didn't make any sense. How could we have gotten close enough to launch a bombing strike on Japan?" Curry thought to himself. He decided to poke his head into the old man's office to see what he knew.

"Come in Curry, come in and help celebrate!" said Roosevelt when he spotted his trusted advisor peeking from behind the door. "How about a glass of California champagne old friend?" Roosevelt quickly wheeled around from behind his desk to a small table set up with several glasses containing various levels of the sparkling fluid.

"Why, thank you Mr. President, but if you don't mind my asking, what the hell is going on?"

FDR smiled as he handed the glass over to Curry.

"We're celebrating our first strike against the damn Japs. Ever since Pearl Harbor, we've been looking for a way to get back at them. The concept for this attack came last January 10th, from Navy Captain Francis Low, who works for Admiral King. This Captain Low convinced King he believed that twin-engine army bombers could be successfully launched from an aircraft carrier after he observed several at a Norfolk Virginia naval airfield, where the runway was painted with the outline of a carrier deck for landing practice. It was subsequently planned and led by a Lieutenant Colonel James Doolittle in which 16 B-25 Mitchell bombers flew off the aircraft carrier USS Hornet, somewhere in the central Pacific. By God did he make it and yesterday was a small down payment for Pearl. What a boost for our civilian morale!!"

"Well congratulations Mr. President, this truly is a great moment for you and the nation. Is there any word on how many made it?" asked Curry.

FDR swung around and grabbed a piece of note paper from his desk, then placed his pince-nez eyeglasses on to read the small print.

"It says here that 15 aircraft reached the Chinese coast after a 13 hour flight and crash landed or bailed out; one crew flew north to Soviet Russia, landing near Vladivostok, where it appears the Russians have confiscated their B-25 and interned its crew. Overall, General Marshall tells me this was the longest combat mission ever flown by the B-25 bomber, averaging approximately 2,250 miles."

"Well, here's to Colonel Jimmy Doolittle and here's to American made medium bombers!" said Jerry as he raised his glass to toast America's newest heroes. FDR quickly followed suit, downing his champagne in one mighty gulp.

As the two made small talk, the President's secretary buzzed FDR, informing him he had a call on line two.

"It's him," informed the protective Presidential secretary. "Do you want me to have him call back?"

The joy Roosevelt had been experiencing quickly evaporated into a scowl. Even his jaunty cigarette holder dipped below lip level, almost dropping into his lap.

"Mr. Curry, would you please excuse me?" asked FDR. "Lydia, you may go ahead and connect me with the Senator."

Jerry got up and headed for the door. Initially he felt relieved he wasn't required any further today by Roosevelt and still might be able to catch an afternoon matinee with his friend Alice before she took the evening train back to New York. But as he briefly listened to the President's conversation before he was out of ear shot, he could tell this was the man who was troubling the President and had something on him.

"*I thought I had the old man's trust,*" Curry thought to himself, knowing his predecessor Harry Hopkins had known what the deal was even since those days immediately after Pearl Harbor.

Curry walked over to the switchboard operator and asked her to connect him to the Hotel Washington. If he was lucky he would catch Alice and maybe see the new Jimmy Cagey movie *Yankee Doodle Dandy* playing downtown.

After connecting with Alice and making a date, Curry hung up the phone, noticing the line connection light to the President was no longer lit.

"Is the President off the phone?" Jerry asked the switchboard operator.

"He sure is. This Senator that calls the President usually calls him during off times for some reason. I guess he's one who wants to spend some private time talking with FDR."

Jerry decided this was the time to confront the President and get to the bottom of the secrecy surrounding those mysterious calls.

"By the way," Curry asked as he turned to leave the switchboard room, "which Senator is it?"

"I think he calls himself *Senator Bee*. Isn't that a strange name for a Senator? I mean who has a last name like *Bee*? I think he comes from the west, at least he sounds like someone who doesn't come from around here."

Jerry waved a quick thanks and headed back to Roosevelt's Oval Office. As he approached, the ever present Alonzo was standing pat – the President's first line of defense to stop anybody from just simply dropping in on the nation's chief executive. Jerry's gave Alonzo a quick glance that said *"Don't try and stop me!"* It was an effective glance as Alonzo not only stood aside he even opened the door to the Oval Office. As the President's advisor entered the office, he quickly closed the door behind him. Alonzo did not want to hear any part of the forthcoming conversation with the President!

As he stepped inside he saw the leader of the United States – sitting in his wheelchair, looking out the main window directly behind the famous *Resolute* desk and staring into space. He seemed crestfallen and hunched over, with all the celebratory glee of an hour ago drained away as if he was a kid's balloon and had sprung a leak.

"Have a seat Jerry," said Roosevelt, not even turning around from his position to confirm who the visitor was. FDR had a concerned look mixed with worry plastered all over his face.

"Mr. President, with all due respect – just what the hell is going on with all these mysterious calls I observed you receiving ever since Hopkins brought me here into the inner sanctum last December?"

"I guess I do owe you an explanation," said Roosevelt, turning his chair and wheeling himself over towards Curry, stopping a few feet from him. He put a fresh cigarette into his holder and lit it, taking a strong drag and then blasting his smoke into the space behind his desk.

"It all started in late 1939 or early 1940. As you and most Americans are aware, I always had a strong antipathy towards Hitler and his dreaded Nazis. However, my hands were tied. At that time, the vast majority of the American people wanted to avoid involvement in the latest European War. There was a feeling our involvement in the First World War had been a catastrophic error and we wanted to insure that the mistake would not be repeated. The Congress as you know was likewise committed to a policy of firm neutrality and had passed the Johnson and Neutrality Acts to make sure that America kept out of war in Europe. Yet I could not stand by and let Hitler march all over Europe. Churchill and the British needed our help, so I took steps that, shall we say, were not in accordance with my powers as President nor would these actions have passed *constitutional* muster."

Curry sat stone faced at this startling revelation, but inside he was shocked. Certainly Roosevelt had pushed the federal government into areas it had not gone before as part of his "New Deal" programs, and had been challenged throughout most of his first two terms by Republicans in both Houses of Congress, but he had been largely successful. This action somehow, was sinisterly different – more complex.

"Mr. President, what exactly did you do?" queried Curry.

Roosevelt took his cigarette holder in his left hand, ready to use it to make a point.

"Jerry, there are incriminating documents out there in the hands of a blackmailer that if released, would generate an enormous public outcry for my removal from office for substantial abuse of my presidential powers. Such a disclosure might even be enough to bring about my impeachment. Certainly the documents provide proof of criminal activity sufficient to warrant my removal from office. Congress will be virtually compelled to begin at least preliminary impeachment proceedings."

"Holy crap! The President himself had committed criminal acts?" Jerry thought to himself. He had wanted to enter the inner sanctum and now he had arrived.

"Mr. President, do you mind if I fix myself a drink? This is to say the least, *extraordinaire!*"

"Only if you pour me a Scotch as well Curry!" responded Roosevelt. "In fact, you might as well make both of them a double."

Jerry handed FDR a tumbler of his finest single malt Scotch, then retuned back to his chair, knocking back a swig in the process. Once Curry was seated Roosevelt continued.

"As I said, it started in late 1939. I began a dialog with Mr. Winston Churchill, who was back then just the First Lord of the Sea. This was completely out of protocol – the discussion about policy and strategy should have been with Mr. Chamberlain. In our dialog, we discussed how our two nations could circumvent the neutrality laws passed by Congress, most notably the Neutrality Acts of 1936 and 1937 among other less honorable things. Apparently at that same time, our London embassy acquired a new 29-year-old cipher clerk by the name of Tyler Kent. For whatever reasons, Kent decided to make copies or summaries of all diplomatic dispatches and cables between Churchill and myself, some of which were before he became Prime Minister. Jerry, many of these documents are fairly ugly and would be a problem if they were ever to get out. Harry believed Kent might have taken an isolationist view and sought to provide copies to those America First oriented senators and congressmen. In May of 1940, the British arrested Kent in a dawn raid at his apartment. Officers from the British MI-5 Counter Intelligence Agency found a couple thousand official documents, cables and letters mostly between Churchill and me, as well as keys to the embassy code room."

Upon hearing that, Curry took an even larger gulp of the FDR's Scotch.

"So what happened to this chap?" he asked FDR.

"Well, we informed our ambassador Joe Kennedy and had Kent's diplomatic immunity pulled. The Brits put him on secret trial; he was convicted and sentenced to seven years' imprisonment. MI-5 rounded up and destroyed the material and so Harry and I though this was the end of the story."

"Apparently not," replied Curry. "These calls you're receiving ..."

"Are from someone who appears to have obtained either some of the original documents or copies of the original cables. Obviously, MI-5 was not as thorough as I thought they would be," finished Roosevelt. "Kent did make an interesting statement at his trial that Harry said might bite us in the ass one day. In his trial, Kent also admitted that he had taken documents from the U.S. Embassy in Moscow, with the vague notion of someday showing them to U.S. senators who shared his isolationist, anti-Semitic views."

"A Senator by the name of Senator *Bee*? Who the hell is that?" Jerry asked.

Roosevelt took another swig. "I can't tell you right now for your safety. It appears they killed once, and they might kill again."

Jerry leaned back in his chair trying to take it all in. He looked at his watch and realized he was not going to make his movie date with Alice.

"Mr. President, may I use your phone?"

FDR motioned his OK to Curry who picked it up. Lydia immediately answered.

"Hi Lydia, Jerry Curry here. Would you relay a message to Alice at the Hotel Washington that I can't make it tonight? I've had a change in plans ..."

Chapter 13

A Dialogue with the Deaf

Fact: Prior to the American entry into World War II, the German Intelligence Agency known as the *"Abwehr"*, under the direction of Admiral Wilhelm Canaris, began infiltrating agents into the United States. By 1942, German agents were operating from within all of America's top armaments manufacturers. In one particular case, a female Abwehr agent infiltrated a US Naval shipyard near Evansville, Indiana, but escaped and was never apprehended. Despite the capture and immediate execution in 1942 of six agents attempting to infiltrate the United States near Long Island, NY, the Abwehr scored some notable successes in America. Its greatest victories were in the area of industrial espionage as agents managed to steal the blueprint for every major American airplane produced for the war effort.

"I only did my duty to my country when I tried to oppose the criminal folly of Hitler"

- Admiral Wilhelm Canaris,
Chief of the Abwehr, OKW's Intelligence Agency

Abwehr Headquarters
76/78 Tirpitzufer, Berlin, Germany
1000 hrs, 4 Jun 1942

The warm, heavy rain had just let up when a black staff car pulled up before the dull gray office complex overlooking the Landwehr Canal. Located within the heart of Berlin's old German military headquarters on Bendlerblock it housed Germany's Intelligence Collection Center and the Defense Office of the Armed Forces High Command, otherwise known to the rest of the world as the *"Abwehr."* Adjacent to Germany's "spy center" the

OKW was brisling with dozens of staff officers charged with running the Wehrmacht's war effort. As such it was the only headquarters in the Third Reich that had a vested interest in obeying Hitler's orders.

Once the car came to a complete halt, enlisted aides scrambled with umbrellas to meet the sole occupant exiting the large sedan. He was a tall, white haired, distinguished looking gentleman with bushy brows who could have been mistakenly recognized as the head of a foreign country or even a diplomat. Yet this man, while not a dignitary, had his finger on the very pulse of the Third Reich.

The "Old Fox" – Admiral Wilhelm F. Canaris, Chief of the Abwehr

"Good morning Herr Admiral," saluted Oberfeldwebel[34] Steiner, in charge of the ad hoc welcoming committee assembled outside the Abwehr's HQ. "How was your trip from Spain?"

The white haired gentleman with bushy eyebrows smiled at his aide as he stretched, relieved from the close confines of the staff car's back seat as well

---

34   Oberfeldwebel: A Non-Commissioned Officer of rank equivalent to a "First Sergeant".

as a 12 hour flight from Madrid. The fresh air, while humid due to the mild summer heat, revitalized the 55-year-old traveler.

"I think you'd enjoy Spain this time of year, Steiner. It certainly beats this damp rainy Berlin weather."

"Ja-wohl Herr Admiral, I hope you keep me in mind as an aide the next time you fly down," replied Steiner. "General Oster[35] has the section heads assembled in your conference room."

The Admiral shook off his black rain coat and hat and handed them to Steiner once they entered the building. Down the main corridor they entered an ancient elevator that slowly took them up to the third floor and walked over to the Admiral's conference room. En route, everyday military and civilian personnel greeted the Admiral, known by his friends and admirers as the "Old Fox." He was obviously respected by those working for him.

"Achtung," cried Lieutenant Colonel Jenke, the Admiral's Adjutant just as the Old Fox entered the room and took his seat at the head of the oak table that sat dead center of the mid size conference room. Already clouds of cigarette smoke fanned out across the room like a thin indoor fog bank, indicating the assembled occupants had been waiting for some time.

"Gentlemen, please take your seats. I am most curious as to why I needed to cut my visit with the illustrious General Francisco Franco short by two days and head back to Berlin. Not that I need an excuse, but dictators can be high maintenance…"

Oster glanced quickly around the conference table, ensuring all the department heads and their deputies were assembled. It was a curious mix of senior officers from both the German Army and Navy. Each had been hand picked for their positions within the military intelligence agency by the very man who they were there to brief and whose cause they too strongly believed in – Admiral Wilhelm F. Canaris.

---

35   Hans Oster was German Army Major General, deputy head of the Abwehr and head of Department "Z" – the controlling head of the Foreign Branch as well as the Counter-Intelligence Branch.

"Herr Admiral," Oster began almost like a school kid with a secret who was just waiting for the right moment to spill the beans about something he was excited about.

"Over the course of the last 10 days a number of, shall we say, remarkable things have occurred that will greatly assist our cause," stated Oster.

The one factor uniting everyone assembled in the conference room was a deep resentment of the Nazis in general and Adolph Hitler in particular, officers who shared the same vision as their chief. So much so, they referred to themselves as "CC" for *Club Canaris*.

Hans continued. "I don't know if the German Embassy in Madrid had informed you, but one week ago SS-Obergruppenführer Reinhart Heydrich, former head of the dreaded *Sicherheitsdienst*[36] or 'SD', and if I might add, your chief adversary, was assassinated down near Prague. From what we could find out on May 27th, 1942 Heydrich was on his way to Berlin when he was ambushed while he rode in his open car in the suburb of Kobylisy. One of the attackers threw a bomb at the rear of his car, seriously wounding the SS Obergruppenführer. He suffered a severe injury to the left side of his body with major damage to his diaphragm, spleen, and lungs, as well as a broken rib. The doctors immediately performed an operation and, despite a slight fever, his recovery appeared to progress quite well. Two days ago, Himmler paid Heydrich a visit, after which he slipped into a coma and never regained consciousness. Reports we received a couple of hours ago informed us he died at 4:30a.m. of septicemia."

The dreaded SS Obergruppenführer – Reichsführer-SS Heinrich Himmler's right hand man and Canaris' chief rival as the head of all intelligence collection for the Third Reich - was dead.

The Admiral sat back in his chair. Slowly a grin began to emerge on his weathered face. For the past two years, the Old Fox himself had been in

---

36   Literal translation: Security or Secret Police. The intelligence branch of Heinrich Himmler's SS.

contact with the head of Britain's MI-6 – Stewart Menzies, leaning on him as recently as last summer to find out the locations of various key Russian units as Germany prepared to invade the Soviet Union. Like Canaris, Menzies was strongly anti-communist, and had no problem sharing this intelligence with the Abwehr. Unfortunately for Canaris, both Himmler and Heydrich became suspicious as to how Canaris came into possession of such valuable information. Heydrich began his own private investigation into the Abwehr chief and ultimately became a threat to both Canaris and the future of the Abwehr[37]. The two were on a collision course but fortunately for the Admiral the Czech's eliminated Heydrich, courtesy of the British. With his chief rival dead, Canaris had nothing to worry about in his agency's quest of ridding Germany of the dreaded Nazi regime. The Old Fox's facial expression made Oster wonder whether the Admiral might have had something to do with this action after all.

"How unfortunate for the poor man. I'm sure that the Reich's Minister Himmler must be devastated," Canaris grinned in a mocking manner, knowing full well that the monstrous SS Chief detested his own SS Obergruppenführer for his high profile reputation as much as the Admiral did. "Is there any indications as to any sort of retaliation?"

Oster responded, "None yet, but there is a lot of talk coming from SS Headquarters that something massive is coming at the direction of Hitler. We've received word that one or two SS Einzatz Commando units were dispatched to Czechoslovakia from Russia for some sort of punitive act of which we are still investigating."

---

37   During Heydrich's posting in Prague, a serious incident put him and Canaris in open conflict. A British agent — the Czech Paul Thümmel — was arrested by Heydrich, but Canaris intervened to save him, claiming he was a double agent actually working for Abwehr. Heydrich suspected that Thümmel was actually Canaris' MI-6 contact. Heydrich requested that Canaris put the Abwehr under SD and SS control. Canaris appeared to retreat and handled the situation diplomatically, but there was no immediate effect on the Abwehr for the time being. With Heydrich's assassination, the matter was dropped.

Canaris' grin faded and his face became blank as he contemplated how ruthless the SS retaliation would be in light of the loss of their great champion, who recently chaired a conference in Wannasee last January to decide the fate of all Jews within occupied Europe.

"Is that all?" Canaris asked. "Certainly that was not the only reason you needed me to come back from Spain?"

"Nein sir," chimed back the Admiral's Deputy. "Our little club has just recruited two new members."

Canaris glanced quickly at the conference room doors, ensuring they were closed so passers by would not hear.

"Before we go on Oster, are we clean?" asked the Old Fox in reference to the Gestapo's nasty practice of planting listening devices within the Abwehr's many offices. Nobody trusted anybody in the Third Reich today.

"Herr Admiral, I had our technicians sweep the conference room just one hour ago, so I assure you this room is indeed spotless!" Oster continued.

"Last week we recruited Major General Henning von Tresckow, currently the Operations Officer for Army Group Center, while he was conducting staff business with OKH in Berlin. This gives us a connection to his uncle Field Marshal von Bock, as well as Field Marshall von Kluge."

Canaris still wasn't quite satisfied with this news. Dissatisfied Major Generals were a dime-a-dozen, especially from the Eastern Front. His facial expression yielded as much to Oster.

"The second officer however, is Lieutenant General Friedrich Olbricht, Chief of the OKW Reserve Army."

"Ah, Chief of the Reserve Army. Now *that* Oster is quite a coup — excellent!"

Oster smiled at the Old Fox's compliment — finally, the boss was pleased.

"Sir, Section III[38], Colonel Franz von Bentivegni, just returned from a meeting with the *Sonderkommando Roto Kapelle*[39] over at Gestapo Headquarters," replied Oster, glancing at von Bentivegni to ready his brief to the chief.

Canaris nodded to his Section III chief to begin.

"Sir, as you are aware, shortly after our invasion of the Soviet Union, the SD and our men began to detect radio transmissions emanating from the Berlin, Brussels, and Paris areas, all directed towards Russia which we believe is relaying critical information and intelligence back to the NKVD. As part of the task force, the Gestapo informed us they recently shut down one of the transmitters in Brussels and felt it was close to nailing the remaining 'pianists' of this so called *Red Orchestra*." With that, Colonel von Bentivegni closed his briefing folder, ending his report to the Abwehr Chief.

"What have we heard from *Herr H* regarding the Americans?" asked Canaris.

It was Colonel Hans "Piki" Piekenbrock's turn to speak to the revered chief. As head of Abwehr Section I his responsibilities included the recruitment of enemy intelligence.

"We've had no further contact with the American named Curry ever since Hans Bernd Gisevius and the American Allen Dulles set *Herr H* up to meet with him in Berne last January. Since his return to the United States he has become Roosevelt's closest advisor, so we know he has taken our message to the President."

Espionage is a game of patience and much like the game of poker, one keeps their cards close to their chest, and Canaris was a master of the game.

---

38   Section III was responsible for armed forces security, combating espionage and treason, infiltration of foreign intelligence.

39   The *Sonderkommando Rote Kapelle* ("Red Orchestra Special Detachment") was a task force set up to combat the Red Orchestra's activities. Including representatives of the Gestapo, Abwehr, and the SD, it was formed in early 1942 on Hitler's personal orders.

"Piki," Canaris responded, "I need to find out where the Americans are in helping us. Time is running out. We all know that while Heydrich is out of the way, it's only a matter of time before Himmler tries again. Every day Der Fuehrer lives means thousands of German soldiers and civilians die, all for this utterly ridiculous madman! Get a message to *H* and arrange a meeting with Curry. I do not intend to have a dialogue with the deaf!"

Piki scrawled a short note on a piece of notebook paper and handed it to his deputy section leader who immediately left the conference room. Everyone present knew Piekenbrock would make it happen.

"Speaking of the Americans," Oster interjected, "we have heard they are involved in a massive make or break naval battle with the Imperial Japanese Navy somewhere northwest of the Hawaiian Island chain near a 'Midway Island'. From what we have obtained from our attaché in Tokyo and confirmed by the Japanese embassy here, our Japanese allies are hell bent on invading the islands as a stop gap against the Americans to keep them as far away as possible. Apparently, that bombing strike that hit Tokyo last April has them quite stirred up..."

Canaris paid scant attention to Oster's words about the Americans or the Japanese – his thoughts were on his adversary's departure from the planet. Inspite of the rivalry between the two servants of the Reich to become the chief intelligence 'Czar' of the country, the two of them were longtime neighbors who shared a common love of classical music. Heydrich, a gifted violinist, would occasionally serenade Canaris' wife Erica with his remarkable music. Some nights, the Admiral would entertain Heydrich with a magnificent dinner prepared by 'Chez' Canaris himself, complete with his famed chef's toque, after a game of croquet in Reinhart's garden. But he was gone and in a somewhat brutal manner. Now all that remained was the question of what sort of retaliation Hitler or Himmler would incite as payback. Whatever was in store for the poor Czech citizenry who happened to be in the locale of bombing, his beloved Abwehr was safe – for the moment.

"Sir, there is one last item," Oster interrupted, "you have a note from a Baron Vladimir Kaulbars. Nothing particularly urgent, but something we just received while you were in Spain."

"Kaulbars eh?!" the Admiral asked. *"I wonder what that ol' White Russian Émigré from the Baltic is up to?"* he thought to himself. Canaris owed the Baltic Baron a lot and their friendship went back quite a few years.

"Have Vera bring me the note once we're finished," directed the Admiral, "otherwise, if there's nothing more to report, I suggest we adjourn so we can continue other more pressing duties."

Canaris returned to his dark wood paneled office located adjacent to the conference room. Typical for a Reich bureaucrat, his desk was filled with piles of papers – reports from agents in the field and from the Eastern and North African fronts, all poorly illuminated by a few scattered lamps that cast islands of light across his dark desk top.

As he sat down to survey his pending workload for the week, his secretary Vera Schwarte came in to deliver the Baron's note as well as offer the Admiral refreshments. Following closely behind was his trusted deputy, Oster, who took a seat to the front right of Canaris' massive desk.

"It's been a while since you've heard from the Baron," said Oster, giving Canaris a moment to quickly read the note. "Does he have anything of particular interest?"

Canaris folded the note and in a mocking manner responded, "Da." Both officers smiled at the irony – Baron Vladimir Kaulbars, in addition to providing a backdoor channel to the Soviet High Command 'The Kremlin', had taught the Old Fox to speak fluent Russian.

Major General Hans Oster, Deputy Abwehr Chief

"Well Oster, seems our Russians friends are interested in opening a back door dialogue with us," Canaris said as he folded the Baron's note and leaned back in his chair. "But why? They damn near destroyed the Wehrmacht six months ago" he mused.

Both stared at one another in puzzlement until Oster stood and headed for a file box on the Admiral's desk and began looking through it for a brown colored file.

"I wonder, maybe they've had enough?" Oster was thinking out loud until he found what he was searching for. "Here you are..."

Inside were various operation closure reports — a type of German after action report which included casualty counts for both sides.

"Herr Admiral, listen to this. Just under one month ago on May 12th, a large Soviet force under the command of Marshal Timoshenko launched an offensive against OKW's Army Group South's Sixth Army from within the Izium Salient, created south of Kharkov during their recently concluded Soviet early spring offensives. Our Sixth Army, under the command of a newly appointed General Fredrick von Paulus, initiated a contingency plan named *Operation Friderikus,* an operation that called for a pincer movement to crush the Soviet armies located within this salient. Apparently the Soviets blundered pretty badly and the Sixth Army bagged the whole gang. Reports here indicate that Timoshenko ordered the official halt of all Soviet offensive actions on May 28th and two days later tried to break out of Army Group South's encirclement. Bottom line is they lost a little over 200,000 while we captured 240,000 prisoners along with the bulk of their armor, while we lost 20,000 – that includes deaths, the wounded and missing. Final field reports state that less than one man in 10 managed to break out of this '*Barvenkovo mousetrap*' and make it back to Russian lines."

Oster closed that report and opened a second one.

"Here's a report from General von Manstein and his Eleventh Army down in the Crimea. It states here that the Eleventh Army launched a counterattack on May 8th, code named '*Unternehmen Trappenjagd*[40]', aimed at expelling Soviet forces in the Kerch area then resuming an offensive on Sevastopol. He broke through and pursued the Russians up to the Kerch straits. Ten days later the Soviets surrendered with a total loss of 176,566 either killed or captured. As of this day, he has moved up his big guns and is pounding the crap out of Sevastopol and it looks pretty good Manstein will capture the port city within a few weeks."

Hans closed the report and replaced the file on the Old Fox's desk.

"Wilhelm, maybe the Russians really are on their final mile? It appears that in just the last few months they've lost over half a million troops on top of the few million they lost in last year's invasion. I've also heard from my good friend

---

40   Operation "Undertake Bastard Hunt".

Colonel Reinhard Gehlen over at OKH who's Head of Foreign Armies – East Intelligence that the American Lend Lease they received in large quantities last year has all but dried up. If that's not enough, within the month OKW will launch Army Group South's *Case Blue* against the Russians in the Caucasus and who knows what that will bring in prisoners and material captured. Hell, yesterday I just finished reading a situation report from Tresckow at Army Group Center where they will shortly resolve another troublesome Russian blunder around the Rzhev-Vyazma salient area. It looks like we'll pocket another quarter million Russians in that action. Maybe Kaulbars is on to something? Maybe..." Oster returned back to his seat and looked back at the Admiral.

"Hans, you served on the Western Front in the First World War. You were present at the Somme when the British, of all people, sacrificed 57,000 soldiers *in one day* back in 1916. Do you really think the Russian are that casualty conscious?" asked Canaris.

"On the other hand, maybe you're right and they simply have run out of warm bodies for the mill? At any rate, I think we should send a response to the dear Baron and see where this goes."

Hans nodded in agreement, while Canaris began drafting a response to his old Baltic friend.

As he got up to leave the Admiral to his correspondence, he turned half way to the door to offer the Old Fox one last comment.

"How ironic Herr Admiral – on one hand we're asking the Americans to help us kill Hitler and bring about a negotiated peace with the Western Allies, allowing us to focus on the Bolsheviks; on the other hand, if Stalin is looking for some sort of armistice, how will the Allies react to them cutting and running?"

Canaris just grinned, returning back to his correspondence. Seeing the need for additional light, he reached over his desk to turn on another lamp. Reaching under the hood, he felt something not at all like a lamp switch chain, but small and cylindrical in shape.

Cautioning everyone in the immediate office area to be silent, he pulled the hood off the lamp, revealing a small slender cylinder approximately three centimeters long suspended by two thin wires. Oster moved to the front of the desk near the lamp and followed the wires, cleverly tucked into the crevices of the desk down to the floor and under the carpet. All present with Canaris office suddenly realized the chief of the Abwehr's office was 'bugged' and others may now be privy to what was just discussed about Kaulbars and the Soviets wanting to meet. Suddenly, someone else knew what Canaris had just discovered, the question was 'who'?

Canaris pulled out a piece of stationary and scrawled a quick note, handing it to Oster. Hans quickly read and acknowledged it with a nod. The Admiral then motioned for everyone to leave his office, holding his finger to his lips indicating they were to depart silently.

Once in the outer office, the Old Fox informed Vera to hold his calls, then told Hans to have Bentivegni and his Section III folks do a thorough 'house cleaning' of the floor for any more of the intrusive electronic creatures.

Before Oster departed, he looked at Canaris, half concerned, half inquisitive.

"Any idea who?" he asked the chief.

Canaris looked back at his deputy with puzzlement – "Who else do you think would be interested in what we do here – the Hitler Youth? It appears there'll be no real relief for us even with Heydrich gone."

A relief in the continuous combat action on the Eastern Front would have been a godsend for General Bernatz, but at this moment it was not on the cards. Ever since taking command, his 2nd Panzer Division had been in almost daily contact with numerous Soviet forces. During last winter's Soviet counteroffensive,

German forces were pushed back from Moscow. Within Army Group Center's area of operations, a large protrusion was formed along the front line in the direction of the Russian capital, which became better known as the Rzhev-Vyazma Salient. It was strategically important for the German Army Group to hold this piece of ground if they expected to use it as a springboard for any future operations against Moscow. Needless to say, an extensive OKH effort was made to ensure it was heavily fortified and strongly defended. The Soviets, on the other hand, had other ideas as to how to deal with this threat to their capital.

Situation of the Eastern Front with the Soviet Izium & German Rzhev-Vyazma Salients

Soviet forces along the Kalinin and Western Fronts broke through the thin German lines west of Rzhev in January, but because of a difficult supply route, the troops of the Soviet 22nd, 29th and 39th Armies became encircled. Slowly German forces squeezed this pocket, ridding themselves of the enemy forces trapped within. There in the heart of all this combat action was the German Ninth Army with Bernatz and his division. By June 2nd, the 2nd Panzer Division along with several thousand German troops had just completed Operation Hannover II and in the process had thoroughly rid the area of partisans and remnants of a failed Soviet airborne operation. Yet the Russian threat to the Army Group was far from over.

Major General Bernatz with the 2ⁿᵈ Panzer Division

Near the small village of Kameski, Bernatz decided to set up his command post on a small hill overlooking the picturesque Lake Beloye. In better times, this site would have made an idea vacation spot, nestled within the soft pine trees and sandy soil typical of the Byelorussian countryside. Now it served as short resting point for a division that had been on the go with non stop combat operations for the past few months. Troops were immediately dispatched to form a circular security perimeter far enough out to prevent Soviet snipers from getting close enough to kill what remained of the division's senior leadership, yet close enough to provide mutual support to one another if needed. After all this is how Bernatz's predecessor General Rudolf Veiel had been seriously wounded – it had ended his command of the division and he was evacuated back to Germany. Much as Johann wanted to display his coveted Knight's Cross, wearing it in the open was tantamount to suicide.

As he jumped off his converted Pz Mk IV Command Tank[41], Johann walked over to his kubelwagen to grab a small pillow, from which he would grab a few winks of shuteye before command would have him on the road again. Within his command car, his aide set his radio loud enough to hear from a few meters away, but not loud enough to betray his rank or position. For the moment command traffic consisted primarily of administrative or "housekeeping" radio communications, eavesdropping on his IIa or 'Adjutant' Hauptman Gustav Siegletz, and calling in the latest casualties and requests for replacements. Within the past months of combat, the division had lost 35 percent of it troop strength and over 60 percent of his officers were lost in action. While the division did receive a fair amount of replacement troops to cover his losses, the quality was nowhere near what it was when the division was stationed in France over a year ago. Bernatz could not help notice many of these fine lads, while very energetic, were not much older than 19 years of age.

"Combat will toughen them up soon enough, especially in this god for-saken place," he thought to himself as he stretched out on the short grass under the Byelorussian pine tree. Even the distant but ever present 'thump – thump' sounds of Russian 120mm mortar fire was not going to interfere with his much needed nap.

As he relaxed, he viewed Lake Beloye, marveling how beautiful such a place could be even in the mist of war. For once the air was sweet, lacking the

---

41   Command tanks carried a mock wooden cannon in lieu of a real 75mm one. Where the cannon's breach would have been located was filled with extra communications equipment.

unremitting reeking of death he had become all too familiar with. Swarms of flies, a constant companion to the stench-filled air, decided to take a holiday from the much harried Panzer Division Commander.

Lying down, Bernatz began to reflect on what they'd been through. They had killed thousands of Bolsheviks over the past few months and yet still more came.

"How many more could the Russians put into the field?" he thought to himself as if he was the only one trying to solve this massive complex equation. Suddenly from above him came a droning sound that could only mean two aircraft were roaming above.

Standing up, he tried to make out what type of plane it was and more important who it belonged to.

Above him in the skies, there it was. Bernatz was now a spectator in front row center of an air battle materializing 5000 feet above him between two Luftwaffe ME-109 Messerschmitts and three IL2 'Sturmoviks'. Eastern Front tankers paid especially close attention to these nasty birds for their dreaded 20mm cannon could easily turn an Mk III tank into scrap iron.

For 10 minutes Bernatz watched in amazement at this aerial version of an old Roman gladiator combat between the five planes, each twisting and turning, trying to out maneuver one another to deliver the killing blow. Soon one IL-2 was sent crashing and a distant thud could be heard, followed by another farther away. John was disheartened when one Sturmovik got a lucky shot off, bringing down one of the two ME-109s. He tried to follow the smoke coming from its fuselage as it dropped but it disappeared behind the Byelorussian pines. He closed his eyes when he heard the distant boom of the crashing plane and said a short prayer for the safety of the pilot, but suddenly he heard a closer, second boom. He looked up and saw the last remaining aircraft, a German Messerschmitt. It quickly did a victory roll over his position then veered off towards the west; returning to base.

Bernatz sat down, amazed at what he had just witnessed. As he sat there his Adjutant Hauptman Gustav Siegletz pulled up in his kubelwagen.

"Did you see that Herr General?" Siegletz yelled pointing to the sky above as he ran over to Bernatz's resting place.

Bernatz's Adjutant was bursting with excitement at having witnessed the Luftwaffe–Soviet aerial dual above the division's command post – it was the most animated Bernatz had seen him in the past few weeks.

"Once again the Luftwaffe's come through, Herr General! Did you see how they cleaned the Rusky's clocks?" the Adjutant proclaimed.

The General smiled, and then asked the Hauptman to take a seat by him. Standing up and waving seemed to have a somewhat lethal effect on senior officers in drawing attention to any snipers lying in wait.

Siegletz took a seat as instructed while Bernatz leaned back.

"Hauptman, we've been in Russia now for some time. By your estimation, how many Ruskies do you think we've killed over the past seven months – hundreds, maybe a couple thousand or more?"

The Adjutant just shrugged his shoulders. "At least a thousand or so I would think," he replied.

Bernatz nodded in agreement, "And yet they still keep coming. Think about what you just saw in the air. We had two fighters go against three of theirs and won, but we still lost one pilot. How long do you think we can keep this up – Siegletz?"

The Adjutant's enthusiasm vanished into a blank, non committal stare, devoid of emotion. He really didn't have an answer to give the General, and didn't want to offer what he actually thought. Suddenly, the war in Russia had caught up with him and he didn't like where it was going.

Bernatz continued, "This is going to be a war like we've never seen before, one of overwhelming brutality and one of utter survival. If anything, we've got to keep our wits about us and keep everything in perspective. You, more than anyone else here in this God forsaken place, know what our losses are especially in trained men and how many we will actually replace."

Siegletz shook his head in agreement. At that moment, a mud spattered kubelwagen pulled up alongside Bernatz's. Though the brown and gray mud unevenly coated most of the vehicle, the General could make out the faint vehicle ID makings of the 1st Panzer Division, located about 20 kilometers north of his current position – a social call perhaps?

Out of the vehicle a natty looking major emerged in a uniform looking very similar to the color scheme his vehicle embodied. By the expression on the staff officer's face, Bernatz could tell this would not be a social call from a sister panzer division.

"Excuse me," the staff officer called out, "I'm looking for the 2nd Panzer Division Command Post!"

Siegletz looked at Bernatz, then with the General's silent approval, raised his arm.

"You've found it Herr Major, what can we do for you?"

The Staff Major approached the Hauptman, coming within approximately 10 meters before he realized he was about to meet the Division Commander. He stopped to pull down his tunic smartly and sharpen his appearance as if he was reporting to a senior officer garrison.

When close enough, the staff officer stopped and offered the customary salute followed by the typical 'Heil Hitler'. Bernatz could only offer a pained expression as a return salute.

"Major, if you've had any serious combat time here in Russia, please refrain from saluting in the field least you have a death wish," the General curtly retorted. "I certainly don't. Now what can my happy-go-lucky band of warriors do for the 1st Panzer?"

"Sir, I am Major Bölter from the Ninth Army Operations staff, here to brief you and your division's role in Operation *SEYDLITZ*. My vehicle broke down while en route to brief the 1st Panzer, so they lent me a kubelwagen for use in coming down to brief you and your staff." While Bölter was talking, he pulled out a briefing file from his leader's bag and unfolded a well worn map of their sector of *Mother Russia*.

Bernatz glanced over to Gustav. A good Adjutant could always read his commander's mind and Siegletz excelled at this. Without uttering a word, the Division Adjutant was on the radio to the command post to reach the Division Ia (Operations Officer), Oberst Karl Fabiunke, whose role in understanding the latest operational nightmare was required. To kill a few minutes of time until the Ia arrived, the General offered the Ninth Army staff officer some refreshment in the from of a lukewarm cup of coffee, while Bölter neatly arranged his briefing orders, overlays, and maps on the hood of Bernatz's command vehicle.

When Fabiunke arrived, Major Bölter began pointing to the large map which covered three quarters of the engine hood.

"In order to eliminate the remaining partisan danger and regain full freedom of action within the area of Russia, General Model, commanding the Ninth Army, has planned Operation *SEYDLITZ*, a concentric counterattack which is to start on July 2nd. During the first stage of the operation, Ninth Army, in difficult forest fighting, is to dislodge the Soviet forces from their positions and hem them into this narrow area located here. We anticipate a quick thrust into the Obsha valley, by the 2nd Panzer Division from the south and the 1st Panzer Division coming in from the north, will split enemy units along the Obsha River, allowing the divisions to encircle the two pockets. An improvised cavalry brigade, the formation of which General Model had ordered prior to the commencement of Operation *SEYDLITZ*, will play a major role in this mission's success. Since most of the terrain within this area is very swampy or covered with extensive marshy forests, this unique cavalry brigade will be organized in such a manner that it can fight in any terrain and under any weather conditions, even if the weather turns to shit. In short Herr General, where your panzers cannot go, this brigade will!"

Both Bernatz and Oberst Fabiunke nodded at the operation's simplicity and understood the role they were to play, but the old panzer commander by this stage in his career knew that even in Russia *'simple was hard enough'*.

As Major Bölter finished his briefing and began handing copies of the wax paper operations overlays over to Fabiunke, Bernatz had one last question to ask.

"Major, what happens once we complete this operation? I seriously need time to rebuild this unit, especially since we can't expect the Ruskies to sit on their asses while there's big time action going on in the south," he said in reference to soon to commence Case Blue operations by Army Group South into the region of Russia known as *'the Great Don Bend"*.

Fabiunke briskly walked back to his vehicle once he had what he needed from the Ninth Army Staff's Major to plan the division's role in *SEYDLITZ*. Once out of earshot, Bölter first looked down at the General's muddy boots, then hesitatingly looked him in the eye and answered his question.

"Herr General, I have both good news and bad. The good news is that once this operation is successfully completed, the division will be placed in defense-reserve for a much needed rest."

"Finally, time to recover and regenerate," responded Bernatz, "and so what could be such bad news?"

"I regret to inform you Herr General; the bad news is you will lose two of your three panzer battalions for redeployment to Fourth Panzer Army for action down in the south towards Stalingrad and the Caucasus. In short, your division's wings will be clipped." With that, Major Bölter closed his briefing book, then strolled over to the borrowed kubelwagen. As he climbed in, he looked at the now down trodden General. Nary was a salute nor good-bye exchanged.

Chapter 14

The End of the Beginning

Fact: In the 1930s, an Italian national while working within the American Embassy in Rome, broke into the safe containing the embassy's secret code books. Within a short time, these books soon reached the Abwehr HQs in Berlin for future use against the United States should war with America occur. Such was the importance of these code books that Field Marshal Erwin Rommel used them to his advantage against American troops in North Africa in 1942 and 1943.

"A general is just as good or just as bad as the troops under his command make him."
General Douglas MacArthur
Commander, Southwest Pacific Area

Southwest Pacific Area Headquarters
AMP Insurance Society Building
Brisbane, Australia
1400 hrs, 1 Dec 1942

Brigadier General Reynolds was utterly exhausted as he got out of the antiquated British army staff car that picked him up from the Royal Australian Air Force Base in Brisbane after a 10 hour flight from Guadalcanal. The tropical summer heat had plagued him ever since he arrived in Hawaii ten days ago on a fact finding visit for General Marshall. The pace of the visits was grueling, even for an old infantry man such as John. While he may have cursed the extreme cold of Washington, he was finding it difficult to acclimatize to the tropical heat of summer in the southern hemisphere, always thinking when his next shower would be. Fort Benning was never this hot, much less humid, even in summer.

After the cursory protocol every General Officer has to endure upon arrival, John soon found himself at the headquarters of the former U.S. Army Chief of Staff – General Douglas MacArthur, Command of the Southwest Pacific Area. It was not his first time meeting the haughty General – after all Reynolds worked for the current Army Chief of Staff General Marshall for well over a year and had even been to the White House with him to advise the President on numerous occasions. Nevertheless, John found MacArthur could be a rather intimidating creature, especially if you had nothing to offer of a public relations value.

But Reynolds's visit was not for public relations, but to evaluate MacArthur's plan as well as gage his optimism in the conduct of his two current operations: the New Guinea campaign, launched shortly after the Battle of Midway concluded in June, and his recently launched Dutch East Indies Campaign. All this was on top of Admiral Nimitz's, and the Central Pacific Front's, ongoing battle on an island called Guadalcanal, located in the adjacent Solomon Islands chain.

As the car pulled up, Reynolds recognized an old friend, Dwight Eisenhower, now wearing the two stars of a Major General on his collar. Moving to the south Pacific definitely had its benefits.

"John, how the hell are you doing?" ask Eisenhower, extending his right hand out and forgoing what would have been the return salute from a junior officer, even if he was a Brigadier General. "Ever see such a headquarters like this in all you life…?"

"Dwight, are you a sight for sore eyes," John replied, scarcely noticing the plush building that before the war had housed a major Australian insurance company, complete with its own club. "How's life here working for the *Big General?*"

Eisenhower responded with his famous grin. Ever the politician, he wouldn't be caught dead in public uttering a catty remark about his superior officer, instead asking John if he could get him some refreshment.

"How about a Coke in the cantine before you meet MacArthur? He's meeting with the Australians and should be back in an hour. That'll give some time to get caught up and give you a chance to freshen up."

As the two headed towards the canteen, Reynolds couldn't resist the opportunity to ask Eisenhower how the Dutch East Indies campaign was going.

"Well, within a fortnight, we've landed 35,000 soldiers within three U.S. Army Divisions; 3rd and 9th Infantry Divisions, the 2nd Armor Division, as well as the 509th Parachute Regiment, on various sites on the islands of Java and Sumatra with the two-fold purpose of recapturing the oil fields seized by the Japanese this February, thus denying them a key source of oil for their war machine. Second, once we've secured Java and Sumatra, we can conduct a build up of forces – a spring board if you will, to further advances north into Borneo, the Celebes, or even back to the Philippines, then eventually across the South China Sea to open a second front on mainland China, thus severing Japanese forces located in southeast Asia that currently are threatening invasion of British India. But you should know the strategy – you wrote it in Warplan *"Rainbow Two"*. Just as you briefed the President last December, I'm sure you have a very keen interest in seeing your creation through to its conclusion, or if a problem is encountered, advise us with the appropriate 'fix'," said Eisenhower, against the background noise of aircraft flying overhead from the nearby airbase.

Reynolds in turned relayed the strategic 'gist' of the war in the Pacific from Washington's standpoint. The overall situation with the Pacific clearly favored the Americans, now undeniably on the offensive against Imperial Japan, rolling up the outer edges of her newly conquered empire less than a year after the disaster at Pearl Harbor.

During the past six months, the two attempts by the Japanese to maintain their strategic initiative and extend their defensive perimeter in the south and central Pacific were thwarted at the naval battles of Coral Sea and Midway respectively.

"Midway was not only our first major victory against the previously undefeated Japanese, we've significantly reduced their Naval offensive capability through the destruction of their major carrier forces. As you know, since Pearl Harbor, we've been on the defensive in the Pacific, but these strategic victories provided us with an opportunity to seize the strategic initiative from Japan," Reynolds beamed, knowing Eisenhower and the other officers present felt the same way. Reynolds continued his 'Big Picture' War Plans recap.

"Admiral King, in conjunction with General Marshall via Admiral Nimitz, chose the Solomon Islands, specifically the southern Solomon Islands of Guadalcanal, Tulagi, and Florida, as their first target. We soon discovered the Jap Navy occupied Tulagi in May 1942 and began construction of a seaplane base near there. Fleet HQs in Pearl grew concerned early last July when reconnaissance spotted Jap construction of a larger airfield at Lunga Point, here on nearby Guadalcanal. By August, our *coast watcher* friends confirmed the Japanese had about 900 naval troops on Tulagi and nearby islands, and 2,800 labor personnel mostly Koreans on Guadalcanal. GHQ believes when these bases are completed, they would protect Japan's major base at Rabaul, threatening our supply and communication lines to the Australians, as well as establish a staging area for a planned offensive against Fiji, New Caledonia, and Samoa. Nimitz relayed to us his Fleet intelligence intercepted transmissions telling us that the Japanese planned to deploy 45 fighters and 60 bombers to Guadalcanal once the airfield was complete. I don't have to tell you what the effect these aircraft would have provided to them in the form of air cover for Japanese naval forces advancing farther into the South Pacific." John stopped to take a drink of water and allow General Eisenhower to soak it in.

"So basically, what you're telling me is how we got involved down in the Solomons? Is this the Navy's idea?" asked Eisenhower.

"You got it. The contingency plan to invade the southern Solomon Islands was conceived by Admiral King. He proposed the offensive to deny the use of the islands by the Japanese to interdict the critical supply routes between the United States and Australia, and to use them as jumping off points towards Japan. With Roosevelt's full support, King also advocated the invasion of the island of Guadalcanal. When General Marshall resisted this line of action as well as who would command the operation, King stated that the Navy and Marines would carry out the operation by themselves – 'with or without the Army', and instructed Admiral Nimitz to proceed with the preliminary planning. I acted as a broker between the two, holding numerous discussions with both senior flag officers, with King eventually winning the argument and the invasion went ahead with the backing of the Joint Chiefs. While the initiative would initially lie with the Marines for now, it would soon be taken over as an 'Army show'," replied Reynolds.

"Do we really have the troops and resources for two such major offensives in the Pacific?" Eisenhower asked, still trying to take in the magnitude of what GHQ War Plans had conceived.

"Absolutely. We had no idea how responsive our industry is and the flexibility it has given us. Guadalcanal was carried out in conjunction with MacArthur's new offensives in New Guinea and the Dutch East Indies in order to capture the Admiralty Islands along with the Bismarck Archipelago, including the vaunted Japanese bastion at Rabaul. From there, the goal would be to sever the Japanese from Southeast Asia by seizing either the Philippines or Formosa," Reynolds replied.

"I can tell you, MacArthur will stop at nothing to reclaim the Philippines and redeem his 'honor' if you know what I mean," retorted Eisenhower.

The jeep continued down the road, slowing for a convoy of trucks they had caught up with.

"So what can you tell me about *Operation Watchtower?*" Eisenhower asked.

General Reynolds took another swig of water before continuing. "As we were getting our act together for a future offensive in the Pacific last May, Admiral King ordered the 1st Marine Division moved from the United States to New Zealand. Other U.S. army, naval, and air corps units were also sent to establish bases in Fiji, Samoa, New Hebrides, and New Caledonia. The island of Espiritu Santo in the New Hebrides was selected as the headquarters and main base for the offensive, codenamed '*Watchtower*', with the commencement date set for this past August 7. At first, our offensive was planned just for Tulagi and the Santa Cruz, omitting Guadalcanal. However, after Fleet reconnaissance discovered the Japanese airfield construction efforts on Guadalcanal, its capture was then added to the plan. Nimitz then had the Santa Cruz operation dropped.

"The *Watchtower* force, numbering 75 warships and transports, assembled near Fiji on July 26 and engaged in one rehearsal landing prior to leaving for Guadalcanal on July 31. Since that date, Major General Vandegrift is currently leading a fighting force of approximately 16,000 American troops on the island and we expect him to conclude operations within the next 45 – 60 days assuming Nimitz and his navy can fend off the Imperial Japanese Navy. To tell you the truth, the Navy is getting its ass kicked down there, but as long as we control the air, this should only be a momentary setback for King and Nimitz," John concluded as the jeep pulled into MacArthur's headquarters.

"You might want to share Nimitz's Navy's problems with the Japanese with the *Big General,*" quipped Eisenhower referring to MacArthur as they disembarked the vehicle and headed inside the air conditioned building. "He could always use a laugh!"

✲ ✲ ✲

While Reynolds and Eisenhower were beaming at the overall successes of America's summer Pacific campaign, it was quite a different story over at OKW HQs on Bendlerstrasse.

During the preceding month of November, Germany's military situation had fundamentally changed for the worse. Retreat had begun on all fronts with resistance possible only at great sacrifice.

Early in November, Field Marshal Rommel began his pull back from El Alamein. By mid-month, Tobruk and Benghazi had fallen. Luck favorably interceded with the great "Desert Fox" when Rommel's retreat was temporary halted due to the cautions leadership of the British Eight Army under the command of General Montgomery, after a trek of over 1,000 kilometers from El Alamein. Still, his western flank was secure courtesy of the Vichy French Government, allied with the Third Reich. Still, while at the Führer's Headquarters, Rommel personally advised Hitler that Germany should retreat from Africa because the problem of transporting supplies across the Mediterranean couldn't be solved. Hitler, in typical form, indignantly rebuked him. The eastern Front was a vastly different matter.

Here, the Wehrmacht was salivating over the success of their summer offensive in the east, achieving and in some cases exceeding the goals set out in "Case Blue".

In the first few weeks of the eastern summer offensive, the Wehrmacht was functioning as splendidly as ever, and had achieved an operational tempo that to many reminisced more of the heady days of Poland 1939 than Russia of the previous summer, with drives by the Panzer spearheads often times achieving 50 km or more in one day. By August, the Panzers were well into the Caucasus Mountain Range and the General Friedrich von Paulus' Sixth Army on the River Volga just north of the city of Stalingrad, cutting the Soviets in half. Yet, strangely enough, something was not right....

Just like the Germans further east, the Soviets chose to simply melt away rather than stand, fight and ultimately be captured as they did the previous summer. Such a lack of captives spurred Hitler on to begin meddling with the plan, coming up with new, more fantastic objectives that couldn't possibly be achieved. When it became all too apparent these new objectives couldn't be reached, he ensured 'heads would roll'. First to go was Field Marshall Wilhelm List, Commander of Army Group A, whose forces were deep in the Caucuses. As List's Panzer's ran out of gas, Hitler continually goaded him on to accomplish the impossible with a diminishing supply line; especially one stretched over 1500 kilometers to Germany. Hitler's impatience got the better of him, sacking List on September 9, and assuming command of the very Army Group himself. List would not be the only one to feel Der Führer's wrath. General Franz Halder, OKH Chief of Staff, noted during the summer that the Wehrmacht should move more cautiously in light of the noted lack of Russian prisoners and repeatedly brought it to Hitler's attention, gaining nothing but the annoyance of Der Führer. Finally, because of Halder's disagreement with his overall conduct of the war, Hitler decided that Halder no longer possessed an aggressive war mentality, and therefore retired the General into the "Führer Reserve" on September 24, replacing him with General Kurt Zeitzler, a more pliable and optimistic Chief of Staff than Halder. He was also thought to be a master of logistics, with solid organizational skills, a talent very much in need in dealing with the ever increasing issues of the Eastern Front. His talents would be put to the test in short order, especially since German casualties in taking 'the City of Stalin' was costing the Wehrmacht over 900 soldiers a week. This blast furnace of German manpower was consuming nearly all the resources Army Group South could muster and these were quickly running out.

Major Massar was walking quickly up the Bendlerstrasse on the morning of December 2. On his, and for that matter, every other German's mind these past couple weeks, was the situation on the Eastern Front, especially at a place called "Stalingrad". On November 19, the Soviets had launched a two prong pincer movement from bridgeheads located north and south of the city, completely cutting off the German Sixth Army within a couple of days. Nearly 300,000 German and Romanian soldiers, as well as Russian volunteers for the Wehrmacht, were trapped in and around the city by roughly 1.1 million Soviet troops. Upon hearing of this calamity in Munich, at a get together of his ol' "Putsch" buddies from 1923, Hitler's initial response amidst the impending disaster was to appoint Field Marshal Erich von Manstein as commander of a newly organized force called "Army Group Don." Hitler further interfered by forbidding an immediate breakout by the trapped German Sixth Army, deciding they would remain in Stalingrad in a bid to hold out until relieved by Manstein's hastily organized force. In order to supply the trapped army, Field Marshal Goering volunteered his Luftwaffe with the daunting task of resupplying the trapped force by air. Massar, as a former logistician, knew that it would requiring roughly 680 metric tons (750 short tons) of supplies per day; however, the latest OKL staff estimate stated that the assembled fleet of 500 transport aircraft within the immediate vicinity were clearly insufficient for the task and everyone within the General Staff knew it. Nevertheless, Hitler gave it his immediate go ahead pending final review at the next evening situation report meeting with him.

Keitel, as per Hitler's insistence, ensured all were notified of the upcoming staff meeting at the Reich Chancellery for that evening to review the options OKW had available to him in relieving the German forces trapped there. The Field Marshall dispatched Massar over to the Abwehr to find out the latest intelligence on Soviet moves and objectives from Colonel Reinhard Gehlen, Head of "Foreign Forces—East".

While Massar sat in on the brief from Gehlen, the Colonel repeatedly told Pierre that this build up of Russian forces along the Don and Volga River's had been briefed numerous times to Hitler, each time dismissed as "fantasy" or sheer "lunacy"!

"I tell you Russia is finished!!" Hitler would shout at Gehlen as he relayed his conversations to the young Major. "After the beating we gave him last year and this spring, he couldn't possibly have that many troops available!!!" Each conversation ended with Gehlen being advised to relook at his figures and check with his sources again — all the while cleaning his glasses of the spittle generated by the Führer's incessant yelling.

After filing the latest Russian intelligence estimates provided by Colonel Gehlen into his briefcase, Pierre quickly walked by Admiral Canaris's office, noting General Oster and another unknown civilian official in discussion with the Abwehr Chief. Had he more time, he would have stopped by and paid his respects to the old Spymaster, but time was short — the meeting with Hitler was scheduled to start in 90 minutes; it was already 1900 hrs — barely enough time to grab a quick bite to eat and pre-brief the Field Marshal before driving over to the Chancellery.

As Pierre entered his boss's office for a quick update prior to leaving for the Führer brief, he could see Keitel looking crestfallen, almost depressed. As Keitel noticed Massar enter, he quickly asked the Major into the inner-office, closing the door behind him per the OKW Chief's request.

"Pierre my boy, we truly live in an unbelievable fantasy world here," started Keitel. "Here we are to brief Hitler on options to extract ourselves for the debacle we've put ourselves in over Stalingrad, and none of the options we're going to present are going to pass muster."

"How so — Sir?" inquired Massar.

"Massar, I want you to think about the outrageous command and control that we've allowed ourselves to fall in. First of all, we have Hitler as the Supreme Commander of the Armed Forces. Last December, when he fired Brauchitsch, he assumed Brauchitsch's position as Commander of the German Army."

"I distinctly remember that moment Herr Feld Marshall," Massar injected. "It was a pretty embarrassing moment for all Staff Officer's in attendance."

"Recently, last September, he fired General List and assumed operational control of Army Group A in the Caucuses. Do you see the absurdity of it all – he's subordinate to himself at all levels! What utter madness!! And we are to brief him on options to tell himself at all levels?" Keitel slumped and put his head into his hands as if the weight of the world rested there.

"At least we have Field Marshal Manstein's assessment of the situation. On November 28, Hitler received a detailed report from the Field Marshal on Army Group Don's situation, including the strength of the German Sixth Army and an assessment on the available ammunition for German artillery inside the city. The dire strategic situation made by him is doubtful on whether or not the relief operation could afford to wait to receive all units earmarked for the offensive. Manstein, along with the rest of us, believed that, due to the inability of the Luftwaffe to resupply our troops in the Stalingrad pocket, it was becoming more important to relieve them "at the earliest possible date"."

"Herr Feld Marshal, I have the Soviet revised troop estimate from Colonel Gehlen – I don't think either you or the Führer will be happy with these figures."

"Just leave them with General Jodl outside and advise him of any details provided by the Abwehr," said Keitel. "Now if you will excuse me, I need a little quiet time to prepare …"

Within a short while, Field Marshal Keitel, General's Jodl and Warlimont (OKW Deputy Chief of the Operations) along with the recently appointed new OKH Chief of Staff General Zeitzler, were in Hitler's Conference Chamber for 'Evening Situation Report', along with the dozens of staff officers and aides to the various Generals and Admirals present. Standing near his boss was Major Massar, by now a seasoned veteran of Hitler's staff tirades. As a precaution, he too had a handkerchief in his pocket in case he became a victim of one of Der Führer's rants.

The first victim of the day was not Keitel, but General Jodl, as he tried to explain the current situation in the Stalingrad area. Hitler still could not grasp where these mythical Soviet units could have appeared from. When he finally calmed down, Keitel handed the briefing to General Warlimont, General Jodl's Deputy, to brief the plan to relieve Stalingrad. The General was prepared – map pointer and all.

"Mein Führer, on the current situation at the southern end of the Eastern front, we had two actions which were successful; the establishment of a loose defensive line along the Chir River and the defense of the a bridgehead at the mouth of the Chir River next to the town of Verchne-Chirskii, barely 50 kilometers away from the Stalingrad perimeter, which you have forbidden Paulus to break."

Hitler nodded in agreement, and leaned forward to study the area in greater detail. Jodl continued.

"South of Stalingrad on the east bank of the Don River, the Russians have already advanced more than 100 kilometers to the south. If we are to launch a relief effort, they will have to come from that direction. As you can see, the Don lies between the Chir front and the bend in the Volga. Other than that, it is relatively stable and quiet in the northern and central parts of the Eastern Front."

Hitler seemed somewhat relieved there was some good news in this evening's situation report and that he didn't have any further headaches in addition to the Stalingrad mess that was rapidly unfurling.

"Jodl, what is the status of the Stalingrad relief effort I directed?" ask the Führer.

The General was ready. "Mein Führer, in conjunction with Field Marshal Manstein, we have developed *Operation Winter Storm*, scheduled to commence operations on December 12. The relief force is composed of the 57th Panzer Corps of the Fourth Panzer Army, under the command of General Friedrich Kirchner, including the 6th and 23rd Panzer Divisions, and Army Detachment

Hollidt, consisting of three infantry divisions and two Panzer Divisions – the IIth and 22nd. In total, we project four panzer divisions, four infantry divisions and three Luftwaffe field divisions to take part in this relief operation; they would be tasked with temporarily opening a passage to the Sixth Army, located approximately 100 kilometers away. Herr Führer, I might also add that the 503rd Schwere Panzer Abteilung (Battalion)[42] equipped with the new Tiger I Heavy Tanks is also committed." While he briefed, Warlimont point to the various assembly areas of the units involved on the Eastern Front map in relation to Stalingrad.

Hitler closely studied the map, then took off his reading spectacles and wiped his forehead.

"General Zeitzler, what is the current situation in Stalingrad itself?"

"Mein Führer, German forces inside the encirclement were too weak to attempt a breakout on their own; half of their remaining armor, for example, had been lost during the defensive fighting, and there was a severe lack of fuel and ammunition for the surviving vehicles given that the Luftwaffe has not lived up to the daily requirements forecasted by General Paulus not able to cope with the aerial resupply. As of today, approximately 100 tons were flown in!"

That comment by Keitel immediately got Goering's attention, and he knew he would have to explain why his Luftwaffe couldn't 'cut the mustard'. Hitler glanced over to the fat Field Marshal with a look requiring an immediate explanation.

"Mein Führer, weather conditions have been extremely difficult for my pilots, that in addition to Soviet fighters patrolling over the area," Goering said.

Hitler wasn't entirely satisfied, but was prepared to let it go for the time being. At that moment, Massar slipped his boss a note passed to him by

---

42   Translation: Heavy Tank Battalion – normally operating as a separate unit.

Gehlen. Keitel briefly reviewed the note, then immediately knew he had Goering over a barrel.

"Sir, maybe the reason the Feld Marshal cannot supply Stalingrad is that many of the aircraft were hardly serviceable in the rough Soviet winter; as of last week, more cargo planes were destroyed in accidents than by Soviet fighter aircraft. By our estimation, our Sixth Army is getting less than 20 – percent or 136 of 680 metric tons of its daily needs."

Before Keitel or Goering could say another word, Jodl spoke.

"Now is the time to launch *Winter Storm*. We must have your approval Führer!"

Hitler again fixed his spectacles on, bending over to study the map.

After a couple of minutes studying the situation, although for many present in the room seemed to last for hours, he stood up and in his customary fashion, pulled his tunic down.

"General Jodl, I don't believe you have sufficient forces available to successfully pull this off. General Keitel, do we have any more forces in France we can dispatch?"

Pierre as usual, looked into his briefcase and pulled out the latest order of battle for the 1st, 7th and 15th Army's stationed throughout the northern portion of occupied France, handing this list to the Field Marshal.

Keitel reviewed it quickly – it had the answer he was looking for.

"Mein Führer, we have the 7th Panzer Division and the newly refurbished 10th Panzer Division's available as well as the rebuilt 2nd SS Panzer Grenadier Division *"Das Reich"* currently in Holland available for immediate dispatch." Hitler took it all in, then resumed looking over the map again.

General Warlimont and Zeitzler quickly grabbed Keitel while Hitler was preoccupied.

"Herr Field Marshal," started Warlimont, "10th Panzer Division is earmarked for Field Marshal Rommel in North Africa. Since his recent defeat at El Alamein, he's going to need everything we can give him to buy time."

Before he could respond, Hitler was again standing straight before the assembled audience.

"Zeitzler, how long will it take to redeploy those divisions from France to the *Winter Storm* jump off points?"

General Zeitzler quickly looked over the map and then replied to Hitler.

"Sir, we can redeploy those units within one week, nine days at the latest, but they will just barely have them ready for Field Marshal Manstein. He'll have no time to apply any winter camouflage paint."

"Keitel, arrange for the 7th Panzer and the SS *Das Reich* Divisions for dispatch to Army Group Don immediately. Notify Manstein he has additional reinforcements. As for the 10th Panzer Division, I heard Warlimont's comments and I agree. We cannot let Field Marshal Rommel fail. Arrange for its dispatch to Panzer Armee Afrika at once."

Simultaneously, Keitel, Jodl, and Warlimont uttered a loud "Ja-wohl".

Satisfied his Generals understood what they needed to accomplish, Hitler issued one last command.

"Now gentlemen, if you don't mind, I have other, more pressing matters of state I must attend to. *Heil Hitler!*"

In one booming voice, the assembled staff officer responded back in kind, as if warming up for a political rally. Just as quickly, they dispersed to return to their various duties throughout the German capital.

As they quickly walked out of the Chancellery to their awaiting staff car, Keitel glanced around, and then commented to Massar, "Someone should shoot that Bohemian Corporal, then maybe we would have a chance to win this war. If we lose this one, this might very well be the beginning of the end of us."

Massar was surprised – Hitler was Keitel's benefactor and the key to his rapid rise to the top of the Wehrmacht and head of OKW. Now, Der Führer's continued harsh comments and criticisms were having their impact on the Field Marshal. As they moved through the corridors, Massar passed by the two staff officers who might make Keitel's comments come true – Major Claus Stauffenberg and Major General Henning von Tresckow. If ever there was a conspirator's get-together, here it was.

Pierre quickly excused himself from the OKW Chief, telling Keitel he would catch up with him in a few minutes.

"Good morning Herr General," said Pierre quickly saluting Tresckow more as a formality since they never knew who was watching. Tresckow, equally informal, offered a weak acknowledgment in return.

"Claus, what are the two of you up to here in 'the Den of the Devil' so to speak?"

Tresckow responded, "He's in considerations as the Ia – Operations Officer for the 10th Panzer which is rumored to be departing for North Africa shortly."

"I can tell you first hand, that's no longer a rumor. I just heard Hitler authorize just a few minutes ago for Zeitzler and Keitel to make it so! Next month if I'm not mistaken," said Massar. "Congratulations Claus, I'll bet you'll be glad to get out of Berlin and head to far warmer place than here if you know what I mean."

Stauffenberg grinned slightly.

"Pierre, I don't think this is a reward for anything I've done here at OKH. I think they want one less critic of Hitler and the war out of the way and what a better place to hide me than down in another lost cause like 'North Africa'. At least I'll be working with General Fischer who just promoted to Lieutenant General last month."

"I'm envious," quipped Tresckow. "We had the 10th Panzer for a time up until this past spring when they were sent to France for rebuilding. Russians beat them up pretty badly last winter. They've just recently cleaned up a botched Allied raid near some town named 'Dieppe'. You'll enjoy working for Fischer - he's rumored to be the best Panzer Division Commander in the Wehrmacht. You could have done a lot worse, especially now in the Eastern Front."

Claus smiled – he knew for the moment his part in the anti-Hitler conspiracy was over.

"Tresckow, you'll tell General Oster of my pending departure and that he'll have to find another army candidate," said Stauffenberg, looking over at Massar.

Pierre was stunned that these two were considering him. He quickly shook his head indicating he wasn't interested. He quickly decided now was the best time to head back to the office.

"By your leave, Herr General. I must return to my duties." Looking over at Stauffenberg, Pierre extended his right hand towards him.

"Claus, my sincerest congratulations on your new assignment and I wish you safe travels to Africa. Come back to us alive."

With that, Pierre turned and quickly departed down the long corridor and ultimately out of the Reich Chancellery, watched by the slightly rebuffed Tresckow and Stauffenberg.

"Do you think he'll turn us in to Keitel?" ask Henning.

Stauffenberg shook his head. "I don't think so. He's never been a Nazi Party man, but I think the fact we are so open about this in front of him will make him wonder whether he's doing the right thing ..."

The weather in London the morning of December 3 was cool with a light drizzle. Typical for this time of the year, many British were scurrying through the streets conducting their Christmas shopping. Unlike Christmas' of the past few years, for many, there was a sense of joy in the air. Despite 1942 starting off disastrously with the loss of everything the Empire owned in the Pacific, many British were joyous of the news coming out of North Africa – General Montgomery's Eight Army has beaten the famed 'Afrika Korps' at El Alamein and Rommel was retreating hard and fast. The Germans could be beaten after all.

☆ ☆ ☆

As Jerry Curry sat at a table under a covered sidewalk in a London pub, he could see the smiles on the British people. Hope, it appeared, had been restored to them.

His current mission was to visit Churchill as an unofficial liaison between the Prime Minister and the President, to reassure him America was still sympathetic to the plight of the British and would continue to lend what support the United States could *legally offer*. Most of the trip so far was the usual courteous 'glad handing' and brandy drinking with '*ol Winny*' as Churchill was often referred to. After all, this was the official reason FDR sent him to London, but Curry also had two other jobs he needed to attend to as part of his hidden agenda.

Once he was free of Churchill, his first task was to pay a visit to Sir David Petrie, Head of Britain's MI-5[43]. Sir David had come highly recommend to Curry by General Donovan when the Director of the esteemed newly formed Office of Strategic Services, or '*OSS*', last came down from New York to brief FDR. Through his OSS channels, Donovan was able to set Curry up with a courtesy appointment with the MI-5 Director General.

The visit was an eye opener for the Presidential assistant. As Sir David and Curry talked about travels and the war, Curry brought up the touchy subject of Tyler Kent, the discredited American cipher clerk currently residing within the British penal system.

"The President asked me to review the evidence collected by MI-5 that was used at Kent's trial," Curry said which was in actual fact a lie – FDR assumed and forgot such documentation existed, but Curry was curious. His only hope was Sir David would comply.

Sir David looked puzzled by Curry's request.

"Mr. Curry, I thought this matter was settled some time ago. You Yanks dropped diplomatic immunity and we, how should I say it '*put him away and*

---

43   **MI5** (Military Intelligence, Section 5), is the United Kingdom's counter-intelligence and security agency.

threw away the key' to put it mildly. I wish I could offer you first hand information, but this did not occur on my watch, rather on Vernon Kell's tour as the agency's first DG. The old man passed away last March or I'd have you talk with him. Still, if you insist..."

"It is most important Sir," Curry replied quickly.

After a short break interrupted by an assistant bringing tea for refreshment, a secretary brought in a mid-sized box filled with papers, official documents and small size photos. British legal jargon indicating the case number and evidence accountability was scrawled on the outside of the box.

Curry could see these were not ordinary documents and papers. As he picked up a few off the top, he could see the U.S. Embassy date/time group postings as well as the various routing stamps attesting to each and every embassy official charged with viewing the information contained on the paper. It was truly a spy's dream come true.

While he was reviewing the information a call came for Sir David requiring his immediate presence in the building. Every bit the courteous host, Sir David excused himself, allowing Curry the luxury of viewing the documentation with a bit of privacy.

"When you're finished, simply pick up the phone and dial '5' and someone will escort you out," said the Director General as he turned to leave the room. "I hope you find what you're looking for."

Curry grabbed a few of the more important cables and documents and sat down to study his catch. Picking up his cup of tea, he almost spilt it on the document in front of him.

The first document was labeled U.S. Embassy Telegram #2720, dated December 25, 1939 – Christmas Day! Kent had intercepted a complete copy of Churchill's message to Roosevelt in which Churchill informed the President that British warships would continue to violate American sovereignty to seize German ships within the U.S. three mile maritime territorial zone. However, in order to keep these violations secret, Churchill promised that the seizures would take place out of view from the American shore.

"We cannot refrain from stopping enemy ships outside international three-mile limit when these may well be supply ships for U-boats or surface raiders, but instructions have been given only to arrest or fire upon them out of sight of United States shores. Signed 'Naval Person'".

This is unbelievable, Curry said to himself. He picked up another document indicating another U.S. Embassy Telegram #490 from *'Naval Person'.* In his message to Roosevelt, Churchill wrote that the British would continue to seize and censor U.S. mail from American and other neutral ships on their way to Europe.

"All our experience shows that the examination of mails is essential to efficient control of information to any neutral or otherwise hostile power to the United Kingdom..."

Curry replaced the document and sat back in utter astonishment. What he just read was a blatant violation of American neutrality and international law.

Hell we fought the War of 1812 against the British for something less serious than this, Curry thought to himself. *If this message intercepted by Kent had been made public in 1940 or 1941, there would have been a hell of a first rate scandal and no doubt, the first successful impeachment of a President since Andrew Johnson in 1868.*

Curry continued to read document after document, all spelling out the same theme. In the secret correspondence between Churchill and Roosevelt intercepted by Kent, the two leaders conspired to insure that the United States government would secretly tolerate British violations of American territorial sovereignty and restrictions on neutral American shipping. The two men wanted to avoid any embarrassing incidents that would provoke public indignation in America over the illegal British actions. The documents and photos showed Curry the two leaders also worked out procedures for joint British-American naval reporting of the location of German surface raiders and submarines which violated at least the spirit if not the letter of United States neutrality.

No wonder they wanted him out of the way, Curry said to himself. *Any Republican or disgruntled, pissed off Democrat obtaining a copy of any of these documents would have himself the ultimate in political dynamite. No small wonder FDR sacked Ambassador Kennedy soon after this.* As soon as he thought it, he suddenly realized someone had.

Curry had seen enough. He picked up the phone and as per instructions, dialed 5. Within a couple of minutes, two secretaries entered the room; one to recover the box of documents, the other to escort him out.

"I'm sorry Sir David isn't available to extend his farewell," said the secretary as the two of them approached the building's main entrance.

As he was about to exit the building, the secretary stopped for a moment.

"Mr. Curry, I almost forgot. This parcel came for you from your embassy while you were with Sir David." The woman handed Curry a small rectangular box wrapped in brown paper tied with twine. "It's from a man named Donovan."

"Thank you," replied Curry as he received the package. "Well, I'm sure Sir David has a lot of things to do, but please thank him from me for all his assistance and I will extend his regards to Mr. Donovan back in the States, especially for his Christmas package for my time in London," Curry responded.

As he entered the fresh air of downtown London, he looked as his watch and realized he had an hour before his second agenda item – a meeting with 'H'.

Time for a pint, he thought as he headed to the arranged pub location.

As he sat and studied the British people strolling by tending to their various affairs, Curry began to think about his discovery. The more he thought about it, the more it bothered him. Here was a standing President, conspiring with a foreign power, to undermine not only the Constitution, but the American people themselves. Worse, now someone else outside FDR's close circle was privy to this and using it to whatever motives they held.

"Mr. Curry?" a very European voice brought him back to reality.

Curry looked up and there he was, tall, dressed in a black coat with a goatee – 'H', his contact from when they first met in Bern last January.

"Welcome to London," responded Curry, extending his hand to shake 'H's'. "I'm so glad you made it here for this meeting. Can I order you something?"

'H' took a seat and signaled the hostess for a pint of ale. After a few minutes of small talk, his pint arrived.

"So what's new in the Reich?" Curry began. "Your message through the Swiss diplomatic pouch has me thinking something's up."

'H' took a sip of his ale and grinned, although Curry wasn't sure if the expression was his reaction to the ale or his question.

"You know Mr. Curry, you can't find this back in Germany," he said referring to the uniqueness of the English drink he'd just sampled. "Just like British Ale, we have something you can't find anywhere else, and that's Hitler. No where else on this planet can you find a madman who can lead a nation to utter ruin. But we are trying. Everyday, thousands of German soldiers are consumed on the Eastern Front. We've got an entire army surrounded and this man, this crazy asshole, won't let them escape. We are going to strike, but we need your help."

"I've talked with the President and he has instructed General Donovan, Dulles, and his OSS folks to assist wherever possible. In fact, I almost forgot – this came through the Embassy's diplomatic pouch for me from Donovan to pass on to you."

Curry handed 'H' the small parcel he was given just an hour prior from MI-5.

"You can think of this as a 'down payment' of what we talked about earlier this year in Berne."

'H' curiously studied the box, and then began to lightly shake it as if such an action would yield a clue to its contents.

"I wouldn't do that if I were you," said Curry, using his hand to stop 'H'. "Those contents might not be agreeable to that kind of agitation."

'H' immediately set the parcel down; unsure what kind of surprise Curry had brought him for the holidays.

Curry continued.

"Before I tell you what Santa Claus brought from the States, I need a little information to take back to my friends in Washington, and I don't mean a sample political statement."

'H' took his gloves off and leaned back in his chair.

"I hear there's a saying you Americans use *'there's no free lunch'*".

"That's about the size of it," replied Curry.

'H' took another swig of his drink, then nonchalantly looked around him to satisfy himself the information he was about to provide was for Curry's ears only.

I don't know what you've heard so far, but we're up to our ass in Russia with the debacle at Stalingrad. Hitler's ordered a number of divisions from France that might get there and breakthrough before the Russians destroy us. Then there's the Kaulbars' initiative...."

Curry held up his hand to pause 'H' as he set his pint down - "The what initiative?!"

'H' continued. "Kaulbars – Baron Vladimir Kaulbars. He's some exiled White Russian who has approached our group representing some high Soviets seeking terms for an armistice in the east. Apparently, Stalin is trying to pull a page out of Lenin's old play book that he used to get the Germans out of Russia during the First World War. By gaining an armistice, he buys time to rebuild and come after Germany at a later time."

"Go on," replied Curry, now leaning forward with interest. "What does that mean for us as the allies?"

"Don't you see? With the Soviets out, he can claim a political as well as military victory. No General or politician will have the guts to stand up to him. As for the

Allies, those forces now in Russia, once redeployed and rebuilt in the Reich, will be more formidable than ever, especially if they are sent back to France. Your precious forces will be slaughtered on the beaches of France and won't have a prayer."

Curry sat back in his seat in amazement. "How far has this gone?"

"The Abwehr has started contact with Kaulbars, but it hasn't gotten too far as long as the Russians think they'll win in Stalingrad. If the Germans break through and relieve the Sixth Army, who knows...."

Both sat for a moment and pondered 'H's' comments and hypothesis. Clearly, a second front would be extremely difficult if not outright impossible given the scenario 'H' had just played out.

"There's something more," 'H' continued as if that wasn't already enough. "I happen to know Hitler has directed a secret weapons program the likes of which until now were only largely found within the science fiction pages of your favorite comic book. As we speak, a massive Luftwaffe rocket program is fully underway at Peenemünde, located up near the mouth of the Peene River, on the easternmost part of the German Baltic coast. Large rockets, that when fully functional, are capable of hitting London with at least two tons of high explosive. They've just had their first successful launch last October. Additionally, I recently witnessed the Luftwaffe field testing a number of prototype jet fighter aircraft, capable of flying more than 900 km/h (559 mph) which I believe is faster than anything in your inventory."

"Tell me this story has a happy ending?" said Curry.

"I wish I could, my friend, but I've saved the best news for last. Forget all that silly allied propaganda you've heard about Germany's atomic weapons program. It is farther along than anyone here is willing to admit. I would say the Germans are within 24 – 36 months from having a functioning atomic weapon. That in its own right is bad enough for everyone, but it is coupled with a rocket that can deliver it and who knows what that will do to the war effort."

Curry glanced down at the parcel. "Maybe this is what it will take to stop him?"

'H' looked at him. "In there?"

"You bet. In this parcel, courtesy of the United States Office of Strategic Services, are fourteen 'time pencil' detonators along with ten pounds of '*Explosive 808*' composition plastic explosives."

'H' remembered Curry's earlier comment regarding the shaking of the parcel – he suddenly gained a whole new respect for its possession.

"I am somewhat familiar with the use of plastic explosives, but how does the pencil detonator work?" he asked.

Curry pulled out a folded piece of paper, and then read the instructions to 'H'.

"Crush the end of the thin copper tube containing the cupric chloride with pliers, or under the heel of your boot. There is no need to crush the end of the tube completely flat. All that is required is to crush and dent the tube sufficiently to break the glass vial, thereby releasing the liquid contained within. Check the inspection hole next to the brass safety strip. If the inspection hole is unobstructed then the countdown has started and the brass safety strip (while holding back the striker) should be removed and discarded. However, if the inspection hole is obstructed the striker has been released so the pencil detonator should be discarded and another one selected. The final step is to insert the end of the pencil which has the actual detonator fitted into the explosives and leave the area."

When he was completed, he refolded the paper and handed it over to 'H'.

"I hope you are successful in getting this to the right folks who will do the most good. I think we all know what the stakes are," said Curry.

'H' gave an unassuming grin as he picked up the package and stood up, in the process tossing down a couple of British one pound notes.

"Trust me, Herr Curry – I know all about stakes. If we fail, there's more to lose than just our lives…by the way, the beers are on me."

Chapter 15

A Change In Plans

Fact: To the complete shock of the world, on the morning of August 24th, 1939, the foreign ministers of Nazi Germany and Soviet Russia signed the now infamous "Non-Aggression Pact" between their two countries, both pledging neutrality if the other were attacked by a third party. What most of the world was unaware of was a secret protocol dividing Northern and Eastern Europe into German and Soviet spheres of influence, anticipating potential "territorial and political rearrangements" of these countries. Per the protocol, both Germany and the Soviet Union planned to invade their respective sides of Poland, dividing the country between them on September 1st, 1939. However, on the scheduled day of the invasion, only Germany commenced with war against the Poles, with the Soviets (in an act of duplicity) citing "technical" reasons for their delay in entering. In due course, the Allied nations (Great Britain and France) declared war on Germany, thus starting the Second World War. Once the German Army defeated the bulk of the Polish forces, the Soviets entered their half of Poland on September 17th, yet there was no Allied declaration of war against them. The Non-Aggression Pact remained in effect until June 22nd, 1941 when Germany invaded the Soviet Union. Strangely enough, on June 16th, 1943, after nearly two years of conflict, it was reported in Stockholm's daily newspaper *Nya Dagligt Allehanda* (New Daily All Kinds) that German and Soviet diplomats were secretly meeting within the Capital.

> *"Stalin may make a separate peace if we cannot help him"*
> *- Sir Archibald Clark Kerr*
> *British Ambassador to the Soviet Union*
> *January 1943*

The Café Järntorget
Vasterlanggatan 81, Stockholm, Sweden
1330 hrs, 16 June 1943

Sitting outside enjoying the mildly warm Stockholm afternoon, Baron Vladimir Kaulbars sat impatiently awaiting the arrival of his appointment. For the past seven months Kaulbars and his Soviet liaison contact, KGB Agent Pavel Sudoplatov, had meet within the old town portion of the Swedish capital to discuss how their two respective, yet ultra politically diverse nations could come to common terms to end the carnage both were inflicting on each other. By this time, millions of Russians and Germans soldiers lay dead on the battlefield, with the war continuing to see-saw back in forth. Would the next upcoming summer months be any different than 1942?

When they initially met in mid 1942, Sudoplatov, under instructions from Lavrentiy Beria, head of the dreaded and world renowned KGB, approached Kaulbars regarding the possibly of opening a dialog with the Germans about an armistice on the Eastern Front. While the idea initially seemed ludicrous when Vladimir brought it up to Admiral Canaris and select members of the General Staff following his first meeting with his KGB counterpart, the Abwehr Chief was quick to point out that is exactly what Vladimir Lenin did to get the Germans out of Russia during the First World War; solidify his control over the Bolsheviks, gain breathing space, and ultimately win the cataclysmic Russian Civil War that shortly followed. The idea had merit and would resolve for the time being the German's present dilemma of a two front war. Make peace with the Russians now, then shift everything back west and finally defeat the British before the Americans eventually (or inevitably) decided to join the effort on the Allied side. Canaris could not help but compare to the parallels to the Treaty of Brest-Litovsk that were very striking and in retrospect, the Germans did come close to winning that spring of 1918. Already the crafty Admiral knew the British and Americans were collaborating about how to coordinate their actions against the Japanese. With no effort at all these meetings could easily involve coordinated action against the Third Reich as well.

Yet, both sides hemmed and hawed during the last half of 1942. The Russians were most receptive when the German Summer Offensive (Case Blue) was fully underway towards Stalingrad and the Caucuses. No surprise that Berlin was taking a wait and see attitude. Yet their fortunes were reversed when the Soviets assumed the initiative in launching a counter attack that surrounded the Sixth and Fourth Panzer Armies within the city they had fought so hard to conquer that past summer. Disaster was once again on the Wehrmacht's doorstep.

As luck or skill would have it, the Germans again gained the upper hand at the close of the year, this time in the guise of Field Marshal Eric von Manstein's 'Operation Winter Storm'. Reinforced with additional Panzer Divisions from France earmarked for North Africa, the Conqueror of Sevastopol was able to break through and relieve the besieged force. In a series of counterattacks against the onrushing Soviet armored spearheads, Manstein carefully calculated when they would outrun their supplies. The rest was sheer folly on the Russian side, as hundreds of tanks and thousands of troops were cut off and destroyed. By March 1943, the front had fairly well stabilized along the same lines as the previous spring. Both sides were too exhausted to think about any offensive operations for the approaching term. Besides, the Russians had additional setbacks. Their much vaunted 'Red Orchestra' spy network was in the process of being rolled up by the Gestapo all over occupied Europe, leaving them increasingly blind to what the Germans were planning. They really didn't have many options left, and manpower was starting to run low in the Soviet armies.

The time was right for both sides to sit down and begin to get serious about imitating an armistice.

Kaulbars was pleasantly surprised when he saw his Soviet contact approach the gasthus. His facial expression indicated he was serious this time around – perhaps a final deal was in the making? As Sudoplatov approached the small outside table, the Baron stood up and extended his hand in greeting towards his KGB negotiator.

"Greetings Baron," the KGB agent offered as he shook Kaulbars' hand. "I must tell you, I've always enjoyed Stockholm this time of the year. Moscow for all its history and political importance is still quite the grey, drab city. I will miss this place when we're done."

With quick session, Kaulbars flashed his prearranged signal to the hostess and in flash two 'Aqua Vitaes'[44] were delivered to the negotiators.

The Baron began. "I take it from your comment you're ready to finalize an agreement?"

Sudoplatov took a swig from his glass.

"I would say the time is right for both our governments. Stalin apparently does not trust the British to come through with their agreement to open a second front; after all they've reneged twice, and he still remembers how the British and French sold out the Czechs back in 1938. Stalin also feels that it's impossible for them to launch any attack into Europe without the assistance of the Americans, who as we know are fully committed against the Japanese with everything they have. But eventually the British will convince them to join the war as an ally, and it would be in your best interests to be ready for that day when it comes."

Kaulbars nodded in agreement. The war in the east had drained German forces from France, leaving it at its lowest level at any time since the French defeat in June 1940. The campaign in North Africa would also need additional support since Rommel withdraw from El Alamain that past November leaving his Panzer Army Afrika to occupy just a small portion of Libya and Tunisia.

---

44 Aqua Vitae – "Water of Life". In Stockholm, it refers to a drink closely resembling vodka.

Sudoplatov reached into his briefcase and pulled out a file folder with a sheet of paper attached on the front cover, sliding it on the table towards the Baron.

"This is a draft of the protocols we've discussed at our last meetings, along with a map delineating the finalized boundaries. I have personally briefed Stalin and the STAVKA and he is very receptive towards ending hostilities between our two governments. If your government agrees, we can have a final agreement and an armistice by the end of the summer."

Kaulbars picked up the document, scanning it carefully. The Russians were notorious for inserting clauses that would later become potential booby traps.

"Herr Sudoplatov, as a safe guard, I've asked for a representative of the German High Command – OKW, to come join us to witness what might possibly be our final negotiating meeting."

At that moment, Kaulbars raised his hand to signal to someone inside the restaurant.

"Pavel Sudoplatov, may I present Lieutenant Colonel Pierre Massar, aid to Field Marshall Keital, Chief of the German High Command."

Massar stood at attention when he heard the familiar sound of boot heels clicking. Even when not wearing a uniform, every German officer responds as if he's still wearing it.

Sudoplatov was surprised. Up till this point, the two met by themselves without any outside 'interference'. The Baron was full of surprises today.

"Colonel Massar's mission is twofold – one is to ensure these documents are real and not some forgery cooked up by parties who stand to lose with its authenticity. Second, he is to brief Keitel as soon as possible in order to enable OKW planners to finalize development of a timetable for withdrawal from those areas of the Soviet Union that are being returned to you."

"Very well," responded Sudoplatov. "Shall we get together again for dinner, say at 2000 hours, and finalize any questions you might have? That should give you sufficient time to convey the protocol to your government for final approval."

"Agreed," responded Kaulbars, looking at his watch. Plenty of time to get over to the German Embassy to telex Berlin with the news.

Sudoplatov finished the remainder of his drink, and then stood up. "Let me tell you, Stockholm at this time of year is extremely enjoyable. I just hope you're prepared for the evening light to extend well past 2200 tonight."

Kaulbars and Massar rose and shook hands, with Sudoplatov departing immediately to contact his KGB masters on his progress. Off to the side, both Massar and Kaulbars noticed two heavy set men in trench coats departing behind the KGB man, undoubtedly his "minders". When Sudoplatov was out of sight Massar turned towards the Baron.

"Why me Herr Baron?" he asked. "Two days ago I was notified by the Field Marshall to depart for Stockholm on a coordinated visit on behalf of the Abwehr. I am not a field agent!"

The Baron smiled. "You're here because we need someone within the War Ministry we can trust. Your friend Claus von Stauffenberg recommended you before he departed for North Africa last December. We needed this to be an Abwehr – OKW operation. Neither Keitel nor Canaris desire to have Himmler and his SS boys gum the works up. Additionally, we couldn't have von Ribbentrop or anyone from his foreign ministry that was involved in drafting the initial Non-Aggression Pact involved since he no longer really has any credibility with the Soviets. We have a golden opportunity here to get out of Russia and perhaps still win the war."

Massar was transfixed. He was a staff aide and logistician, not a 'spy', yet here he was at the backend of a complex and highly secret negotiation – one that could greatly change the course of the war.

"Here, study the file. Inside you'll find a map with the negotiated boundaries", Kaulbars said sliding the file across the table to Massar. "Do not discuss this with anyone, not even your wife…"

Before the Baron could finish, the figure of a tall man in a black coat suddenly appeared out of nowhere at the two German's table. Both the Baron and Massar were startled by his presence and immediately suspected the man's intentions were sinister in nature - cheerful people just didn't wear black.

"Excuse me gentlemen," the stranger interrupted. "Allow me to introduce myself. My name is Reinhard Inman."

"And what is your business with us, Herr Inman?" asked Kaulbars. "Whatever it is that you trying to sell us, I can tell you we're not interested."

Inman took off his gloves and pulled out the just departed Sudoplatov's chair and took a seat.

"I think not, Herr Baron, if you knew the people I am working for."

The Baron was rattled on the inside but didn't let it show. His mission was a secret at the utmost highest levels of the German government. Obviously, this stranger knew who he was and perhaps what his mission was. Massar however was terrified.

"And who do you work for...?" the Baron asked.

Inman smiled and then produced his billfold. Inside he pulled out his identify card and a picture of another German, one of exceedingly high rank.

"Let's start with my boss who I'm sure you are quite familiar with."

Both Massar and the Baron immediately recognized the picture of *SS Gruppenführer* Heinrich Müller, chief of the dreaded Gestapo. A deep chill passed through the two Germans of the prospect of having been discovered by the most sinister of secret police organizations.

"You recognize him I see," said Inman. "As you can tell, my identify card is proof of who I am and work for."

"What exactly does that prove?!" responded the Baron flipping the card back to Inman. "During the revolution, we were able to make dozens of these a day, and of better quality I might add." He tried to sound defiant, hoping to either bluff or shake the stranger.

"If that's the case, how is it I know what General Hans Oster, your Abwehr colleague, is up too – huh? Undoubtedly you might have heard but we've have him involuntarily 'released' from your organization."

Kaulbars and Massar exchanged glances. Massar didn't know who Inman was referring to, while Kaulbars appeared slightly stunned.

Inman continued. "We've had our eyes on your folks from the Abwehr for some time. My boss, General Müller, believes everyone there is suspected of betraying the Fuehrer and the Third Reich. What we have here is proof of your treachery!"

"What proof?" the Baron injected. "These documents will end the war in the east! We are saving German lives. How can it be considered treachery to save the Fatherland?"

"Treachery is whatever I define it to be Herr Kaulbars!"

"So what are you going to do? The Gestapo does not have any authority over us in Sweden. You simply cannot just 'arrest' us."

"No Herr Kaulbars, here in Stockholm I cannot do anything to either of you, nor do you have any family in Germany. But the Colonel here does, and we are in a position to, shall I say, make new accommodations for them."

"So what do you propose Herr Inman?" asked the now anxious Colonel Massar.

"General Müller is not without 'an understanding of the situation'. All we want is to be the party that finalized the agreement instead of the Abwehr. If we get credit for this it will improve our lot within the party."

"And if I refuse…?" suggested Kaulbars.

Inman grinned.

"Just how in touch have you been with the Abwehr lately besides this little behind the scenes project Herr Baron - hmm? Along with having Oster relieved of duty, we also arrested another colleague – Hans Dohnanyi."

The Baron knew Dohnanyi from the Abwehr as well. He had been employed as a special leader on the staff of the High Command of the Armed

Forces under Oster, but Kaulbars also knew they had released him for lack of evidence. *Perhaps letting the little fish go would lead the Gestapo to even bigger ones* he thought.

"There is no shortage of people to arrest over at *Tirpitzufer Strasse*," Inman continued, referring to the Abwehr HQ's location. "As far as General Müller is concerned, everyone there from Canaris on down are all traitors."

Baron Kaulbars sat silently and then slowly turned to Massar who looked as if he would be facing the firing squad at any moment. For the moment it appeared there was nothing they could do.

"How much time do I have to make a decision?" asked the Baron.

"I will give you one hour," replied Inman. "One hour from now you will give me all your papers, documents, and maps on this agreement; delivered here to this gasthaus."

"And what guarantee do we have that no harm will come to my family?" asked Massar.

"Well, you have my word – Colonel! You'll just have to trust me that no further action will take place against you or that nest of spies for that matter."

The Gestapo man stood up and quickly departed the restaurant.

Once Inman was out of earshot, Massar spoke.

"So what the hell are you going to do – are you going to hand all this over to those jokers? I strongly suggest you do and that's the end of this!"

The Baron was not amused.

"Get a hold of yourself Colonel! Nobody is giving anything away, not just yet, and not if I have anything to say about it."

"What are you going to do?" asked the anxious Lieutenant Colonel.

"I want you to go to the embassy and contact Admiral Canaris. Send a telex informing him we have an agreement now in place with the Soviets and that Operation '*Curtain Call*' — the armistice plan - is in the immediate making."

Kaulbars then grabbed Massar's arm.

"Do not tell the Admiral anything more. Stay at the embassy until you hear from me later — do you understand?"

The Lieutenant Colonel nodded his head in agreement and then headed off towards the embassy. The Baron reached into his billfold, threw a Swedish 100 kronor bill on the table, then headed towards his apartment.

Shorty after 3:00p.m Massar walked onto the embassy's third story balcony overlooking Stockholm's old town. He was successful in getting the encrypted telex to Canaris who relayed 'a job well done' back to him and Vladimir. *But where was the ol' Baron?* Massar thought to himself.

Suddenly Massar saw a brilliant flash immediately followed by a tremendous boom coming from the side of the old town square where 90 minutes previously the two of them had their meeting with the Baron's KGB contact. To Massar's complete amazement the blast briefly shook the balcony he was standing on, knocking a plant off the railing. Within a few minutes the wails of emergency vehicles — Swedish fire engines specifically - could be heard traversing the city's streets towards the scene of the explosion.

What the hell? Massar thought. By the sound of the explosion, he thought an artillery round had landed within the old town. All that was missing was the all too familiar tell-tale whine of the rounds' incoming trajectory.

"Quite an explosion," a voice from behind Massar injected. "I wonder how many people were killed down there?"

With a tap on the shoulder, Massar turned to see the stoic, but slightly amused face of the Baron.

"Where in the hell have you been?" Massar demanded.

"Taking care of a little business. I think one or more of Germany's fine Gestapo men will be 'missing' next time they take inventory" responded

Kaulbars. "I guess Sweden is just not that cordial toward secret policemen, much less black costumed *thugs*."

Colonel Massar couldn't believe his ears.

"How did you do it?"

Kaulbars quickly scanned the room, noting most of the embassy personnel had gone to the roof to get a better view of the calamity unfolding within Stockholm's old town center.

"What I have to tell you cannot be repeated to anyone!" instructed the Baron in a low whisper. "Some time ago, many of us were provided with British 'pencil detonators'. They look like a pencil but they contain a small capsule inside that, when crimped, will explode within about 10 to 15 minutes. Stick one of these into a small piece of plastic explosive and *voila* your problem is eliminated!"

"I don't believe it!" an astonished Massar stuttered, relieved that his problem with the Gestapo was now suddenly no more. "How effective are these devices?"

The Baron stroked his beard and smiled. "Sometimes they work well, other times — who knows? Do you remember Hitler's recent trip to Army Group Center a few months ago, last March I believe, the one he took to Smolensk?"

Massar nodded. "Yes - I was almost on that mission, but got bumped at the last minute."

"Good thing. General Tresckow, Chief of Operations at the Army Group had such a device planted on Hitler's plane disguised as a bottle of Cointreau. We thought that would have done the trick and brought him and his cronies down. Unfortunately, it appears the pencil detonator froze and the bomb obviously didn't go off, sparing Der Fuehrer's life. Pity 'cause had it done the trick, all this probably would not have been necessary."

General Tresckow, Pierre thought to himself. "I met the man last year and I'm not at all surprised at what you've said," he replied to Kaulbars.

The Baron smiled. "Well Herr Colonel, we've got work to do if we're to meet Sudoplatov tonight and fortunately, Inman will not be joining us for dinner."

✵ ✵ ✵

Halfway across the world, midnight was fast approaching in Tokyo. Emperor Hirohito had just summoned the key leadership of the Imperial Japanese High Command to convene a new General Staff strategy session, but this time around, the back slapping and congratulatory atmosphere of 1942 was as removed from the room as the Imperial Fleets prized four aircraft carriers immediately after the disaster at Midway. As Admiral Yamamoto predicted early on in the aftermath of Pearl Harbor, the Americans were on the move and with a vengeance.

Across their maps of the Pacific Ocean were the tell-tale depiction of arrows pointed directly towards the Imperial Home Islands — arrows displaying the approach of American army and navy fleets closing in, each one looking as menacing as daggers at the throat of the country.

In the South Pacific area Australian forces under General MacArthur, after a short, but tough fight coupled with an infusion of American forces, had cleared Imperial Japanese forces from New Guinea. They subsequently seized the Dutch East Indies Islands of Sumatra and Java, with the assistance of British forces from India who landed in the northern part of Sumatra; posing a threat to Japanese units in Singapore and their ability to control the strategic Malacca Straits. The impact to the Japanese was immediate — from now on all supplies destined for Burma now had to be transported via land routes through Thailand, adding three more weeks delivery time to their soldiers fighting the combined British-Indian forces there.

"Where will they go from here?" was the question on every Imperial General Staff member's mind who understood the current situation.

Another staff officer redirected the audience to events in the Central Pacific. While the situation was bad in the Dutch East Indies, everyone present, but especially the collected naval talent of the Imperial Japanese Navy (IJN), knew that a major campaign of epic proportions was to erupt here.

By early 1943, under Admiral Chester Nimitz, Guadalcanal was secured and the threat to the Solomons and Australia was largely erased, however its capture had not been easy.

During the campaign, both sides lost thousands of soldiers before the Imperial General Staff decided to cut its losses and pull out. In the surrounding waters, American and Japanese navies traded combat actions, clashing at night, literally littering the ocean bottom with a collection of ships from both side – such was the staggering amount of loss that the very waters north of Guadalcanal were renamed 'Iron Bottom Sound'. In most of these engagements, the Americans came out on the bottom end, but for every ship they lost, dozens more were built to replace them. The Admiralty knew as well as the other Japanese strategist present, that every IJN ship lost could not be replaced, but by far their biggest loss to date wasn't ships, troops, or aircraft; it was the very strategist that had brought them to their apogee – Admiral Yamamoto. Just a few months prior, the beloved Admiral was killed during an inspection tour of forward positions in the Solomon Islands when his Mitsubishi G4M bomber was shot down during an ambush by American P-38 'Lightning' fighter planes. His death, only announced to the nation last month, was a major psychological blow for Japan, once and for all forcing the imperial government to acknowledge that the Americans were quickly rebuilding their military capacity and were on the offensive. It was only a matter of time before they would be on the move again, but where? Would it be Rabaul, their prized naval fortress on New Britain Island, the Philippines, whose capture would dearly cost the Americans much blood and treasure? Would they plunge deep into the Central Pacific perhaps striking towards the Gilbert Islands and Tarawa, or more to the north striking the Marshall Islands and Saipan?

While the assembled strategists were pondering Nimitz's possible options in a manner not unlike an opposing chess player, they were made aware of the American's recent capture of Attu and Kisa Islands in the Aleutian Island chain. The Japanese conquest of these islands in June 1942 had been the only true victories in their ill fated Midway venture, but now they too were lost to the Americans. Within a fortnight, U.S. Army Air Corps B-24 'Liberators' began flying bombing missions towards the northern island of Hokkaido, a harbinger of things to come.

For all the gloom of the strategic situation briefed to the Imperial General Staff, the worst news was saved for last.

"As you all are aware," the Naval Lieutenant Commander conducting the briefing began, "We are an island nation that must import all our goods in order to survive. Yet, within a short while, this will no longer be possible. From our communication intercepts, we believe the American Navy has thrown an almost impenetrable submarine net around our Home Islands, sinking nearly every ship approaching our ports. Over the past month, they have successfully intercepted and sunk over 100,000 tons of shipping. At this rate, they will cut our fuel stocks to about 20 percent. Additionally with the loss of raw materials from Indochina, we can expect to see war production drop dramatically."

The combined Army and Navy flag officers present reacted in shock.

"How can this be?" asked Vice Admiral Gunichi Mikawa, one of Admiral Koga's fleet commanders, recently assigned to the Naval General Staff after extensive action in the Solomons. "Certainly we are conducting convoys and all the appropriate anti-submarine measures?"

"Sir, I cannot answer to the effectiveness of the Imperial Navy's protection of our convoys, I can only comment that many of our convoys were intercepted and sunk. If I had to guess, I would say the Americans have taken a page from the book of our German allies regarding the organization and employment of '*wolf pack*' submarine tactics. For a nation that cried foul about the way the German Kriegsmarine operated in the Atlantic Ocean, the Americans have successfully emulated the Germans with a high degree of efficiency. You could say they have placed an effective blockage around Japan and are slowly tightening the noose."

"Commander!" Mikawa stood up and shouted. "What you are saying is hearsay! This simply cannot be. I caution you to be careful of speaking defeatist talk to this assembled audience."

"Sit down Mikawa," came an unmistakable command voice from the rear of the conference room. "The Commander is speaking the truth. It is you, Admiral Mikawa, who is doing his country a disservice by not waking up and seeking the facts."

The entire room looked back at the ashen face of Admiral Mineichi Koga, the new Commander of the Combined Fleet.

Koga, who had finally joined the brief, was listening from the rear.

"I am here to explain what he is telling us is correct. If you recall, my predecessor, Admiral Yamamoto, pointed out in late 1941 that without a strategy we are doomed. We have all been caught up in the hubris of victory over the past year, but now the Americans are coming at us with everything they have mobilized. Guadalcanal and our loss of the Solomons was our wake up call. Gentlemen, I am here to tell you that I predict they will be here by this time next year."

The Razor - General Tojo, the dreaded Imperial War Minister, stood up to address the group.

"This is utter nonsense," Tojo responded. "We will continue to bleed the Americans for every piece of ground they wish to contest from us. They have no stomach for war, and after awhile they will tire and begin to sue for peace. Everyone here needs to be reminded of that! Everyone here needs to stand firm with the plan and not cower just because of some success and good luck on their part. We will fight them to the very end. If they come, it is because you, Koga, have failed to do your part!" The gauntlet had been thrown.

The old Admiral shot back. "You speak of *the plan*? What may I ask is this plan?"

"We stand and fight them everywhere. We bleed them; hurt them every which way possible. Only then will the decadent Americans tire of war and sue for peace. But to make this occur and set these conditions, we need to be tough."

Koga shook his head in utter disagreement. "General, you offer platitudes and phrases. We need ammunition, fuel, aircraft and ships to fight them and all of these are in short supply. What do you suggest we use in lieu of these?"

The Razor was not accustomed to having one of his prized naval commander's mock him in front of the combined army navy audience.

"I suggest Admiral that you take a hard look at what is left of the Combined Fleet and find a solution as quickly as possible, or has the defeatist mentality claimed you and your staff as well?! I charge you with repelling the Americans – the quicker the better!" he shrieked at Koga.

Off to the side, at the head of the conference table, sat the Emperor. Quiet, almost detached from the clash of army and navy chieftains, the Admiral had almost wished for Hirohito to intervene on the side of reason. Alas, he too was under the sway of Tojo.

Koga was not about to back down in the face of the War Minister. To do so would not only bring shame to the senior naval officers present, but the threat of assignation from a hot headed junior officer for having shown cowardice. It was their way...

"General, in order to defend the home lands and hold our current outer perimeter, I will need army troops. My navy can defend the seas and react to the Americans, but only troops can hold the key islands the Americans wish to seize."

"Out of the question," responded Tojo, "the army is too busy in China winning the war there!" Everyone present knew the real truth, everyone that is except the Emperor who the comment was undoubtedly directed to.

The old Admiral would still not back down. "Then I am willing to make you a deal. If the Americans seize Saipan, Tarawa, Guam, or the Philippines with their present army garrisons, I will insist on your resignation to the Emperor."

"And you Koga, what do you plan to put on the table if you fail?"

"I am in the middle of a plan to revitalize our naval operations by reorganization of the Combined Fleet into task forces built around what aircraft carriers we have remaining, much like that of the American Navy, and have organized our land-based naval air fleet to work in coordination with the carriers. Should the opportunity present itself, I plan on luring the American fleet into a major naval engagement to avenge Midway. However, if the Americans seize our base at Rabaul, even with its 100,000 man garrison, then I will offer the Emperor my resignation as commander-in-chief of the Combined Fleet," replied Koga.

Both Koga and Tojo glanced at Hirohito, who was nodding silently in acknowledgement of the deals struck. Maybe he wasn't as ignorant of the situation as many thought he might be?

Once the two hot headed flag officers regained their composure and took their seats, Admiral Mikawa stood to address the assembled Imperial Staff brain trust.

"Is there anything further we need to know about our overall situation commander?" he asked referring to the staff officer conducting the overall situational brief. "There is an old Prussian saying that bad news does not get better with age."

The commander nervously glanced across the room; first at the Emperor whose facial expressions indicated a clear interest in the subject at hand. Admiral Koga nodded for the officer that it was OK for him to continue – after all how much worse could their situation get?

"Your Majesty, Honorable Admirals and Generals, there is one bit of intelligence we have recently been made aware of. One of our contacts operating in the United States outside the city of Seattle brought to our attention a copy of a newspaper covering the crash of a large bomber built and tested by their Boeing aircraft company. Apparently, this large bomber is intended as a replacement of their current B-17 with a range we believe of approximately 5,300 kilometers[45]. Should the Americans begin production of this bomber, they will be able to hit us from bases in China."

The commander's comment caught everyone by surprise, not the least of which was Admiral Koga.

"How close do they have to locate their forward bases in order to bomb us from the west?" asked Koga.

The staff officer knew this question was going to be asked and was dutifully prepared. "If the American Navy captures any island within the Mariana Islands such as either Saipan or Guam, we at General Staff and Fleet Intelligence believe they will begin their bomber offensive against us with planes so large as to make last year's Doolittle raid look like a brief joy ride in the Ginza."

The *Razor* was not willing to let pass this last comment without one final word. Standing up and taking one last puff from his cigarette, he looked directly at Admiral Koga.

Before he could speak, a messenger burst into the conference room, followed closely by Admiral Koga's aide-de-camp.

"Honorable General," the messenger uttered, trying to gain his breath. "This message just came in from our command in the Gilbert Islands. The

---

45   Approximately 2,800 nautical miles or 3,000 miles

Americans are invading as we speak, landing a large force on the small island of Betio on the western side of the Tarawa Atoll!"

"I would strongly suggest Koga that you have your work cut out with the navy," said the now furious Tojo. "The quicker you get to it, the better!"

Deep inside the cool, damp Smolensk forest within the Army Group Center Command Post, Major General Tresckow finished up his daily journey entry of the day's events. With some occasional artillery barrages exchanged between the Russians and themselves, the war had ground down to a dreary lifestyle tailored on staying alive. In a few days it would be the inglorious second anniversary of *Operation Barbarossa*, the German invasion of the Soviet Union. It was clear to everyone that the Wehrmacht had no chance of winning against the Soviet Union, but on the other hand, the Russians did not at this time possess the strength or professional talent to end it on their terms. All in all, on what should have been a good day, Tresckow was once again plotting.

His aide-de-camp and cousin, First Lieutenant Fabian von Schlabrendorff, quietly entered Henning's tent and noticed his usual optimistic General frowning in thought. The young aid pulled out a bottle of cherry brandy from his coat pocket that he had liberated from another General Staff officer, reached for a small cup, and poured the General a small portion.

"You looked like you needed a little 'morale' boast Herr General," commented Fabian.

Henning smiled and held the cup up in the form of a mock toast.

"To the Fuehrer," the General uttered, and then quickly gulped the brandy down in one large swig. Slamming the cup down, he looked as his aide with disgust.

"How the hell does he do it Fabian? How the hell does that *pig* manage to avoid being killed?"

Schlabrendorff knew who his General was referring to. Anybody over-hearing such comments could have the two of them shot for treason but he had his boss' total confidence. Looking quickly around the tent entrance, he concluded it was safe to talk.

"This son-of-a-bitch is the luckiest pig around. First, I was going to have Captain von Boeselager and his Cavalry unit serve as armed escort to Hitler's motor-cade last March during his visit to our headquarters. The Fuehrer's car was to be gunned down in an ambush during the drive from the airfield by Boeselager, but he had to abort when Hitler arrived with his own armed escort of 50 SS guards."

Fabian shook his head in agreement, "Ya, I remember that. Boeselager almost pulled it off."

Tresckow continued. "You remember the next attempt? The bomb we placed on his plane failed to explode. I had to send you to Berlin to recover the *Cointreau* from Colonel Brandt before that idiot either found out what he was carrying or blew himself up by simply setting it down too hard. After that disappointment, I dispatched Colonel Rudolf von Gertsdorff, the Army Group's Chief of Intelligence, to kill Hitler in the Zeughaus. His plan was to conceal a bomb within his coat while he stood close to Hitler at an exhibit hall. Unfortunately Hitler left the building before the acid within the bomb could act and Gertsdorff immediately entered the men's room and flushed the fuse down the toilet."

"You know there will be other opportunities to get that madman, Herr General," commented Schlabrendorff.

"The man leads a charmed life," replied Tresckow. "If that's not enough, we then lost General Oster within the Abwehr. The Gestapo picked him up a couple of days after Hitler's last visit."

Henning took another swig of brandy, finishing it off, and then pulled a telegram out of his breast pocket.

"I just received this today from my friend Lieutenant General Friedrich von Broich, Commander of the 10th Panzer Division in Tunisia, that his Operations Officer and my ol' friend Lieutenant Colonel Claus von Stauffenberg, was seriously wounded in action last April as a result of a British air attack."

"How bad?" ask the aide.

"Bad enough to get evacuated to Munich apparently. This dispatch is dated mid May and says he lost his left eye, most of his right hand, and two fingers of his left. It also says his body was riddled in the back and legs with shrapnel. General von Broich wrote 'It's a miracle he's still alive'."

Tresckow sat the telegram down, then stood up and pulled another cigarette from his pocket. As he lit it, he blew the smoke in the direction of *Der Fuehrer's* picture, customarily found hanging within the command post.

"Fabian, I refuse to be disheartened. If you'll forgive my cliché, there's an expression '*where there's a will, there's a way*'. I have an idea how we can make it occur."

"I'm all ears, Herr General."

Henning once again glanced around the tent and then took another drag from his cigarette.

"What if we were to take the Home Army Plan, code named '*Valkyrie*', and rework it?"

Schlabrendorff appeared confused. "I don't understand Herr General. What is '*Valkyrie*'?

"Quite simply, it's the plan the Home Army designed to deal with internal disturbances in emergency situations, such as an insurrection or the possible riots of the millions of forced laborers brought into the Reich. But what if the plan was reworked to trick the Home Army into the seizure and removal of the civilian government of Germany under the false pretense that the SS was attempting a coup d'état that included the assassination of Adolf Hitler? The key requirement would be to ensure that the rank-and-file soldiers and junior officers, who were supposed to execute this plan, are motivated to do so based upon their false belief that it was the Nazi civilian leadership who had behaved with disloyalty and treason against the state, and therefore had to be removed."

"It is possible it might work, given you have someone with balls in Berlin to rewrite it and ensure it is executed," replied Fabian. "You also realize that the very pretext required to implement this plan is Hitler's death?"

Tresckow took another puff from his cigarette then threw it down, crushing it out with his boot.

"Isn't that what we've always wanted to do? We will have to ensure that as the plan is executed, we implement a secret declaration beginning with the words: *The Führer Adolf Hitler is dead! A treacherous group of party leaders has attempted to exploit the situation by attacking our embattled soldiers from the rear to seize power for themselves.* I tell you Fabian, it might just work!"

"Do you think General Olbricht will help us?" replied Fabian.

"Of course he will. As Chief of the Armed Forces Replacement Office, he was *Valkyrie's* original author."

Schlabrendorff nodded in agreement.

"If you don't mind, I'm going to take a stroll and clear my head to ensure I think this through thoroughly. I believe we need a new change in plans."

Chapter 16

"Call me – Franklin"

Fact: In 1943 alone, the industrial output of the United States reached 86,000 planes, 45,000 tanks, and 648,000 trucks. In addition, American companies that year made 61 million pairs of wool socks and every day another 71 million rounds of small-arms ammunition spilled from army munitions plants.

"""The war has been variously termed a 'war of production and a war of machines'. Whatever else it is, so far as the United States is concerned, it is a war of logistics."
– Fleet Admiral Ernest J. King, 1946

The Presidential Oval Office
The White House, Washington, D.C.
1030 hrs, 3 October 1943

Fall was definitely in the air in Washington. The dreadful heat of the past summer typically for the residents of the District of Columbia had finally passed, evident by the many citizens strolling along Massachusetts and New York Avenues on that cool morning.

Jerry Curry appreciated the change in weather. Spending long hours working alongside a President surrounded by the ever constant cloud of cigarette smoke, the change in season would finally allow him to step outside the Oval Office and breathe the clean fresh air of Fall.

As he strolled along the White House's back portico, the change in colors reminded him of his old home in Kentucky; it seemed 100 years since his last visit.

My how so much has changed over the few months, he thought to himself, reflecting on everything that had occurred since returning from London that past December. Who could have imagined a year ago that the US Army would have mobilized over seven and a half million soldiers, many now fighting deep in the Pacific alongside another two and a half million sailors and Marines, far more than what was mobilized for the Great War in 1917. And still the basic training camps were filled with raw draftees learning their deadly craft.

With so many forces in the south and Central Pacific, the US Navy and US Army were pushing the Japanese back on all fronts; Java, Sumatra in the Dutch East Indies, Guadalcanal and the Northern Solomon Islands, and Tarawa in the Gilbert Islands, while the north Pacific islands of Attu and Kiska in the Aleutians ensured Japanese ambitions for Alaska as well as against the West Coast were finished. After destroying a massive convoy of Japanese reinforcements bent on reinforcing New Guinea in what is now known as the *'Battle of the Bismarck Sea'*, the US Navy had positioned itself to isolate and cut off many of the remaining Japanese forces located throughout the Bismarck Archipelago, including their major naval based at Rabaul; virtually turning the entire area into an abstract prisoner-of-war camp.

Curry also reflected back to his last meeting with "H" in London, wondering what he was up to, which still left him bittersweet. Through Dulles and his OSS, he heard that there had been two attempts against Hitler – one using the very bomb making material he provided 'H' with, which gave him a sense of pride had they succeeded.

But he was still bothered by his discovery of the President's pre-war duplicity with Churchill and the possibility of it being revealed to the public before the end of the war. On more than a few occasions, he thought about letting Roosevelt know he was on to him and his possible blackmail situation, only to lose heart when he saw his President – the man who picked him as Harry Hopkins' trusted replacement - steadily become worn down by the day-to-day decisions of war. The President clearly didn't have long to live at this hectic pace.

After a few sweet minutes enjoying the fresh air of autumn, Curry finally made his way back to his office and immediately noticed the fresh layer of messages strewn about his desk as if they were leaves newly fallen from some hidden tree. If ever there was a person whose job seemed never ending, it was his.

Most of his messages were reminders of meetings – events requiring his presence at the behest of the President.

Let's see, he thought to himself as he thumbed through the various notes, trying to establish their respective priorities.

This one deals with the Manhattan Project brief, conducted by Bill Armstrong in lieu of the recently promoted Brigadier General Groves. Curry was sorry he wouldn't be able to meet the distinguished General, especially now that his construction project for the War Department – the world's largest office building aptly named 'The Pentagon' was now completed and in full operation. He continued thumbing through what seemed an endless amount of dispatches, noting most dealt with war production, finance, war bond status, etc; all appearing boring and ultimately mundane considering what his role to the President was all about.

Curry threw them back on his desk, then sat back and began mapping how the remainder of his day would shape out. As he looked at his daily calendar of events, the buzzer on his intercom sounded, almost like an annoyed hornet looking for a victim.

"Mr. Curry," his secretary announced, "The President would like your presence in the Oval Office as soon as possible."

Here it comes, he thought, the first of the day's interruptions to whatever schedule he had planned. He snapped down the intercom reply button to acknowledge.

"Is he with someone?" he asked. He was not aware of any meeting with anyone of real importance.

"Yes, he is. He's meeting with General and Mrs. Chiang Kai-shek and he asked me to see if you were available to attend. I left you a note early this morning as a heads up."

Curry scooped up the notes and quickly reviewed them again; sure enough, there it was, scheduled for 11:00a.m, Oval Office.

"Tell the President I'm on my way!" he said as he reached for his coat and briefing pad, hightailing down the hall towards the Oval Office.

Within a few minutes, Alonzo Fields announced his arrival to Roosevelt and his Chinese guests. The Generalissimo was impeccably dressed in his forest green dress uniform adorned with dozens of badges, medals and other regalia, many of which he'd probably awarded to himself. On first appearance, the General reminded him of the Charlie Chaplin character in 'The Great Dictator'.

Madame Chiang on the other hand was stunning. Dressed in a long and slender, elegant purple dress she could have easily passed as an exotic oriental movie star. Curry recalled that during the past winter he had seen her picture on the cover of *Time* magazine when she became the first Chinese national and the second woman ever to address both Houses of Congress. Up close he realized her cover picture did not do her justice.

After a short glimpse of Madame Chiang, he also noticed two General Officers present for the meeting; General Marshall and Brigadier General Reynolds from War Plans. This meeting was by no means a diplomatic 'social call'.

"Well Jerry, please take a seat," the President instructed Curry.

Looking over to his guest, FDR opened the discussion.

"Jerry is my right hand man and key advisor, and I don't like keeping him the dark when it comes to major policy items."

Chiang nodded in understanding of the civilian's presence at such a high level discussion. FDR continued.

"We were just getting ready to discuss how we can help our General Chiang and our distinguished Chinese allies with their problems dealing with the Japanese. Isn't that right General Chiang?"

Again, the General nodded, this time smiling for a change, but still studying Curry, wondering what this man could possibly bring towards China's salvation.

"Mr. President," the Generalissimo began, "As you know, we have been fighting in an almost constant combat against the Japanese for almost six years. My armies are holding back approximately one million Japanese soldiers as you can see from my map."

Chiang Kai-shek then unrolled a map he had brought with him to help plead his case.

Generalissimo Chiang Kai-shek's map

"Even before the Marco Polo Bridge incident in 1937, the Japanese Kwantung Army[46] was ravaging my country; we have had to deal with these ruthless people since 1931."

"We have provided extensive aid to your country over that same period General Chiang," Marshall inserted, "Since late spring 1941, the United States has provided over $145 million in lend-lease funds for China to acquire both ground and air equipment. If you recall, in May 1941, Secretary of War Henry Stimson approved your request for sufficient equipment to outfit 30 infantry divisions. On top of that, we also financed the creation of the American Volunteer Group led by General Claire Chennault and his famed 'Flying Tigers', then turning to the President, Marshall continued. "President Roosevelt, I believed they're racked up a pretty impressive record of over 300 Japanese 'kills' before reforming as our 14th Air Force."

Roosevelt following the dialog between the two distinguished military figures, nodding in agreement with the Chief of Staff's claim.

BG Reynolds raised his hand, catching Marshall's attention.

"Sir, I need to comment on the obvious; the biggest challenge to your war effort in the Chinese theater is logistical. In fighting your war, our efforts in supplying you involve shipping material over enormous distances from the United States. Right now, our only real way of supplying you is by air over the Himalayas or as they say 'over the hump'."

"Precisely, General Reynolds," Chiang responded. "In spite of your great efforts to date, the U.S. military simply cannot sustain the logistics effort required to build a modern Chinese army. Without sufficient arms, ammunition, and equipment, let alone doctrine and leadership training, my Nationalist Army is incapable of driving out the Japanese invaders, let alone deal with the Communist bandits that I have had to face for over 20 years!"

---

46   The **Kwantung Army** was an army group of the Imperial Japanese Army (IJA) in the early 20th century, becoming the largest and most prestigious command in the IJA. One of its Chiefs of Staff "*Hideki Tojo*" would later go on to become the Imperial Japanese War Minister.

"Well then General, what are you proposing?" asked a now inquisitive Roosevelt, complete with his telltale cigarette holder held straight as a flag pole. "If we can't supply you, how do you intend to continue the fight?"

Before Chiang Kai-shek had a chance to respond, Madame Chiang raised her hand. Given her distinct beauty, all eyes soon turned to her to see what this *Lady of the Orient* had to say.

"Mr. President, you must understand we need American forces to land in China and help us with this dreaded fight. Until the Burma Road is re-opened, you must invade to save my country."

"Does your Chief of Staff, General Stilwell share your opinion?" asked Marshall.

The Generalissimo immediately gave Marshall a vengeful scowl for questioning his wife – he was not used to having Generals question him or her about consulting others - but quickly regained his composure because after all he was dealing with the second most important man in America today behind Roosevelt.

"General Marshall, there are times when my distinguished Chief of Staff General Stillwell and I will disagree. He thinks my Nationalist Army is too defensive minded, but I tell him, without heavy weapons or airpower, my armies are slaughtered by the Japanese. I must keep sufficient forces on hand to deal with the indignant Communist guerilla forces that operate mostly in this region!" Chiang pointed to a section of northwest China near Yenan. It was apparent the mountainous terrain would not make it easy to route them out in the near future.

Roosevelt looked over at Marshall and Reynolds.

"Well Generals, what do you have to say about that?"

Marshall spoke first.

"Mr. President, when I heard from Lieutenant General Stillwell that President Chiang Kai-shek might propose to you the possibility of a land invasion, I had General Reynolds and the War Plans' folks draw up a series of concepts how this might be possible. As of today, we have 90 army divisions organized into seven armies, five Marine Corps divisions and 18 corps' headquarters mobilized. As you can see by looking at President Chiang's map, China is far too large to invade and take over the war effort there, but if we were to land a two corps sized force and seize the port city of Shanghai, we would be able to control the flow of Japanese material up the Yangtze River into the interior. Since the port city is half way between Hong Kong and Peking, we will have a strategic position what will allow us to cut off the Japanese operating in Southeast Asia, as well as provide us with a staging area for launching strategic bombing against the Japanese home islands."

FDR leaned forward in interest.

"And what does the rest of the Joint Chiefs of Staff have to say about this?" he asked.

Marshall glanced over to Reynolds. It was now his turn in this strategic level tag team brief. Reynolds immediately redeployed himself between Marshall and the Generalissimo.

"Mr. President, when General Marshall and I discussed this yesterday with the Joint Chiefs, specifically with Admirals King and Nimitz, in concept they support it, especially since this will undoubtedly bring the whole Japanese fleet out in the open for us to destroy. However, before we go the distance, we will need to seize the island of Formosa, located here," Reynolds pointed to the large cigar shaped island off China's southeast cost. "The Deputy Chief of Staff, LTG McNarney, and General Hap Arnold both favor bypassing the Philippines and seizing Formosa."

"By seizing Formosa, we will truly cut the Japanese lines of communication to the south and southeast Asia," Marshall added. "We can even begin using the new B-29's bombers from there if we have to, instead of from Shanghai!"

"What do we know about Japanese forces there?" FDR asked.

"From reliable estimates we have on the island, we believe there are approximately 170,000 troops stationed there of varying levels of combat proficiency," replied Reynolds. "We have identified the 10th Area Army Headquarters also known as 'the Formosa Army', five army divisions, seven brigades of varying strength and one air division, as well as the usual support troops associated with an Area Army Headquarters. Nothing we haven't dealt with before."

Roosevelt asked that Chiang's map be brought to his desk in order for him to study it closer.

"Hmm, you know that Douglas MacArthur is not going to like to hear any talk from you and the other Joint Chiefs of bypassing the Philippines, but I must comment – it does make perfect sense though."

Standing beside FDR, Marshall pointed to the Philippine Archipelago.

"You know, Admiral Nimitz and some of the other senior naval commanders in the Pacific favor at least reoccupying the southern or central Philippines before striking on toward Formosa. These officers believed it would be impossible to secure the Allied line of communications to Formosa until our land-based aircraft from southern Philippine bases had neutralized Japanese air power on Luzon. This might be something General MacArthur could accomplish."

The President sat back in his chair to take it all in, letting out a large puff of smoke in the process, much like a departing steam ship leaving port. Marshall gagged slightly, standing back to catch what little fresh air he could.

"So tell me the bottom line," the President asked Marshall. "What can we do different in order to better aid President Chiang and China?"

"The 'bottom line' Mr. President," the Army Chief of Staff responded, "is that we are well into the planning cycle to help China, by seizing Shanghai via Formosa. Thus, the longer we delay an attack on Formosa, the more the operation would ultimately cost. General Reynolds' Army planners suggested that we might be able to reach Formosa during February 1944 if the

Joint Chiefs immediately decided to bypass the Philippines. Moreover, based on what General Chiang and General Stillwell tell us, the Joint Chiefs were beginning to fear an imminent collapse of Chinese resistance within the China-Burma-India theater could occur. Most of Reynold's best planners feel that the only way to avert such an eventuality would be the early seizure of Formosa and the port of Shanghai."

Both the Generalissimo and his wife smiled in agreement at the Chief of Staff's words of wisdom. American aid would save China.

Roosevelt turned to Chiang Kai-shek and his wife. Their display of pleasure at Marshall's comments convinced him they would leave satisfied with their visit.

"How does that sound to you?" FDR asked his two distinguished oriental dignitaries, already knowing the answer.

"Mr. President," Madame Chiang began, "we will be eternally grateful for what you've informed us of today. We are most pleased you will help us with support and most importantly with American troops. You will not let us fall to the Japanese."

Chiang Kai-shek nodded in agreement. "At last, I know with direct American support, we can see the light at the end of the tunnel!" he added to his wife's comment. "I only wish we had American troops to assist us as we prepare to for our upcoming offensive in Hunan Province, which is scheduled to commence the first week of November."

The Generalissimo glanced at his watch and then rose.

"Mr. President, distinguished guests, you must forgive Madame Chiang and myself, but we must depart for a very important reception at my embassy. I will have General Stilwell cable General Marshall for further coordination of our conversation as well as have a one of my military liaison officers from the embassy report to your Joint Chiefs of Staff for immediately use."

Everyone within the Oval Office, with the exception of the President, rose and bid General and Mrs. Chiang Kai-shek farewell, who were escorted out by Roosevelt's trusted aide – Alonzo.

When the President's guests had departed the room, he instructed his two Generals to take a seat. Clearly, they were not leaving soon.

"Tell me General Marshall, do you believe the Generalissimo?" asked FDR. "After all that aid we've provided, can the Chinese army be that bad?"

Marshall knew FDR would want to know if there was 'the rest of the story' – that left unsaid by the Generalissimo.

"Mr. President, from what General Stillwell tells me, Chiang and most of his army commanders are incredibly corrupt. On top of that, he holds back his Nationalist troops in order to keep a handle on the communist forces under Mao Tse-Tung, a long time rival he nearly wiped out back in the early 30s. As for the quality of his Nationalist forces, nearly every time they meet the Japanese, they get their asses kicked, and pretty badly I might add. If we're to keep them in the war, we will need to get directly involved, more so than what we're doing now, and with American boys."

FDR grimaced. He was not exactly thrilled at the prospect proposed by the army's Chief of Staff.

"Tell me about the Communist Chinese forces. How strong are they? Can they fight?" asked the President.

"We really don't know much about them, other than under this Mao character they've survived Chiang Kai-shek's assaults for the past 15 years, so it's pretty much survival of the fittest. They're a pretty tough bunch and they've done better against the Japs than the Generalissimo has. We do know that they are not controlled by Stalin and Moscow."

"All right," summed up Roosevelt, "I want you to dispatch a team to meet with this 'Mao' and find out for me all you can about them. We'll call it the '*Dixie*' mission. Contact Stillwell and let him know about this, then clear it with Chiang of course; I don't want him thinking we're operating behind his back, but on the same token, I don't want him to think he has a monopoly on information as to how the war in China is going. Meanwhile, begin your planning as per our discussion today."

"Acknowledged Sir," was Marshall's reply. "I believe we have enough here to have the Joint Chiefs' planning group finish up JCS Plan #924 for your review and approval within the month. If there is nothing further for us Mr. President, General Reynolds and I must depart to the Pentagon to give the Joint Chiefs a heads up on what was just discussed."

"Splendid, thank you gentlemen for your time today. I believe we had a most fruitful discussion, but General Marshall, this conversation must not go any further than the Joint Chiefs' planning staff.

"Yes Sir," replied Marshall, displaying what many would have considered the ultimate poker face revealing neither pleasure nor displeasure with his commander-in-chief.

As per custom, the two General Officers immediately stood at attention and saluted, departing in an instant. Curry got up thinking this was his cue to escape as well.

"Hold on there Jerry, have you got a moment to talk?" asked FDR. No one left the President when he wanted to talk. Curry knew his escape back to his office was just aborted.

"Of course Mr. President, what is on your mind?"

"What is your opinion of this whole China matter? Do you think we should land troops in China and back the Generalissimo?" FDR asked.

"Well Mr. President, for starters, our involvement in China is what ultimately got us into a war with the Japanese. With all the trade embargoes against the Japs for all the havoc and hell they were raising in China, we all knew it was inevitable something was going to happen. We just can't walk away from them and leave them on their own just because of Pearl Harbor. After all, the Chinese lobby is extremely powerful here. Just look at the reception Madame Chiang got from the Congress last spring. I'm surprised this issue wasn't brought up back then!"

Roosevelt sat back in his chair, all the while replacing a cigarette with another in his cigarette holder. He then lit up, letting out a large cloud of smoke. Curry quietly winced, knowing the acrid air within the Oval Office would not improve anytime soon.

"Ya' know Curry; this job doesn't get any easier with time. My schedule fills up daily with meetings, briefs, what have you. To make that all happen, I need you to be there to help assist me, but of late you seem distracted, almost as if you're putting distance between yourself and me; ever since you returned from London last spring. Am I correct or just reading the cards wrong?"

Curry immediately felt uncomfortable. Was it all too obvious? If ever there was a time to get it out into the open, now was it.

"Mr. President, I apologize if I've given you the impression of putting distance between you and me, but there has been something on my mind. For starters, I feel in order to truly be your advisor, there has to be trust between us."

"That goes without saying, Jerry," FDR replied.

"Well Mr. President, in London, I met with a representative of MI-5 recommended to me by General Donovan. He showed me documents, damaging documents about your communications with the First Sea Lord Churchill from 1939 and 1940."

FDR kept his usual non expressionless political face. "Go on," he said.

"You told me about the blackmailer and what he might possess, but after seeing these documents first hand, I can tell you without a doubt, this truly is political dynamite that would leave the country with no choice but to impeach you for criminal conduct against the constitution and the country itself!"

"Does this change your desire to continue working for me?" a now somber Roosevelt asked. "I still need you as does the country. I did what I had to do, but if you cannot accept this, then I'll understand if you wish to tender your resignation."

"No Sir, I do not wish to at this time," said Curry, finally relieved he could get what was weighing him down off his chest. "On a side note Mr. President, where are you with this whole blackmail matter?"

FDR grinned, telegraphing to Jerry an upbeat note.

"It appears Jerry, that we have a sort of Mexican standoff. As long as we pursue the war against the Japanese, he will not release that material to the press or Congress, nor has he sought any money in exchange for it. I guess this senator is a type of warped patriot."

Curry was surprised at FDR's response.

"So no FBI or police?" he asked.

"You've seen the material. Do I risk it? If we knew positively we could recover it with no release to the public, I'd have J. Edgar and his G-men over there in a flash. Otherwise, I have a country at war with the Japs and we can't afford to have a massive scandal hit now, not while we haven't defeated them yet."

Jerry took a huge sigh of relief – his conscience was now at ease.

"Well Mr. President, now that we've cleared the air, if you don't mind, I need to tend to matters that will help you win this war," he stated as he stood up to leave the President.

"Thank you Jerry, and by the way, you can call me Franklin when it's just the two of us."

"I'll remember that Mr. Pres… I mean – Franklin. See you for drinks at 6?"

"Looking forward to it," echoed the now revitalized Chief of State in his classic Harvard twang.

Curry stepped into the hallway outside the Oval Office feeling a sense of liberation. He had finally entered that inner circle of the President's earning the honor afforded so few men of calling the man by his first name. That was worth more than any medal or bonus he thought, strolling back to his office.

As he neared his office, a messenger he recognized from the OSS approached him.

"Mr. Curry, I have a message for you from General Donovan. He instructed me to get it to you ASAP." He handed the brown envelope over, making Curry sign for it as per the usual protocol.

After thanking him, he closed the door behind him and sat down. In the short time he was with FDR, another snowfall of messages, notices and other correspondence had descended on his desk, reminding him of a winter scene. He opened the envelope from Donovan and carefully read the contents of the one page document.

Crap, he thought to himself, *the President's not going to like this. How the hell could something like this happen? Who could possibly have thought — much less predicted — that Germany and the Soviet Union would produce an armistice?*

Half way across the world, the sun had just set on the German capital, bringing Berliners out for their evening after dinner stroll. Despite the past few years of deprivations and rationing within the city, many Germans in general were in a festive mood and for good reason. For the past few weeks, rumors had been circulating about a cessation of hostilities on the dreaded Eastern Front. While there had been no official word from the Reich Chancellery, Eastern Front Wehrmacht casualties had dropped to their lowest level at any time since the fall of France in the summer of 1940, leaving many to wonder whether the Soviet Union had finally had enough. Troops unlucky to have been wounded since were due largely to accidents or from running into unknown minefields. After all, minefields do not discriminate…

Lieutenant Colonel Massar knew better. As he accompanied Field Marshall Keitel to a special meeting at the Reich Chancellery hastily scheduled for that evening, he couldn't help but feel a sense of pride at his part in the momentous occasion. While Keitel officially reprimanded him for acting outside his prevue once the Field Marshall found out the real reason for his mission to Stockholm that summer, he privately thanked him for saving both German soldiers and the Reich from what might have been a modern day version of the

First World War Western Front – untold millions of casualties in an attrition war Germany couldn't possible hope to win.

After negotiating the various checkpoints, searches, and other security protocols in place by the Gestapo within the greater chancellery, the elite of the OKW General Staff were assembled within Hitler's office; all wondering what the purpose of this meeting was.

"Actung," thundered Hitler's Adjutant, SS Obersturmbannführer[47] Richard Schulze-Kossens, as the massive doors swung open allowing entrance of Der Fuehrer himself, accompanied by a procession of faithful toadies and party hacks led by Herman Goering.

Yet to all assembled it was very apparent this was a different Hitler, one with an optimistic, almost boyish look about him, as if today was his birthday and a special gift waited for him. In his usual fashion, he took his place at the head of the large staff situational briefing, positioned near a map of the Soviet Union. Everyone studied him as he unclenched his hands, then promptly placed them behind his back as if standing at parade rest.

"Gentlemen," he began, "today I am extremely pleased to formally announce the cessation of hostilities with the Soviet Union and the establishment of an armistice." With that, Hitler raised his hand, signally two SS officers to unroll a new map across the briefing table.

"As you see, I have instructed our units to pull back along this line here, largely following the Dnieper River within the Ukraine, due north along this line running east of the Baltic States. As per our agreement, I have directed there will be no more combat operations against the Soviets. Units found in violation will be severely punished." Looking at Keitel and Jodl, both Senior OKW officers acknowledged their usual agreement with Hitler, nodding while uttering the customary "Ya-wholl Mein Fuehrer!"

"And I will ensure my Luftwaffe units also abide by your instructions Mein Fuehrer," Goering abruptly inserted to feel part of the General Staff

47   SS Rank equivalent to Lieutenant Colonel.

group. He was largely ignored by the still stunned audience reacting to his armistice announcement.

"With the Soviet Union neutralized, what is your new guidance Mein Fuehrer?" asked Jodl.

Hitler smiled; a rare sight to the assembled General Staff. His piercing blue eyes revealed a man who had given that very question deep thought and now was presented the opportunity to provide that answer.

"We must now contend with the unfinished business at hand," said Hitler, motioning to the map in the direction of Great Britain, "as well as prepare for our eventual conflict with America!"

One could hear the subtle but distinct gasps from the various senior officers present. Common sense was to leave the United States well enough alone.

First to speak his mind was General Kurt Zeitzler, OKH Army Chief of Staff.

"Mein Fuehrer, before we begin this new endeavor, I beg you to consider that we need to rebuild the army. The army we sent into Russia two and a half years ago is not the same one today. We need time to make good our losses and re-equip our forces."

Hitler glanced across the room. He could see in the eyes of Zeitzler's peers he was right, but then again, Hitler rarely would consider a Senior General's point of view. He had a politician's instinct and was first and foremost a gambler, not a military 'technocrat'.

"We must prepare as rapidly as possible to destroy the British before the Americans bring their weight of numbers against us. Right now their army is deployed against the Japanese who will cut them down by the thousands, perhaps even inflicting a million casualties. Assuming they invade and conquer our allies, what shape do you think they will be in to face us after that Zeitzler? They are a soft people. The Americans will not have the stomach for another bloodbath!"

Hitler raised his voice to ensure the Army Chief of Staff as well as any other doubter present understood his annoyance at such a comment.

This wasn't the General's first public dressing down; Hitler had continually scolded his OKH Chief of Staff on many occasions over the past year, ever since Zeitzler's near panic attack just prior to last winter's Stalingrad debacle.

Jodl took over.

"Mein Fuehrer, do you propose we invade the British Isles? Surely, you can't be serious? As I believe Admiral Doenitz will attest, we have nowhere near the shipping or air assets required to take on such an endeavor."

"Who said anything about an invasion Jodl?!" Hitler snapped back. It was Jodls' turn to be stared down.

"Mein Fuehrer, I just assumed..."

"You assumed incorrectly!!" the German leader yelled back at the now humiliated senior Wehrmacht leader. "Within a short time, we will be able to bring Churchill and the British people to their knees using our new 'wonder' weapons such as the V-I and V2 rockets. Our new jet fighters will sweep the annoying British bombers from the skies. But yes, we do need to buy some time before they are fully tested and ready for deployment, so my directives in this matter are such. First, I want Doenitz and his U-Boats to begin tightening the screws around the British Isles. If this includes sinking American boats that are approaching the British, so be it. I have tolerated their presence long enough! Second, I want Speer and his organization to begin fortifying the Atlantic coast line from Brittany through to the Dutch coast. Take whatever labor he requires from the local population. Should the Americans get involved, I want them to know if they thought invading Japan was tough, wait till they see what kind of a reception I will have awaiting them in France! Meanwhile, bring as much of the army we can from Russia back and begin the rebuilding, starting with reequipping the Panzer Divisions with the new Tiger and Panther tanks."

Der Fuehrer's directives to the assembled General Staff were crystal clear — it was just a short intermission before the next act of this grand tragedy would commence.

As the high ranking staff officers left Hitler's conference room, many felt a mixture of emotions. On one hand, their nightmare with the Soviet Union was abated for the time being providing a brief sense of relief. Yet, with these new directives, it was apparent his actions would clearly bring the Americans into the war — a war that now appeared to have no end in sight.

While Keitel stayed behind to confer with Speer on his labor requirements, Massar headed to the Field Marshall's waiting car parked in the courtyard. As he approached a group of Generals, he recognized his old friend Henning Tresckow talking with another senior officer he recognized from the Reserve Army — General Olbricht.

"Good evening Sirs," saluted Massar. "I guess you'll be coming home soon from Russia."

"So I heard," Tresckow replied, "So I heard. So what new madness has now brewed in the Chancellery?"

Massar quickly glanced around, knowing they were about to once again descend into comments of a treasonous nature.

"He is again considering taking on the British, only this time he knows his actions will seriously provoke the Americans and he's preparing for that as well. A war with no end..."

"Oh Christ!" Olbricht uttered. "Instead of leaving it alone with the armistice in Russia, he's committed us to more insanity and won't be satisfied until he destroys the nation!"

"He's got to go," replied General Tresckow, "I'm telling you, the sooner the better."

Looking at Massar, Henning turned deeply serious. "Are you with us?" he asked the young Lieutenant Colonel.

Massar couldn't answer the question, at least not immediately. He truly believed the armistice with the Soviet Union would be the end of it. *With the war in North Africa at a stalemate, the British sooner or later would see the light and begin negotiations but this would not be the case, he thought.* Hitler was intent on the inevitable entry of the Americans with its eventual 'Gottdammerung'.

"Are you with us?" Tresckow asked again, pressing the young staff officer further.

"Massar, there you are!" came the all too familiar voice of his boss, the Field Marshall, heading straight towards the conspiring group. Without any acknowledgement, Lieutenant Colonel Massar turned on his heel and walked away towards Keitel.

"Do you think he'll betray us?" asked the incredulous Olbricht.

Henning shook his head. "The young man's confused. Give him time. Meanwhile, I want you to contact Colonel Stauffenberg. Once I inform him what's Hitler's going to do, I believe he's more than ready."

Chapter 17

Death of an Empire

Fact: Nearly 500,000 Purple Heart medals were manufactured in anticipation of the casualties resulting from the invasion of Japan. To date all the American military casualties of the sixty years following the end of World War II—including the Korean and Vietnam Wars – have not exceeded that number. In 2003 there were still 120,000 of these Purple Heart medals in stock. There are so many in surplus that today combat units in Iraq and Afghanistan are able to keep Purple Hearts on-hand for immediate award to wounded soldiers on the field.

"What it must have been like for some old-timer buck Sergeant... who had been through Guadalcanal, Bouganville, and the Philippines, to stand on some beach and watch this huge war machine beginning to move and stir all around him and know that he very likely had survived this far only to fall dead in the dirt of Japan's Home Islands."

- James Jones, Author

Aboard the USS Enterprise
Off the coast of Kyushu, Japan
1330 hrs, X+35, 5 April 1944

Major General John Reynolds hated flying. For 20 hours he had bounced from nearly every type of aircraft the U.S. armed forces possessed; traveling from Andrews Air Field outside Washington to California in a C-47, then from San Francisco to Pearl Harbor, Hawaii in a B-24 bomber, then various PBY Catalina patrol planes, until finally reaching his destination: the *USS Enterprise*. After hours of flying over boring ocean views, suddenly he saw what was perhaps the largest armada he had ever beheld – the American carrier fleet 250 miles off the southeastern coast of Japan – all supporting the ongoing invasion of Kyushu. While his trip was highly unpleasant at best, he was not prepared for what he saw as his small plane circled the massive aircraft carrier on its final approach.

Dozens of Navy fighter pilots buzzed about the 'Big E' as the carrier was fondly referred to, like hornets protecting their nest. As he looked down on the carrier, he could see the tell tale blackened scars, no doubt a result of recent fires on the ship's superstructure and flight deck. Off in the distance, many of the fleet's screening vessels had smoke billowing off their decks, indicating receipt of punishing damage delivered by the Japanese.

Reynolds got on the plane's intercom and asked the pilot what caused the damage.

"Kamikazes," the flight officer replied. "Japanese suicide planes bent on crashing into any American ship in an attempt to sink her and her crew".

'So this is what kamikazes are capable of doing,' Reynolds thought to himself. He recalled the post-action report submitted by the III Amphibious Corps after *Operation Broadaxe*, the invasion of Formosa last fall. Here, the U.S. Fifth Fleet reported that hundreds of Japanese suicide planes flew out of bases in China and Okinawa and assaulted the U.S. invasion fleet, killing 15,000 sailors and sinking 12 ships; three of which were precious aircraft carriers. That was just the beginning.

Sixty days later, in *Operation Longtom*, two Marine Corps Divisions, the First and Fourth, seized the Chinese port city of Shanghai. The conquest of the city itself, though bloody, was over within three weeks, with the Japanese quickly melting into the surrounding country side. In a déjà vu reminiscent of Formosa, Japanese kamikaze's again returned from outlying bases to harass the fleet, killing more sailors and Marines than the actual fighting within Shanghai. And once again, the fleet suffered grievous losses and serious damage, losing another 10 ships. Clearly, the closer the Americans came to invading Japan, the more ferocious they were expected to be.

Once on board the "Big E," Reynolds descended below deck to the Enterprise's master conference room to hear the report from the assembled members of the Sixth Army Corps commanders and the Third Fleet admirals. He learned firsthand the to-date progress on *"Operation Olympic"*, the first of a two-part invasion of the Japanese islands, coded named *"Operation Down Fall"*. He was in essence, General Marshall's, as well as the Joint Chiefs of Staff's, "eyes and ears" and, most likely, the deciding factor on whether or not the second part of *Downfall*, code-named *"Operation Coronet"* for the invasion of the main Japanese island of Honshu, would take place.

As he entered the conference room, Reynolds recognized a few old friends, some of which he hadn't seen in years. One old friend, MG Randy Postell, who currently commanded the U.S. First Corps, immediately recognized him from their days training the Georgia National Guard in the 1930s down at Fort Benning. Another was MG Tommy Stewart, former Second Corps Commander and representing General Walter Kruger, Commander of the Sixth Army responsible for the success or failure of *Operation Olympic*.

"All right, gentlemen," the all-too-familiar voice of the U.S. Navy — Admiral Chester Nimitz said, "now that our distinguished guest from the Joint Chiefs of Staff — General Reynolds - is present, I suggest we get started. First of all, General Reynolds, let me give you an overview of the Navy's participation in *Olympic*."

"From what I saw flying in, you must have at least 100 ships as far as the eye can see," replied Reynolds.

Nimitz laughed. "Between the Third and Fifth Fleets, we have nearly two dozen battleships, 100-plus carriers of all types, 70-plus cruisers, nearly 700 destroyers and destroyer escorts, many of which are serving as radar pickets against the kamikazes. I also have 200 submarines, as well as hundreds of support ships oilers etc to protect the two fleets. In short, over 2,700 ships of all types are supporting this affair."

"Very impressive Admiral, very impressive. Amazing what we can build since Pearl Harbor."

"John, if you do not have further questions for the Navy or I, the Sixth Army's Deputy Commander, General Stewart, will bring us up to speed with *Operation Olympic*."

Tommy stood up and headed over to the massive six by six foot map board of the island of Kyushu illuminated with various colored lines and arrows in red, black, and blue, and interspaced with a mosaic of colored squares; blue ones representing American regiments, red representing various identified Japanese forces.

"Gentlemen," Stewart began in his typical Georgian accent, "it appears as of today, with five weeks of the campaign, we have secured everything south of the Six Army northern objective line across the island." He used the four-foot pointer to draw an east-to-west line that evenly bisected Kyushu into two halves.

"At this time, the army is securing this line and establishing defensive positions to prevent the ongoing Japanese counterattacks we are subjected to on almost a daily basis. Meanwhile, we've got the 98th Infantry Division and a whole lot of Army Corps of Engineers and Navy Construction Battalions [Seebees as they refer to themselves], working nonstop to repair and restore the port of Kagoshima for our immediate use in the forthcoming 'Operation Cornet'. Additionally, all major airfields captured are being repaired for use by army and Navy air forces to support ground forces in repelling further Japanese counterattacks. At this time, MG Postell will brief us on First Corps' operations."

Tommy handed over the map pointer to Randy as he stood up. He winked at Reynolds, letting him know he acknowledged his presence.

"Fellow Generals and Admirals. I'm General Postell and I'm going to tell you that this operation began as one gigantic 'kick-in-the-pants,' so to speak."

Randy was also a born and bred Georgian, and by the sound of the last two speaking senior officers, Reynolds chuckled that maybe the South didn't lose the Civil War after all. Postell continued.

"We hit right here at the "Town Car Beach Zone" on March 1st with three infantry divisions, the Twenty-Fifth at Cord Beach, Thirty-Third at Chevrolet Beach, and the Forty-First at Dort Beach. And let me tell you we suffered approximately 5,000 casualties right off the bat with them damn kamikazes going straight for the landing craft instead of the supporting ships as we had experienced off Formosa. We lost a lot of damn fine American boys that morning hitting those beaches, if you could call them that. General, take a close look at those contour lines on the map."

Reynolds closed the distance to the map and squinted, viewing the close set lines contour lines nearly mashed together.

"Sir, those close lines represent cliffs. C-L-I-F-F-S. And we have to navigate through a few of those bad boys to deal with them Japs. Even with fire support from five battleships, I still had the devil of a time defeating their defensive positions and destroying their gun batteries, which thanks to the Navy we were prepared for. After defeating numerous counterattacks — and mind you gentlemen many of those fellows went as part of massed suicide attacks - we were able to pivot the Corps to a line extending from the East China Sea inward with the Thirty-Third Division less the 130th Infantry Regiment along the coast south of the town of Tsuno, and the Forty-First Division alongside to the Thirty-Third's west after they initially linked up with the Eleventh Corps down south near the town of Aburatsu. My corps was reinforced with the arrival of the Eighty-First

Division and I have found a nice home for them in the central highlands. My farthest western boundary is held by the Twenty-Fifth Division, adjacent on the east with the Eighty-First and Eleventh Corps' Seventy-Seventh Division to its west. With all that, we're doing OK, but it sure hasn't been pretty!" said Postell to Reynolds as he visually inspected the area indictaed on the map by Postell .

"Randy, what have your losses looked like so far?" asked Reynolds.

Postell exposed a pained sour grin.

"Well sir, we've lost somewhere in the neighborhood of 75,000 men in five weeks of this campaign. I've some regiments that are pretty banged up and down to rifle strength of 1,500 men and no senior officers. In the case of the Thirty-Third Division, the Jap Twelfth Infantry regiment launched a night suicide against the Thirty-Third's 130th Infantry Regiment, catching them by surprise and virtually destroying it. If it hadn't been for my Corps' artillery fire smashing them sons-a-bitches, it would have been much worse; hell, they might have gotten down to the Chevrolet Beach-head."

Randy looked depressed as he mentioned the losses his beloved First Corps had incurred but, overall, his Corps had made the army's objective and were digging in.

General Stewart brought MG Matt Carlisle up next to discuss Eleventh Corps operations. Receiving the pointer, Matt began.

"Gentlemen, like General Postell, at 0500 hrs on March 1, I hit the assigned Station Wagon Beach Zone within the Ariake Harbor area with the First Cavalry Division hitting Ford Beach, Forty-Third Infantry Division hitting Dusenburg Beach to the right of Ford Beach and the Americal Division landing on the largely deserted Franklin Beach. As you can tell from the map, we're about 35 miles to the south. As with the First Corps, we had six battleships supporting our operations, but we too were also hit with about

400 kamikaze planes and suicide speed boats, but only lost approximately 3,500 soldiers in the initial assault.

"As we moved inland we weren't so lucky. Once they sensed we were on the ground and off the beach, the Japs immediately threw in two regimental counterattacks, one of them being a suicide attack against the 132nd Infantry Regiment of the Americal Division, overwhelming and like General Postell's unit virtually destroying the unit as a combat force with an overall cost of about 10,000 men. I had to have BG Kendall commit his 164th Infantry regiment to save Franklin Beach head and stabilize the situation."

Matt pointed to his assigned beach heads within the vicinity of the southeastern part of Kyushu, near Ariake Wan Harbour, approximately 32 miles southwest of the First Corps' beach zones, then continued.

"I can assure you after that, our progress was slow but steady, linking up with First Corps here near the village of Nichinan, cutting off and destroying Jap units located within the Osumi peninsula. Forty-Third Infantry Division fanned out inland, reaching the eastern shore of Kagoshima Bay. They continued northward blocking any lateral shift of Jap forces from Kagoshima over against Postell's First Corps, forging up the valley on the western side of Mount Kirishima. Meanwhile, my First Cavalry Division, once off the beach, fanned out and cleared my western flank, capturing the town of Kushira, after which they assumed a 'follow and support' mission behind the Forty-Third Division. Currently they are the Corps' reserve behind the Seventy-Seventh Infantry Division."

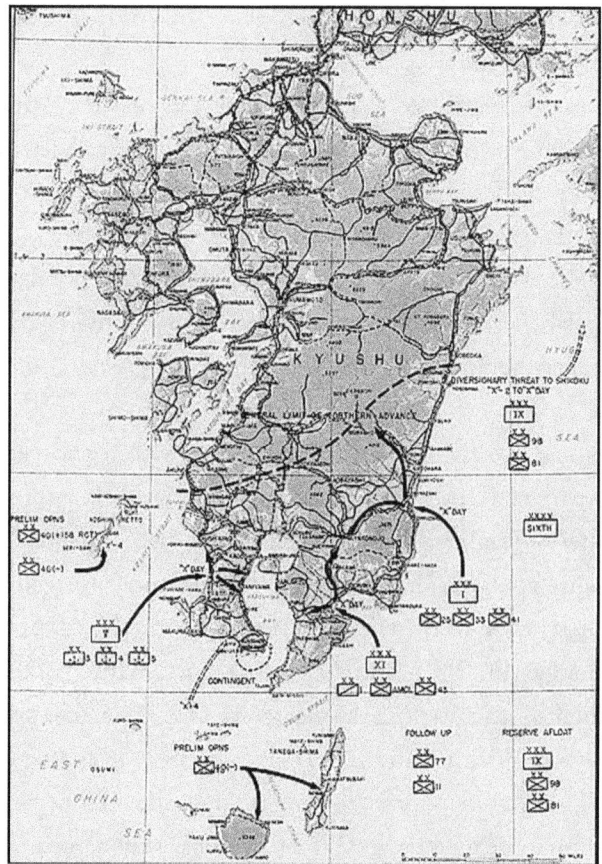

Sixth Army's Invasion of Kyushu, March-April1944

"Matt, how many casualties have you incurred to this date?" Reynolds asked, informally acting as General Marshall's casualty accountant.

"Well, it isn't pretty. Like General Postell, I believe I'm also upwards of 60,000 casualties."

The news caused everyone to stop and think for a moment. Between the two Corps that briefed, the butcher's bill for *Operation Olympic* was well over 140,000 soldiers and sailors killed, wounded or missing, and that wasn't the end. Next to brief was Lieutenant General "Iron" Mike Karpen's V Amphibious Corps – U.S. Marines one and all.

"Gentlemen," Iron Mike began, "I guess I drew the big prize, landing along Roadster Beach Zone near the town of Sendai here on Kyushu's western shore." Using his pointer, General Karpen displayed the length and array of his morning objective: securing the Roadster Beach Zone.

"About four days ago, the Navy had four battleships pound my beaches with preparatory fire, silencing whatever Jap gun batteries were there. Starting at 0600, first to land was the Third Marine Division, here at Winton Beach. Alongside the Third to the south, landing at the same instance, my Second Marines hit Stutz Beach. A short time later, at 0730, Fifth Marine Division landed at Zephyr Beach. In spite of all the prep fires, we got hit with over three dozen suicide speed boats coming out of nowhere plowing into the Higgins' boats. I damn near lost a regiment before hitting that damn beach."

"I had the same issue as well!" General Postell chimed in. "These damn suicide boats just appeared but fortunately, the high surf screwed them up in my beach zone and navy aircraft was able to shoot most of them up pretty good!"

Karpen continued. "Overall, the beach itself is hard white sand but is backed within about 15 feet by 10 foot (3m) high dunes made of soft sand. Immediately behind the dunes is an area of scrub pine followed by an area between one and five kilometers deep that is solidly agricultural with both ploughed and irrigated fields. Beyond that, the fields are backed by high hills. These give way after about six miles (10 kilometers) to a range of small mountains, around 300 – 600m high, which are packed very closely together."

John studied the map noting the tough terrain the experienced leathernecks had to deal with.

"Go on General Karpen. Tell me about the landing."

"Sir, we succeeded in getting ashore, but my casualties amounted to approximately 5,000 Marines. It could have been higher if the Japs had decided to defend Stutz Beach with something more than a couple dozen local militiamen. However, I did lose D and E Companies from the Second Battalion, Twenty-Six Marine Regiment due to kamikazes attacks. Once off the beachhead, Third Marine Division headed northeast towards Sendai, while Second Marines headed towards Kagoshima City and into the Ozato Gawa highlands towards the town of Kushikino. Fifth Marine Division attacked towards the northwest to expand Zephyr Beach head, attacking and eliminating the Jap 126th Infantry Brigade, but losing 2,000 Marines in the process before establishing a blocking position to protect the overall Roadster Beach Zone. By March 27th, the V Amphib Corp was successful in expanding our beach zone, and was poised to seize Kagoshima. By the first week of April, my Marines established northward blocking positions in conjunction with General Carlisle's XI Corps, and had successfully captured the Port of Kagoshima, with some help from the newly landed Ninety-Eighth Infantry Division. Overall, we repulsed several Japanese suicide counterattacks from those units trapped in the Sendai peninsula, resulting in their ultimate destruction. At present, I have the Fifth and Second Marines along the Army northern objective lines, repulsing numerous Jap counterattacks, with the Ninety-Eighth Infantry Division securing Kagoshima. Additionally, I received the Fortieth Infantry Division at the conclusion of Sixth Army's diversionary action off the coast and I have them securing the various local towns and villages within my zone of operation. At present, Third Marine Division is in reserve due to recent serious losses."

"What do you mean serious losses General Karpen?" Reynolds asked. "What the hell happened?"

Karpen looked down, not quite ashamed, not quite embarrassed, but at a sudden loss for words.

"I do regret to inform you that last week, I too had a Jap suicide attack that took down the Twenty-Seventh Regiment/Third Marines near the town of Izumi. During the night of April 3rd, in a sudden sneak attack the Jap 212th Infantry Regiment of the 330th Infantry Division launched a massive banzai attack against the Twenty-Seventh Marines, overrunning their Command Post and destroying the regiment at a loss of 5200 marines before off shore naval guns and help by the Twenty-Six Marine Regiment was able to seal the breach and restore the front. Overall sir, I am still in shock at this loss. I knew many of the Marines killed or wounded in action, including the CO, Colonel Tom Sullivan. I'd like to put ol' Tom in for the Navy Cross, along with a few other of his boys. Good troops one and all."

Everyone in the conference room knew the casualty estimate for *Olympic* would be high, especially after the losses U.S. forces sustained in the recent *Broadaxe* Formosa invasion. For few senior officers present, it brought back memories of the horrific losses they experiences in the First World War.

When LTG Karpen finished, Stewart resumed the brief.

"Overall General Reynolds, we have successfully secured Kyushu and project having Kagoshima marginally up and running within five to six weeks if the estimates provided by Admiral Nimitz's Construction Battalion folks prove true."

Reynolds was still thinking about the overall casualties sustained by the invasion force.

"Tommy, what is the total casualties estimate to date?"

General Stewart reached into his right shirt pocket and pulled out a 3 x 5 card. He knew this question would sooner or later be brought up and he, as bad as the news was, was prepared.

"Sir, as of today, I regret to inform you that in this campaign, we have sustained over 216,000 killed, wounded, or missing in combat..."

The gasps of many of the staff officers in attendance could be heard, while MG Postell uttered a barely audible, "My God!!...'"

Stewart continued.

"Yes, these casualties were high, there's no denying that, but I have to tell you they would have been far worse if we hadn't employed a few countermeasures based on experience brought about in Formosa and Shanghai.

For instance, the fleets didn't do a good job of nailing the Jap aircraft on the fields before they could take off. Most of the carrier based planes were protecting the beaches which allowed the kamikazes to get off the ground, mass, and attack. Second, in *Broadaxe* and *Longtom* they attacked the carriers and supporting ships. Our experience here in *Olympic* is they have shifted targets, going instead for the troops carriers and Higgins boats as they approached the shore, making protective fire from the supporting ships difficult. Basically, as we change our tactics, it is not unreasonable that they would as well, and quite effectively.

"Gentlemen," Reynolds began, "The Battle for Formosa ran up 74,000 U.S. casualties in 82 days, of whom 12,510 were killed or missing. If the projected U.S. casualty rate for this operation was only been five percent as high per unit area as it was at Formosa, the United States would still have lost 297,000 soldiers – killed or missing! *Operation Coronet*, the invasion of the Japanese main island of Honshu, is scheduled to commence in 120 days. The Joint Chiefs of Staff have casualty projections of upwards from 500,000 to a 1,000,000 men, depending on who you talk to in Washington! Speaking for General Marshall, I can tell you he wants a thorough analysis of what happened during *Olympic* and a recommendation of countermeasures to mitigate future kamikaze and suicide boat attacks. I can also tell you the American public will go *'ape shit'* when they read this, especially based on what we've seen so far with the casualties published in the papers over the past year."

Stewart nodded in agreement.

"General Reynolds, I can assure you that General MacArthur and Admiral Nimitz are in agreement with the Joint Chiefs that we can learn from this operation. I don't know if you've been briefed, but as per General Marshall's planning guidance, we are prepared to use chemical weapons in future operations rather than expending American lives chasing after Japs hiding within their caves and underground bunker complexes," explained Stewart.

"Chemical weapons? Can you elaborate? Is this even legal?" asked Reynolds.

"Well, first of all, regarding the question of legality, I can tell you that we haven't stopped them from using it against the Chinese. They've never used it against us, but what's to say they might change their minds considering we've got their back up against the wall? Second, because of its predictable wind patterns and several other factors, Japan is particularly vulnerable to gas attack. Using chemical weapons would seriously neutralize the Japanese tendency to fight from caves, as caves would only increase their exposure to gas, the more they enclose themselves, the more powerful it acts."

"That still hasn't answered the question of legality," said Reynolds, still fascinated the idea had gone this far.

Stewart continued.

"Well sir, chemical warfare has been outlawed by the Geneva Protocol, but neither the United States nor Japan were signatories at the time. While our policy is that we would never initiate gas warfare, as I mentioned before Japan has in fact used gas against the Chinese on numerous occasions. Finally if I might add, the army Chief of Staff has always been an advocate in its use against the Japanese and if I might quote General Marshall; 'The character of the weapon was no less humane than phosphorous and flamethrowers', so I think that pretty much sums it up."

"OK, but if we go ahead and initiate usage, what's to say they won't retaliate?"

Stewart smiled at hearing the question, for he had a trump card up his sleeve to play for just such a moment.

"John, what if I told you we don't have to fear Japanese retaliation because their ability to deliver gas by air or long-range guns had all but disappeared. We have received ultra information revealing that the Japanese doubt their ability to retaliate against our use of gas. We have intercepted a communiqué, where they are quoted as saying *'Every precaution must be taken not to give the enemy cause for a pretext to use gas'*, their commanders were warned. So fearful are the Japanese leaders that they plan on ignoring the isolated tactical use of gas in the Home Islands by our forces because they feared escalation."

General Reynolds realized as deadly gas warfare was, this just might be the answer they were looking for in reducing American casualties in *Coronet*.

"So what is the preferred chemical weapon of choice?" Reynolds asked.

"Well sir, we have approximately 1,800 tons of cyanogen chloride, mustard, and tear gas with us aboard the S.S. Henry James, with additional stocks of Lewisite and Phosgene available from facilities on Luzon. If we have to use anything, I prefer Lewisite – think of this stuff as a super mustard gas. I'm told its nickname when they tested this stuff in the 1930s was the *'Dew of Death'*. Much of this is in the form of 105mm artillery rounds, but we do have a few 4.2" mortar rounds for those folks in the infantry regiments that require immediate support. And to round out the list, we also have good ol' fashion bombs we can drop from our bombers.

Reynolds was impressed they had an answer, the weapon available for use as well as the delivery system, but still didn't know if he would recommend its usage to the Army Chief of Staff, much less the Joint Chiefs.

"General Stewart, one last question. If you use Lewisite in *Coronet*, what can you tell me about collateral damage and deaths among the Japanese populace?"

Stewart was transfixed at the question.

"Say what? Did I hear you correctly General?" he asked.

"What about civilian casualties when we start using this stuff?" Reynolds inquired. "Gas doesn't adhere to any tactical boundaries. You know this stuff will drift into the local towns and villages, afflicting the non combatants."

Stewart was transfixed at the question.

"Sir, did the damn Japs give a shit when they bombed Pearl Harbor about all the innocent American civilians killed in their sneak attack? How about the Philippines – all the Filipino and American civilians killed outright when they invaded back in '42, much less all the folks who died in captivity since then? How about all the American prisoners of war who have perished at their hands just because they were captured? How about the numerous islands we've invaded where Jap civilians launched suicide attacks at our soldiers even after they had hoisted white flags of surrender. No sir! I tell you, we shouldn't give one God damn about Jap civilians – the only good Jap is a dead one! They're going to attacks us one way or another – let the gas take'em out before they have a chance to do us any harm."

"I will take the suggestion up with General Marshall," John replied, not liking being put on the spot.

Suddenly, the conference room was filled with the blare of Claxton horns, loud enough to wake even those staff present out of a year's growth.

"Battle stations, Battle stations!" blasted the loud speakers. "Enemy aircraft approaching from the northeast."

Karpen grabbed the conference room phone, connecting them directly to the ship's bridge.

"Bridge, this is the Conference room, what's going on?" asked General Karpen.

"Radar has picked up a large swarm of aircraft, perhaps 80 to 100 coming on us from the northeast. Kamikazes no doubt. There'll be here in approximately 20 minutes. I suggest your group get its gear on and seek protection down below!"

Reynolds suddenly realized the helmet he was given when he boarded the Enterprise was now his immediate protection should the ship receive bomb damage - more than likely given the size and importance it was. Reaching over to where he placed it, it felt odd – different from the ones he had worn in the past and certainly very different from the one he wore in the First World War. No longer a staff officer in the Pentagon War Plans Office, he now found himself on the front lines as part of the greatest invasion the world had ever seen. An invasion the Japanese clearly still had a say in. As

Reynolds donned his helmet and followed the other senior officers down amidships, he hoped today was not his turn to become an army casualty on a U.S. Navy ship.

The situation was no less tense on Kyushu as First Sergeant Sam Posavec took stock of the mission he was handed by his Company Commander, Captain John MacPherson. As the First Sergeant for Company B, 1st Battalion, 511th Parachute Infantry Regiment, 11th Airborne Division, Sam had been with his boys ever since their formation at Camp Mackall, North Carolina, where the 511th Parachute Infantry Regiment trained long and hard for the pending airborne mission – any mission by this stage of the war. Bloodied by seizing airfields in landings on various small islands in the Pacific, followed by rest and recuperation on their now conquered private beach, then a regime of training replacements, Sam's regiment longed for continual action – the type most conventional infantry units found and would soon ultimately regret.

The 11th Airborne Division came ashore through Zephyr Beach head as reinforcement for the V Amphib Corps three weeks into the campaign. After two hard weeks supporting the Marines fighting in the Ozato Gawa highlands, Sam's 100 man airborne company was reduced to a mere 42 soldiers – a reinforced infantry platoon, bivouacked just outside the village of Tsusedo, 15 miles from their beachhead.

The mission Company B received was frightful. Along with the remainder of 1st Battalion, 511th PIR, they were to assault and seize a Japanese artillery forward observer outpost located on the south side of Mount Yae, an ugly chunk of hill located two and a half miles northwest of Tsusedo. "Simple enough mission for this outfit," Captain MacPherson informed Sam; but to date nothing Company B encountered was 'simple'.

As the company moved up the hillside, their sister unit, Company A, moved alongside on their right flank as the battalion's main effort, moving against a dug in Japanese infantry platoon the Regimental S-2 said was guarding the observation point or 'OP' as they were referred to.

Twenty minutes up the hill, Company A found itself under intense artillery fire from a battery of camouflaged Jap 105 mm guns.

With the battalion main effort stopped for the moment, MacPherson signaled the unit to continue moving up the hill towards the OP, when suddenly, machine gun fire from three positions raked across the company's front, instantly killing four airborne troopers and pinning them down as well.

"Sam, move one of your squads over to the left and see if you can flank the far left Jap gun!" MacPherson yelled. But Sam was already on it, taking the broken remains of 1st Squad augmented with those left from the 2nd, moving slowly through the brush in a series of rushes, followed by short bursts of carbine fire to keep the enemy heads down.

While Posavec was moving forward, MacPherson yelled for his Radio-Telephone Operator or 'RTO'. Once he reached the CO's position, John grabbed the mic.

"Kidnap Six, this is Kitfox 61. Contact, 12 o'clock, 100 meters. I have a fire mission for Keynote - over!"

Over the din of exploding shells and rounds, MacPherson heard a faint, "Roger – send grid coordinates".

MacPherson reached for his map which he'd left in his rucksack, but couldn't find it. Looking behind him, he saw where it had dropped out, just five meters on the trail from where he and his RTO were crouched.

"I'll get it sir," Private First Class Powell yelled.

"No, you stay here and protect the radio. If anything happens to it, this company gets creamed and I mean real bad!" the Captain replied. Rushing over quickly, he grabbed the map and immediately stuffed it into his shirt.

As the CO squatted to rush back, Powell watched in horror as a Jap sniper's bullet found its target. MacPherson's upper body immediately snapped back, forcing his helmet to fly off along with portions of his head. Company B's commander was dead before he hit the ground.

"Kitfox 6I, this is Keynote 25!" the radio blared. "Send your target grid coordinates — over!"

Powell in a state of shock grabbed the microphone "The CO's been hit. I think he's dead!" he screamed into the mike.

"Roger," the radio replied. "What are your coordinates? Over!"

"How the hell do I know?" Powell yelled back into the mike as if it was human. "The CO's dead and I don't know where the hell we're at!"

"Is your First Sergeant still alive? Over."

Powell clawed over to a tree for cover then slowly stood up ensuring the tree provided him the maximum amount of protection available. *'Where the hell is the First Sergeant Posavec?,'* he thought to himself.

At this time, Sam and his 1st Squad leader Corporal Sam Herron were flanking the far left Jap machine gun. An exchanged signal between the two of them and within seconds, three grenades found their target, as the airborne troopers watched the four man crew fly upward and out like rag dolls from the machine gun nest. One down, two to go.

"Corporal Herron, take your squad and lay down covering fire from 11 o'clock to 2:00 o'clock and give me all your hand grenades," yelled Posavec. Herron promptly complied with his six man squad laying down a heavy covering fire, while Sam again moved towards the next machine gun position, 50 meters behind and to the right of the first one they just knocked out.

Within five minutes, the tell-tale thump, thump of grenades detonating informed Company B that the second position had met the same fate as the first.

Posavec and Herron then linked up to coordinate taking out the third position, 20 meters and to the right of the second position Sam just took out.

"Sarge, let me take this one?" Herron asked. The First Sergeant made it look so easy. "Besides, I want to get in on some of this action for myself before you kill them all!" said Herron as he grabbed the grenade bag and made his way over to the last Jap position.

Sam maneuvered his squad over and gave the command for covering fire. Herron crawled closer to the position using the machine guns firing to mask any sounds he made in the bush.

Five meters, four meters, three meters from the gun. Herron rolled on his back and pulled out a 'pineapple' - as G.I's referred to the green shaped bomb. Rolling back onto his stomach to prepare to throw, he snapped a branch just as the Jap gun ceased firing its last burst.

He froze for what seemed an eternity, but suddenly as if out of nowhere, a Japanese soldier emerged, plunging his bayonet into Herron's chest. Before he slipped into perpetuity, all Herron would hear is the resumed clatter of the gun he failed to knock out.

After five minutes, Posavec knew something was wrong. Telling the acting squad leader to continue cover firing, Sam made his way to Herron, lying motionless next to the machine gun nest. Grabbing the bag, he pulled one grenade out, pulled the pin, then returned it into the bag. Counting to five, he flung the bag into the pit, then rolled over and covered his head.

Baaaabooom! To those soldiers still alive from Company B, it was as if a battleship's 16" naval gun had scored a direct hit on the nest. For at least one minute, debris in the form of wood, metal, and human flesh rained down on the surviving company like a bloody volcanic eruption. It also seemed Sam's grenade bag had also detonated some explosives the Japs kept in store for use against anyone trying to take their position.

As Posavec got up, he couldn't help notice the lifeless body of his colleague — a friend he knew from their early days at jump school at Fort Benning. He could feel rage building up inside. In three weeks he had seen so much death and destruction on Kyushu. Much of his company was now gone and now the war had claimed his friend as well.

Finding an intact Japanese Type 99 light machine gun lying near him, Sam grabbed it and immediately started off towards the observation post just 50 meters behind the now destroyed machine gun nest.

Within minutes, he charged into the position from behind, firing his weapon widely in all directions like a man possessed. Those Japanese who didn't immediately flee from this mad man were cut down instantly.

Once his gun ran out of ammo, Sam smashed it against the OP's targeting optics, then the radio; smashing anything and everything within his sight. Finally, exhausted, he collapsed on to a nearby Jap army stool and took his helmet off. Looking down the hill side, he could see exactly what the Japs could – nearly every American position within the 511th PIR's area. Clearly they were sitting ducks and the Japs knew it. It was a well developed ambush "kill zone".

Sam sat back and took a swig of water from his canteen. Hearing approaching soldiers, he grabbed a Jap bayonet lying on the ground and prepared to defend himself. A counterattack?

"First Sergeant, you in there?" the voice belonged to none other the PFC Powell, along with the 20 or so remaining Company B troops.

"Yea, it's me," Sam replied, lowering the bayonet. "Tell the CO we took the position."

"Hate to tell you this First Sergeant, but looks like you're now the CO," replied Powell breaking the news that MacPherson too was dead. "What do you want me to do?"

Sam looked out over the hill side they'd just climb up and wiped his face. 'How much more of this can we take?' he thought to himself as he looked north toward the Japanese lines. There were more hills as far as the eye could see and he was out of troops.

"Tell battalion we took the damn OP and we're digging in," he said, then sat down, mentally and physically exhausted, falling into a deep sleep. As he drifted off, he could faintly hear his CO's radio uttering, "Any Kitfox element, this is Kidnap Six. What is your status? Over."

✮ ✮ ✮

Half a world away in another ocean, the surface of the North Atlantic was broken by the emergence of a four foot periscope belonging to the German U-boat *U-315*, commanded by Oberleutnant Herbert Zoller. As part of a nine boat Wolf Pack code named '*Blitz*', it was Zoller's turn to troll the open Atlantic in search of any shipping headed towards Great Britain. Once a convoy was spotted his boat would become a '*shadower*' and would chase the convoy and report its heading and speed to the U-Boat Tactical Command, known by its initials 'BdU'[48]. The BdU knew the daily positions of all the Third Reich's U-boats and would coordinate the operation against the convoy by ordering nearby boats to form up around a convoy and attack with as many submarines as possible during the same night to overwhelm the escorts. Here the U-Boats would execute their time tested attack pattern against the convoy, sinking as many allied ships as possible before the arrival of any convoy escorts or naval aircraft.

A year earlier, guidance from his command, the IIth Flotilla HQs, made it clear they were not to engage American shipping, but since the armistice with the Soviet Union, they were now given a free hand to sink any shipping that happen to stray within the British Isles' war zone. Up until now, there had been slim pickings within '*Blitz's*' assigned patrol sector, but Zoller felt his luck was about to change for the better.

At 1615 hours, Captain Zoller could not believe his eyes – headed across his bow about five kilometers away were approximately 20 cargo ships, traveling at 15 knots.

"Mein Gott," Zoller yelled out. "Radioman, get this message and our position out to Lager Koralle![49] Sighted about 20 ships headed west at 15 knots."

Rechecking his periscope, Zoller knew there were nine sister ships within the area, all licking their chops at a taste of such a fat cow as what this

---

48   BdU – Operations abteilung (operational department) U-boat Tactical Command. The BdU-Op is the tactical command for all boats in the Atlantic, the North Sea and in the Indian Ocean.

49   Base location for BdU OP. A large communication hub located in a forest north of Bernau, 20 km northeast of Berlin.

convoy offered. As he looked through the scope he still couldn't believe his eyes. Twenty ships heading right for the pack and by his count, eight were flying the stars and stripes of the United States. Today was his lucky day.

"Helmsman, set a course for 087 degrees, set your speed for 10 knots" commanded Zoller.

Seaman Mohrs, the boat's radioman, acknowledged that BdU received U-315's message.

"Captain, the U-277, 355, and 361 also acknowledge and are moving towards our position."

Zoller smiled. '*Finally some action!*' he thought to himself as the various ship's departments relayed their status. The U-315 would be ready for combat.

"Captain, message from BdU — we are to rendezvous with all boats of '*Blitz*' at map point XT-21 at 1900 hrs. Looks like we'll have all nine boats in this one," said Mohrs.

"Down scope," cried out Zoller, "Helmsman, set course for map coordinates XT-21. Let's not keep the Americans waiting any longer than we have to. We have a little over three hours to get ready to throw the Americans a party they'll never forget."

As Oberleutnant Zoller stood on the bridge, he could feel his U-boat surge with excitement. After 25 days at sea with nothing to show for it, many of his crew as well as himself felt their prayers would now soon be answered.

The unseasonably good seas helped the U-315 make good time. By 1900, all '*Blitz*' boats were in their positions awaiting final confirmation. A quick air check by the U-277 made sure weather conditions would hinder any British or American air patrols.

"Berlin says GO!" yelled Seaman Mohrs. Zoller knew all the other U-Boats assigned to his Wolf Pack received the same word as well.

Raising his periscope, a quick scan revealed his favored target less than 3,000 yards amidships — a nice fat tanker carrying approximately six million gallons of fuel.

"Helmsman, change course left 090. Torpedo room, load tubes one and two with Falcon contact torpedoes!" barked Zoller. The various crewmen within the control room scrambled into their positions.

"Torpedo tubes one and two loaded Herr Kaptain!" the forward torpedo room replied.

As Zoller continued his fix on the tanker, he reached into his pocket and pulled out his stopwatch.

"Mohrs, tell the other boats to commence their attacks at my signal," commanded Zoller.

"What would that be Herr Kaptain?" asked the radioman.

Zoller smiled as he continued his periscope observation of the convoy. Without looking at his radioman, he grinned, "Trust me, they'll know. Torpedo room, fire tubes one and two!"

"Aye Kaptain," the forward torpedo room responded.

With that, Herbert clicked his stopwatch. If all went well, at 3,000 yards they should hear something in 15 seconds.

Tic, tic, tic, tic. The small stopwatch could be heard by everyone within the control room.

Zoller studied his watch. Ten, 11, 12, 13....

Suddenly, a deep thunderous sound echoed, like an underwater thunder-clap, followed immediately by a second equally ominous one.

Herbert looked through his scope, but was slightly blinded by the brilliant glare that met his eye. Before him lit up like the arrival of dawn, was his tanker along with her six million gallons of gasoline in flames, courtesy of his two Falcon torpedoes. In the light of the burning vessel, another five ships of the convoy were prominently silhouetted.

Looking at his radioman, Zoller motioned towards the burning tanker. "Now that's a signal the rest of the pack will understand to commence their attack!"

By 2215 hours, the convoy code named RU-86, bound for Belfast Lough, was no longer recognizable as an organized convoy. By this time, the 'Blitz' Wolf

Pack had laid waste to seven freighters and two tankers by this time, many of them still burning, continuing to illuminate the local area and providing just enough light to identify the remaining fast departing ships. As an added bonus, two escorting American destroyers also met their demise, throwing additional confusion into an already chaotic evening. All in all, it looked like 45,000 tons of allied shipping along with over 13 million gallons of precious gasoline had found a new home on the bottom of the North Atlantic.

The next morning in Washington D.C., Jerry Curry was eating breakfast upstairs within his White House apartment when Alonzo, FDR's personal assistant interrupted.

"Sir, the President desires to see you as soon as possible!"

Curry cleared his mouth with a napkin. One thing that shouldn't have surprised him was the President's constant interruptions into his private life, after all living in the White House made you subject to the President's every beck and call.

"Inform the President I will be down shortly," he informed Alonzo. "Do you happen to know what's got him excited today?"

"He wasn't this way earlier, but I believe it had something to do with what's in today's paper," Alonzo responded. "If you like sir, I can get you a copy of today's *Washington Post*."

Curry nodded a yes, then proceeded to make a sandwich out of his remaining bacon and eggs.

'*Can't keep the ol' man waiting,*' he thought to himself as he quickly downed his coffee, then finished dressing for FDR.

Within a few moments, Alonzo returned with a copy of the *Post*.

"I think you'll find what's upsetting the President is on the front page," Alonzo quipped before departing as quickly as he'd come.

There in big, bold letters on the front cover of the *Washington Post* was the headline: "*Two Warships and Eight Freighters Sunk, Navy Given a Black Eye by Hitler!!*"

'*That's just what FDR needs right now,*' Curry said to himself as he preceded, newspaper in hand, downstairs to the west wing and the President's Oval Office.

As he approached the outer office, the President's secretary flagged him to go straight in. As he opened the door, there was FDR – gray, gaunt, and looking every bit like he was feeling the strains of his 11 year stint as a crisis leader. He also was suffering the consequences of 20 years of physical immobilization caused by polio and a lifetime of chain-smoking. Curry knew the President had been in declining health for the past four years, but by this time Roosevelt had numerous ailments including chronic high blood pressure, emphysema, and systemic atherosclerosis, along with a host of other heart ailments. If managing the American war efforts wasn't enough, there was also his decision to seek another unprecedented term as President – no other President before him had opted to seek a fourth term.

FDR was on the phone when he entered. He immediately waved Curry in for a seat while he continued his conversation; not minding Curry eavesdropping.

"Help yourself to some coffee young man," FDR said as it appeared he was in listening mode to the conversation.

Curry poured a cup, then returned to his seat. He could see the same newspaper on the President's desk, a strong indication that Alonzo was right all along.

"I don't care what it takes," FDR bellowed. "I want whatever ships we can pull together to make sure we don't get our ass kicked again by those Nazi bastards. Is that clear Admiral King? By the way, I've been trying to get a hold of Secretary Knox, but haven't been successful. If you happen to contact him before I do, please inform the Secretary what we just talked about, and have him call me as soon as possible!"

It was no secret who was getting taken out to the wood shed and getting his butt blistered – the Chief of Naval Operations Admiral King. And as shit typically rolled down hill, Curry suspected that Secretary Knox would soon be hearing from King. It was strange however that the Navy secretary was unavailable during this crisis in the North Atlantic.

As he hung up the phone, Roosevelt immediately burst into a coughing seizure, in the process knocking over his cup of coffee and numerous papers piled all over the Chief Executive's desk. The coughing lasted well over a few minutes, but the sound emanating from Roosevelt indicated a seriousness far worse that he had witnessed in past coughing attacks.

Curry immediately leaped to his feet to assist FDR, scooping up the scattered files while also grabbing a napkin to soak up the spreading coffee. FDR meanwhile pressed his servant call button which immediately brought Alonzo into the Oval office.

"Yes Mr. President?"

"Alonzo, I need you to bring me my pills in the yellow bottle over on the credenza," replied the gaunt Roosevelt. "I'll also need a glass of water."

As if executing a precision battle drill, Alonzo had the requested medications and water to the President within seconds. As FDR downed the prescribed pills his calm demeanor seemed to return as if it were nothing more than a sneeze.

Curry was still trying to take it all in as he placed all the files back on Roosevelt's desk, then returned to his seat.

"Now Jerry, where were we?" FDR asked.

"Well sir, you asked me down here to discuss something important – I believe it has to do with this morning's headline in the paper as well as your conversation with Admiral King," Curry replied.

"Can you believe the audacity of Hitler? Sinking unarmed merchant ships in international waters. It's utterly barbaric! And they call themselves a cultured civilization. Ha!" Roosevelt uttered, ending his commentary in another short series of coughs.

"Well Franklin, it's to be expected. Once he and the Russians settled their war in the east, it was only a matter of time before he would become increasingly bolder in taking us on. Certainly this isn't the first time we've had our ships sunk by the Nazis?"

"No, but this is the first time the newspapers have been so graphic with this," Roosevelt said indicating the newspaper. "I guess they're looking for a little diversion from the massive casualties we're experiencing with our Japanese invasion," Roosevelt responded. "Hitler picked the right time to begin his little war of annoyance against us knowing that our attention is focused resolving our fight in the Pacific."

Curry stood up and walked toward the large Oval Office window overlooking the grounds immediately outside the West Wing, all the while stirring his cup of coffee.

"You're thinking about something Jerry, what is it? Spit it out young man!"

Curry turned away from the window and towards the President.

"Well Franklin, I was thinking about your friend – the one who periodically calls to remind you about getting involved in helping the British and in getting involved in Europe. Certainly he's thinking what the hell are we doing getting our ships sunk supporting Great Britain. Quite frankly I'm surprised he hasn't called already today and added to your inbox of problems."

"You don't think that hasn't crossed my mind Jerry?" FDR retorted. "It's like having this dagger hanging over my head every day. Every fiber in my body wants to somehow get us into a war against Hitler and his Nazi thugs, especially now that I'm receiving all sorts of reports about them putting Jews into concentrations camps for the sole purpose of extermination. I need to do something, but I simply cannot afford to get the Presidency involved in any sort of a scandal, especially now that we're on the verge of victory against Hirohito and the Japanese Empire. But it is absolutely imperative we continue to support the British in their endeavor and end this madness in

Europe. I know the American public can only take so much of seeing our boys killed and ships sunk before it's April 1917 all over again!" replied FDR referring to the circumstances that brought the United States into the Great War now known as the First World War. "Talk about being caught between a rock and a hard place, eh Jerry!"

Curry finished pouring another cup of coffee. "It does seem like we're heading down the same path as before, only this time with a blackmailer calling the shots."

As FDR thought about his situation, he instinctively placed another cigarette into his long black holder, then lit up, sending a large billowing cloud into the surrounding area. Much to Curry's chagrin, Roosevelt did his best thinking after lighting up a Camel, even if it was cutting his life ever shorter. Within a few short moments, the holder was in the up position – FDR had an idea.

"Jerry," Roosevelt whirled around, "I want you to go back to Britain and inform Mr. Churchill that for the time being, I'm going to have to scale back our support to him and the British. However, the real reason I want you over there is to have a get together with your German contact in the resistance and find out what support they need from us to knock off this madman. I believe he is called 'H'. Get in touch with him. Get me any new information to help me steer through these troubled waters. If we can't do anything, maybe we can help the Germans who care enough to get rid of him."

'*Another trip to Europe,*' Curry thought. It meant another month to six weeks away from Washington. FDR immediately sensed the hesitation.

"Give it some thought young man!" the President suggested. "I could sure use your help on this one."

For a few minutes the two sat in silence pondering the President's suggestion, when suddenly they were interrupted by the sound of the intercom on Roosevelt's phone indicating an incoming call.

"Now what?" FDR asked as he looked at the phone's blinking light. He studied it for a while, considering whether to pick it up or ignore it. After the second buzz was immediately answered by the annoyed President who did not wish for a third incoming call announcement.

"Yes," FDR quizzed the secretary. "Go ahead, put the Admiral on."

Curry thought it had to be Admiral King from the of the President's voice, closing the loop on their earlier conversation about protecting convoys. FDR's sudden facial change could only indicate more bad news.

"Thank you for that information Admiral King, please inform Mrs. Knox I will be contacting her shortly." Roosevelt once again looked gaunt, slack jawed, and at a loss for words.

"Bad news Mr. President?" asked Curry.

"Today seems to be the day for it," the President responded. "My secretary for the Navy, Frank Knox, died of a heart attack last night. It's no wonder why I wasn't able to reach him."

"Frank Knox!" exclaimed Curry. "You just had a meeting with King and him a few days ago."

FDR looked out the large Oval Office window towards the grounds, suddenly more despondant than any other time Curry could remember.

"I shouldn't be surprised," FDR quipped. "He's had a series of small stokes now for the past few months. And now, now that we are so close, he's gone."

"I'm sorry Franklin. I knew the two of you were fairly close."

FDR continued looking out at the pale, gray skies of a Washington spring.

"Besides you, he's probably my only other Republican friend. Ya know Jerry, it's tragic that in light of the disaster at Pearl Harbor, he's re-built the Navy to the point it's second to none on this earth and now that we are on the verge of victory, he will not be able to witness the death of an empire."

Chapter 18

"I owe you one!"

Fact: Though the Japanese Imperial High Command talked about "Total War," the fact is they didn't understand it, nor did they grasp the requirements to wage it. Astonishingly they failed to understand the military potential of a nation is directly proportional to her industrial potential. This was particularly true in naval expansion; throughout the war, the United States out-built Japan in large and heavy cruisers by a ratio of 27:2 hulls laid down (13:0 ships commissioned) while in destroyers, the United States laid keels for 365 ships, launched 362, and commissioned 323, with the Japanese only able to commission 31 (10.5:1).

""The Army must provide 600,000 replacements for overseas theaters before June 30, and together with the Navy, will require a total of 900,000 inductions by June 30."
- GEN George Marshall and ADM Ernest King, 1945

The Café Brasileria
Rua Garrett, 120, Lisbon, Portugal.
1135 hrs, 8 November, 1944

Jerry Curry sat in the open air café of the Café Brasilera, enjoying his time people watching various Lisbon citizens strolling along the riverside. Since it appeared that 'H' was going to be late again, he decided to while away the time with another cup of coffee and sampling a mouth-watering freshly baked croissant. For a November day, it was rather enjoyable outside and Curry clearly enjoyed the fresh ocean air, so typical for a historical sea port.

The weather for once favored Curry. Usually wet this time of year, Lisbon was having a moderate Fall, clear and surprisingly dry with a comfortable 62 degrees outside, making this mission far more enjoyable than what he would have had to face in London had Roosevelt decided to send him there.

But weather wasn't the sole reason Curry found himself in Portugal. Normally, London was where the two of them would meet after Curry conducted his business with Churchill and White Hall, but the London of November 1944 was not the same city he had visited a few months prior on FDR's request. London was a city under siege, but not the kind of siege in the classic sense, but a newer, more sinister form, courtesy of Der Führer of the Third Reich – Adolph Hitler!

Since mid June, the Nazi had begun a new form of aerial attack against London, using a newly developed rocket fired from various launch sites along the Belgian coast. These small 'buzz' bombs – literally cigar shaped missiles approaching the city with a distinct buzzing sound - would be observed by keen eyed watchers wondering what the hell they were, until they found their unsuspecting target – a building in London or a nearby small town, and delivered its nearly 2K lb warhead of death and destruction. Nearly 7,000 Brits had become casualties of this new form of terror.

The British scrambled as best they could to deal with these new wonder weapons, using everything they could get their hands on. Initially using anti-aircraft weapons, the 'Doodlebugs' as the Brits nicknamed them, simply could not acquire the fast moving targets. Barrage balloons proved equally ineffective, as the leading edges of the flying missiles wings were equipped with chain cutters. Finally the Brits were able to employ interceptor squadrons whereby planes could dive down and carefully attack the 'buzz' bomb before it found its programmed target.

By mid September, just as the Royal Air Force was gaining the upper hand on the German 'Doodlebugs', a new threat emerged, this time in the form of a combat ballistic missile, traveling at incredible supersonic speeds and carrying a larger warhead. For this new threat the RAF could not offer any defense and Londoners suffered accordingly.

Unlike the earlier employed 'buzz' bomb, this new missile's speed and trajectory made it invulnerable to everything the Brits had in their inventory - it dropped from an altitude of 100–110 km (62–68 mi) at up to four times the speed of sound, making it far too fast for any interceptor or anti-aircraft to acquire much less destroy. Between these two new wonder weapons, over 12,000 Londoners perished, making it unsafe for any covert, much less diplomatic get-togethers, and Roosevelt was not about to risk losing his valuable and trusted advisor to a stray missile.

"Herr Curry?" came a familiar voice over Curry's shoulder. "How are you doing this fine day?"

Curry immediately recognized 'H's' accented voice.

"How are you enjoying Lisbon my friend?" asked 'H' as he pulled out a chair and joined his American colleague. "I've usually favored Lisbon in August, warm enough to get a tan, but not as hot as say – North Africa."

Within a few minutes, the hostess had an espresso and freshly baked croissant set in front of Curry's newly arrived friend.

"Have you had any of their pastries here before? Their croissants are highly recommended. I thought you might like it, so I took the liberty of ordering you one."

'H' smiled as he began consuming his without saying a word.

"Now you know why I chose this place," 'H' replied as he washed the delicious pastry down with his coffee.

"So what would you like to discuss this time Herr Curry?" asked 'H'.

"Well, as usual, my President wants to know what your folks are going to do with Hitler. Hell, look what's going on in London today. You can't go out to take a piss without some missile landing in your water closet."

'H' sat back and smiled at Curry. "Looks like the Vergeltungswaffen weapons have been more accurate than the Nazi's believed."

"The what?!" Curry responded. "What the hell did you call it?"

"Vergeltungswaffen. In English you would call it a *vengeance* weapon. The Luftwaffe has invented two such devices which we aptly called the *V-1* and *V-2*. Nasty weapons if you ask me, and this is just the start of what Hitler has in mind to knock the British out of the war before the Americans find the guts to get involved. These '*V*' rockets are one of the first of such weapons with more to follow. Last year the Kriegsmarine started sending out a new type of U-Boat – the type "XII" series U-Boats. These babies have much better crew facilities than the current type VIIC class out there, much more silent underwater, freezer for foodstuffs, a shower and a basin and little things like that. More important, they also have a hydraulic torpedo reload system that enables the commander to reload all six tubes in something like 10 minutes which is less time to reload one tube on the VIIC under normal conditions. To top it off, these boats have three times the electrical power of the current boats which gives them an enormous underwater range compared to the older types and they can stay submerged far beyond the Bay of Biscay so as to be undetectable by the Royal Air Force of Navy. Your Navy will have a hell of a time finding, much less getting close enough to sink one in the mid North Atlantic. I believe you've tangled with a few already," said 'H' as he signaled for another espresso.

"Like I said, this is just the beginning" 'H' continued. "I haven't even begun to talk about their atomic weapons program. The Nazis are working on a secret crash program to develop an atomic bomb and with the effort in Russia complete, they just might complete it in less than a year. Good thing for you that many of the key scientists fled Germany to America including Albert Einstein."Curry remembered a recent conversation with General Leslie Groves and Bill Armstrong while he was at the White House briefing FDR on America's own atomic bomb project, code name '*Manhattan*', but decided against mentioning it to 'H'.

'H' continued. "Aside from the special weapons development, my brother talked to me about hearing a brief about a so called '*Atlantic Wall*'. The massive amount of work going on in Northern France to fortify the coast on a scale beyond what you experienced in the Great War will make any invasion of the continent just a pipe dream..."

Curry sat back dumbfounded. He had hoped his meeting with 'H' would provide FDR some good news, but that clearly wasn't on the menu for the day.

"How do you know all this information?" Curry asked, utterly mystified. "Our agents in the field haven't reported anything like this. How do I know all of this and all that you've told me in our past meetings is true?"

'H' quickly scanned the immediate perimeter of the outdoor café to make sure no one nearby was eavesdropping. In war, all walls had ears.

"Have you ever heard of a Heinrich Hoffman? Does that name mean anything to you?"

Jerry shook his head. "Why, should it?" he responded.

"Heinrich Hoffman is Hitler's official photographer, and as it so happens, is also my brother. Everywhere Der Führer goes my brother is right there to capture his image for Dr. Goebbels and his Propaganda Ministry. Must have seen a few of his books – he's written and published a couple dozen courtesy of Der Führer, making him quite a rich man. In the course of his duties he overhears a lot of information about Hitler's movements, strategy briefs, new weapons, all sorts of things. I get together with him monthly when I'm in Berlin. We have a few drinks, he opens up. It's that simple."

Curry was absolutely thunderstruck. Here was the man who knew everything about the world's greatest enemy, sitting in a Lisbon café talking to him over coffee and pastries. General Donovan and the OSS would have had an absolute field day if they knew this.

'H' once again scanned around the local area. Espionage tended to make many a person slightly paranoid.

"I find I live a lot longer being precautious, especially after informing you of the source of all my information."

The hostess promptly arrived with 'H's' espresso along with a fresh napkin. Curry was still speechless.

Once he gained his composure, he asked, "So how come you haven't been able to knock him off, especially since you know all his movements? It really should be a breeze at this point. You know where he's going; you plant a bomb, or send in an assassin..."

'H' uttered an amused chuckle. "If you thought so we wouldn't be having this conversation now would we? Seems Hitler is a lot harder target to nail these days. Would you believe we have conducted 13 assassination attempts against him to date? The last one was this past February; a Captain Axel von Bussche agreed to blow up Hitler and himself while he was demonstrating a new army winter overcoat to Der Führer. Fate intervened the day before when during a British air raid the uniforms were destroyed and Bussche was returned to duty at the front. A few weeks later another 'overcoat' attempt was made. This time the volunteer model was Ewald Heinrich von Kleist, son of one of the original conspirators. Again the RAF saved the day with an air raid just before the demonstration was about to take place forcing its cancellation. If I didn't know any better, I would swear that Hitler truly had a charmed life."

As he concluded, 'H's" facial expression changed from amusement to slight depression. "I think one mass bombing attack in the right spot at the right time is what it would take to end this *antichrist's* life!"

At that point 'H' stopped talking. A suspicious young man in a dark suit and hat had taken a table immediately adjacent to the two. After carefully studying the occupant for a few moments until he was quite sure the man was not a threat, 'H' continued, but in a much lower, inaudible voice.

"So I understand congratulations are in order!"

"How so?" asked Curry, curious about 'H's comment. Did his information network extend into Curry's life too?

"Well, it's in all the newspapers. Your President Roosevelt won an unprecedented fourth term in office. I don't see how this is possible in light of all the massive casualties you're taking in your invasion of Japan," replied 'H' referring to *Operation Coronet* which had just commenced a week prior, half a world away.

'H' continued.

"I see that in just a few days, you've already lost well over 75,000 soldiers, and are just getting started. Even during the worse time on the Eastern Front, the Wehrmacht never lost this many troops in a month, much less a few days. And this matter of using poison gas on the Japanese – very nasty stuff! In the case of world opinion, this puts you in virtually the same barbaric league as the Nazis."

"Well, we have to do what we have to do!" retorted a defensive Curry. "You should've seen the butcher's bill for the first part of that operation we did last spring as well as what we encountered in China. These people have no concept of defeat, much less surrender. The President made the decision to save American lives – pure and simple. In case you hadn't noticed, they started the whole mess at Pearl Harbor!"

"And so the end justifies the means, if what your saying is true, eh! Well, all I can tell you my friend is that since you've used chemical weapons against the Japanese, the Wehrmacht will be more than ready should America get in the war, and make no mistake my friend, she will eventually get in the war. Hitler has started his intimidation campaign against the United States until…"

"Until we either declare war against him or you guys find the balls to knock him off!" Curry finished.

"Yes," 'H' replied, "I fear you will be in this war well before we have the next opportunity to kill him and end this madness. Now, if you'll forgive me, I've exposed myself quite enough here and I have a flight to catch to Madrid, so if you'll excuse me Herr Curry, I'll bid you Auf Wiedersehen until we meet again."

As 'H' departed, Curry decided the weather was much too nice to head back to his hotel room, instead signalling to the hostess for one last Brasilera espresso, while pondering the magnitude of the source of 'H's' valuable information. He virtually had a mole in the very heart of the Third Reich. While he stared out towards the bay, a second, older man joined the young stranger sitting on the adjacent table enjoying his pastry.

"Well Jani," the stranger stated in a light Hungarian accent, "Sorry I'm late. Anything good on the menu?"

Jani smiled at the older gentleman as he doffed his hat and took a seat next to him. "I highly recommend the dessert, but the real treat to share isn't on the menu..."

At that moment across the Atlantic in Washington D.C, another somber meeting was taking place in the Oval Office. All across FDR's desk were congratulatory telegrams from congressmen, senators, and foreign leaders alike. In this unprecedented election, Roosevelt scored a comfortable victory over his opponent, Thomas Dewey. Despite the casualties from *Operation Coronet* and having dumped his previous Vice President Henry Wallace for Missouri Senator Harry Truman, a moderate who had become well known as the chairman of a senate wartime investigating committee, Roosevelt took 36 states for 432 electoral votes, while Dewey won 12 states and 99 electoral votes. In the popular vote Roosevelt won 25,612,916 votes to Dewey's 22,017,929. Dewey did better against Roosevelt than any of FDR's previous three Republican opponents, and he did have the personal satisfaction of beating Roosevelt in his hometown of Hyde Park, but in the end Roosevelt triumphantly returned to the White House.

But the campaign to become the first President ever to win a fourth term in office clearly had taken its toll on him. Wheelchair bound, ashen gray with a constant cough, many of his fellow democratic political leaders wondered why he chose to run despite his declining health.

Because of his deteriorating situation, many of these key political leaders just prior to the summer's convention pushed and ultimately succeeded in having FDR dump the left-wing Wallace from the ticket and replace him with the more moderate Truman. This move succeeded in ensuring Roosevelt's capture of all southern states and thus a return to the White House, but all those close to Roosevelt knew that this ultimately would be his final term – the end was only a matter of time.

With the election out of the way, FDR was now free to assess the progress of *Operation Coronet*, by holding an impromptu meeting with his closest military advisors. Deep down, he may have felt his end was coming soon and was hoping to live long enough to witness the final collapse of the Japanese empire.

Assembled in the Oval Office were the nation's military brain trust; General's Marshall, 'Hap' Arnold, Reynolds, Admiral King, and War Secretary Stimson. New to this distinguished assembled group was FDR's new Navy Secretary James V. Forrestal along with Brigadier General Leslie Grooves - few present knew what this man represented within Joint Chiefs of Staff and the War Department. Rounding out the group was British General Alan Brooke, Chief of the Imperial General Staff, and Field Marshal Edmund Ironside, a recent arrival to Washington tasked to carry on the duties of the late General Sir John Dill, the unofficial British Army liaison to the U.S. Armed Forces Joint Chief of Staff who died of natural causes nearly a week prior. Both British Generals were there representing the United Kingdom's role in Japan's final defeat as well as conducting unofficial coordination of convoy passage through the North Atlantic.

Reynolds began with his brief to bring FDR up to date; specifically how the current invasion of the Japanese main island of Honshu was going.

Overall *Coronet* was the largest undertaking ever taken by a great power in the history of the world – breathtaking in scale and scope. In total, two U.S. armies; the Eight Army with four corps assigned, and the First Army, commanding five corps. Each corps in the *Coronet* invasion force was composed of three infantry divisions except for the First Army's' II Armored Corps, which commanded the 1st and 3rd Armor Divisions. Overall General MacArthur employed well over one million American soldiers available for combat operations in Honshu arrayed in 28 army and Marine divisions, five times the number of troops used in *Olympic*, and that was just the army side of it.

"Mr. President, if I may direct your attention to the map of the island of Honshu, Japan, where *Coronet* is presently taking place," Reynolds started. General Marshall uncovered the large six by six foot map board revealing a large swath of Honshu with Tokyo in the middle. Reynolds continued.

"*Coronet* basically is an attack across the Kanto plain to capture Tokyo. Naval bombardment by guns and air commenced on October 17th designed to silence Japanese opposition and nail as many kamikazes on the ground as possible. The overall concept is very simple; as Phase I commences a blocking force lands at Mito on the coast north of Tokyo, then moves west to establish a position north of Tokyo. The main force, which is First Army, conducts landings on Kashima Beach south of Choshi with a goal to clear Chiba province including the east side of Tokyo Bay. One of their tasks is to build airfields and the II Armored Corps, composed of the 1st and 3rd Armored Divisions, before moving across the Kanto plain to attack Tokyo from the east." Reynolds stopped for a second to allow the President to study the map and the array of American dispositions depicted on it before continuing.

"Phase II starts on Y+31, 30 days later with Eight Army conducting a southern landing at Sagami Bay with the goal of seizing Yokosuka naval base and moving rapidly north to be west of Tokyo. We then anticipate capitulation of Japanese forces shortly thereafter."

FDR was impressed, nodding his approval at the concept of the operation.

"So General, how are we doing one week into this invasion?" the President asked.

"Per the plan, on November 1st, First Army landed on the southern half of Kujukuri Beach with four divisions and secured a beachhead. On November 6th, two more divisions landed, allowing First Army to begin movement across the peninsula to clear the east side of Tokyo Bay, then move north to take the port city of Choshi. While this is going on, all available engineers and other Service troops are building land-based air bases under the cover of carrier aircraft. This will allow us to fly in additional supplies and reinforcements."

"We project 30 air groups to be in place by November 30th," inserted General Hap Arnold representing the army Air Forces. With FDR nodding his understanding, Marshall signaled Reynolds to continue.

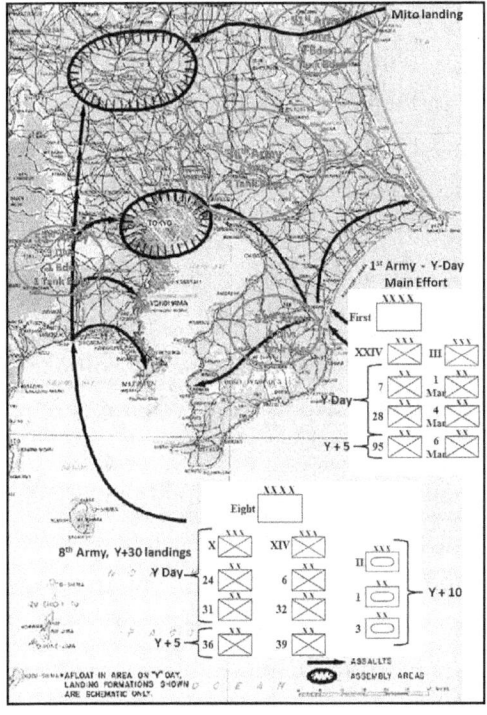

Operation Coronet Campaign Map

"Almost simultaneously, Eighth Army landed at Sagami Bay with four divisions, securing their beachhead, and is currently moving to secure the Miura Peninsula and Yokosuka naval base. A critical part of the Eighth Army's mission is to secure and establish crossing sites over the various rivers in the area, since many of the Japanese bridges will not be able to support the weight of our armored vehicles that are part of this fight. Three days from now on November 11th, the 1st and 3rd Armored Divisions of the II Armored Corps — with 230 M-4 Sherman tanks each - will land and move straight north, behind the industrial cities on Tokyo Bay to establish a blocking position north of Tokyo. Other elements within the Eighth Army are tasked to take the port cities of Yokohama and Kawasaki to provide supply points for the troops. That concludes Phase I. Do you have any questions at this point — sir?" Reynolds asked.

For a sick man, Roosevelt's mind quickly grasped the operational plan. Nodding, he signaled John with his ivory cigarette holder to continue.

"Prior to Phase II, First Army will then attack across the Kanto plain to Tokyo about December 1st to secure positions east of Tokyo. With the cold weather, we are anticipating frozen rice paddies that typically populate this area. I believe General Arnold concurs that Tokyo has already been extensively destroyed by bombing. We hope by this point they will throw the towel in."

"What makes you say that?" quizzed General Brooke. "From what we've seen, we expect them to go down fighting. What makes you think that will make them surrender?"

Marshall was ready to jump in and help his colleague from the British.

"Sir, *Coronet* is a much larger operation than *Olympic*, but the landings this past spring on Kyushu was expected to be the more expensive because all of the Japanese homeland defenses expended there. Any promised replacements to ward off *Coronet* are industrially impossible and any competent units from China have already been siphoned or sunk by us."

Hap Arnold joined the fray as well. "Several thousand Air Force fighters and medium bombers have flown from a hundred airfields on Kyushu, along with XXI and XX Bomber Commands. We've conducted a systematic aerial destruction of all industrial targets and cities. Hell, Major General Curtis LeMay's begun using phosphorus incendiaries on Japan's larger cities, creating massive fire storms and burning dozens of square miles of city each night. According to our strategic bombing chief – General Spaatz - , in just six months of bombing we've estimated to have killed between 175,000 to 200,000 people and rendered eight million civilians homeless."

FDR seemed impressed with the operation so far, but his face indicated he still wasn't quite satisfied with the answer. Marshall still was on the hook.

"However sir, if necessary, follow up operations after Tokyo are planned to be initiated in the south, central, and north of Japan with additional U.S. troops from home, as well as any Commonwealth troops our distinguished British guest care to volunteer. If the campaign continues beyond seizing Tokyo, we have a contingency to seize the next largest industrial cities with landings to take the peninsulas of Ise Bay and Nagoya, then march overland to Osaka, Kyoto and Kobe. In the north, we will conduct a landing at Sapporo on Hokkaido followed by taking the anchorage at Mautsu."

While *Coronet* was more or less on schedule, the American casualty figures were appalling even by World War I standards. Despite the lessons learned from the earlier *Operation Olympic*, the Japanese employed a few surprises on the cautious Americans. One such device was the suicide mini submarines, while another was a remote controlled device called the *"I-Go"* - basically an unmanned miniature special vehicle that would break open a passage in an obstacle. These were in addition to the constant swarm of kamikazes and suicide speed boats that harassed the invading Americans. Even with a vast number of destroyers serving as radar picket boats, Japanese plane still managed to evade; flying low and through the various mountain passes that propagated the island of Honshu.

Nor were the Japanese armed forces as prostrate as believed. Despite strategic preparatory bombing provided courtesy of the XX and XXI Bomber Commands newly fielded B-29 'Super fortresses' bombers flying from bases in China and the Marianas Island chain, augmented with hundred of U.S. Navy carrier strikes proved by the Third and Fifth Fleet's 28 plus aircraft carriers, advance army units found stockpiles of aviation fuel – enough for thousands of suicide planes, manned torpedoes and other such suicide 'crafts'.

Japanese desperation in defending the Home Islands also extended to the civilian population – through either patriotism or more likely coercion, thousands of civilians were pressed ganged into militia units, many employed as simple cannon fodder into the awaiting America guns. Far more deadly for the invasion force were the many fanatical civilians acting individually, each with explosives strapped to their bodies as a form of walking suicide bomb. These individuals would wander within the U.S. Army rear areas; find a group of G.I.s, then detonate themselves, in the process taking upwards of a squad or more down. Such action would ultimately result in the wholesale slaughter of Japanese non combatants, in many cases killed due to the failure to understand simple commands given in English, a language very few Japanese understood.

Where heavily fortified positions were encountered, both mustard gas and Lewisite were quickly employed by either mortar or artillery to subdue defenders with horrific effects. The Americans simply were not about to undergo the same arduous rigors they encountered digging put the Japanese defenders on Kyushu that past April. The unfortunate side effect was weather – winds would often carry the selected toxic gas to nearby towns and villages, contaminating water sources, while maiming or killing local non combatants. Such was the viciousness of this invasion campaign. Union General William Tecumsea Sherman said it best nearly a century prior – "War is Hell!"

"At this rate, how much longer will this campaign last?" asked a somber FDR, clearly with his eye on the massive casualties and their potential explosive impact on the American people.

Reynolds looked over to his army godfather – General Marshall. FDR's question had the hint of a political agenda and this was something John clearly wanted to stay away from. Wars were had enough to manage, but if there was a political agenda – all bets were off!

"Mr. President," Marshall began, "The Joint Chiefs want to end this nightmare as soon as feasibly possible. This is why I asked Brigadier General Groves here to discuss his '*Manhattan Project*' and the new weapons system he has under development."

All eyes within the Oval Office bore down on the portly General Groves. Many knew him from his previous assignment building the new War Department Office building across the Potomac – '*the Pentagon*' as many now called it due to the building's unique five-sided shape.

"Sir, as you are aware we are in the process of developing a uranium weapon or what many call an 'atom bomb' capable of destroying a whole city with a single blast. We have recently transferred a substance we call plutonium from our Oak Ridge research center out to Los Alamos in New Mexico where the bomb design will continue as practically possible."

"Do you have a time line of when this weapon will be available? In other words, will it be available to end the current campaign in Japan?" asked FDR.

"Unfortunately sir, we are still quite a ways out, possibly a year."

Grove's assistant, Bill Armstrong interrupted.

"Excuse me Mr. President. We are currently working on two designs; one that uses plutonium, the other using uranium. I am very confident between the two we will have a weapon by this time next year."

Roosevelt smiled. "You're quite sure of this young man?"

"Mr. President, when Bill makes a statement like that, you can take that to the bank. He's the best civilian operations manager the program has out there," replied Groves.

"Alright, so you have this 'bomb'. How are we going to deliver it?" asked FDR.

Now it was Hap Arnold's turn at bat.

"Sir, we are planning on forming a bomb group that will be specially trained to fly and deliver this weapon using a modified B-29. It's the only plane big enough to carry this uranium bomb. We'll train them here in the States and employ them anywhere in the world you and the Joint Chiefs see fit!"

"General Arnold," FDR responded, "Any idea who you have in mind to command such an outfit?"

"Yes sir, right now we are looking at a number of army Air Corp pilots who have had experience flying in the Pacific. On the top of our short list is Lieutenant Colonel Paul Tibbets."

'Tibbets,' Reynolds thought to himself, "Very impressive choice." He'd met the pilot when returning from the *Olympic* brief that past April and needed to hitch a ride on a B-29.

As Hap concluded his comments, the Oval Office suddenly became very quiet. While the immediate objectives of the meeting had been met, it now appeared there was a hidden agenda waiting to be sprung and it was Roosevelt's.

"Gentlemen, before you depart for your various duties, I need to discuss the situation in Europe. As you can tell from reading the newspapers, Hitler has stepped up his campaign of intimidation against the United States. I hate to say it, but by all accounts we have an undeclared naval war going on against the Nazis. There isn't a week that goes by where we don't have a clash or a ship sinking out in the North Atlantic. As our British friends here will attest, they are under siege and having a hard time striking back against the Germans. I am seeking your collective counsel as to what are our options?"

Marshall started. "Mr. President, we can't declare war, not now while we are in the middle of Operation *Coronet*." Many present nodded in agreement with the army chief.

Secretary James V. Forrestal spoke next. "We can take more aggressive action in the Atlantic, seek out and attack the U-Boats before they hit us."

Admiral King shook his head. "Mr. Secretary, with all due respect, if we attack and sink them undoubtedly Hitler will declare war on us and we are in no shape to deal with him, not when the majority of the fleet is in the Pacific cleaning the Japanese clocks. Let's wrap up *Coronet* as soon as possible, then we'll have Reynolds and his JCS plans team review our options."

FDR looked over at General Brooke and Field Marshal Ironside. It was apparent their hidden agenda to get the Americans in the war was not going to happen and they looked despondent.

"Gentlemen, you heard my military advisors. Until *Coronet* wraps up we're in no position to help beyond what we're presently doing. I hate to use a cliché but it appears you're going to have to carry on with that English *stiff upper lip* until circumstances change."

Coronet was far from wrapping up. Outside the village of Shimi, 50 kilometers north of Yokohoma, First Lieutenant Sam Posavec was leading his *'Baker'* Company, Ist Battalion, 53rd Infantry Regiment, across a large frozen rice paddy. The Sixth Infantry Division badly needed veterans with experience fighting the Japanese and Sam fit the bill. Rather than sit with the IIth Airborne Division back in Formosa while it rebuilt its combat power in the wake of *Olympic*, Sam, now the proud recipient of a battlefield commission, accepted assignment as a company commander within the 53rd Infantry Regiment. Good company commanders were hard to find – the average life expectancy as one fighting the Japanese was often times measured in days.

But Sam was not the typical average "shake-n-bake" officer fresh from Officer Candidate School at Fort Benning. Years with the airborne had taught him a thing or two about soldiering and experiences on Kyushu had tightened him up. He knew he might not make it through Honshu, but he was determined to save as many of his soldiers as possible.

Up to this point, 53rd Infantry followed the front, conducting mop up operations against by-passed Japanese positions that refused to surrender. These actions allowed the 53rd to achieve a slow seasoning in battle, teaching the 'green' soldiers valuable lessons of combat. Yet, many of these Jap positions were equally green — third line reserve forces barely equipped with a rifle and hand grenades, much less the heavier equipment found in more experienced veteran forces, many of which had combat experience gained from years of fighting in China.

Today, 1st Battalion, 53rd Infantry Regiment had conducted a passage of lines through its sister battalion — the 2nd - and had now assumed the main effort toward the village of Shimi. As the main effort, the Regimental Commander assigned a platoon of M-3 Stuart light tanks to 1st Battalion, who in turn assigned them to the battalion's lead company — Baker Company and ILT Posavec.

If Sam had his druthers he would have preferred heavier tanks such as the M-4 Sherman found in the armored division to accompany him. But many of the bridges they had encountered since moving inland simply could not accommodate the 30 ton weight of these tanks. Stuarts on the other hand, at 16 and a half tons, stood a better chance of being available when the going got tough, and *Coronet* was definitely that.

Up till recently the men of Baker Company welcomed the daily sight of U.S. Army Air Corps and Navy carrier planes — seeing hundreds of Army Mustangs and Naval Corsairs over the Japanese landscape making any tactical movement by them during the day towards the invading Americas — suicidal! But today's weather was anything but cooperative for the fliers. Heavy clouds filled the gun metal gray skies, giving indication of either rain or snow coming; not a welcome sight for the army boys on the ground relying on the invaluable support the pilots provided them. If the crap hit the fan they were on their own...

As Baker Company crossed the frozen rice paddy, Posavec ordered three of the platoon's tanks to move forward on a road that patrolled the company's advance, having them function as a screen to his right flank. He anchored his weapon's platoon on this left to provide cover while his first platoon led them towards a small clump of woods to his direct front.

'If the Japs were going to be anywhere, it surely would be in the woods,' he thought to himself as the company slowly moved forward. As 1st Platoon closed to fifty meters there was still no contact – the silence was surreal except for the clanging of the soldiers' poison gas protective gear.

"Ripper 16, this is Ripper 6 – I want you to send a squad over and quickly check out wood patch to your direct front – over," Sam instructed his 1st Platoon Leader, 2LT Quin.

"Roger," Quinn replied, and within seconds, 10 soldiers rose and raced over the 50 meters to the ominous, yet quiet patch of green.

Just as the squad approached the woods, machine gun fire suddenly erupted, but not from the woods as anticipated, but from Sam's left flank, approximately 150 meters to his 10 o'clock.

"It's a God damn bunker!" he cursed, finally finding its position by the repeated burst of Japanese machine gun fire. "I have just the cure," he said as he reached for his radio.

"Phantom 5, this is Ripper 6," Sam called over to the lead Stuart tank.

"Ripper 6, Phantom 5 – over," the tank platoon leader replied.

"I have a job for you – from my 10 o'clock, 150 meters, I need a bunker busted – over!"

As Baker Company hugged the earth, Posavec watched as the platoon's two lead Stuarts turned sharply to the left and began to dart across Baker's front towards the enemy bunker, still emitting its deadly spray of lead in search of soft infantry targets. Within seconds Baker Company's troubles would be over for the moment.

The two tanks moved quickly across the frozen rice paddy, firing their coaxial machine gun towards the bunker in an attempt to force the Japs to keep their heads down.

'Boooomb.' The sound of a cannon erupted, echoing across the landscape. The Company continued to keep their heads down.

'Wait a minute,' Sam thought to himself. 'That's not a Stuart's signature fire.' As he raised his head, a second 'booomb' identical to the first again echoed across the rice paddy. Slowly he rose to see the remains of the two Stuarts in flames, one missing its turret. From the size of the flames, there couldn't have been any survivors.

'Holy shit,' he thought. Grabbing the mike, he called the tank platoon leader.

"Phantom 5, this is Ripper – what the hell happened – over!"

The silence that answered Posavec could only mean one thing – Phantom 5 was either dead or too seriously injured to reply.

"Any Ripper element, this is 6! Anybody see where that came from?"

2LT Quinn came on the air. His voice betrayed an air of panic typical of that found in a new 'Butter bar' second lieutenant.

"Sir, it came from that patch of woods directly in front of me. Looks like a Jap anti-tank gun. What do you want me to do?"

'What do you want me to do?' Posavec thought to himself wondering what type of platoon leader he had inherited. "16, this is 6 – what is your status over?" he asked Quinn.

"Sir, I have two wounded, and two who I think are dead," the shaken Lieutenant replied.

Sam slowly scanned the company's direct front. Pretty clever of those bastards; normally, a Jap 47mm AT gun couldn't do squat to an American tank if firing towards its direct front, but by tricking them with the machine gun firing off to the side in order to get them to expose their thin side flanks towards the wood, the tanks in essence became as vulnerable as tin ducks at a shooting arcade.

"Screw'em," he said, switching the frequency over to their direct support artillery.

"Bad Ass 55, this is Ripper 6. Fire mission, Jap AT piece direct front, Grid Yankee Papa 23627858. We are 100 meters south – over!"

It took a few seconds to call in the artillery fire mission that seemed an eternity.

"Ripper 6, this is Bad Ass 55 – splash over!" Within a heartbeat, everyone within the area could hear the faint but distinct multiple thumps of artillery fire – American 155mm heavy artillery.

Sam yelled out over the company radio, "Incoming – get the hell down!"

Fifteen seconds later, the earth erupted into vast fountains of flying dirt, as if a giant shovel had scooped up a large acre of earth into the air, only to flip it over and let it fly.

Rising up, the Baker CO could see that most of the rounds landed in the area between 1st Platoon and the tree clump. If Quinn hadn't crapped in his pants by now, that volley surely would have helped.

"Splash out! Add 50 – fire for effect!" responded the Lieutenant. Now the fireworks would truly get going.

Twenty second later, Posavec once again heard the radio utter "splash over," immediately followed by a distant but longer announcement of multiple thumps, sounding as if everyone was listening to the Almighty's heartbeat. Five, four, three, two, one - booom, booom, booom! For 45 long seconds, Baker Company was treated to a rare glimpse of hell! As the company clung to the ground dirt, debris, and ice from the rice paddies rained over their positions.

Crouching cautiously, Sam raised himself high enough to see a direct hit on the Japanese antitank gun, watching it not only be hit by an American artillery round, but fly high into the air courtesy of its ammunition detonating as well. 'Good riddance,' he thought guessing no enemy soul could have possibly survived that hit.

As the artillery fire let up Baker Company began to collect themselves and their equipment. Almost immediately Sam ordered his 1st and 2nd Platoons to quickly move and occupy what remained of the clump of wood, now a mix-ture of broken and burning tree limps and brush. As the platoons established a hasty defensive position, Sam was glad to hear the remaining two Phantom tanks decide to join the program. He quickly dispatched them to eliminate the bunker, which they did quickly but cautiously; each tank moving and covering the other. Once within a 50 meter range four rounds of 37mm high explosive ensured that the Japanese troops occupying the bunker joined their brethren anti-tank mates.

1st and 2nd Platoon speedily scrambled into the remains of the broken woods, taking cover behind any foliage and broken tree trunks available. The remains of at least a squad of dead Japanese soldiers, many torn and twisted into distorted shapes, littered the immediate area generating a stench of burnt human flesh. A few of Baker Company's soldiers vomited at the horrible sight.

Once the two platoons were set in a hasty position, Sam called to his weapons platoon.

"Ripper 36, this is 6. Need you to move up and join us at the woods – over."

"Ripper 6, roger. Be there in a jiff!" the platoon leader replied back.

Booom, boom, boom! That sound heralded the tell tale arrival of Japanese mortars, usually followed by the counterattack. Apparently they weren't through with Baker Company, at least not yet.

"Holy shit sir! Here they come!" yelled a rifleman.

Posavec moved over to the edge of the tree line to see for himself.

"Oh my God!" he said to himself. There, racing across the 200 meters of open frozen rice patties they came – dozens of Japanese soldiers, screaming 'Banzi' towards the bewildered Americans, transfixed at this awesome spec-tacle about to befall them.

"Open fire! Fire everything you got!" Sam yelled at those soldiers within earshot. Within seconds, Baker Company quickly came to their senses and began firing, throwing a wall of lead at the advancing human tidal wave.

Grabbing his radio, Sam called out to his weapons platoon.

"36, this is 6 – over your asses here fast or there won't be anything left!"

"6, this is 36 – roger" the platoon leader huffed back.

By this time the Americans were feeling the effects of mass Japanese fire all over their positions; sounding much like an angry hornets' nest buzzing about a picnic area as rounds impacted or ricocheted off the broken trees.

But Baker gave as good if not better than it was receiving. In the 50 meters the Japanese had crossed, clearly a third was dead in their tracks, a testament towards the accuracy of the American infantryman and his rifle. Yet still they came, continuing to yell 'Banzi' as if that alone would scare the Americans away.

The Japanese mass continued closing in. Suddenly 37mm high explosive tank fire, mixed with .30 cal machine gun fire, was added to the fight courtesy of the remnants of the Phantom tank platoon.

'Thank God for the damn tankers,' Sam thought, seeing another dozen Japanese fall with each volley fire from the two Stuarts. Time for another taste of deadly American artillery.

"Bad Ass 55, this is Ripper 6 – over!" Posavec heard nothing, not even static that typically is heard while awaiting a reply. All around him the continual 'swish-thud' of bullets striking the ground or 'ping-ping' of them whizzing around their heads meant if he didn't find help soon he and Baker Company were goners.

"Bad Ass 55, this is Ripper 6 – over!" Sam again yelled into the mike. Again, nothing. As he picked up the radio to move to another position, he suddenly noticed three holes in the back side of his radio - .30 cal rounds that could only have come from a Jap light machine gun. He threw the radio down and knew that Bad Ass wouldn't be coming to the company's rescue this time.

"Here they come!" yelled 2LT Quinn. Sam turned towards the screaming lieutenant. There, at least two dozen Japanese soldiers, armed with bayonets, swords, and rifles fell upon the American position in a whirl of frenzied man-to-man combat, reminiscent of an old 'Cowboys and Indians' western movie.

A Jap soldier lunged towards Posavec trying to pierce him with his bayonet. Sam stepped to one side then pulling out his pistol, fired point blank into his attacker's head, causing the soldier to immediately crumple up like a rag doll. Within seconds, he fired point blank at five more enemy soldiers screaming all around, as if they were in a trance, oblivious that the Americans were returning fire, fighting for their very lives.

Seeing one Jap soldier bayonet a 2nd Platoon soldier, Sam took aim at him with his .45 cal pistol, determined this one was going to meet his oriental maker.

'Click.' That sound meant one thing and one thing only; he was out of ammo. As he stood there, the enemy soldier spied him as his next target, and then turned towards him with the obvious intent to bury his bayonet into the now hapless company commander standing with an empty weapon.

"Die!!" yelled the fanatical Japanese soldier uttering the only English word he probably had ever learned in his life as he raced over toward Posavec. In a moment of desperation, Sam threw the .45 caliber pistol at the charging soldier in an attempt to stop him in his tracks, but missed.

'Wham' – suddenly, the enemy soldier tumbled to the ground, dead, with an entrenching tool buried in his back just below his neck, nearly severing his head in the process. Behind him stood 2LT Quinn, bloodied and wounded in the shoulder, but still capable of enough strength to plunge the tool into the enemy soldier's backside. Posavec just stared at the two entities before him in amazement - one friendly, the other an enemy.

Suddenly, as quickly as the banzi suicide attack started, the silence that now surrounded them indicated it was over, and they were alive.

Looking around, both Posavec and Quinn saw dozens of dead Japanese troops scattered about, some in heaps two to three deep.

"Cease fire," yelled Posavec, only to realize his voice was barely audible.

"Sir, did you say something?" responded Sergeant Kingman, a section sergeant within 2nd Platoon.

Clearing his voice, he again yelled out, "Cease fire! Count off, who's still with us?"

After 10 minutes, 110 soldiers sounded off alive, 83 didn't. Posavec stood still listening to the silence that had descended on their position, trying to comprehend all that had taken place over the past 15 minutes. The sound of a track squeal, belonging to a Phantom Platoon M-3 Stuart tank moving into the unit's defense position brought the Baker Company CO to reality.

"Sergeant Kingman," Posavec barked out, "Grab a detail and get these Jap dead out of here. Put'em into a pile and set it on fire if you have to. Quinn! Get the weapons platoon set up around the perimeter. I want to be ready for the next counterattack if it comes."

Quinn acknowledged then saluted Posavec, holding it in place until his CO returned it.

As Sam returned the salute, he looked Quinn straight in the eye.

"I owe you one," the Baker CO responded, "now find me a radio and let's get this mess cleaned up."

Both officers knew that this was just the beginning of what was going to be a long campaign. Would the Japanese run out of troops and patience before the Americans?

Chapter 19

A Whole New Ball Game

Fact: At precisely 5:30 a.m. on Monday, July 16th, 1945, 18 year old Georgia Green was traveling in the front seat of a car next to her brother-in-law, Joe Willis. They were 50 miles north of Alamagordo, New Mexico driving north along Highway 85. Joe was driving her down to Albuquerque for an early morning music lesson. As they passed the town of Lemitar along the empty stretch of highway, a flash of extraordinary brilliance suddenly filled the landscape. Georgia grabbed her brother-in-law's arm. "What was that?" she cried out in shock. Joe started at her reaction for a brief minute in stunned silence because his sister-in-law Georgia Green was blind! At that very moment with the detonation of America's first atomic bomb, the Nuclear Age was born.

"The Japs are asking for an invasion, and they are going to get it. Japan will eventually be a nation without cities — a nomadic people."
- Vice Admiral Arthur Radford, 1945

"I told the President that a so-called negotiated peace was impossible in this kind of war where one side was fighting for civilization and the other side represented barbarism; there was no common meeting ground and there therefore necessarily had to be a fight to the finish; that a fight to the finish meant a long, horrible contest where we needed all the manpower that we could summon."
- Henry L. Stimson, diary entry, January 1945

Apartment 209,
4701 Connecticut Ave, NW, Washington D.C.
0635 hrs, 2 February, 1945

Harry was up earlier than usual this crisp, cold Washington morning. He stepped outside his apartment in search of the Washington Post and into the freezing blast of arctic air typical for this time of the year. But he soon realized the newspaper must have already been scooped up inside and went back in quickly. Despite living in this spacious residence nearly four years he still had problems getting used to the size of the five room apartment at a cost of $120/month and the amenities available to him, plus he was also still adjusting to the ins and outs of Washington D.C., even after 10 years.

'I tell you, things were never like this back home,' Harry thought to himself as he entered the kitchen and quickly found the objective of his search – his newspaper - along with a tepid cup of coffee recently poured by his wife who'd heard him getting up. By this time she had already dressed and was at her job as an office clerk in the capital, while it appeared his daughter was already up and off to class at George Washington University.

Grabbing the newspaper and cup of coffee, he strolled into the living room and settled down to digest the past day's news. Washington was always a town that lived for news and rumors; both in plentiful supply these days. The only way he was going to find out what was going in this big town was in the *Post*.

Lately the *Washington Post* had consisted of a full spectrum of information from the current situation in Europe ranging from Great Britain weathering the fall of rockets from the Nazis, to the Germans once again taking the offensive in North Africa. In the Pacific, after three incessant months of heavy fighting on the island of Honshu, it appeared the United States had finally broken the back of the Imperial Japanese Army. Three weeks ago, U.S. Army units had seized the Imperial Palace in Tokyo – albeit without capturing Emperor Hirohito and the rest of his royal family. But this set back was only temporary, for one week later a battalion from the 53rd Infantry Regiment, Sixth Infantry Division, captured the royal family dressed as peasants traveling towards the interior in a cart. With the Emperor in U.S.

custody, Hirohito opted to save what remained of his country and issued a 'call to surrender' speech over the radio. Each day brought mixed results; some Japanese units took heed of their leader to surrender – others continued the struggle, ultimately meeting their end in a tragic, inglorious manner similar to the countless million other Imperial Japanese Forces throughout Asia. All this on top of five million Japanese civilians dead and thousands of square miles of countryside contaminated with various concoctions of deadly chemical agents.

'Looks like the formal surrender is scheduled to take place this Friday the 9th aboard the USS Missouri,' Harry read to himself, feeling proud the surrender was taking place on one of the largest battleships in the U.S. fleet – a ship named for his home state.

As he finished the newspaper, he realized he was running behind schedule and needed to get dressed quickly. As he started to tie his signature bowtie, he stopped and looked at himself in the mirror. A year ago he had been a powerful senator, head of a major committee fighting waste and mismanagement in the war effort. But since last fall's election Harry now felt he was just another bureaucrat in a city filled with them doing a worthless job. Looking at his reflection he drew his breath in with a sigh and finished his tie. A knock at the front signaled that his driver, Tom Harty, was right on time to drive Harry to his job downtown. He grabbed his hat and coat and headed for the front door when the phone rang.

'Damn, who the hell wants me now at this time?!' he thought to himself as he set his hat and coat down to let Tom in, then reached for the black ringing irritation in the living room.

"Hello, can I help you?" Harry asked in an irritated mood.

"You sure can Harry," the voice replied. "You can pick up the tap for lunch today at the Senate dining room over at Capitol Hill. Don't tell me you forgot about it?"

Harry smiled once he recognized the voice at the other end.

"B.K. Wheeler, you ol' Montana rascal you, of course I didn't forget. I still owe you for all those times you bailed my ass out years ago starting in 1935 when I first got to this detestable place." Harry was referring to Senator Burton K. Wheeler, his good friend ever since those days 10 years agowhen he arrived on Capitol Hill as a freshman senator. Wheeler had taken a shine to the young novice and showed him the interworkings of pre-war Washington D.C. as well as where all the skeletons were buried.

"Good, see ya at 11:30 a.m. sharp. Don't want all those Republicans stealing all the Navy Bean Soup!" Wheeler said, and then hung up. Harry smiled, grabbed his coat and hat, then headed downstairs with Tom to his black Mercury limousine. Outside by the car Harry was greeted by George Drescher, a Secret Service man who had the dubious honor of being the first such agent ever assigned to protect the nation's Vice President.

Right on schedule, Harry found himself at the appointed place, grabbed himself a tray and started through the buffet line. The Senate dining room was more than a cafeteria for the country's senators to eat — it was a place where backroom deals were consummated, voting alliances forged and friends betrayed. Every time Harry came to dine, he thought that one day he might find a statue of the Roman Senator Brutus, who brutally assassinated the Roman leader Julius Caesar at the steps of the senate, as a reminder to those who thought they are in control of the Republic.

Senator Wheeler was waiting at the end of the line just as Harry approached to pay.

"Mr. Vice President," Wheeler asked, "Are you trying to skip picking up the tab 'cause I'm late?"

Harry smiled, "Come'on, grab a tray and git on over and join me at that table. I don't have all day to fuss about much as I'd like to."

The two sat down and caught up on the business of the Hill; pending bills and legislation, latest congressional gossip, and finally, the discussion on the President himself — FDR.

One thing Harry Truman immediately recognized was Wheeler's passion against Roosevelt. The more Truman listened, the more he was convinced Wheeler thought FDR was a bigger threat to the nation than Hitler.

"Harry, I tell you, he's a no good lying son-of-a-bitch, just trying like mad to get us in a war with Germany now that we've licked the Japs fair and square!" Wheeler thundered. "What's he planning to do with the army and Navy now that we've won the war in the Pacific?"

Truman looked Burton square in the eye. "I can't tell you 'cause I don't know anything going on over there in the Oval Office. Other than routine stuff and ceremonial things, being the Vice President is one of the most worthless jobs I've ever held. The President pretty much keeps me in the dark as far as national strategy goes. Hell, I only was sworn in a little less than two weeks ago."

Wheeler frowned upon hearing this disappointing news from Truman. "Ya know, the old man is pretty sick and his days are clearly numbered. Are you prepared for that big day when it comes?"

At that moment, Harry briefly thought back to FDR's recent State of the Union speech, where he sat behind the President during its delivery. Throughout the speech, Roosevelt constantly threw out ad libs and side statements, making it one of the most poorly delivered speeches he ever made. At that point Roosevelt's very apparent frailty made Truman convinced that the President would not last through his fourth term.

"If the day comes, the day comes. I'll just have to make the best of it — God willing!" Harry fired back, feeling a little disadvantaged at his apparent vulnerability.

"All right Mr. *Vice* President," B.K. as his friends referred to him, quizzed on, "What are you going to do about that whole mess in Europe once you're in charge?"

Truman knew from past dealings that Wheeler was an adherent isolationist and an *'America First'* Committeeman.

Truman smiled at the challenging question. "I think you've heard me say about four years ago that if we see that Germany is winning we ought to help Russia and if Russia is winning we ought to help Germany, and that way let them kill as many as possible, although I don't want to see that son-of-a-bitch Hitler victorious under any circumstances. But until that time comes, I think we'll leave those Europeans to sort out their own mess! Hell, as far as I'm concerned, they brought it on themselves. Now if Hitler decides to tangle with us, then that's a different story all together."

Wheeler smiled; apparently Truman and he were still more or less in sync with foreign policy as it pertained towards dealing with Europe – hands off for the time being.

"Did I tell you Harry, my favorite cousin Tom decided to join the Navy. Thought it might make a man out of him."

"Well, I can tell you as a former artilleryman in the Great War, being under fire in France has a way of making a man out of you quicker than a Missouri mule shooing off a fly. I truly feel sad for all those tens of thousands of soldiers and sailors lost over there in Japan during the invasion. A true tragedy if ever there was one!"

The two sat in silence and finished up their lunch. At one o'clock Wheeler looked at his watch.

"Well Harry, time to go back to the chamber and see what kind of sausage we're making for legislation today. It's a pleasure seeing you back here on the Hill, even if it's only been a couple of weeks!"

Harry smiled at the compliment, then stood up and shook his former mentor's hand. While he did miss the camaraderie of his fellow senators, he didn't miss the slime associated with backroom dealings. He had been exposed to plenty of that back in Missouri. Putting his hat and coat on, he trudged over to his old office at the Senate Office Building to see what was going on. If he was lucky, he might even get a chance to go over to the White House, visit his boss and get a chance to see what he thought of the war…

✬ ✬ ✬

Across the Atlantic in northern France, a Wehrmacht train pulled into the station at the town of Rouen, France. Off in the distance, the passengers could view the famous 4th century Rouen Cathedral, with all its high gothic architecture on vivid display on this clear but cold February day. Also on display front and center of the station's platform was the escort entourage of staff officers and drivers, courtesy of Lieutenant General Bernatz and his XV Panzer Corps Headquarters.

"Hopefully lunch is the first thing on the agenda," the head of the Wehrmacht's inspection team, Major General Henning von Tresckow told his attached operations chief, Colonel Stauffenberg. "I hate to inspect anything on an empty stomach!"

With the war on the eastern front set at an armistice, OKW at Hitler's behest began the titanic rebuilding of the Wehrmacht from its losses suffered in the campaigns to date, most notably the campaign against the Soviet Union. Concurrently vast resources of labor and building materials were pouring into northern France to construct the ultimate Atlantic Wall; one that stretched from the Bay of Biscay up to Denmark.

But this was not to be a wall in name only consisting of just simple coastal defenses, obstacles and shore batteries. Hitler was most explicit with the OKW General Staff on how this fortified zone was to be engineered, based largely on his recollections and experiences as an infantryman in the First World War as well as his close up inspection of the French Maginot Line back in late 1940. To make sure all agencies of the Reich were behind this project, special inspection teams were formed to assist where needed in alleviating bureaucratic turf wars, so as simple as eliminate commanders who didn't quite share the same enthusiasm for the project as Der Führer.

One such team that was drawn up was Team #14, lead by Major General Tresckow, who had handpicked his 25 members that comprised mostly of engineers, logistics, and special operations soldiers. To cap it off, Tresckow borrowed Stauffenberg from the War Ministry to serve as his Operations

Officer. As liaison to OKW, Stauffenberg recommended Colonel Massar, which Field Marshal Keitel agreed to for only a short duration. In that manner, Massar as the eyes and ears of OKW would only receive that information Tresckow and Stauffenberg felt the General Staff needed to know.

Officially, the inspection team was to ensure that resources were properly used, local labor was procured, and construction timelines met. Unofficially, Tresckow had a hidden agenda and the true reason he had volunteered to lead this inspection team was to solicit and recruit army members into the conspiracy to remove Hitler, a list growing longer each day thanks largely to Himmler and the SS.

Since the army's return from Russia, Hitler thought it was time to purge the armed forces of commanders and officers who he felt were not fully behind his National Socialism, or performed cowardly on the battlefield. Many of the senior officers, such as Field Marshal von Kluge, who had been injured in an auto accident in October 1943 as the Army Group Center was preparing to withdraw, were simply pensioned off to retirement onto confiscated estates provided by Hitler as gifts. Other officers weren't quite so lucky, instead receiving a summons or a visit at night by the Gestapo, only to disappear in the vast maze of Nazi bureaucratic prisons or concentration camps. While not as dynamic or as well publicized as the dreaded "Night of a Thousand Knives" where Hitler eliminated his brown shirted '*Sturm Abteilung*' or 'SA', this time the practice was more subtle, conducted quietly behind the scenes.

As Team #14 departed the train, a senior officer with the rank of Colonel approached Tresckow and his group and saluted.

"Good afternoon, Herr General, I am Colonel Kiesel, General Bernatz's Chief of Staff. The General sends his regards and his regrets that he is unable to meet you in person due to some enemy activity he is personally taking care of."

Tresckow looked at Stauffenberg and Massar. "Enemy activity? Really, what's going on?"

Kiesel responded. "Last night, a British commando unit landed within our sector, apparently to sabotage a radar early warning tower recently erected. The General is personally hunting these bastards down as a message to send to both the British and the local French resistance elements that wish to hinder our efforts."

With that, Kiesel escorted Tresckow and the team to a number of assembled and waiting staff cars, where in a short bit of time, they raced over to the XV Panzer Corps Headquarters, approximately 20 kilometers outside Rouen, located well within the French countryside.

The seven car convoy sped down the dirt roads turning past an army checkpoint towards an imposing château that clearly had to be 500 years old.

"Welcome to the XV Panzer Corps Headquarters," Kiesel informed Tresckow and Stauffenberg as the car approached the château's covered entryway. Nearby, a German army ambulance was parked with four soldiers on stretchers near its open rear doors; two were British, while the identities of the other two were covered up with white sheets.

"I can tell you General Bernatz is back, as indicated by the captured commandoes, and is probably in a good mood," said the Chief of Staff.

Within seconds of the convoy's arrival, the entourage was escorted into the château's main entry parlor, down the vast hallway, into the headquarters' conference room, where the inspection team found Bernatz on the phone.

"Ya, ya, Herr Field Marshal. Tell Der Führer I nipped this action in the bud. I have captured all of them, along with their equipment. How many? Five captured, two wounded, and two dead. Very good, if anything further develops, I'll keep you in touch – Heil Hitler!"

Tresckow uncovered his glove and extended the customary salute to General Bernatz.

"General Bernatz, it's good to see you again after that miserable time we had in Russia."

Bernatz immediately recognized the former Army Group Operations officer, recalling their first time meeting with the Field Marshal at Bernatz's promotion and award ceremony three years prior.

"A lot has happened since those days – Henning," Bernatz reflected."A lot has happened... and we can catch up when you come as my guest for dinner tonight, say 1800 hours. Kiesel will fill you in on the details, as well as have your team meet with the appropriate staff officers here in this headquarters. Now, if you'll forgive me, I have some unfinished business to attend to regarding this British commando incursion."

"Gentlemen if you'll follow me, I have lunch awaiting you in the *kanteen*," said Colonel Kiesel, directing the now famished team down the main hallway towards the smells of sausage emanating from within the building's kitchen.

Later on that afternoon, once the team was fully engaged with their counterparts, Tresckow and Stauffenberg took a short stroll along a path outside the majestic château as it could be their only chance to talk without anyone eavesdropping.

"Well Claus, what do you think? Do you think we have a chance to convince Bernatz otherwise and join our cause?" asked Henning.

Stauffenberg continued looking directly ahead. "Herr General, I don't think so – look at how he's faired in the wake of all the General Officer sackings? Three years ago, he was a Panzer Regimental Commander. Today, he commands one of the most powerful Corps in the Wehrmacht. This man loves war, and his record in Russia proves that. As long as he delivers, Hitler will take care of him."

Von Tresckow stopped on the trail and immediately grabbed Stauffenberg. "That's my point exactly. As long as he '*delivers*'. What happens to him if he doesn't deliver, if he runs afoul of Hitler? I swear Claus; this is like playing the kid's game *musical chairs*. As long as you have a chair when the music stops, you're in good shape. But if you don't, the men with the black suits come to visit."

The two continued down the path, enjoying the cold, clear sky and winter gardens surrounding the French château.

"General Tresckow, we still haven't resolved the Massar issue yet, whether he's with us or not."

"I thought that was settled – that's why I agreed to have him along on this trip. Didn't you succeed in convincing him these past few months since your recovery from hospital?" the General asked.

"Nein, Herr General, between all the convalescent time and reworking your Valkyrie drafts I haven't had too many opportunities. Those I did have, Massar was either too busy to see me or avoided me altogether. As far as I'm concerned we have nothing to worry about. If he wasn't along for the ride, he would have turned us in a long time ago."

"How can you be so sure Claus?" von Tresckow asked. "How can you be so sure?"

"Trust me, Herr General. We have far more important things to worry about than a fence sitting staff officer. Whether he wants to admit it or not, he's along for the ride in more ways than one."

That evening once dinner was completed, Generals von Tresckow and Bernatz both grabbed a brandy and cigar, then strolled out onto the patio to reminisce about their days in Russia with Army Group Center.

"How's your uncle von Kluge taking retirement?" asked Bernatz.

"Not too well, especially since he was more or less forced out for speaking his own mind and trying to save German troops."

Bernatz took a drag off his cigar, then blew the smoke into the cold night air. "Most unfortunate for the Field Marshal, but one must do what one must do to save lives."

Tresckow saw an opening and decided the moment was ripe.

"Even if it means a change of leadership; change that will save a country?" responded Henning.

The comment puzzled Bernatz, who then cocked his head at the suggestion.

"What exactly do you mean — Tresckow?"

It was Tresckow's turn to pull a drag from his cigar and stare at the stars about. After a small swig of his brandy, he turned to Bernatz.

"There are people out there who feel the same way, that we need a change of leadership or be destroyed as a race, a culture, by the Allies."

John was utterly stunned by the suggestion. He had suspected there were such traitors, but never suspected for a moment they were as close as von Tresckow, standing in front of him.

"You must realize Henning, that what you are saying is treason — high treason! You have no chance, no chance what so ever."

"How do you know Bernatz?" von Tresckow replied. "Our organization is fairly vast and wide throughout the Reich and composed of people - soldiers, politicians, industrialists, and others - who feel the same way. Think about it Johann, one day you're in the Führer's favor; decorated and promoted. The next day, you could find yourself up against a wall because of a stray rumor, innuendo, or gossip courtesy of the Gestapo. Is this how you see the future of Germany? At least with Hitler gone, we have a chance to negotiate with Great Britain and end this mess!"

John reached up to his throat to adjust his collar, touching his prized Knights Cross with oak leaves and swords. He had heard through the military grapevine he was going to be presented with another award in recognition of his actions against the commando incursion from the previous day. If he threw in his lot with the conspirators, all he had achieved or could advance in the present regime could be lost.

"Very intriguing words Henning, very intriguing," said Bernatz, knocking back his brandy. "So what do you want from me — to join?"

"I want to know if you're willing to join us," replied Henning. "Are you with us or against us?"

Bernatz placed his glass down on the table, then once again reached for his Knights Cross as if to reassure himself it was still there.

"I'm afraid you've made a mistake with me, Herr General. You and your people might have problems with Der Führer, but I don't. In case you haven't read the paper, look around. We are winning this war. We have modern weapons like rockets that are pounding the British to pieces. We have forced the Russians to quit the war, and we are preparing to slaughter the Americans when they decide to join the allies by the tens of thousands. No, I cannot join you and your group. If anything, I owe him my command and my life. Don't you recall, when you accepted your commission as an officer in the German Army, you took an oath, an oath of allegiance to the Führer?"

"I don't need to be reminded of the past. Who in his right mind would have elected this madman if we knew it would lead us to total war with the world!" retorted Tresckow.

"I think you do. Let me remind you and I quote *'I swear by God this sacred oath that to the Leader of the German state and people, Adolf Hitler, supreme commander of the armed forces, I shall render unconditional obedience and that as a brave soldier I shall at all times be prepared to give my life for this oath.'* Do you recall these words General Tresckow?"

Tresckow was not prepared for confrontation, least of all from Bernatz.

"I have a loyalty to Germany and to its people!" Henning replied. "If you don't want to join us, fine! I would greatly appreciate your discretion in this matter."

Bernatz looked Tresckow square in the eye. Silently, both could tell from the other they were totally committed to their cause and were unwilling to give in.

"Tresckow, I'm going to forget this conversation ever occurred for the sake of your uncle, the Field Marshal who I greatly respected. I would not want to bring any shame to him mentioning this to the Gestapo."

Tresckow finished his brandy, replaced the glass on the table, then crushed out his cigar on the patio grounds.

"I believe our informal business is concluded, General Bernatz," stated Henning. "My team will finish up in a couple of days and then be out of your hair, and trust me, I won't bother you again. I'll pass on your compliments to the Field Marshal the next time I see him." He turned and left Bernatz by himself in the cold, starry night while he returned to his guest room.

High over the afternoon skies near the Salton Sea in southern California, five B-29 *Superfortress* bombers approached a practice target bombing area. Throughout the trip, crews repeatedly practiced their long range navigation and target approach skills in hopes of placing their practice bomb within a 300 foot radius concrete ring. Of the five, only two carried a special practice bomb; a bulbous shaped, 12 foot long, 10,500 pound practice bomb filled with cement, plaster, sand and water to replicate Composition 'B' which the crews referred to as 'pumpkins'. The other three planes came along to photograph the bombing approach and drop for after action review purposes. Visual bombing, by use of the secret Norton bomb site, was the group commander's preferred technique for bombing, especially from 30,000 ft. Previous test runs by the group had discovered that use of high altitude radar bombing had yielded poor results, with a typical crew having only a one to two percent chance of hitting a 1000 ft radius circle.

The lead plane, call sign '*Victor-82*', was typical of the new brand of bombers equipping the 509th Composite Group as they were called. She was a brand glittering new beautiful plane with a large '82' adorned on her side and a big black arrow on her tail. These planes could fly faster, farther, higher, and carried a bigger bomb load than the standard U.S. Army Air

Corps' bomber workhorse currently employed – the B-17 *Flying Fortress*. On the ground, *Victor-82* was as tall as a three story house with four massive Wright R-3350 Duplex-Cyclone engines – the most powerful radial aircraft engines produced in the United States to power this aerodynamically perfect weapon of war to whatever target was selected to meet its destruction.

"Form up into approach formation," the group commander radioed *Victor-82* and the following plane *Famous Glory*. Within seconds, the change in engine tone indicated the planes were descending to their assigned bombing attitude of 30,000 feet. The clear desert skies yielded the sight of the massive Salton Sea, 10 miles dead ahead. At the northern edge was their target, an inconspicuous concrete circle in the midst of sand and scrub.

"Go for it," radioed out from the command B-29.

Victor-82 leveled out, opened her bomb-bay doors, and within seconds, the large bulbous inert bomb descended, causing the plane to lift with the release of the large load. Following closely behind, *Famous Glory* mimicked Victor's exact actions, shortly later releasing her 'egg' onto the southern California desert. All the while *The Great Artiste* filmed every second of their 'pumpkin' drops. Once *Famous Glory* delivered her payload onto the ground, the signal was given for the group to fly the four hours back to Wendover Field.

It was 6:00 p.m. and dark when the last B-29 landed and taxied over to the ready area. Once the ground, jeeps were on standby to pick up the crews and take them over to the special hanger for debriefing, while a special photographic crew rapidly developed the film shot by *The Great Artiste* for use at the debrief. For the crews' relief, hot chow was available for them in the building adjacent to where they would be debriefed.

After two hours, the crews watched the effects of their practice bombing run with the group commander. *Victor-82* hit just inside the circle, but *Famous Glory* missed the circle entirely by approximately 100 meters.

"Gentlemen," the commander began, "you have got to put your entire focus on delivering that bomb within that circle – period! I am not settling for near misses, or that clumsy cliché – *Close enough for Government work!* You were all handpicked for this group and assignment. If you can't get it right within the next two week, you're out of here! Now are there any questions?"

Captain Ed Donovan, commander of *Famous Glory* raised his hand in response.

"Sir, what exactly is the big deal? The war with Japan is over, and I heard they're shipping folks home and discharging them."

The group commander was not amused. "Well Donovan, in case you haven't read the papers, I haven't seen the Germans going home, and you never know what will happen if they get in a real shooting war with the Navy in the Atlantic. Just focus on the bombing and let the Generals worry about what they have in store for us. Understood?"

Donovan replied with a weak, "Yes sir". It was late and the crews had had a long day. In two days, they would be back at it again and again until they could hit the circle with the pumpkin.

As the commander dismissed the flight crews, the Operations Officer, Major James Hopkins entered the room.

"Colonel Tibbets, here is the schedule and assignment of tomorrow's practice crews."

Colonel Paul Tibbets had a lot of work still ahead of him to get the 509th ready for whatever mission the Joint Chiefs of Staff had in store for the group.

✦ ✦ ✦

Outside the Gasthaus *Dietrich Herz* in downtown Berlin, two highly inebriated brothers staggered in the early morning light under the weight of a full nights drinking. They had not seen one another for a couple of months, so tonight was a night to get caught up on each other's lives. But the older brother had cause for celebration – he had just published his seventh book on his favorite subject and was set to make another large sum of money. What better way to celebrate than to spend time with his younger brother the business man!

They staggered into the older brother's downtown apartment, each finding a suitable place to crash for the time being and sleep it off. Within a couple of hours, they had sobered up enough that coffee and Danish were in order for breakfast.

"Ah Harold," the older brother clamored, "You need to spend more time in Berlin. I really miss you around here. It's just not that much fun when you're off on one of your business trips going to wherever you go and do."

Harold, with a slight hangover, sipped his coffee shaking his head in disbelief. "What are you talking about? With the entourage you keep, I would think you'd be at parties having all sorts of fun all the time!"

"No my dear younger brother, the folks you refer to don't do a lot of partying, so all the Party hack and cronies pretty much tend to their own selfish needs. Hitler doesn't party and never drinks at all. The biggest party horse of all is Göring. That fat man can really drink everyone under the table. I guess having all that 'fat' slows the drink down!"

"Still Heinrich, I can't get over it. After all these years, it still has to be a head rush being Hitler's official photographer. That alone must have you traveling a lot keeping up with him."

Heinrich smirked. "Well, Harold all in all, it has its up and downs. I usually get a three day to one week advance notice on where he's going, so I can prepare accordingly. Makes for hell on security and any visitors, but for me, it's not a problem. As a matter of fact, he gave me this small pocket knife the last time I saw him, about three days ago."

Heinrich pulled about a small four inch red pocket knife, emblazoned with the Nazi swastika on both sides, then handed it to Harold.

"Der Führer received that from the Swiss Ambassador last month and gave it to me as a token of his appreciation and now I want to give to you. Call it a belated birthday gift!"

Harold didn't immediately know what to say. He was utterly touched by the gift – receiving something owned by Hitler. He stood up, walked over to his brother and gave him a hug.

"Thanks brother. Thank you."

Harold put the knife in his pocket, then returned to his seat where he then finished up his half eaten Danish, then poured himself another cup of strong coffee.

"So what's your next Führer photo assignment?"

"In three days, I'm to accompany him to the new OKW Command Center in Zossen and get some pictures of him directing those freckless Generals around," replied Heinrich.

"*Zossen Command Center?* – Never heard of it. Where is it located?" asked a now curious younger brother. This was a bit of useful if not welcome information.

"The OKW Zossen Command Center is just a short hop, about twenty kilometers south of here. Quite a big place actually."

"This is fascinating. I though OKW and the High Command did all their operations out of Berlin, but you tell me they have a separate facility that commands everything – wow! Tell me more," said Harold.

"If you insist. There are actually two complexes at Zossen; *Maybach I* and *Maybach II*. The first command center *Maybach I* consists of 12 concrete structures disguised as residential houses, each 36.2 m x 16.39 m. There are three levels: a fortified underground cellar, a single ground level floor and another level in the roof; all sub-divided into rooms. The houses were hermetically sealed against gas attack should the British consider such use if they ever found out. Water is supplied from underground springs. All buildings are connected by an underground gallery. The OKW command center used to be downtown, but was transferred to Zossen in March 1943."

Harold continued intensely listening to his older brother describe this secret Wehrmacht command center and urged him on.

"The second command center *Maybach II* was recently completed as a Führer-HQ; it consists of 23 more buildings similar to those at *Maybach I*, seven of which were allocated for Hitler and his entourage. This is where I stay when I'm with him. The other buildings are occupied by army transport folks, so I don't get a chance to see any of these, and why would I? Are you interested in accompanying me for this upcoming trip?"

"No Heinrich, much as I would like to, I too have travels awaiting me. My export business is sending back to Lisbon in a week to 10 days to cut another import deal, this time regarding the acquisition of Tungsten for munitions. While I'm down there, I also plan on getting some much need sun! Berlin can be pretty dreary this time of year, and Lisbon is just the place to get some color if you know what I mean."

"Ah the life of a playboy! And you think I have the life. I might even be a little jealous of all the time you spend down there. Maybe you can take me down there sometime; after all I could use a little color too. You could take me to some of those sangria places and introduce me to a cute Portuguese Fraulein. Then we can have some serious fun, assuming Hitler could do without me for a short time."

Both had a good laugh at the prospect, then spent the remainder of the morning reminiscing of the good times they had while growing up and getting into trouble as kids, all the while consuming the remainder of the coffee and pastries.

By late afternoon, Harold had said his goodbyes to his brother, then headed off to the Hotel Europa. As he strolled down the street still slightly hung-over, he thought about the information his brother had inadvertently conveyed to him about Zossen; did the British know anything about this and what if they could take out Hitler with a massive bombing strike at just the right moment? The *Kreisau Circle* could certainly use this information to act upon at just the right moment Hitler was killed and enact their coup on the government. It had possibilities.

As he thought about it, a black Mercedes sedan pulled alongside him, with the driver rolling his window down as if to ask Harold a question. As he approached the driver, two men in dark suits sprang out from the back seat, grabbed him from behind, while placing a chloroform rag over his face. Harold struggled as best he could before fading out.

As he came to, Harold slowly scanned the immediate environment he now found himself in, all the while trying to fight off the after effects of the chloroform, which was already compounding his late night hang over. The light was dim; he could barely make out his surroundings, but from the mildew-musty smell, he ascertained he had to be below ground. As he looked up, he could see over hanging pipes crisscrossing the ceiling. A basement perhaps, but where, and more importantly why had he been brought here?

He could hear the muffled voices of people walking above him — the telltale creaking of floor boards told him there were three, maybe four men above him.

As his head continued to clear, he realized he was now a captive in someone's basement. As he looked down, he saw he was tied securely to an old wooden chair with arm rests. Escape was not on the cards at this time.

The opening of a door at the top of the staircase followed by the footsteps of two men descending heralded the start of the answer as to who was behind this kidnapping.

"Well, Mr. Hoffman, I'm glad you're accepted our little invitation to join us," the older of the two men started with a distinctly Hungarian accent. "Sorry for the accommodations, but hopefully, if you are cooperative, we can end this little inconvenience and you will be on your way."

"Alright," replied Harold "What exactly do you want from me? Is this some sort of shakedown or something?"

The two men looked at each other amused. "Ya, you might consider this a shakedown if you don't tell us what we want," the younger man quipped, as he reached into his front pocket and unveiled a six inch switchblade with the pop of his finger.

"If you want money, I have some from the business I could arrange to get," said Harold.

"We are not interested in your money my friend, what we are looking for is information. We've been following you for some time since your last trip to Lisbon and are very interested in why you visited this man," said the older man as he held up a picture of Jerry Curry in front of Harold.

"Do you know who he is?" asked the younger man, all the while using his switchblade to clean under his fingernails.

"He's a business associate. We met before the war and he and I occasionally conduct business together." Harold amazed himself at his quickness in inventing such an ad hoc cover story off the top of his head, while still with a slight hang over.

"Bull-shit," the older man responded. "Yes, he is a businessman, but that's not what he does these days."

"Well then, if you know what he does, please share with me since it's obvious you know more about him than I do," Harold sarcastically replied back.

"This is a waste of time," said the younger man. "Give me five minutes and I'll get the truth from him!"

The older man shook his head disapprovingly. "Jani put your toy away for now. We have some time with Mr. Hoffman. Doctor Shimmel from Gestapo Headquarters will be here within the hour to administer a serum that will tell us all we need to know from this gentleman. Then you can have your fun with him."

'So I'm not at Gestapo Headquarters,' Harold thought to himself. 'Why am I here then?'

The sound of the doorbell upstairs caught the attention of the two captors. The older man looked at his watch in amazement.

"Dr Shimmel isn't due for another 45 minutes. Jani, keep an eye on him while I go and see who could be visiting."

As the older man departed up the stairs, the younger man Jani began to pace back and forth across the basement floor.

"So who do you work for?" asked Harold.

"Who do you think?"

"If I was arrested by the Gestapo, we wouldn't be having this conversation here now would we?" Harold retorted.

"You're a smart man. Who do you think we are?" replied Jani.

"By your accents, you sound Hungarian; Hungarian Intelligence perhaps?"

Jani smiled, "Good for you. I told you you're a smart man."

"Then why haven't you turned me over to the Gestapo?" quizzed Harold.

"Well, you might say we are on contract. If we find out anything of interest to the Gestapo, we let them know and they pay us – handsomely of course. Good information and intelligence are worth their weight in gold, and it frees them up for mundane things like arresting and torturing disloyal German civilians and enemies of the state."

Harold leaned back in the chair in an attempt to stretch his legs. The old chair let out a creaking sound that let Harold realize this chair had been retired down in the basement for a reason.

"So again, why am I here?" Harold asked Jani again. "What is it you think I know?"

Jani again took out Curry's picture, displaying it for Harold to see.

"This man, the one you say is a *business man*, is really an agent for the American OSS."

Harold faked surprise. "Oh really, how do you know this?" he asked.

"We've had him under observation for the past year. We know that he works directly for President Roosevelt and all of a sudden, we find you having coffee with him in Lisbon. Small coincidence?"

"So I had coffee with him. I tell you he's a businessman and I might add, has helped us arrange numerous shipments of material in spite of the American trade embargo," Harold lied, hoping it might deflect Jani.

Jani grew impatient, reached into his pocket and grabbed his trademark switchblade and snapped it open, then approached close to Harold, waving it within inches of his face.

"This Dr. Shimmel. His drugs may or may not work. I might not wait for him, but start with cutting the information out of you one finger at a time, starting with your right hand. How does that sound to you?"

Jani looked Harold square in the eye, their foreheads just inches apart. "Ya, how would you like that *smart man?*"

Harold saw his chance. As a former rugby player, he instinctively head butted Jani squarely across the bridge of his nose, causing him to fly back against the back wall. He appeared out for the moment.

Leaning back on the chair again, Harold attempted to lift both him and the chair in the air, then slam down against the concrete floor, which in turn resulted in the chair collapsing into a dozen wooden fragments.

Reaching into his pocket, he found the pocket knife Heinrich gave him, then immediately began to cut the ropes around his legs.

Jani began to stir, still groggy from his head butting, and now displaying what appeared as a broken nose, but this didn't stop him from seeing his captive was nearly free.

Harold finished freeing his legs as Jani made a move to recover his knife, lying half way between the two. He immediately lunged at the young Hungarian. The two men scrambled across the floor, each trying to recover the instrument that would mean the others demise.

Jani grabbed the knife, but before he could use it against Harold, he felt a sudden painful sensation across his neck, just below his left ear.

Harold was instantly blinded by the fountain of red fluid rushing from the Hungarian's neck, as his pocketknife found its intended target; Janis' jugular.

As he stood up, he could see Jani attempting to stop the rhythmic geyser of blood, now pouring all over the basement floor.

"It will all be over in a few minutes my friend," he said, as he picked up the switch blade, wiping Jani's blood off the device. As Harold predicted, the young Hungarian fell back on the ground, dead to the world, life still oozing from the three inch slit in his throat.

Scanning the basement Harold immediately seized upon the coal shuttle doors near the back end. He scrambled up the loose pile of coal until he reached the door, which he quickly unlocked and opened up to the clean, crisp early evening air. Night was beginning to descend on Berlin and with it, the blackout conditions Berliners had come to expect of the past couple of years. These very blackout conditions most Berliners came to hate became the covering cloak that would protect Harold's escape into the night.

Running a mile down the road, he hailed a taxi and instructed the driver to take him to the Hotel Europa then to the train station. As the taxi sped down the now darkening boulevard, Harold knew his first and foremost act was to get out of Germany – alive and fast, before his late acquaintance and his older colleague decide to get the Gestapo get into the act. It would be a long time before he would see his brother Heinrich again, if ever.

Three weeks later, Jerry Curry was hastily called over to the Oval Office for an impromptu afternoon meeting with FDR. Also present was the newly appointed Secretary of State Edward Stettinius, Secretary of War Henry Stimson, Secretary of the Treasury Henry Morgenthau, General Marshall, Admiral Knox, and General Donovan of the Office of Strategic Services – "OSS" for short. Also present was Dr Ross McIntire, the president's personal physician and then Surgeon General of the U.S. Navy. Since the November election, FDR's physical decay was plainly evident even to non-physicians. To all present, the President had noticeable weight loss, brought about by a severe case of anorexia as well as his custom of obstinately obeying a rigid diet.

"Jerry, come in my boy, and join us," FDR motioned for his advisor to take one of the open seats on the couch next to Secretary Stettinius. "We were just discussing post war Japanese policy and I thought you might be interested in sharing your views on the topic. General Marshall and Admiral King were bringing me up to date on the wrapping up in the Far East. Please precede gentlemen."

Marshall placed his reading glasses back in place, picked up his briefing notes and continued.

"Gentlemen, as I said earlier, we have interned approximately 500,000 Japanese soldiers with no issues or incident to date. In China with the assistance of Chiang Kai Shek's Nationalist Forces, we have accepted the surrender of approximately another half a million Japanese soldiers from their Kwantung Army. We've also sent troops into Korean and accepted the Japanese surrender of forces there as well. For the time being, we're using these troops as 'policemen' under our control until the State Department can organize a local government."

"I'll bet with the surrender of the Japanese Army, Chiang must be having an absolute field day over there," said Curry, sipping a cup of coffee.

Marshall continued. "As a matter of fact, with a sizable American troop presence along the coast and key cities complete with supplies and equipment, the Nationalists have literally thrown themselves against the Chinese Communists — damn near destroying them in the process. Mao has taken what's left and fled to the far western hinterlands, as far from Chiang as he possibly could get."

"How about in southeast Asia, how are wrap up operations going?" asked the President.

Marshall turned to King – it was the Chief of Naval Operation's turn to brief.

"Well sir, since we took over the Dutch East Indies a couple of years back, we've set up a provisional government there for lack of any real Dutch colonial government, not that the people are real crazy about having them return. Currently, the Brits have returned to Malaysia and Burma, and a naval contingent is on its way to reestablish control of Hong Kong. The Aussies are in control of New Guinea and don't plan on pulling out anytime soon. Other than that, we control all the remaining real estate in the Pacific basin."

Roosevelt seemed satisfied, nodding his head in approval. As he reached over to pour himself a glass of water, he suddenly erupted into an uncontrolled spasm of coughing, growing in intensity with each cough. His color, grayish and gaunt on a good day, became reddish, no doubt brought on by his already sky high blood pressure.

Dr McIntire, FDR's now ever present physician was ready. Once the spasm seemed to subside, he quickly gave Roosevelt a couple of pills, quickly followed by a glass of water he poured while the President was hacking away. Within a couple of minutes, FDR's color returned to the paltry gray and he was now in control of his functions. To everyone present, the show was a shocking reminder and a clear message that his days were limited, with many present wondering where the Vice President was and how soon he could be read in on the current situation.

Apologizing for the unforeseen outburst, Roosevelt asked King to continue.

"Well Mr. President, the only thing left on the official agenda is the occupation of Japan itself. Basically General MacArthur flew into Atsugi on January 30th and set up temporary Supreme Allied headquarters at Yokohama. Also on the 30th, Yokosuka Naval Base was taken over to provide a convenient facility to support future naval undertakings. We still don't have the official plan yet from MacArthur's Supreme Command of Allied

Powers Headquarters, but we expect it anytime now. The biggest problem will be feeding the millions of homeless civilians that survived the carnage. A great deal of the countryside is laid waste and highly contaminated due to all the chemical munitions used against their armed forces and militia. This stuff will be around for a long time."

"So, what do we care?" chimed in Secretary Morgenthau. "Japan has always been a threat to our trade, our friends, especially the Chinese, and our security since the turn of the century. I have plans ready to implement that basically calls for Japan to be dismembered, partitioned into separate independent island states, stripped of all heavy industry and forced to return to a pre-Industrial Revolution agrarian economy. It's due justice for a war making society such as theirs and I am looking forward to converting that area that isn't contaminated into a country primarily agricultural and pastoral in its character."

"I completely disagree," stated Secretary Stimson. "It's barbaric what you propose, even if they did start the war. We need to win the peace, and what you propose is something out of the Punic Wars."

As the two cabinet secretaries began their heated argument, FDR's phone light indicated he had an incoming call. As he picked it up to answer, his secretary Grace Tully informed him he had a confidential caller on line one. FDR's somewhat upbeat mood of the afternoon quickly disappeared.

Covering the mouthpiece, FDR announced to the assembled guests they would need to please leave the room for a few minutes including his personal physician. As the distinguished visitors stood up and silently departed, FDR motioned for Jerry to remain and pick up the phone extension in order to listen in. While the departing dignitaries wondered who the important caller could be, Jerry immediately guessed their identity. When the room was clear, Roosevelt responded that it was safe to talk.

"You should be very proud Mr. President; you have your victory in the Pacific, but the purpose of this call is to remind you that you should not get any ideas of getting involved in Europe. Just as quickly as you mobilized our armed forces, you can easily demobilize. We have no business in Europe and I just wanted to remind you of that."

Roosevelt was flushed. He hadn't heard from his blackmailer in nearly six months, each time playing the blackmailer's game to the limit, but by this time he was a tired, old man.

"I hear you, but what makes you think I haven't had the FBI put a trace on this line?" he bluffed hoping to shake up his mysterious caller.

"Be my guest," the caller retorted. "I'm sure the FBI would be very interested in what I have to tell them. In fact, you would be doing me a service and who knows how far the publicity will go. At any rate, as a warning, I know everything you do, so don't think you can be cute and try to pull the wool over my eyes!" And with that the mysterious caller hung up.

Curry and FDR stared at one another as two powerless mortals, in charge of the greatest armed force seen in the world today, yet unable to get out of the situation the President had placed himself in some four years prior.

"Have our guests come back in," FDR asked Curry, who immediately departed to the outer office to signal their return. Once they were all seated, he asked General Marshall if that concluded the agenda.

"Well sir, the formal agenda is concluded. We will take your guidance and coordinate it with the Joint Chiefs and the War Plans Division," replied Marshall.

"And I'll see that the other cabinet secretaries also get a back brief on our little session here," added Stimson. "But there is a 'white elephant' in the room that we do need to talk about Mr. President."

Roosevelt as best as he could, sat up in his high backed wheel chair ready for his Secretary of War's final comment. '*What now?*' he thought to himself, still drained by his blackmailer's latest reminder.

"Franklin," Stimson began, "We need to discuss the situation in Europe in general, and dealing with the Nazis in particular. Whether you like it or not, we have the equivalent of an undeclared naval war going on in the North Atlantic. American boys are dying by the week in U-boat attacks, and yet, the press is tepid."

Curry quickly jumped in to defend FDR.

"Sir, you can't be serious. We still have things we need to accomplish in the Pacific before we undertake such a massive action." Curry was lying of course. The present size of the U.S. armed forces mobilized against the Japanese was more than capable of handling the situation in the North Atlantic.

"That's utter bullshit Curry and you know it," responded Stimson. "Hell, we have all sorts of forces stateside just waiting for deployment to the Pacific. We can just as easily shift them as well as a portion of the fleet. Isn't that correct Admiral King?"

"Well, technically, you are correct," answered the Admiral, but King was no fool. He wasn't any more interested in assisting the British with their present predicament than Hitler himself.

"It would take the better part of four months to withdraw pieces of the fleet from Japanese waters, give them a quick overhaul at any one of the west coast ports, them redeploy over to Norfolk."

FDR raised his hand, a telltale signal he was going to provide the final word.

"Gentlemen, I am not prepared to discuss the situation in the North Atlantic at this time. We will carry on with the way we've been conducting business at present. You must remember, I am fully aware of the situation and how the majority of the American people feel about our getting involved in another European war *at present*. Do I make myself clear?"

Try as he might the majority of those present in the Oval Office were not convinced by Roosevelt's comments, with many wondering *what was going on and why?*

As the assembled group began to leave, FDR asked General Donovan to stay behind for a few minutes.

"Bill," FDR asked, "What's the latest bit of information or intelligence about the anti-Hitler groups? Are they doing anything considering the amount of material we've provided them to date?"

"Well Mr. President, we do know that they have made a number of attempts on Hitler's life; all unsuccessful."

"What about anything from 'H'?" asked Curry? "Everything he's told me I've passed along to your folks in New York."

Donovan reached into his uniform pocket and pulled out an envelope, withdrawing a short message.

"Jerry, this is from Allen Dulles in Berne. Seems your contact had to leave Germany rather suddenly, somehow getting a message to Dulles's place last week. We don't know if he's OK or not, nor do we know where he is, but he did inform us he's alive somewhere in occupied Europe and he provided us the location of the German OKW Command and Control center, located outside Berlin. This is a strategic bit of good news."

'H' was been found out,' Jerry thought to himself. *'My one contact throughout the war is now on the run in Europe.'*

"Tell me Bill," asked FDR, "Just how strong are the Nazis in Europe today? What are your contacts telling you about what's going on in the occupied countries?"

"Mr. President, from what the British have provided us, it's not good. They are constructing a massive fortified zone 40 miles deep along the Atlantic coast from the Spanish border all the way to Denmark. If we do get into the war, invading occupied Europe will be carnage on a scale I can't hazard to guess. We can get to Britain, that won't be a problem for our Navy, and once we're in, we can assist the Brits with strategic bombing; but a cross channel invasion is clearly out of the question."

Roosevelt sat back in his chair crestfallen. On one hand, his cabinet and conscience were advising war against the Nazis, but common sense, coupled with his current situation told otherwise. It wouldn't be too long before political pressure demanded he either declare war, or demobilize the army and navy.

Before Donovan and Curry's eyes, the President once again began another coughing spasm, this time laced with saliva, flem, and blood.

Curry quickly ran around the Chief Executives desk to help Roosevelt where he could, pouring him a glass of water, while Donovan raced out to the outer office to fetch Dr McIntire. As McIntire entered, FDR endured one massive coughing spasm, then passed out. McIntire quickly checked for a pulse, then tried unsuccessfully to revive him, while the two witnesses wondered if this was it.

"He has a pulse, very faint, but he's still alive," said McIntire. "I've got to get him to a hospital and fast."

Within 15 minutes, an ambulance was on its way to Walter Reed Army Hospital with the stricken President, still unconscious.

As Donovan and Curry watched FDR depart, both wondered what would happen next.

"General, I'll go inform Eleanor what just occurred as well as inform the Vice President and the cabinet. Would you go inform the Joint Chiefs of Staff?" Curry asked the OSS Chief.

For one week, Americans sat by their radios pondering the condition of the nation's thirty second president, hoping for the best, but expecting the worst. None were more concerned than Harry Truman, who like every other American, was praying nightly for Roosevelt's recovery.

At 1:37 p.m., February 24th, the phone rang at apartment 209. Truman was home listening to music with his daughter Margret, while Bess was out shopping.

Harry reluctantly picked it up, fearing the worse.

"Harry Truman here," he answered.

"Mr. Vice President, Jerry Curry here. It grieves me to inform you that at 1:05 this afternoon, the President succumbed to a massive coronary and has passed away. You are now the thirty third president of the United States."

At the same time, the door bell rang. While Truman was on the phone with Curry, Margret went to answer it. Standing in the doorway were two tall men, one introduced himself as Greg Cornell from the White House, the other was Truman's Secret Service man George Drescher. Margret quickly asked both men in, wondering what was going on.

As she escorted the two men into the living room, Harry finished his call with Curry.

"What's wrong Dad, what's going on?" she asked.

"Ma'am," Drescher began, "President Roosevelt passed away about an hour ago. Your father is the new President of the United States."

Truman still really hadn't absorbed the full impact of the call. Yes, Roosevelt's condition was bad, but he really didn't think it would have come to this, not now.

"Mr. President, we need to take you over to the White House to be sworn in," said George. "Greg Cornell is here to assist you where ever he can."

As Truman grabbed his coat, hat, and family Bible, it started to sink in that he was now the nation's new Chief Executive.

"So what do you think Mr. President?" asked Cornell as they entered the awaiting limousine.

Truman sat looking out the car window at the leaden gray Washington skyline.

"Well boys, it looks like it's a whole new ballgame..."

While Truman was sped off to the White House to accept the Presidential oath of office, a large convoy, 35 ships in all, code named BX-45, was departing Boston for Halifax, Nova Scotia, then on to Liverpool. Standing on the bow of the USS Suffolk as it gained speed clearing the harbor, Seaman Tom Dandridge watched the lights of Boston twinkle against the shimmer of the old bay. He was his first mission he wrote to his uncle – an esteemed senator from Montana, and he was filled with excitement at his first visit to Halifax as well as trepidation at his first voyage. Little did Tom know that he would never see the lights of Halifax nor Boston again.

Chapter 20

The End Justifies the Means

Fact: By May 1945, the Manhattan Project's Oak Ridge Enrichment Facility had produced approximately 15 kilos of weapons grade U-235, yet bomb designers required a little over 65 kilos to make an atomic bomb. This caused the Manhattan Project officials to express reservations about the insufficient amount of uranium available to make such a bomb. Testing the 'device" would consume an entire years worth of produced enriched uranium, yet President Roosevelt had authorized the test as petitioned by the Los Alamos scientists.

Coincidentally, on May 14, 1945, after nearly one month at sea, the massive German submarine U-234, at 294 feet long and 22,000 tons fully loaded, was intercepted by the destroyer USS Sutton south of Newfoundland Banks. The U-boats' captain, Lieutenant Johann Fehler, had recently found out the war in Europe was over and he opted to surrender his boat to the Americans. Prior to this action, the U-234 carried two Imperial Japanese Naval officers; Lieutenant Commander Hideo Tomonaga (a leading Japanese submarine designer) and Lieutenant Commander Genzo Shoji (an aircraft expert), who both committed suicide upon hearing of the submarine's pending surrender and were subsequently buried at sea. Sutton's crewmen boarded the ship and redirected her to the Portsmouth Naval Shipyard.

On board it was discovered the U-boat contained two dismantled ME-262 jet fighters, as well as ten gold lined barrels, each labeled 'U-235', containing 560 kilograms of highly enriched uranium – 1,235 pounds in all - along with wooden barrels of 'water' and infrared proximity fuses. None of the crew, with the exception of Lieutenant Fehler, knew of the significance of the barrels on board. Also on board was German Luftwaffe Lieutenant General Ulrich Kessler, the former commander of special bombing and attack wings, based in Norway. Within days of the ship docking at Portsmouth, the barrels mysteriously 'disappeared' most likely finding their way to the Manhattan Project's Oak Ridge diffusion plant. It has been calculated that it would have yielded approximately 7.7 pounds (3.5 kg) of U-235 after processing, approximately 20 percent of what would have been required to arm a contemporary fission weapon. America now had sufficient uranium to build the bomb later known as 'Little Boy'.

"I remember when I first came to Washington. For the first six months you wonder how the hell you ever got here. For the next six months you wonder how the hell the rest of them ever got here."
"The atomic bomb was no 'great decision'. It was merely another powerful weapon in the arsenal of righteousness."

- Harry Truman, 33rd President of the United States

The Presidential Oval Office
The White House, Washington, D.C.
1035 hrs, 15 April, 1945

In the days since his was sworn to the presidency in the wake of Roosevelt's death, President Truman continued to struggle with the situation he and the nation now faced. With Roosevelt's death, the presidency had transitioned to a man who had no deep experience in foreign affairs, diplomacy or military matters beyond the rank of reserve colonel. For all of FDR's faults, the President had maintained a tight control on all aspects of leadership, especially as it pertained towards fighting the Japanese and supporting the British against the Germans.

Truman's days were spent in Roosevelt's basement 'map room' consumed with reading the various diplomatic cables spawned by FDR in directing the nation's energies; war production, strategy, diplomatic, intelligence and the intrigue that came along with it. When seated at Roosevelt's Oval Office desk handling affairs of state, he felt befuddled – as if the former President's ghost was mocking him. When it became too much he asked his administrative assistant to remove Roosevelt's navy prints and personal effects from the office.

What Truman couldn't remove, at least not at this time, was FDR's cabinet – wartime advice was something he would need if the situation with Nazi Germany was to boil over; something many now expected. Over the course of the transition, each of the various cabinet secretaries visited Truman to offer their advice to the baffled Chief Executive, so for the moment they would remain. Those that did visit found the new Chief Executive very snappy, wanting quick answers to his questions in contrast to Roosevelt's long drawn out soliloquies. Truman's approach to his presidency would be as crisp as his double-breasted suits and bow ties. Clearly, he was a different type of leader, especially for those Cabinet members accustomed to having things pretty easy.

Also to remain in position for the moment was Jerry Curry. When Roosevelt passed away, Curry thought his job was done. After FDR's funeral, he began the process of packing up his belongings in the White House and looking for suitable lodging elsewhere, possibly even returning to his business in Kentucky. But just like the other cabinet folks, Truman liked Curry, even took a 'shine' to his direct, unvarnished style of advice – so untypical for Washington. Truman asked Curry to stay on for a few months longer in order to "get my feet wet" and get his new administrative assistant – Greg Cornell - up to speed on White House operations.

As Truman continued his reading 'homework', Curry wandered into the Oval Office to see whether Truman required anything since he was heading over to the Pentagon for an informal meeting with General Marshall.

"I have to ask ya Jerry!" Truman erupted, "how the hell did Roosevelt keep such a lid on everything? As a Senator and as the Vice President, I had no idea all this was going on behind the scenes from the American people. You might as well stick around, General Donovan and his OSS folks have a short 'cloak and dagger' briefing for me in about ten minutes. I'll need you to tell me whether the General's pulling my leg or not."

While they exchanged small talk about growing up in small rural towns, Alonzo brought the morning's edition of the *Washington Post* into the Oval Office; his faced indicated the lead story was not good news.

"*Nazi subs score big victory, sink 15 ships and 3 US Navy Destroyers!*" Truman read out loud. "Tell me Jerry, we have the largest navy in the world and we can't deal with the buzzards out there!" he howled, "Why did FDR put up with this?"

Curry knew the answer, but didn't know Truman well enough to share the dark secret with him. But it was strange though; in the nearly sixty days since Truman had assumed office, FDR's mystery caller had not uttered a word, nor made his blackmailing presence known with the new president. Curry could still recall his voice as if it was yesterday when he delivered his message that in all likelihood caused Roosevelt to have his coronary. Right now, a blackmailer was the last thing Truman needed to deal with, especially one who held the keys to FDR's skeleton closet.

Right on time for his appointment, Major General '*Wild*' Bill Donovan informed Truman's appointments secretary Matthew Connelly, of his appointment to provide an intelligence briefing with the President. As Connelly ushered Donovan into the Oval Office, Truman asked the distinguished OSS chief if he minded Curry sitting in on the classified brief.

"Well Mr. President," began Donovan, "here's the current situation as we have analyzed it. In the Pacific, most of the former European colonies are discovering the pitfalls of putting a government together have settled just fine. We've seen this in particular in the Netherlands Indies, which is now called Indonesia. Korea is also doing well. The Brits have moved back into Burma, Malaysia, and have their bastion in Singapore up and running. Meanwhile in Indo China, Chinese Nationalist Troops have occupied the northern part of the country, setting up shop in Hanoi, while the Vichy French are more or less in control of the remainder of French Indochina; but unless they reach some sort of accord with the Vietnamese, we are predicting the French will have their hands full in a short while."

"Outstanding," the President responded, "shouldn't be too long before we have most of our boys home soon. How's his majesty General MacArthur doing with Japan?" It was apparent to both Curry and Donovan that Truman cared little for the five star general now running the occupation of Japan.

"Well, the Joint Chiefs basically approved the plan, and we are sending large amounts of material to assist in decontaminating the country side. It will take years Mr. President, and no doubt until the fields are decontaminated, we will have the responsibility of feeding the Japanese people."

"Jerry, make a note for me to talk with Morgenthau and Stettinius about this at our next cabinet meeting." Curry quickly wrote the President's comment on his note pad.

"Now General," Truman said as he sensed the OSS Chief was winding down, "we need to talk about this." He handed Donovan the front page of the *Washington Post*.

"I've seen it Sir," Donovan replied. "I'm afraid you need to talk with Secretary Forrestal or Admiral King. If you'll forgive me, navy operations are a little out of my league."

The General's comment lightened the mood within the Oval Office, but Truman still had his concerns.

"General Donovan, we are on the verge of war with the Nazis. From the OSS viewpoint, how does this situation stack up if I am to declare war on them?"

Donovan sat back in his chair for a moment to ponder the question. He wasn't really prepared to fully answer, but everyone at the OSS had been thinking about it for the past month.

"Well Mr. President, here is my opinion. If you declare war, there's no question we will clear the whole Atlantic of German U-boats – no question at all! It will not be easy as Admiral King will assure you, but it can be done, in a manner similar to what we did in the First World War. There is also no question we can bring a number of Army Air Forces over to Britain and start a strategic bombing campaign against the Germans in much the same manner we did against the Japanese, but ..." and Donovan went quiet.

"But what General?" asked Truman?

"Sir, but what do we do once we have the army in Britain? Our sources inform us, and it has been collaborated by the British, that a cross channel invasion into France is tantamount to suicide on a massive scale. Even by the luck of the Irish we get ashore, by even the most conservative of estimate, we would have a forty to fifty mile fortified zone to bore through which I know the Army G-2 has already briefed you on before. The casualties would be staggering; on a scale making the 375,000 we lost last year in Japan seem paltry. Hitler's had a couple of years to plan and build this 'Atlantic Wall' on the anticipation of our eventual entering in the war."

"So General, what are our options? Without getting into the War Plans details or the Joint Chiefs business, what are our options?"

Donovan was getting a little uncomfortable, squirming from one side of his chair to another, and all the while rubbing his right hand over his mouth as if he were looking for the right words.

"Well Mr. President, as I mentioned if we go to war, we can attack across the English Channel from staging bases in England. Another option is to attack Europe through North Africa, coming in from the south. The British Prime Minster, Mr. Churchill, has always been a fan of this concept, but in the end this will get us into war with Vichy France as well as Italy."

Truman sat back contemplating the options. His facial expressions yielded distaste for all presented so far.

Donovan continued. "Or we can sit back and bombard Germany, eventually pounding it to pieces. It is a crap shoot though. From what we have gleaned from our contacts, the Nazis are developing all sorts of 'wonder weapons' and have a few in production now, such as giant bombers, and jet aircraft. One look at London confirms they have missiles. I suspect they are as far along the atomic research program as we are. On the other hand, maybe the army or the people will eventually overthrow Hitler. We do know there are a few resistance groups in the Reich. Isn't that what Roosevelt had you doing for a bit Jerry? You had a number of groups in Germany you and Allan Dulles had contact with."

Truman looked over at Curry. "I didn't know that," he said. It was another example of something Roosevelt failed to inform him about.

Over the next thirty minutes Curry explained to Truman about his contact Harold and his various trips to London and last year – Lisbon, coordinating the delivery of material and support to the more prominent resistance groups in Germany, ending with his being compromised last fall to the Gestapo.

"Last I heard a couple of months ago; he was trying to escape Germany," Curry finished, slightly depressed at the apparent loss of his friend.

"Well maybe not," Donovan inserted. Opening his coat, he pulled out a message and opened it.

"I just received this earlier today from our London embassy, but it appears your friend Harold made it safely to London. I was saving this for the end of the meeting, but I can't think of a more appropriate time."

Curry's face lit up like a little boy at Christmas – *Harold was alive after all,* he thought. *Hallelujah!*

"Does this still have a chance?" Truman asked the two men.

Donovan shook his head disapprovingly. "Not by itself Sir. Our reports indicate since the armistice with the Soviet Union, Hitler has been conducting a lot of housekeeping, with a lot of our former contacts arrested and sent to special concentration camps. Just last year, the head of the German Abwehr, Admiral Canaris, was arrested with the Abwehr merged into the SS Intelligence system. They're still there, but have gone down deep."

Truman looked over at Curry. "Do you think your contact; this Mr. Harold, could contact them if we need to?"

Curry shrugged his shoulders. "I can't answer that Mr. President until I talk with him. He is a man of unusual talents and capabilities, and does have an impressive list of contacts *if they haven't been compromised at this time.*"

"All right Jerry, it's off to London with you. I have to tell you though, I'm not like Roosevelt in sending all sorts of special envoys and troubleshooters out all over the place, undermining the Secretaries of War and State, but in this case, I'll make an exception. I want you to ask this Harold if he's still willing to work with us should we get into the war," said Truman.

"Yes, Mr. President. When would you like me to go?"

"The sooner the better. Also pay a call on Churchill and let him know I haven't forgotten him. He's already called me about four times over the past seven weeks working me over like a salesman trying to sell a housewife vacuum cleaner."

At that moment, the white-haired, blue-eyed Secretary of State Ed Stettinius popped his head into the Oval Office.

"Private meeting, or can anyone join?" the smiling Stettinius asked.

"Nah, you can come in Ed, hell I was just about to call you on a matter I want you to pursue, based on our little conversation here that we're just wrapping up," replied Truman.

Stettinius entered the room and closed the door behind him. "Yes Mr. President, what can I do for you?"

"Ed, I want you to draft up a message to the Germans, informing them of my intention of cutting off diplomatic relations. I am not going to let that jack booting son-of-a-bitch run ramp shod all over the North Atlantic. Next, I want you to set me up with an appointment with the Senate Majority Leader, Nick Fletcher, as well as the Speaker of the House, Sam Rayburn, and see if you can make it for this week sometime. I need to talk to the both of them about options, especially if I'm going to ask Congress for a declaration of war against those buzzards over there."

Curry was shocked at what Truman uttered. He could tell Donovan was trying to take it all in stride, but was also overwhelmed at the potential course Truman was taking the country to.

"I'd better get going Mr. President," said Curry as he grabbed his hat and headed for the exit.

"Good luck my boy!" replied the President. "Unless things get out of hand, I'll try and hold off any big decisions until you get back from your meeting."

High over the North Atlantic, a special Luftwaffe airplane was conducting a reconnaissance training flight. The plane was a Junker-390, code named 'Honey Bee', and was one of two massive six engine prototypes flying on mission out of a secret airbase near Oslo, Norway. In command of the 'Honey Bee' was Luftwaffe Major Frtiz Spangel, a seasoned veteran of the Battle of Britain as well as two years combat in Russia. Serving as his co pilot was Captain Hans Pancherz, a test pilot ultimately familiar with the development and testing of the Luftwaffe's massive aircraft.

Junkers Ju 390 V1

The two men and eight others had been airborne approximately sixteen hours and after flying through intermittent cloud cover the crew was getting antsy.

"Major, we should be within sight of the target within a few minutes," chimed in the aircraft's navigator, Lieutenant Strossel.

"Roger," replied Spangel. "Are you sure you'll be able to recognize it? How long has it been since you were last there?" he asked.

"I lived there for about ten years before coming home to the Fatherland," replied the confident navigator. "I would recognize that place anywhere!"

"Pancherz," said Spangel "I'm going to take her down to 6100 meters (20,000 feet) and take a quick look."

As Spangel descended, the crew's ears began to pop and stomachs churn with the sudden drop in altitude. All views outside were obscured with the whitish swirl of clouds as if the plane were flying inside a light bulb. After a couple of minutes, the crew of the Ju-390 broke into clear air. Twelve miles before them, laid out in all her beauty and magnificence, was the target of their mission.

"Strossel, get over here and confirm whether we're in the right place," cried Spangel over the intercom. In s matter of seconds, Strossel was up in the cockpit. Even he was taken in by the sight that awaited him.

"Oh Mein Gott," the navigator uttered into his intercom. "Herr Major, allow me to introduce you to New York City!"

"How can you be so sure?" replied Pancherz.

"Look down there, by that large wharf. See the little island between the wharf and the larger island. That my friend is the Statue of Liberty, as clear an indication my navigation brought us to the right spot!"

The three flight officers observed with awe the 'Big Apple' for as long as they could within the cramp confines of the Junker's cockpit. For Major Spangel and Captain Pancherz, the sheer size and brilliance of the city was more than either had ever seen before, far grander than Berlin even before the war.

The 'Honey Bee' over New York City,

"Okay, enough sightseeing gentlemen, we have work to do!" Spangle reminded everyone before their return sixteen hour flight. As Strossel returned to his station, he flipped a switch that activated two high aperture, wide angle cameras. At last, they would be able to complete their mission of photo reconnaissance, with New York City as their target. For the Luftwaffe, it would be proof that if this mission could be accomplished, a bomber delivering a special package was possible. When completed, Spangel and the crew of the *'Honey Bee'* would have flown for 32 hours and proved to the High Command of the Luftwaffe their ability to pilot the massive bomber 6,000 miles to whatever mission she was assigned - even possibly the much rumored German *atomic bomb*.

By the end of the week, the German Embassy in Washington was formally notified of Truman's severing of diplomatic relations, giving the embassy staff one week to clear out and head back to the Fatherland.

In Berlin, the German Foreign Minister, Joachim von Ribbentrop, was hardly surprised at the American reaction. He and most of his ministry staff had expected it for the past six months and had even drawn up contingency plans to deal with the crisis. After briefing Hitler, the Foreign Minister retaliated in a similar fashion and limited the movements of American diplomatic personnel in Berlin to within the city limits.

Whatever the dour mood of the Americans in Berlin at their predicament, the British, and Churchill in particular, were ecstatic.

The American's were half way to declaring war, Curry thought upon hearing the news. The day before after visiting the U.S. Ambassador John Winant, Jerry Curry stopped by 10 Downing Street to bring Churchill up to speed on how the Americans were now conducting business under its new President, all the while surveying the damage brought about by the German V-rockets. Over the course of the meeting Churchill realized Truman was not the same manner of fellow as Roosevelt, who Churchill found could be swayed by passionate commentary or past colored experiences with the Nazis. Churchill also found his most dangerous act was to overplay his hand while the Americans deliberated what course of action they would undertake now that Imperial Japan had been vanquished.

That afternoon, Harold was at his much loved pub, enjoying his favor pint of ale. As he sat back awaiting Curry, he reflected how close he had come to capture, using many of his aliases to escape through Spain to Portugal, then on to Britain. Yet, in all the intrigue of his evasion from the Gestapo, he had rather enjoyed the battle of wits with his pursuer. While it was now certainly dangerous traveling in occupied Europe, he was able to easily outwit the bureaucratic and dim witted border police and security forces. It was such an embarrassment to them, he really wondered whether his brother knew he was working for the Allies or not.

While sipping his ale, he happened to glance across the pub at a young demure woman with long brown hair, sitting alone at a table reading a book. As he tuned into what the lovely lass was saying he realized she wasn't British, but American. The more he studied her, the more he realized how beautiful she was, unlike any women he happened to have been with for years. He just had to get to know her, find out all he could about this beauty, but how?

"Hey buddy, is this seat taken?" came a voice over his shoulder, causing Harold to come back to reality from his sudden daydreaming.

It was Curry, a few minutes late for their meeting. Curry pulled out a chair, sat and then signaled the barmaid for a pint.

"Thank God you made it out of there," Curry said, grabbing Harold's shoulder more as a sign of relief than as a greeting.

Harold sat back in his chair in a manner that displayed little concern what-so-ever. There he was, cocky, alive and well, sitting right next to Curry.

"It really wasn't that bad getting out. If you have enough money or attitude, you can get out of anything," he said. It was BS, but Jerry didn't know that.

"Well, I for one am glad you made it out, safe and sound," replied Curry, "and I might also add, so does my new boss, President Truman."

Harold took another sip of his ale. He remained focused on the woman, with Curry sitting just to one side.

"So what's going on with the new president?' asked Harold. "Is it more of the same ol' shit, or are the Americans finally going to get into the act?"

Curry grinned at the comment. "For now, the wheels are rolling. No doubt you've probably heard from your sources we've broken off diplomatic relations with the Nazis."

Harold nodded, even though this was the first he had heard of it. He was not about to let Curry know he was in the dark.

"So how does this affect me?" Harold asked. "Why should I care?"

"Well, because it's no longer a case of 'if' but 'when' and I think in a matter of days, maybe weeks. But make no mistake - we are getting in, especially since we've defeated the Japanese. If that's not enough, you said it yourself; if we don't get in, it's only a matter of time before those 'wonder weapons' will completely flatten Britain and they use them against us. We've already seen the new submarines and the rockets. If what you said in Lisbon last year is true, they should have an atomic bomb before too long."

"Okay, so what does your president have in mind for me this time?" asked Harold.

"We want you to go in one more time, assess the state of the anti-Hitler resistance groups, in particular you folks within the *Kreisau Circle*. We need to ensure that whatever they're planning, we can capitalize on it. Hopefully, you can convince them to time their actions around us, and you're the best source to ensure this success. Our OSS man in Switzerland, Dulles, will equip you with whatever you require; papers, money, explosives, radio – the works. He'll arrange passage through Vichy France while we still have relations with them."

Harold was intrigued at the prospect of sneaking back into occupied Europe. He had played the security folks for fools once and he knew he could do it again. In the back of his mind, he knew he couldn't allow the Germans to win this war, not at the cost already paid or the cost yet to bear.

"Can I get back to you on this?" he asked Curry. "When do you need to know?"

Curry downed the last of his ale. "Don't take too long. I have roughly another day here and then I have to get back to Washington. I have to get over to the embassy, so give me a call at this number with your decision and we'll fix you up from there."

Curry stood up, left two quid on the table, then departed.

Harold noticed the young lady had departed, but left her book behind. He immediately went over to her vacated table to see what was of such interest.

'The Art of Rabbit Raising' - now that is a peculiar unusual subject for an American to study in London during war. Harold thumbed thought the book, viewing the various pictures of rabbits found within, as well as the mysterious woman's notes written inside the well worn book.

"Excuse me, but I believe you have my book," said the shapely brown haired woman, who suddenly appeared out of nowhere.

"Err, excuse me. You left this here and I was making sure the barmaid didn't pinch it," Harold stammered, caught completely by surprise by the object of his attention. He immediately handed the book back to its owner.

"So tell me, if you'll pardon the ol' movie cliché, what's an American gal like you doing studying 'rabbit raising' in the middle of London during a war?" asked Harold.

The young lady smiled at the question.

"This isn't the sort of opening line one would expect upon meeting a man in a pub, but if you would like to know, it's a hobby of mine back in California where I come from. I'm here in London taking a one time course at a veterinarian college just around the corner. I would have finished if it hadn't been for the damn war. Looks like I'll have to finish my classes back in the States."

"Well, before you go back and at the risk of being forward, can I buy you a pint?" he asked, motioning the young lass towards an empty table.

"Well, I guess one drink couldn't hurt," she said as she pulled out a chair and sat down.

"My name's Harold."

"I'm Kathryn, but you can call me Kate," she replied.

Within a minute, a barmaid brought two pints of ale, while the two strangers sat down and attempted to cobble together a conversation. To each other's surprise, they found out they had a number of things in common.

They talked endlessly into the evening hours, oblivious of the time that had passed. To the casual observer, the two of them appeared to be very smitten with each other, as Kate and Harold thoroughly enjoyed each other's company, telling stories of their upbringing, schools and places they had traveled.

"Excuse me," the barmaid interrupted much later, "but if you don't mind, we're closing up."

The two of them looked at the clock hanging over the fire place – 2:00 a.m.– closing time!

Harold settled the tab while Kate waited outside.

"Can I see you home?" he asked, not wanting the night to end.

"I would like that," she replied, looking into his eyes and reaching for his hand. "I can't tell you home much fun I've had tonight or when the last time I've enjoyed the company of someone since coming to England."

Harold squeezed her hand in acknowledgement as the two walked the dark English streets very close together.

After what felt like a short stroll, the two arrived at Kate's flat, a nondescript building in an otherwise common looking portion of the city.

They looked into each other's eyes, neither wanting to make the first move to end the idyllic night. Then, slowly moving together, they embraced, becoming two people now hopelessly falling in love.

As they held each other looking into the night sky, their moment of bliss was abruptly interrupted by the sudden loud boom brought about by an explosion, possibly an errant V-2 rocket fired from the continent, causing the surrounding apartment windows to rattle and crack. London was still not a safe place to be.

The couple soon heard the sounds of British fire engines racing down the darkened streets towards the source of the explosion, bringing both to reality of the here and now.

Kate looked up at Harold. "This is why I have to go home," she said, looking away.

"When do you leave?" Harold asked.

"Tomorrow afternoon," she replied, trying to hold back her sense of disappointment. "I'm sailing on the S.S. America, heading for my home in Long Beach, California."

Suddenly, a second, more distant explosion passed through the neighborhood.

"If only this madness could end. If only it would go away..." she said. Kate turned, and then headed for her front door, leaving Harold behind, alone on the street.

Harold watched her disappear behind her door, saddened, knowing that as long as the war continued, the two of them could not have a future together.

Perhaps, he thought, *something can be done...*

In the week following Curry's departure to London, Capitol Hill was the focus of intense congressional lobbying action, with legislatures lining up either for or against going to war in Europe. While the decision to go to war against Japan in the wake of Pearl Harbor three and a half years earlier had been fairly straight forward, going to war against Germany was another matter. For many Americans, it was déjà vue, eerily reminiscent of April 1917, when Germany's unrestricted submarine warfare brought the United States into the First World War; the memory of how that conflict ended and the ramifications that followed in the wake of the flawed Versailles Treaty haunted the nation.

In order to measure how much congressional support he could muster with the 79th Congress, President Truman set up a meeting with two of the hill's most influential men: Senator Kenneth McKellar, President Pro Tem of the Senate, and Congressman Sam Rayburn, Speaker of the House of

Representatives. Both argued that while a declaration of war was possible, it was not guaranteed. The Democrats held the majority in both houses, but this was also the case in 1917. Less than four years following America's entry into World War I, that majority would vanish like a snowflake in hell, returning the Republicans to power.

Truman nominated April 25 as the date he intended to go to 'the Hill' and make his case, working up till that point on his speech to Congress. The day prior, he asked his old friend, Senator Nick Fletcher of South Carolina to join him in the Oval Office for a chat over 'bourbon and branch'.

Fletcher was the stereotypical *good ol' boy* from the heart of the Confederacy – South Carolina - with southern roots as deep as a palmetto tree. His family had fought for the southern cause during the Civil War, which struck a sympatric chord with Truman, whose family came from a Missouri confederate heraldry. In his mid thirties Fletcher went into politics, eventually reaching the statehouse where he served as Governor for 20 years before running for the Senate. He had been in the state capital of Columbia for so long, people still referred to him as 'Governor' years after he left to serve as a U.S. Senator in Washington.

It was late afternoon on the 24th when the 'Governor' stopped by the Oval Office.

"Come on in you ol' rascal," Truman announced as he came from behind his desk to shake Fletcher's hand. "Can I fix ya' an *eye opener?*" he asked.

In a heavy southern twang, Fletcher responded with, "How about the usual if ya' don't mind Sir."

Fletcher toasted Truman on his presidency, congratulating him on having made it so far without having screwed it up – such was the nature of their relationship, which is why Truman often sought the 'Governor's' political advice.

"Nick, tomorrow I'm going up on that damn hill and asking for a declaration of war against Hitler and his damn Nazis. I know most Americans are getting fed up with his thumbing his nose blatantly at us, sinking our ships and killing our boys, but why the hell am I getting all sorts of grief from everyone about going to war against the Germans?"

Fletcher swirled his drink around a few times, watching the ice form a mini-whirl pool before knocking back a chug.

"W'all Harry, something y'awl need to consider. The first question you have to answer is 'why are those ships there in the first place?' Y'awl provokin' them Nazis or what?"

"I've considered that. I believe most Americans are in favor of aid to Great Britain. Roosevelt started it to keep Churchill and the British afloat," commented Truman.

"Well, maybe yes and maybe no," replied Fletcher. "The fact remains it's still their war. Another thing you need to consider is Corporate America, by which I mean Standard Oil and General Motors, who over the past few years have all made sizeable investments in Germany. You just can't declare war, wipe out their fairly hefty investments, and expect them to keep on smiling. Hell, I know for a fact that since 1931, General Motors owns Opal, who by the way is making all those trucks for the German Army? I'll bet-cha you didn't know that throughout the 1930s, the du Ponts invested heavily in Hitler's Germany through their corporate empire. Through their controlling interest in General Motors, they had GM invest thirty million dollars alone into I.G. Farben. Is it any reason why a few Senators who have received fairly generous campaign contributions from these companies are your major adversary? Y'all have to make good on these potential losses in order to gain their good will." Nick knocked back another chug of his bourbon and branch.

"Well 'Governor', I knew about the Standard Oil connection. I accused them of treason back in March 1942. I point blank asked the President of Standard Oil at my senate investigating committee if they had delivered the oil to Japan that made the attack on Pearl Harbor possible as well as if he made deliveries to the Germans. He answered me that Standard Oil was an international company! Can you believe that son-of-a-bitch? I should have thrown him in jail," thundered Truman, nearly spilling his drink in the process.

"Wa'll there you have it – Suh! That's the opposition y'all have to deal with. You have the Corporate owned clowns and the isolationist ones like Gerald Nye from North Dakota and ol' B.K. Wheeler from Montana," said Fletcher, heading back to Truman's bar for a refill.

"Wheeler I'm all too familiar with. He was a great help to me when I first came to Washington. I'll tell you, he's dead set against anything Roosevelt did and in many regards, I agree with him. However, he and I clearly do not see eye to eye when it comes to dealing with Europe and the Nazis. By the way, would you fix me another eye opener 'Governor'?" Truman handed his glass to Senator Fletcher, who lavishly filled it with the President's bourbon, topping off with just a splash of branch water.

"Yeah, I hear ya' Harry, but Wheeler's been fairly quiet on the Hill lately – not his usual boisterous self. For now, that works in our behalf. Tell ya' what, I'll go over and work with Sam Rayburn and continue building a consensus tonight, so when you give your speech tomorrow, we might be able to get on with the vote and hopefully get your declaration of war."

The two men stood and shook hands, with Harry slapping his right hand across the Senator's back.

"Give my regards to Vicky," said Truman as he escorted the 'Governor' towards the Oval Office exit.

"And likewise to Bess and Margret," replied Fletcher. "How ol' is Margret nowadays, twenty?"

"Twenty going on thirty if you ask me. Take care of yourself and we'll see ya' tomorrow on the Hill." With that, Truman returned to his desk to continue polishing up his speech to Congress.

At 11:30 a.m. the President's limousine picked up Truman, his aide Cornell, and his Secret Service man George Drescher outside the south portico, then on to Pennsylvania Avenue, surrounded by a half a dozen Secret Service and military escorts. The sky was sunny and warm, with just a hint of thundershowers possible later on in the day.

As they traveled the short distance towards Capitol Hill, both Truman and Cornell were taken by the number of protesters picking along the route, dozens maybe one hundred in all. Many carried anti-war signs, warning viewers about the dangers of getting involved in another European War. Three women held up a large banner with the phase 'Is this the United States of Great Britain?' written in large, bold red paint. Up another block was another large group of protesters, urging for the U.S. involvement in Europe to save humanity from Hitler.

As soon as they parked, the Secret Service quickly ushered Truman into the building. Bess and Margret had arrived earlier in order to give the President time to finish his speech as well as simplify security matters.

At 11:50 a.m., the Speaker of the House, Sam Rayburn, gaveled, signaling for the representatives of both houses to take their seats. The clerk of the House of Representatives solemnly intoned, "The President of the United States!"

Truman strolled down the aisle, while everyone on the floor and in the galley came to their feet. Many cheered, clapped and shouted 'Remember Pearl Harbor' with wild emotion. A few Republican senators remained seated, offering only token clapping as an indication of their indifference towards the President.

While Truman was no stranger to this chamber, knowing nearly every senator and a great deal of the Congressmen, this was his first major speech to the nation since taking office. He strode up to the rostrum, his eyes looking out towards Bess and Margret, finding both of them within the sea of legislators. He took his speech out of his coat pocket and opened it up on the lectern, allowing for the ovation to subside.

Within moments the huge chamber was silent. Truman cleared his voice for a final time.

"Gentlemen of Congress, I have called the Congress into extraordinary session because there are very serious choices of policy to be made, and immediately, which it was neither right nor constitutional permissible that I should assume the responsibility of making. We as a nation have achieved a great victory against the forces of Imperial Japan in ridding the world of fascism in the Far East, yet this victory becomes increasing mote so long as there remains no freedom of the seas when it comes to the North Atlantic. For the past year and a half, American ships have been needlessly attacked and sunk, with American lives lost due to the actions of one man and a rogue nation. They have put aside all restraints of law and humanity. The United Kingdom has stood alone against this menace to mankind for the past five years, incurring unbelievable civilian suffering and incalculable damage defended the rights all nations possess. Many of the occupied nations of Europe have had their peoples shipped off to camps, never to be seen again . . ."

He stopped briefly to take a sip of water located on the lectern, then continued.

"What choice do we as a nation have at this point? In the words of a former President, Woodrow Wilson, who faced a similar choice back in 1917, 'There is one choice we cannot make, we are incapable of making, and that is we will not chose the path of submission. The wrongs against which we now array ourselves are no common wrongs; they cut to the very roots of humanity.'"

With that last line, many Democrats within the chamber raised their arms in the air and rose to their feet in applause. Soon the members of the

Supreme Court, led by Chief Justice Harlan Stone, also joined the chorus, all shouting and cheering. Several Democrats Senators and Congressmen began shouting, "Give 'em hell Harry! Give 'em hell Harry!" which soon resonated through the chamber. Truman felt more confident with each thunderous applause. Once again he looked over towards Bess, where she signaled her approval with a thumb up.

The President raised his hand for the chamber to quiet and then he continued.

> "Twenty – eight years ago, I was a farmer in Missouri watching in horror what the German navy was doing to this fine nation and how as a country, we rose to the challenge to make this world safe for democracy. I listened as President Wilson transformed my neighbors and my attitude from one of bored indifference to one of standing up for something. It is that same attitude that I ask the Congress to declare the course of the Nazi Government to be in fact nothing less than war against the people of the United States, and that we take immediate steps to exert all her power and employ all her resources to bring the Nazi Government to terms and end the war!"

The entire chamber was on its feet cheering. Becoming louder, a Democrat chorus continued shouting 'Give 'em hell Harry!' Many legislators began waving flags, and in some cases, began sobbing at the emotion brought about by the President's speech. A few people noticed that a few senators made a point of doing nothing. A small, sardonic smile on his wide, creased face, Republican Senator Gerald Nye from North Dakota, folded his arms across his broad chest and stood there in silent disagreement. Nye opposed all major defense measures in the Senate, as well as led the fight against Lend Lease. On the floor of the Senate he charged that the British and not German submarines had sunk the *Robin Moor*, only later did he withdraw the baseless charge. Another senator, Robert Reynolds, a Democrat from North Carolina, also sat in stony silence. Reynolds had at one time openly praised

Hitler on the Senate floor. A third senator, Montana's B.K. Wheeler, quietly left the chamber, keeping his emotions to himself.

The President shook a few hands as he departed the House chamber, heading immediately back to the Oval Office. Accompanying him in the limousine was Senator Fletcher, coming along to provide a '*Monday morning quarterback*' review of the speech.

"Well Mr. President, no question you hit that one out of the stadium!" Fletcher said as he poured himself a drink out of the car's mini-bar. "Damn, no bourbon?"

"I didn't know you were coming, otherwise I would have stocked up," replied Truman. "So you really think I hit a home run with that?"

Fletcher found a small bottle of Jack Daniels tucked behind a bottle of seltzer, immediately making use of its contents.

"Absolutely — ya'll heard the chamber. They're ready to go, but I really believe the true test is how quickly Rayburn and McKellar put it up for a vote, and how much resistance you get from Nye, Wheeler, and Reynolds. Those three son-of-a-bitches didn't so much as crack a smile for fear of their faces falling off."

"Well 'Governor', trust me. I'll need all the help you can muster to get this thing approved and passed. Once that vote is in, then I'll rest. I'd look pretty stupid after that speech only to have the Congress throw it right back in my face," replied Truman, looking at the demonstrators still picketing outside Capitol Hill.

In a region of the Hartz Mountains, deep in the forest of Thuringia known to the Germans as the *Dreiecks* or 'Three Corners', German civilians and key Wehrmacht personnel were assembling. The building they met in was non-descript concrete and overlooked a medium sized valley recently cleared of foliage near the mediaeval town of Arnstadt. The building could have easily been mistaken for a bomb shelter with massive walls possessing the smallest of observation ports and thick metal doors. Overhead, the building was obscured from the air with heavy forest green camouflage netting that draped over the complex. Dozens of smaller wooden structures were also located nearby, dwarfed by the blockhouse. Scores of antenna masts from these buildings poked through the netting as if an imaginary large porcupine was residing underneath. Surrounding this secret installation were dozens of gray green tunic SS Security personnel, located in strategic outposts within the area, with each sentry heavily armed and ready for the unexpected.

Inside the blockhouse, Dr Robert Abraham Esau, plenipotentiary for the nuclear physics section of the RFP Reich Research Council[50], was giddy with excitement. Along with his fellow scientists, Doctors Werner Osenberg, Head of the RFP Planning Board, Walter Gerlach, Esau's assistant, and Erich Schumann; each was present at 'Site Siegfried' as a witness to what may be the culmination of a decade's worth of theoretical research and construction. Located eight kilometers below in the center of the valley was a small wooden building next to a fifty foot tower that contained a large black barrel, approximately two and a half meters tall and one meter wide. Nearby, hundreds of concentration camp inmates were also located within a large fenced in area conducting various construction and other camp labor related support operations.

Dr. Esau looked at his watch. It was nearly 1800 hours and the sun was beginning to set over the isolated forested area. He motioned a technician who reached over and flipped a switch, resulting in an obnoxious claxton sounding; a signal alerting the security and scientific community they had five minutes to get to their assigned stations.

---

50   An organization that fell under the Reich Ministry for Armament and Ammunition.

Gerlach looked nervous, while Osenberg and Schumann tried to remain aloof and cool. No one had any expectations, yet they all reached for their black welder's goggles, securing them over their heads and around their eyes. Nervous security personnel followed suit — like the scientists, they also didn't know what to expect.

All eyes were fixed on the clock. At one minute to 1800hrs, everyone moved over to one of the small viewing ports, each straining over the other to get a view of the now inky black countryside.

"10...9...8..." the announcer called over the installation's intercom system, "7...6...5...4..."

Everyone's heartbeat picked up, with some technicians and engineers holding on to whatever fixture that was located nearby.

"3...2...1...0..." For what seemed an eternity nothing happen. Just as the assembled group began to exhale, the room, which just a second ago was illuminated by the dim lights of switches and desk lamps, was suddenly a glow with a brilliant light, brighter than anything they had ever witnessed before. Each and everyone was stunned, transfixed by the beauty of a brilliantly illuminated and fast rising cloud, a cloud that began to resemble that of a yellow and purplish mushroom, boiling its way into the equally illuminated night sky. Along the cloud base, was a donut shaped mixture of fire, dust, and the debris of the surrounding area, swept up briefly into the stem of the rapidly rising mushroom cloud. Then as if exhaling, the donut seemed to expand outwards towards the complex. Before anyone could react, the donut swept past the building, scattering all the surrounding wooden structures as if they were mere paper houses and swept out to sea by the surf.

Within the blockhouse, lights and other electrical items rapidly blinked off and on, as if the generators were running out of fuel. Osenberg and Schumann both departed to the back of the building to view the damage to the complex. As a precaution, the scientists had ensured 'Site Siegfried's' security personnel were briefed to occupy various slit trenches dug throughout the complex perimeter, cover their eyes and not look into the blast.

"Mein Gott," uttered a technician in the back that was answered by a half a dozen "yas" from the group. After five minutes, the stunned group finally removed their goggles to view what their 'wonder weapon' had accomplished. Viewing out the ports, all were aghast at what had become of what was once their private, peaceful, valley below.

Germany's Site Siegfried's successful atomic detonation

Illuminated by the now burning timber of a flattened forest, nothing but a large crater remained within the immediate area where the small wooden building and tower once stood. The forest itself had been cleared from where it once existed just 200 meters from the building/tower to at least three kilometers away; blasting and burning timber and brush in every direction.

While the distinguished scientific group was awed and even marveled at their creations new found destructive power, they could not help but notice the large group of concentration camp inmates were gone, vaporized along with their working materials and tools by the hellish fire they had just released ten minutes prior.

Esau, Osenberg and Gerlach checked their instruments. Geiger counters crackled indicating radiation was present, but in a low, dispersing registry.

"I calculate a three and half, maybe four kiloton blast," called out Schuman, also known as the leading explosives expert for the Third Reich.

As Doctors Esau, Schumann, and Osenberg began to come to grips with their accomplishment, the room was suddenly filled with the sound of a large 'pop!' Turning around, the group was surprised by Dr. Gerlach opening a prized bottle of champagne, then spewing its effervescent contents into a variety of coffee cups and drinking glasses.

"Comrades, we have done it, we have done it!" cried out Gerlach, drinking directly out of the bottle itself, dancing around the control room area.

"A toast," said Osenberg. "Dr. Esau, you may have the honor."

Esau and Schumann, along with a half a dozen technicians picked up the randomly filled champagne cups and held them up high.

"I propose a toast to the Second *Uranverein*[51], and our successful detonation of Germany's first atomic bomb!"

"Here! Here," cried the group, throwing their arms up high, then gulping the bubbly contents.

"To Der Fuhrer," came another toast, which in turn was echoed back by the group as well.

As the scientist began their erstwhile celebration, Esau strolled over to the installation's communication officer.

"I need you to get a radio communication back to Berlin informing them of our success at 'Siegfried'."

The Communications Officer, Captain Heinman looked at Dr. Esau, then shook his head negatively.

"I'm sorry Sir, I regret to inform you that shortly after the blast went off, we lost all communications with everyone on all frequencies. I believe none of our communications equipment functions anymore," replied Heinman.

---

51   Translation "Uranium Club" the formal German nuclear energy project under military auspices.

☆ ☆ ☆

In the week following the President's speech to Congress asking for a declaration of war, Washington became a grid lock of protest marches. Many favoring bringing the boys home and staying out of Europe's entanglements, while others encouraged the move to stop the Nazis and aid Great Britain. Daily clashes between the groups became more common, resulting in the District of Columbia Police requesting assistance from the surrounding cities in Virginia and Maryland.

Studying the situation from Number 10, Downing Street, Winston Churchill furiously scribbled cable after cable to every Pro-British American legislator he knew, encouraging, even imploring their support in declaring war against his dreaded foe, while at the same time, being careful not to 'over play his hand'. Such was his desperation that he secretly ordered his military chief of staff, General Alan Brook, back to Washington to work with Field Marshall Ironside and other key British embassy staff to coordinate, lobby, and if necessary cajole as many congressmen and senators they could to ensure the passage of the declaration. If this was Monte Carlo, Britain was stepping up to the craps table and getting ready to throw the dice.

On the Hill, an ugly debate raged daily between Senator Nye from North Dakota, leading the opposition against war, and Senator Richard Russell from Georgia leading the group supporting Truman. While on the surface, the Democrats possessed a 57 to 38 Republican seat majority advantage in the Senate, and a 242 to 191 majority in the House, many Democrats were still haunted by the specter of 1919. Hearing the latest German victories over the various overseas radio broadcasts gave them further reason to doubt American success in what might be a tremendous folly.

Yet, steadily working behind the scenes virtually nonstop over the course of four days, Senator Fletcher worked his magic, backslapping a colleague here, promising support on a fellow senator's bill there, even threatening to blackmail a key supporter caught in a Washington brothel if he didn't support the President.

By May 1, Fletcher informed House Speaker Rayburn and Senator President Pro Tem Carter Glass he had as many votes as he could lobby for, with about thirty lawmakers still 'sitting on the fence.' In swift order, Glass and Rayburn had debate cut off and a vote scheduled for that afternoon. All over Washington, as well as across America, citizens turned their radios to their local news and held their collected breath awaiting the outcome. Across the street from Capitol Hill, the British Broadcasting Corporation or 'BBC' leased a special office from which to broadcast the results live to its overseas listeners, among them the British Prime Minister.

At eleven minutes after two, the Senate voted. The crowded galley listen in absolute silence as each vote was conducted. Many a legislator's voice quivered with the emotion of the moment. When it came to Gerald Nye's turn, he thundered out a loud "no" which echoed throughout the chamber. The biggest surprise of all came from Montana's B.K. Wheeler, uttering a meekly "abstain", causing the audience to gasp at his utterance. When the clerk announced the final tally; 61 votes for, 21 against, not a hand clapped nor a voice cheered in the galleries.

At 5:00 p.m. it was the House of Representative's turn. While the House galleries were usually only half full during the debates, with the same antagonism that was displayed within the senate chamber alive and well in the House. Sam Rayburn limited speeches to ten minutes. One congressman from Iowa argued that sinking a handful of ships and killing some American sailors did not constitute a cause for war, pointing out the Mexicans had killed far more Americans in Pancho Villa's raids and skirmishes.

Debate continued well throughout the night until finally at 2:45 a.m. the following morning, the lawmakers at last fell silent. Wearily, Rayburn called for a vote. Over the next two hours, various "yes" and "no" voices echoed dully in the empty galleries, long devoid of spectators having departed home for the night. The roll called droned on until the clerk reached the last name and reported back to the Speaker Rayburn. The House of Representatives had voted 373 for war and 62 against. With both houses in approval, the U.S. was now officially at war with Nazi Germany.

Speaker Sam Rayburn immediately signed the war resolution on the spot, but since Truman had assumed the presidency in the wake of Roosevelt's death, there was no Vice President available to sign as President of the Senate. In swift order, a telephone call was made and a car dispatched to pick up the Senate President Pro Tem Carter Glass from his slumber. By 6:00a.m., with both signatures affixed to the war resolution, Truman's aid, Greg Cornell, immediately rushed to the White House where the President was having breakfast with Bess and Margret.

"Here's the resolution Mr. President," said Greg, as he was escorted into the dining room.

Margret immediately jumped up to hug her dad. Bess was equally pleased, rising to give the President a congratulatory kiss, adding, "Job well done dear!"

"Now the only thing holding this up is a pen. Does anyone have a pen for me to sign this thing?" Truman asked everyone present, half joking.

Cornell reached into his coat pocket and produced a cheap pen for Truman and within seconds, with the President's signature, America's declaration of war was complete.

In London as noon passed, Prime Minister Churchill was also celebrating along with U.S. Ambassador Winant and Jerry Curry, having started with champagne as soon as he was made aware of the successful vote from Field Marshal Ironside who was discreetly present within the appropriate congressional gallery as each vote was taken.

"We are finally together again as a crusade against evil!" chimed Churchill as he poured Winant and Curry another glass each, pitching the empty bottle into the fire place. He then raised his glass for all to see.

"A toast! To your President Truman! May his vision and strength be as great as his predecessor, Mr. Roosevelt. I will truly miss him once we beat the Hun at his game!"

"Here, here!" the two Americans replied. "To the President!"

As all three polished off their champagne, Churchill was ready for business, despite his inebriated condition.

"Tell me Mr. Ambassador, how soon can America apply her vast resources over here to aid us?"

Winant looked at Curry, hoping he might know that answer. When he didn't reply, the Ambassador shrugged his shoulders.

"I'm sure quite soon Mr. Prime Minister. I think it's more a matter of redeployment from the Pacific."

Churchill smiled, then pulled out one of his customary cigars and lit it. At this point, it really didn't matter where the Americans were coming from, but that they were coming.

"Gentlemen, as a welcome to the war gift, I have a present for President Truman. Please have a seat."

As the two Americans sat down, Churchill pulled a chair out and sat directly in front, facing the two curious spectators.

"Since the United States has now joined us in war against Hitler and the Third Reich, we are now prepared to share highly classified information we have received from a source we call *Ultra*."

Curry and Winant looked at each other.

"Is *Ultra* a person?" asked Curry. He briefly thought of Harold and the intelligence he had provided the OSS.

Churchill shook his head. "No, *Ultra* is more of a thing, in fact it's valuable information we obtain through our signals intelligence. Key to *Ultra* is what we acquire through a German 'Enigma' machine that deciphers their cipher traffic, a device we obtained courtesy of our Polish allies. Used properly, the German military 'Enigma' machine was virtually unbreakable; in practice, our Government Code and Cypher School 'Boys' had broken their codes, giving us a fairly good idea of what the Nazis are up to. I think it's high time we stared this intelligence with our new allies."

"On behalf of President Truman and the Americans, I thank you" replied Ambassador Winant, standing up and thrusting his right hand towards the Prime Minister in appreciation.

"Just promise me you won't dilly dally getting over here," said Churchill, taking a long drag from his cigar, then blowing a large smoke cloud away from the two.

A knock at the Prime Minister's door heralded the arrival of a messenger with a diplomatic cable from the American embassy. He immediately handed the sealed envelope to Winant.

"Good news I hope?" asked Churchill as Winant opened the large envelope.

Quickly reviewing the various documents that comprised the package, the Ambassador began sharing the contents.

"Mr. Prime Minister, this document authorizes direct coordination between your General Staff and ours regarding the planning of joint operations in the Atlantic, the transfer and staging of American forces into Britain..."

Churchill smiled, taking another long puff from his cigar.

Winant continued. "This one directs the coordination between General Hap Arnold and your Air Ministry regarding the pending arrival and stationing of the Ninth, Eighth, and Fifteen Air Forces."

Churchill reached behind him and grabbed a pad of paper and pencil, scribbling down notes as quickly as the Ambassador rattled off coordination documents and actions.

One document gave Winant pause. "Jerry, this note is for you. Seems your friend Harold wanted you to know he's 'in', and is heading for Marseilles this evening. Your man?"

Curry sat back and smiled, winking at Winant. "You bet. He's one of the best guys we have in coordinating with the anti Hitler folks."

"With the Unites States now in the fight, I'm sure the Nazis will be even more paranoid than at any other time," responded Churchill. "Sounds like you might be sending him on a suicide mission. Are you sure it's worth it?"

Curry cocked his head to one side as a sign of agreement with the Prime Minister. Churchill was more right than he knew — he was not aware of Harold's close call escaping from Germany a couple of months prior, but somehow Curry had convinced him to go back.

"Well Mr. Prime Minister, if he does what we've asked, I can tell you the ends will justify the means!"

Chapter 21

"Well Gentlemen, we have work to do..."

Fact: In the twilight hours of October 11, 1944, Hans Zinsser was piloting a Heinkel twin engine bomber high over the Baltic Sea near the island of Rügen, an area that was highly classified within OKW circles. Zinsser knew flying at this particular time was the safest since Allied fighters owned the skies over Germany. At about 12 to 15 kilometers from Rügen, he noticed a strong, bright illumination of the entire night sky, lasting for two seconds. As he closed in, Zinsser noticed a clearly visible pressure wave escaping the approaching blue-violet cloud formed by the explosion. He noticed the wave had a diameter of about 1000 meters when it became visible, with the color changing rapidly. After ten seconds, the sharp outlines of the reddish rimmed and colored cloud became more visible, taking on a lighter color against the pall gray overcast. Zinsser's plane soon encountered a sensation he described as a "push-pull" as the apparent shock wave of the explosion overtook his plane. As the wave passed, he turned to see a spectacular cloud in the shape of a mushroom with turbulent billowing sections rising to approximately 7,000 meters from the spot where the explosion took place. Along this cloud, he witnessed strong electrical disturbances, making it impossible for him to notify ground control of what he just observed. What Hans Zinsser had just witnessed was the detonation of an atomic bomb, eight months before the first American A-bomb detonation at Los Alamos, New Mexico.

""If our most highly qualified General Staff officers had been told to work out the most nonsensical high level organization for war which they could think of, they could not have produced anything more stupid that that which we have at present. . .We took this challenge before our Lord and our conscience, and it must be done, because this man, Hitler, he is the ultimate evil."

– Colonel Claus von Stauffenberg, 1943

Latitude 37 Degrees, 30', 02" North
Longitude 69 Degrees, 50', 04" West
Off the eastern coast of Massachusetts
1515 hrs, 18 Jun, 1945

Captain Herbert Zoller was in an uptight if not arrogant mood. As the new captain of the newly commissioned German U-boat *U-2520*, he was more than ready for his next go around with the American Navy. When the United States finally declared war against the Fatherland over a month prior, he was at La Rochelle putting the final touches to his new ship, the *U-2520*, a newly constructed Type XXI boat which would have made his old ship seem like something out of the First World War. Fast, and with the ability to traverse deep water 'silently', this boat had far better crew facilities as well, making her the dream of the Kriegmariner submariner.

But while Zoller was conducting his final 'sea trials' on this new boat, many of his colleagues were having a tremendous time attacking and sinking American shipping off the eastern coast of the United States, racking upwards of 60 – 80,000 tons of shipping descending to the bottom of the North Atlantic. Most of the American fleet had not redeployed from the Pacific, so now was the time for easy spoils. Finally, when the U-2520's trials were complete and her crew certified as trained, Zoller issued the order to sail to his assigned duty location within the *'Faust'* Wolfpack as fast as he could, traveling at flank speed.

Captain Herbert Zoller, Commander of the U-2520

As the navigator informed Zoller the ship was at its assigned station, Zoller reached upwards touching the Knight Cross he was wearing around his neck. The award, as well as the command of one of Germany's newest boats was the Kriegmarine's way of thanking him for the extraordinary successful patrol the year prior.

Touching the medal, he thought to himself that maybe this tour would bring him the next grade of the Knights Cross with oak leaves perhaps or maybe even a promotion to Kapitänleutnant!"[52] At 26 years of age, he had done pretty well for himself.

Zoller wasn't alone. His ship was now part of a nine boat wolfpack code named 'Faust' with an assigned patrol section approximately 30 miles off the eastern shore of Massachusetts. What made 'Faust' special was nearly every ship was a Type XXI, more than a match they believed for anything the United States or Great Britain for that matter could throw at them – or so they thought.

Arriving on station at 1515 hours, the U-2520 signaled both BdU and the Faust Commander of her arrival and for further orders. Within a minute, fresh intelligence flowed back, indicating a large forty ship convoy originating in Curacao was cruising northward up the Atlantic seaboard no doubt bound for Great Britain. The U-2512, acting as the pack's shadower, broke radio silence confirming the convoy sighting as well as providing a current position fix of 30 miles southwest of Faust's location, traveling at a standard convoy speed of 15 knots before she abruptly signed off. At its present course and speed, the convoy was expected to be in Faust's patrol box within two hours. 'Fresh meat for all' many of the ship commander's thought to themselves as they readied their respective boats for action.

Zoller took in a deep breath as he quickly scanned his control room. While no stranger to action, this was his first time with a new and highly inexperienced crew, with only a few of his boys barely out of their teens. While he had a few experienced 'sea dog' petty officers, he didn't have the

---

52   Equivalent to Lieutenant Commander

depth that he had on his old U-315. Hopefully, his new boat with all its latest technology would see them to victory. For now, it was a waiting game.

At 1710 hours, Zoller ordered the U-2520 to periscope depth for a quick look around. With summer fast approaching, sunset would still be a couple of hours off; plenty of light available to see what this convoy looked like.

Scanning in the direction of southwest, he could faintly make out the silhouettes of something, possibly a number of ships on the horizon. The question on his mind was to surface and have a better look, or sit and wait for them to approach?

Minutes seemed like hours. Scanning through his periscope again, he could clearly make out a number of American 'liberty' ships, a few tankers, along with a healthy dose of U.S. Navy destroyers, more than he had seen in a long time. Still, the *Faust* wolfpack, now equipped with the latest U-Boats the Fatherland could produce, should be more than a match for a few American 'tin cans' as they referred to the destroyers.

A quick signal from the *Faust* commander on the U-2501 informed everyone to fire at will. Zoller immediately ordered "Battle stations" causing his boat to immediately shift into a heightened combat mode, with Claxton's blaring, crewmen scrambling towards their assigned sections.

Within seconds, Zoller could see the lead American destroyer erupt in a geyser of water at the bow. Someone in *Faust* had scored the first kill.

"Torpedo room, ready tubes one and two with G7 Wren torpedoes," the Captain ordered, while scanning to a target of opportunity. Suddenly, three destroyers charged out of the pack like old fashioned cavalry in pursuit of the enemy, in this case the U-2520.

"Helmsman, adjust course to 045 N, steady as she goes," Zoller yelled out. He decided to take out the lead destroyer before it would be upon him in a matter of minutes.

Once the helmsman acknowledged aye, Zoller ordered opened fire, then ordered tubes three and four loaded.

"Down scope," he yelled as he clicked his ever present stop watch. At 6,000 meters to the lead destroyer, it should take 15 seconds for contact, yet everyone heard a distant sounding explosion after ten seconds. Everyone in the control room looked at Zoller who was just as puzzled. Five seconds later as expected, ka-boom! – the familiar sound of a Wren torpedo making contact with a ship. Suddenly everyone started to breathe easier again.

Before Zoller could order up periscope, Crewman Franze, who was manning the ship's sonar station, called out he could hear another destroyer at approximately 3,000 meters and closing.

"Chief, take her down to 100 meters – now!" called Zoller. Almost immediately, the ship began to pitch forward and down, as if everyone was riding a gigantic sled going down a hill.

Franze signaled he could still hear the U.S. warship circling above, along with the sounds of splashing – depth charges being dropped by the destroyer.

The boat's 'watch officer' or executive officer Lieutenant Schweiger ordered all quiet, while Zoller order a course change to 045 NW, diagonally away from the circling destroyer.

'Kaaa-boom!!!' The ship suddenly pitched to the left flinging everyone against the bulkhead walls and railings. Within seconds, a second explosion, this time on the right side, sent all unprepared crewmen again against the ship's bulkhead, this time on the right. Two pipes directly above the navigation station erupted, showering all crewmen within the immediate area with hot, scalding steam. Those affected hollered in pain as the stream literally pealed the skin right off their hands and faces.

Schweiger quickly reached out to the cut off valve, closing it while trying to maintain his balance against the rocking boat, pitching from port to starboard. Zoller could see though his crew was well trained, they had the look of terrified men, typical for a crew with no experience. If he could only keep it together for the moment.

The ship slowly moved forward on battery power at three knots at a depth of 100 meters. To play it safe, Zoller ordered Schweiger to take her down an additional 50 meters. He knew his boat could take the pressure; her hull was fabricated from one inch thick steel aluminum alloy, which allowed a maximum crush depth of 280 meters[53]. That coupled with her streamline hull should reduce any American sonar contact for the moment.

Zoller looked over at Franze, hoping they had broken off contact with the enemy above. Franze slowly shook his head – the destroyer was still above on their tail. He held up two, then three fingers indicating he had three sonar targets above. Within seconds, three explosions took place, shaking the sub to such an extent values busted, pipes burst, and various electrical boxes controlling the many sub functions popped off or exploded in a shower of electrical sparks.

Suddenly, the U-2520 was plunged into darkness. Within seconds, the ship's battery lights kicked on giving a dull, surreal, eerie look to the inside of the boat. Gently, the ship continued to gracefully glide at a depth of 150 meters with a fitful enemy ship in pursuit.

"Schweiger, take her to 200 meters," whispered Zoller "then pass the word, rig for silent running."

Quietly, the terrified crew responded, slowly climbing through the debris filled room that was once their tidy control operations.

After about ten minutes, Schweiger compiled a damage report of the ship's condition.

"We have two dead, twenty five injured, but other than that, we're okay I guess," he informed Zoller.

"Good, I'm going forward to check out the torpedo room Schweiger," replied Zoller "you have the con. Continue on course 045 at 200 meters at

---

53   919 feet

three knots. Let's see if that will work. If after 10 minutes we haven't shaken them, order full stop."

"Aye Kaptain, good luck!"

☆ ☆ ☆

At that moment in Berlin, Field Marshall Keitel and General Jodl, along with their immediate senior staff and aides, had just arrived at the Chancellory for a secret meeting with Hitler. As they entered the vast briefing room, already present were Field Marshal Goering, Reich Minister Himmler along with another senior SS officer – SS-Obergruppenführer[54] Hans Kammler. Array on the conference table was a map of the North Atlantic as well as a map of New York City.

As LTC Massar walked in, he immediately recognized Kammler. He was Hitler's "go to" man for all sorts of infamous projects, most notably his installation of the crematory system at the Auschwitz death camp and now in full use throughout the Reich. After that, Hitler had Kammler appointed head of all missile projects, most recently he was the *"Fuehrer's general plenipotentiary for jet aircraft"* giving him full range from V-2 rockets to the fielding of jet aircraft. Rumors swirled he was going to be given an even bigger project to manage.

Once everyone was present and gathered around the table, Hitler spoke.

"Gentlemen, as predicted the cowardly Americans have now entered the war against us. This was not unforeseen and I can tell you, we will be ready for them once they come across the Atlantic and threaten the Reich. Six months ago, I assigned Obergruppenführer Kammler with overseeing our atomic weapons development program. He had developed a plan to strike vengeance at the Americans at their very heart should they even think of

---

54   SS rank equivalent to a US four star general

invading Europe. For that, I will let Obergruppenführer Kammler speak about this project."

At that point, Hitler turned to Kammler, shook his hand, then turned the conference over to him.

"Thank you Mein Führer. A little over six weeks ago, my team successfully detonated a three kiloton atomic device at 'Site Sigrid', deep in the Thuringia Wald, proving we have the capability to build and test such a device. We are now assembling four more devices for use as our Führer sees fit. I now draw you attention to the large map you see before you. On it, you will see a large arch drawn from our secret Luftwaffe base near Oslo, Norway, over to New York City. Recently, we concluded our second proof of principle test flight of a specially configured Ju-390 bomber, flying a reconnaissance mission round trip in just under 30 hours, with absolutely no interference or detection by the Americans or British."

"Very impressive," replied Keitel, "but so what does this mean to us? Are we now going to start bombing the Americans in such as manner as we bomb London?"

"Not quite, Herr Field Marshall. I now draw your attention to this targeting study map of New York City, focusing on lower Manhattan Island. Notice the various rings radiating out from the center of the city. My team in conjunction with the Luftwaffe conducted this study detailing the blast and heat damage radii of such an atomic blast over this city."

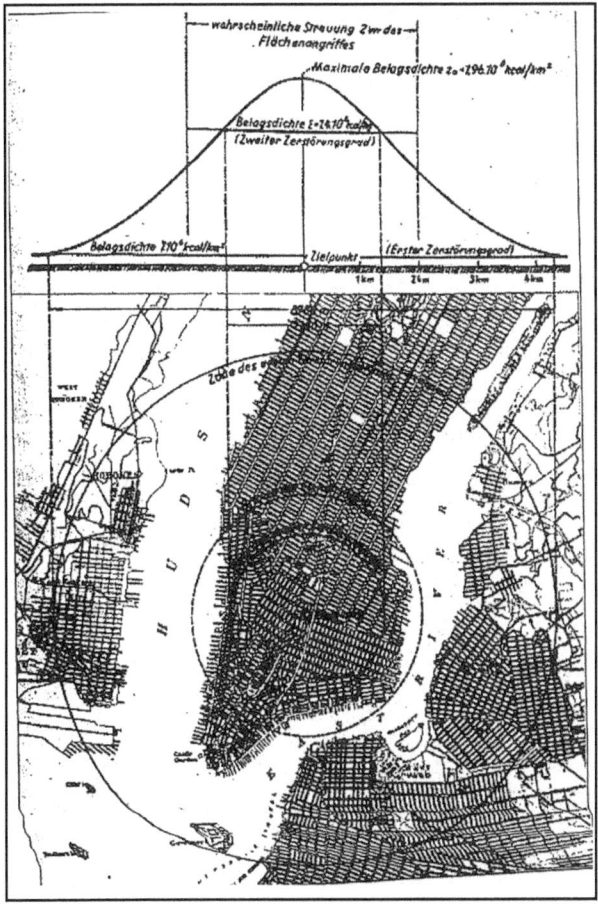

OKL Targeting Study of an Atomic Bomb over New York City

"Why New York, as opposed to bombing their capital Washington, or Boston, or even Philadelphia?" asked General Jodl, looking for the strategic sense of the target.

Before Kammler could answer Jodl's question, Hitler cut in.

"I selected New York City, Jodl!" yelled Der Führer furious at the mere suggestion of someone questioning his choice.

"When we destroy this city, we will destroy America's financial and business center. This will create an immense military and psychological blow to their war effort, perhaps shake them against any future attacks against us. We will destroy their ability to ship troops and material to the British, destroy any navy presence, and utterly wipe out any transportation systems servicing the entire northeast. But most importantly, it will show the Americans we mean business and that Germany can strike them at the very symbol of their decadent lifestyle! Then, if they do not sue for peace, we will hit another target of my choosing."

The entire audience listened to Hitler in stunned silence. Development of an atomic bomb was one thing, but possessing the ability to deliver to a target, much less one over three thousand miles away was entirely a different matter. The question as to '*could it be done*' was now looking more a fact of '*when will it be done*'? Hitler continued.

"Kammler will be given your full and total cooperation in the matter – am I clear?" he loudly stammered out with a focus half in enthusiasm, half with furry.

As the General Staff officers studied the maps and queried among themselves, Massar knew he had to get this information out to Tresckow as soon as possible. Hitler would soon have the capability of dropping an atomic bomb on the Americans and who knows where it would go from there, but he did know Hitler had to be stopped and General Tresckow and his circle were the only ones capable of doing it.

After cruising on battery power deep under the North Atlantic for 19 hours, Zoller felt comfortable enough to bring his ship up to a depth where they could employ one of the newest devices on his ship – a 'schnorchel', an apparatus which enables the U-boat to stay submerged while running the diesels to recharge the batteries and also to ventilate the boat. The device or 'mast' would deploy upwards to the surface, allowing them to operate while under water, while allowing him to recharge the ship's batteries after their long usage. It had been over 15 hours since they lost contact with the destroyers on the surface, so he ordered the U-2520 up to periscope depth. A quick scan of the surrounding waters revealed no ships whatsoever. *It is now or never*, he thought as he had the scope descend down.

Zoller ordered the ship to slow down to three knots, then gave the order to deploy the schnorchel. Once U-2520 slowed down, the apparatus would fold out from the deck up to the surface. After a few minutes, it was apparent it had not. A seaman checking the indicator alarm within the bridge confirmed it had not. The Captain's only choice – to recharge his batteries, he had to surface.

Within minutes, the U-2520 broke the surface of the rolling seas of the North Atlantic. Zoller and Schweiger opened the hatch of the ship's coning tower to take in the salty, but sweet air of the sea. The skies were a heavy, leaden gray, but that didn't matter to the submariners having been underwater for the past ten days. Crewmen were given the opportunity to go on deck in order to check on the schnorchel as well as inspect damage from the American destroyers.

From the conning tower, both officers could see the various indentations caused by the depth charges within the hull as well as broken fixtures on the ship's deck. Bad as it looked they were all thankful to still be alive.

"Schweiger, have the Chief put together a detail and check out the schnorchel. I don't want to be here any longer than I have to," instructed the captain, seeing the obvious damage around the schnorchel area.

Grabbing the intercom mike, Zoller called down to his senior radioman, Chief Petty Officer Kruger.

"Kruger, contact BdU and give them our location once the navigator figures that out. Also contact Faust and let them know we're still alive."

The radioman acknowledged Zoller's order and proceeded to contact the pack once the navigator obtained the location, approximately 60 miles northeast of where they initially made contact with the American convoy.

Meanwhile, Zoller continued inspected the U-2520 from the conning tower while Schweiger assisted a repair crew with the schnorchel. The depth charges had bent the device to such an angle it would require the mounting of a lift boom to wrench it out of storage location, an operation that could take upwards of one or more hours depending on sea conditions.

A quick scan of the surrounding seas by the Captain revealed no dangers, so the order was given. While the crew assembled the boom, Zoller called down to Kruger inquiring whether contact had been made.

"Negative with Faust, Sir!" the senior radioman replied "but I have raised BdU and informed them of our situation. They haven't heard anything from Faust either."

Strange, Zoller thought. Protocol called for all ships to let BdU know their positions and status, unless under attack. He looked down at the work crew scrambling to bring all the tools on deck to fix the device as quickly as possible.

While the repair detail continued, Zoller drew his binoculars up and began scanning the horizon. Since his whole crew was involved in conducting repairs to their various stations, he would serve as the ship's 'air watch', scanning for any activity that could threaten the U-2520.

After thirty minutes, the crew was able to winch the schnorchel upright, adjusting it in the process. As he watched their progress, Zoller felt great pride in his crew's ability to fix his ship under the most austere of conditions.

They may have been inexperienced prior to this voyage, but they more than made up for it in enthusiasm out on the high seas, he thought to himself as they neared completion of their task. *This patrol will clearly make a man out of every boy that stepped aboard.*

Taking one last scan towards the west, Zoller spotted something high in the sky. Refocusing his binoculars, he could make out four aircraft, about nine miles out as they began their descent directly for his ship. He didn't recognize the planes, but they clearly were not German. He had maybe five minutes before they would be upon him.

"Schweiger, get everyone below deck – now!" he yelled from the conning tower. Grabbing the mike, he called for the second watch to prepare the ship for an emergency dive. Looking back down on the work detail, he saw various crewmen picking up their tools, others disassembling the repair boom.

"Get the hell off the deck and go below now!!" he again yelled down to Schweiger.

"Herr Captain, we can't afford to lose this equipment" the First Officer yelled back. "We need this stuff down below as well."

Zoller was in no mood to quibble. "If we don't dive now, there will be no need for any tools in the future, so get your detail inside!!"

Looking back up into the skies, the planes were now lining up for each to take their turn in trying to sink the sub. The U-2520 had maybe one minute before the first plan would drop its load.

Looking back on the deck, he could see there were two crewmen and Schweiger left to descend down the amidships hatch.

Suddenly, the splash and immediate boom followed by the load sound of a passing plane directly overhead heralded the arrival of the first attacker. A clear miss! The U-2520's luck was holding out, but for how long?

Zoller popped up to see Schweiger was now in the hatch. "Crash dive, crash dive," he yelled into the mike before he too descended down inside the conning tower, pulling the hatch closed behind him. Heading to the control room, he directed an immediate course change to 120 ESE, at a depth of 100 meters. As the ship slid deeper in the water, the crew could hear the dreaded sounds of explosions above; reminding them once again they were back in danger.

With the amidships hatch secured, the ship's First Officer joined Zoller in the control room.

"How did they find us so quickly?" he asked Schweiger, who was holding a bandage to his head. Apparently, in his haste to close the hatch, he slammed it on his head, causing a seriously bleeding head wound.

"I wish I knew," he replied back. "It was as if someone at BdU had given our grid coordinated to either the Americans or British. It's as if they're inside our heads!"

Zoller shook his head in bewilderment, puzzled at how they found him, and still puzzled at where the remainder of his wolf pack was located or if they were even still around.

Schweiger still holding the improvised bandage over his head asked, "What are your orders now Herr Captain?"

Zoller looked incredulously at Schweiger and the crew within the control room.

"Orders? Ha, all right, I have two for now. First, set course back to La Rochelle. We're in no shape to do anything out here. Second, get yourself down to sick bay and get that head looked after. What do you want to do, bleed all over my charts?"

What Captain Zoller and the crew of the U-2520 were not aware of was his ship was the sole survivor of the *Faust Wolfpack*, destroyed largely through *Ultra* and the boys from Bletchley Park; intelligence shared by the British with the Americans on U-boat locations in what was now shaping up as the Battle for the Atlantic. Not only had the U.S. Navy successfully redeployed from the Pacific to the North Atlantic, but in addition to the massive numbers of ships and aircraft, they brought with them their deadly skills of sub killing, honed from experience gained killing the Kreigmarine's major ally — the Imperial Japanese Navy. The German Navy may have better submarines, but they were no match for the numbers, intelligence, and experience of the American Navy.

✲ ✲ ✲

The Battle of the Atlantic was the German's first taste of the might of the United States, now fully directed towards them. Even as thousands of American vessels began the process of clearing the North Atlantic of German U-Boats, the skies above were filled with thousands of aircraft streaming towards Great Britain via Iceland.

Within sixty days of America's declaration of war, the United States deployed the Army's First, Eighth, and Fifteenth Army Air Forces across the Atlantic upon which in conjunction with the British colleagues in the Royal Air Force Bomber Command, began the systematic bombing of the dreaded V-1 and V-2 rocket sites across the English Channel, which brought almost immediate relief to the besieged British in general and Londoners in particular. While V-1 and V-2 rocket attacks diminished, it did not come without cost – the German's anticipated the U.S. Army Air Corps action and had the Luftwaffe positioned in airfields along the coast to extract a deadly cost in American planes and airmen lives. Much like the ongoing Battle of the Atlantic, the air war over Nazi occupied Europe would boil down to a massive attrition war of Allied bombers and fighters against the Luftwaffe, with 100 American B-17 and B-25 bombers going down every two to three weeks across the country sides of France and Germany.

Yet, still they came, complete with a new family of fighters that could meet the Germans on their own terms and beat them. While the Allies were losing men and machines across Europe, so too was the Luftwaffe who had become somewhat complacent since the Reich's armistice with the Soviet Union.

In the twenty some months since the cessation of combat air missions over the Soviet Union, the Luftwaffe under Goering opted to maintain a "status quo" mentality in dealing with their British counterparts while flying patrols across the channel, opting to attack the British only if they clearly were making a mistake or were off course. The Luftwaffe was desperately trying to make up their losses from combat action over Russia, siphoning just enough combat qualified pilots to aid their Italian allies in North Africa from the ever increasing British threat from Egypt.

In addition to pilot training, the Germans were also hampered by the quality of their current workhorse fighting machines; the ME-I09 and FW-I90, both of which were suffering from their age, with the ME-I09 nearly a decade old. Their replacements, the new ME-262 "Swallow", unquestionably the world's first jet aircraft, was expensive to build, and even more difficult to train on. While Germany ruled the continent, she still required oil, and clearly there was an insufficient amount to keep both the army and the Luftwaffe fueled to meet their needs, and Allied intelligence knew this.

By mid July, the U.S. First Air Force, in conjunction with the British Bomber Command, in addition to destroying the rocket launch sites, now began a calculated campaign of destruction of the Wehrmacht's 'Atlantic Wall', raining hundreds of tons of bombs on the concrete fortifications along the coast, often times working well inland. Hundreds of interned French and captured prisoners of war were killed during the First Air Force campaign in an attempt to stop its continued construction in its tracks. While the bombing campaign showed initial success, it soon became apparent that while the Allies bombed during the day, the Germans would use night to repair as much of the damage as possible. Many of the massive concrete emplacements simply shrugged off the dozens of bombs landing on its impervious roofs.

Concurrent to the First Air Force bombing campaign along the coast, the Eight and Fifteenth Air Forces took the fight to the German heartland itself, bombing the various cities of the Ruhr. Here too, the Luftwaffe gave as good as it got, with ME-190s and 262s meeting American P-51 'Mustangs' and British 'Spitfires' for control of the skies over the Reich, often times shooting down three aircraft for each one of their losses. Try as they may, the Germans simply didn't have the qualitative much less quantitative edge over the Allies, instead extracting a deadly attritional cost for each mission launched from Britain towards the Reich. As the Luftwaffe lost its edge in pilots, steadily the German cities began to burn.

In June 1945, General Marshall authorized the commitment of the Twentieth Air Force, complete with the latest B-29 'Superfortress' along with 509th Composite Group, directing them to work directly for the Supreme Commander Allied Expeditionary Force (SCAEF) himself, newly appointed General Walter Kruger, the experienced commander of Operation Olympic, chosen for his familiarity with large scale invasions. Should the opportunity present itself, the Allies wanted to be prepared to use its secret weapon.

In the Reich itself, the euphoria many of the people felt since the armistice with the Soviet Union soon turned to concern and dread. Since June, their cities began to be bombarded from above, leveling them to rubble and there was nothing they could do but attempt to endure it.

On the ground deep within the Third Reich to observe the impending destruction was Harold Hoffman. Since returning to Germany from England, he carefully made his way to Berlin, cautiously approached his brother, Heinrich. To his surprise and good fortune, he discovered Heinrich was not aware of his entanglement with the Gestapo. For whatever reason, Heinrich believed he was out of the country on business as usual.

As the two of them had dinner and drinks at their favorite restaurant, the 'Gasthaus Dietrich Herz', the brothers once again reminisced over old times when they were interrupted by the now all too familiar sound of an air raid siren, with Berlin's popularity with the British Bomber Command and the American Air Force. In accordance to local command, everyone descended down into one of the local array of underground bomb shelters located throughout the city suburb.

Once down in the shelter, the Hoffman brothers could hear the faint thumping of explosions in the distance, slower growing louder with each passing minute.

"God damn Americans," Heinrich swore under his breath. "They will pay, I swear to God Hitler will make them pay!"

Harold looked at his brother in the candlelight and could tell he was deadly serious.

"And how is he going to do that?" he asked. "The Luftwaffe bombed London in 1940 and the British didn't cave in. How's Hitler going to make the allies pay? How is he going to stop all of this?"

Heinrich looked up at Harold and smiled.

"You've been out of the country far too many times — I can see dear brother you don't have much faith in the Reich," Heinrich replied.

Harold tilted his head to one side trying to understand what his brother was getting at. "Well, since we have all sorts of time down here in this cellar until the bombers clear, please enlighten me as to what you're talking about."

Heinrich quickly look around, making sure no one else was in ear shot.

"What if I told you we now have the ability to wipe out an entire city in a single blast? Think about it — one bomb and whoosh, no more city!"

"You mean like an atomic bomb? I think you've been reading too many science fiction books, either that or you're starting to believe that what ol' Goebbels is shoveling out," said Harold, shaking his head at the notion.

"And I tell you it's true. I've recently heard Hitler talking with some high ranking Nazis and they informed him not only have they tested it, but flown a special bomber from Norway over the Atlantic to New York City, proving it can be done. I tell you, vengeance will be ours!"

Harold knew his brother and he could tell Heinrich was dead serious.

"Okay, so we have a special bomb. I've also heard that a weapon that isn't used is a useless weapon. When does he plan on using it?" Harold asked.

"Very soon, possibly in a couple of weeks, perhaps the first of August if the weather holds out. That will teach the Americans and the British once and for all they cannot defeat the Third Reich!"

Suddenly, the 'all clear' siren sounded, announcing to everyone that it was now safe to rise to the surface and survey whatever damage the departing bombers created. As the two brothers emerged to the surface, they were surprised at what little damaged was immediately visible, yet in the distance towards Berlin, everyone stood to observe the glow of many fires burning in the city center, interrupted by an occasional muffled thump of a late detonating bomb. Many citizens wept, others simply hugged one another that they had survived another attack. Heinrich cursed under his breath, while shaking his fist up at the sky as if an American or British pilot was watching.

"We will get even, I swear it..." Heinrich uttered.

As the two headed towards Heinrich's apartment, Harold took the opportunity to leave his older brother, using the excuse he had a girlfriend for the evening. Once back at his hotel, he called a phone number provided to him by Alan Dulles while in Berne. Dulles had arranged for a contact Harold could communicate with should he run into trouble or need to get information out of the country.

Once he dialed, he heard a faint dial tone, interrupted by an increasing level of static on the line.

"Ya, may I help you?" answered the other end.

"I wonder if you might help me, I am looking for directions to the Berlin Zoo," Harold uttered, using the pre arranged code signal Dulles provide him should he find a need to use the phone number.

"It is too difficult to provide to you over the phone. I can give it to you direct at the corner of Leipzig and Bismarck Strasse, say in 20 minutes," said the caller, then hung up.

In fifteen short minutes, Harold made his way to the arranged location. It was quarter to midnight, but the sky was still aglow with the various fires still burning within the city. It would be another long night for Berliners in general and the Firewehr in particular.

As the local church clock tower struck midnight, a hardy, tough looking stranger built like a soccer player suddenly emerged out of the darkness.

"Are you looking for directions to the Berlin Zoo?" the stranger asked.

When Harold nodded, the stranger came closer, pulled his glove off and extended a hand to him.

"Kurt Steege," he said, changing from a German to a midwestern American accent. "Dulles sent me as your OSS contact, sort of like your Guardian Angel. So what's the deal, do you need help un-assing the country?"

Harold shook Steege's hand, then the two sat down on a nearby bench. "No, but I do have information that needs to get out of the country – fast! Is there somewhere we can go?"

Steege took Hoffman to his local safe house, then had Harold debrief him on what he just learned from his older brother. Steege seemed skeptical at first, but Harold reminded him of all the other wonder weapons the Nazis had employed and he began to agree it might be not only plausible, but highly possible.

"So let me get this straight. Not only do the Nazis have an atomic bomb, but a bomber capable of dropping it on the States? Where is this base in Norway?" asked the incredulous OSS agent.

"I believe Heinrich said it was just north of Oslo," Harold replied. "Should be pretty easy to find it, and once you do, just send a couple hundred of your bombers over and flatten it!"

Steege shook his head in disbelief.

"Son, it's just not that easy. We blow that base up, Hitler will just build another base and bomb, even more secret, and then what? He drops it on London, or ships it via a U-Boat off the U.S. coast and pulls the pin, or who knows what? You need to leave strategy to the big boys."

"But if we can take out the government, then blow the base, wouldn't that change things?" Harold responded.

"That all depends on whether you're successful at an over throw of the Nazis, which I thought was the main reason you're back here, to meet with your 'Circle' folks, that is if they in fact exist?"

"As a matter of fact, the Circle as you refer to it as, is meeting tomorrow night, at 2100 hours. If you don't believe me, I'll take you there and show you for myself." Harold didn't care for the insinuation or thought that the resistance was simple fantasy invented as a way of getting funding and attention.

"Okay, you make the arrangements, and I'll inform Dulles of this news as well as get any further information from him to pass on to your group. Meet me back here at a quarter to nine," replied Steege, who then turned and disappeared into the night.

In Washington, another get together of a more pleasurable nature was commencing at the White House. President Truman, on the advice of Margret and Bess, decided to throw a reconciliation reception to help mend the wounds within the Democratic Party brought about by the war vote. Truman hoped that such a gesture might help get the various legislatures working together again, at least those within his party. Among those invited was Jerry Curry, fully recovered from his latest London adventure and enjoying the 'grip and grin' of the Washington power elite cocktail circuit.

Curry wandered through the various senators and congressmen, shaking hands, listening to various tales of intrigue and amazement, and generally enjoying himself for a change. As he sipped his champagne, he spied Senator B.K. Wheeler standing by himself, hands in his pocket, looking out across the south portico.

"Hello, Senator Wheeler I presume," said Curry extending his hand, "Jerry Curry. I don't believe I've had the pleasure."

Wheeler politely smiled and returned Curry's handshake.

"Quite a party the President is throwing," responded Wheeler, attempting to make small talk with the President's aide.

"This, this is nothing, at least not yet. Wait until the ol' man gets warmed up and hits the piano keys. Then you'll know we've got a party going down. In fact, the President once told me if he hadn't been President of the United States, he'd probably would have ended up a piano player in whore house!" Jerry's comment got Wheeler to grin, if only for minute.

"You'll have to forgive me if I'm not exactly in a party mood," said Wheeler. "Ever since my favorite nephew was killed at sea earlier this year, my attitudes and convictions have become confused."

Curry remembered Truman's administrative aide Cornell telling him that the senator was uncustomary low key during the war vote debates.

"That's quite all right Senator; you don't need to explain anything to me."

Wheeler continued. "It's just that this President is a far cry from that left leaning commie loving Roosevelt. He sold us out in a big way and I can tell you this from firsthand experience, and I was so ready to nail his political carcass on the wall and end it for all time, for the good of the American people. But now, with all that's occurred in the past few months, FDR's death, the U-boat attacks, maybe I was wrong…., I just don't know."

Wheeler placed his empty glass on the nearby table, then buttoned his coat.

"Please pass on my regards to the President and let him know I will support him where I can." He became crestfallen, turned and departed out the south portico doorway.

Curry stood there trying to understand what just transpired, while at the same time, was struck by something the senator said — something he had heard before. The more he thought about it, he had heard that voice and mannerism before, but he couldn't quite place where.

A waiter passed by with another tray of champagne. Curry grabbed a glass all the while pondering the question that was now ricocheting inside his head. As he thought about it, Greg Cornell entered the room along with an army major, both seemed as if they were searching for someone.

Making eye contact with Curry, Cornell approached and asked him if he knew where the President was.

"He's somewhere in the immediate area having a good time, why?" Curry asked.

"I've got a hot message from Major General Grooves relayed from New Mexico that I've got to get to him," Cornell responded, almost out of breath.

"Can you share it with me, after all I'm probably as close to him as his cabinet folks, perhaps even closer?" asked Jerry.

Cornell quickly scanned the room, then stepped close to Curry to ensure no one was within earshot.

"I have a telegram for the President from the Trinity Test Site near Alamogordo, New Mexico. Take a look at this," Cornell then showed the message to Curry.

'Operated on this morning. Diagnosis not yet complete but results seem satisfactory and already exceed expectations. Local press release necessary as interest extends great distance. Dr. Groves pleased. He returns tomorrow. I will keep you posted.'

Curry handed the telegram back to Cornell. "What exactly does all this mean?" Curry asked.

"It mean that Grooves and his team have successfully tested *the contraption* as they refer to it. We now have a fully functioning atomic bomb!"

Trinity Site Testing of the First US Atomic Bomb

As Curry took in the fantastic news, the sound of piano music erupted throughout the reception area. Sure enough, the President was behind the keys rendering his favorite piano piece '*Happy Days are here again. . .*' The reception had now transitioned into a true Truman party and soon a celebration.

✵ ✵ ✵

Steege and Hoffman pulled up in front of a mid 19th century, imposing gray black gothic house, surrounded by a wrought iron fence, located in the Berlin suburb of Schöneberg, a place known as the birthplace of the actress Marlene Dietrich. The large house was not far from Tempelhof airport, making it easy for the various *Kreisau Circle* conspirators to fly in and out of the vast Nazi capital city. The two noted the numerous cars parked nearby, indicating this was a rather sizable get together. The two quickly scanned the various automobiles, looking for any Gestapo presence that might be observing the home's occupants comings and goings.

Harold and Kurt entered the building through a special side door, making their way to the second floor study were the Kreisau Circle members typically met. While the study was large enough to accommodate most meetings, tonight it was virtually standing room only. The immense cloud of cigarette smoke hung mid air like a thin fog bank, precluding a clear look across the room.

Harold quickly introduced Steege to the key conspirators present; Dr Carl Goerdeler – the former Mayor of Leipzig, Ludwig Beck – retired General and former Chief of Staff of the German General Staff, General Friedrich Olbricht – Chief of the Wehrmacht Replacement Home Army Office, and Major General Henning von Tresckow – presently with the OKW Inspector General's office. A dozen other military and civilian officials were also present, patiently waiting for the meeting to come to order. Off to the side in a nearby separate room, Harold observed Colonel's Claus von Stauffenberg and Pierre Massar, waving a short acknowledgement to both. Truly, this was to be a 'come to Jesus' meeting for the anti-Hitler conspiracy.

Goerdeler brought the meeting to order, introducing Harold to those present who were not familiar with him, then asked Harold to inform the assembled audience of Hitler's latest gambit; the successful testing and proposed dropping of an atomic bomb on the United States.

Colonel Massar then chimed in, validating what Hoffman reported, informing everyone he was present when Hitler informed the General Staff of the newly developed 'wonder weapon', hearing it *"straight from the horse's mouth."* The assembled audience gasped at the news and its implications.

"Do you realize that if this action occurs, there would be absolutely no chance at all of negotiating with the Allies for an armistice, none at all!" Goerdeler responded. "We need to remove Hitler immediately, and we need to do this quickly! Henning, where are you and Stauffenberg with your plan?"

Tresckow stood up and motioned for Stauffenberg to join him in the main room.

"Gentlemen, we have Operation *Valkyrie* developed and ready to go once the word gets out we have killed Hitler. With his confirmed death, General Olbricht through his boss General Fromm, will mobilize the Home Army, allowing us to seize the government before the SS gets involved. Up till now, we've been stymied as to how we can get close enough to Der Führer to use either a bomb or poison to do him in. Perhaps our OSS guest might have a suggestion that would be of assistance?" asked Tresckow.

All eyes were on Kurt – the Allies expected much from the conspiracy, but to those assembled here tonight, the question was upon what exactly could the Allies be counted on? Kurt thought, *time to put up or shut up.*

Kurt looked Goerdeler and Tresckow straight in their eyes. "What exactly do you want?" Steege asked. "We've given you munitions, explosives, money, and even intelligence assistance. Isn't that enough?"

"Maybe what we need is direct assistance," Goerdeler replied. "What good are explosives if we can't get close enough to Hitler to use them? Money? The Gestapo have our contacts arrested if they begin to show any signs of wealth where they haven't taken a cut in." Clearly he wasn't satisfied with Steege's answer.

"What we need is something massive, something that we know is guaranteed to either kill Hitler or keep his head to the ground long enough for us to take over, long enough for *Valkyrie* to take effect," said Tresckow.

"How about one massive bomb strike by the American Air Force," asked Beck? "If we could get intelligence that Hitler was at a command post or visiting an installation, could the Americans arrange a large enough bombing that might do the trick?"

Stauffenberg shook his head at all the discussion, especially at the comment about using the American Army Air Corps to 'bomb' Hitler in order to kill him. "Is there no officer over there in the Fuhrer's headquarters capable of shooting that beast!?" he said in disgust.

Harold raised his hand. "My brother informed me Hitler is scheduled to be at the Zossen OKW Command Post around August 5, for a command post exercise test. Suppose, just suppose, Steege could arrange for the Americans to strike them?"

"Three weeks from now," said Steege. "I suppose it could be arranged, hell anything can be arranged, but how can any of you guarantee he'll be there, for one and stay there long enough to plaster the place for two?"

"Leave that to us," responded Stauffenberg. "He's our problem, we'll figure out a way to keep him pinned down long enough for your air force to ensure do its job so that we can do ours with *Valkyrie!* Hoffman can provide you with all the specific locations such as Hitler's briefing building, his residence when he stays at Zossen, where the General Staff hold up, etc."

Kurt scratched his head pondering the proposition the conspirators just presented to him.

"All right, I'll take this up with Dulles and we'll see what we can do – no promises, but if you're telling me you can ensure that Hitler will be at this place – Zossen on August 5, we'll be visiting with a squadron or more of B-29 *'Superforts'*, just the ticket to clean that place out an set the stage for your *'action'*. Now as a favor to me, can you brief me on the specifics of *Valkyrie*, so I can bring Dulles and our folks up to speed on what you're doing?" replied Steege directly to Stauffenberg, who nodded to his assistant Major Hans Ulrich von Oertzen, standing behind him to his right. Oertzen in turn opened his briefcase and produced a number of manila files filled with documents and photographs.

"If you'll follow me over here Herr Steege, I can brief you in on *Valkyrie* in the adjacent room without bothering these gentlemen here." Steege followed the Major allowing the remaining Kreisau Circle conspirators to talk uninterrupted or overheard by the OSS agent.

"What do you think Hoffman?" Stauffenberg asked, with Beck joining the two of them. "Can he be trusted and do you believe he can get the American's committed?"

"I believe so," Harold replied. "My coming back was so important the American President sent his special assistant over to London with a personal request for my return, especially to deliver his message offering whatever we need, provided we're doing something to take the beast out. I firmly think Oertzen is worth supporting, hence why Steege is going over the detail to convince his folks of our intent to take Der Führer out, and then we can seek an armistice with the Allies and end this stupid, senseless war once and for all!"

Beck interrupted. "It's the only way the Allies are going to talk to us. If what you say is true about this atomic bomb, with Hitler out of the way, we can stop this attack literally before it gets off the ground." Beck then looked around the room.

"Where's Massar?" he asked Stauffenberg and Hoffman.

Stauffenberg pointed towards the far end of the study. "He's on the phone with someone to find out about Hitler's Zossen visit and what specifically it's all about."

While the three awaited Massar to finish his call, Steege and Major Oertzen returned back to the study.

"Well, what do you think?" asked Stauffenberg.

"Fairly impressive if you ask me," he answered, speaking in a half German, half midwestern American twang of an accent. "Someone sure did their homework putting that plan together, but still, if you can't cut off communications from that OKW command bunker, you're all a bunch of sitting ducks!"

"We'll take care of our part of the plan. You make damn sure you Americans come through on your end," retorted Beck. "Tresckow and Stauffenberg were very thorough in this plan's development and I trust them completely with it."

Colonel Massar finished his phone call, then quickly scurried over to Beck, Stauffenberg, Hoffman and Steege.

"Well, I found out what was going on at Zossen on August 5" said Massar. "It appears that it's the day Hitler plans to send a special Luftwaffe mission out against the Americans as a warning."

"It must be the bomb!" said Beck, eyebrows raised. "He's planning on dropping the bomb."

"Where is this 'bomb' coming from?" asked Steege. "Is he launching this from Germany? What plane do you have that has that kind of range?"

Massar quickly replied "I believe it's coming from a secret base in Norway. I have to find out where it is from my Luftwaffe counterpart in Field Marshall Goering's office, then somehow get that information over to you and the Allies. Maybe a separate strike by the Americans can take this out before the fifth."

"I can guarantee you 'maybe' won't cut it if you can't find out that air base location and if get the chance, finding out what kind of air defenses the damn thing has." Steege quickly opened his notebook to jot down this late breaking piece of information, scribbled alongside his notes on *Valkyrie*.

Beck now looked at the small circle of conspirators composed of Stauffenberg, Massar, Hoffman, and Steege, encapsulated within the large study, all reacting to Massar's news with stunned silence. Breaking the silence, he utter to everyone present, "Well gentlemen, we have work to do, so I suggest we get on with it."

Chapter 22

End Game

Fact: Anybody familiar with Nazi Germany will be familiar with Heinrich Himmler, Albert Speer, Martin Bormann and such, but few have ever heard of SS Obergruppenführer Dr. Ing[55] Hans Kammler. What is interesting is that Kammler, a high ranking 'General 'in the SS, was regarded by many in the Nazi hierarchy as the most powerful man in Germany outside the Cabinet. Kammler held a position of authority directly under Himmler, initially starting out his career by designing facilities for the extermination camps, including gas chambers and crematoria, after which SS Reichsführer Himmler assigned him the task of demolishing the Warsaw ghetto. By late 1944 he was in charge of Hitler's most secret projects, specifically projects such as the world's first jet engines and rockets. From January 1945 he became head of all missile projects and just a month later was given charge of all German aerospace programs as these came under SS authority as well. He had over 14 million people working for him mostly building underground factories. Some writers have equated his projects of equivalent importance to being in charge of building the Great Pyramids or the Coliseum in Rome. Towards the end of the war, Hitler even made Göring and Speer subordinate to Kammler. General Eisenhower admits in *Crusade In Europe* that the Nazis were within six months of developing advanced weapons that would have changed the outcome of the war, nearly all under this SS General's control.

In April 1945, Kammler disappeared. Some reports suggest that he was assassinated by a member of his staff, acting on orders from Himmler not to allow personnel with detailed knowledge of the rocket program to fall into Allied hands. Others indicate that he may have been killed in action or committed suicide somewhere around Prague. The fact that his exact fate is unknown and that his body was never recovered led to some speculation that he continued his work in the United States after the war, where it is alleged he worked on anti-gravity and other advanced devices. There have been

---

55   Doctor of Engineering.

no "Kammler sightings" since the end of the war, contrary to the cases of other Nazi war criminals such as Dr Joseph Mengele – the dreaded physician Angel of Death at the Auschwitz-Birkenau concentration camp. There is a trail of evidence that indicates in the closing days of the Reich that Kammler used a long-range multi-engine aircraft to ship a large body of research material and prototypes out of the Reich. References to this SS General in the official literature relating to the Nuremberg trials have been deleted, and was he never formally indicted, much less brought to trial even *in absentia*. In fact, despite the knowledge that he was, in many ways, the number three in the Nazi hierarchy in 1945, his name only comes up once, in an indirect reference by Walter Dornberger, the original chief of the V-2 program. SS Obergruppenführer Dr. Ing Hans Kammler simply went *'missing'* never to be heard or seen of again.

"Pilsen and the Skoda Works were captured by Combat Command B, Third Armored Division, the same unit that captured Kammler's unique metropolis, with its treasure trove of missiles and jet engines, at Nordhausen, in Saxon, on April 11."
- Tom Agoston, 'Blunder! How the U.S. Gave
Away Nazi Super secrets to Russia
(New York: Dodd, Mead and Company, 1985, p. 65).

The White House 'Map Room'
Washington, D.C.
0845 hrs, 21 July, 1945

The President's Map Room was ablaze with activity. It had only been a week since Hoffman and Steeges had passed information pertaining to a possible coup d'état[56] against Hitler by the *Kreisau Circle's* through Dulles in Switzerland. And these details coupled with the possibility of a German 'atomic bomb', had led Truman to call a meeting of his closest advisors.

---

56   Also known as a **coup, putsch,** or **overthrow,** is the sudden, extrajudicial deposition of a government usually by a small group of the existing state establishment – typically the military, to replace the deposed government with another body; either civil or military.

Truman called a secret get together of his closest key advisors down in the White House basement 'Map Room' to come up with a strategy on how to best deal with this latest, and possibly game changing, news from within Germany.

Assembled in the tight confines of the austere room were Generals Marshal and Reynolds from the Pentagon, Secretary of War Stimson, OSS Chief General Donovan, and Jerry Sherman representing the Manhattan Project's General Grooves. As usual, Jerry Curry accompanied the President, still reading the classified dispatch sent late that night by Dulles in Switzerland. As the President entered, he asked everyone present to take a seat. As per his direction, the doors to the room were closed, closely guarded on the outside by two heavily armed Marine sentries. No one would carelessly wander in to such a highly classified meeting.

Truman took his seat at the head of the horseshoe shaped table, with the military on his left, civilians on the right. He poured himself a cup of coffee from a container and then turned to General Donovan.

"All right General, without any varnish or bull, what's the straight story? Are these folks, this *Kreisau Circle* gang serious and going to conduct a coup?" Truman asked in his straight forward 'take no prisoners' approach towards getting to the truth.

The General was well prepared; opening up his file containing all the latest intelligence Dulles had supplied him with for the past three weeks.

"Mr. President, not only do I believe it's true, but it's been confirmed by Curry's own man, Mr. Harold Hoffman. Is that right Jerry?" the General asked Curry, sitting to Truman's left side.

Curry nodded in agreement, informing the group he was in possession of a separate dispatch from Hoffman not only confirming the existence of *Valkyrie*, but also of the possibility of the Nazis possession of an atomic weapon.

"Alright, we know they plan on removing Hitler, and that they are requesting our help. As I mentioned before, I'm committed to doing whatever we can if it will shorten the war and save American lives," said the President. Looking over to Generals Marshall and Reynolds, Truman then asked, "Well General Marshall, so what is our response to this proposal and what can we do about this atomic bomb they have? Do we know where this base is, and if so, why can't we just bomb it to hell?"

At this point, Donovan inserted himself between Truman and Marshal.

"We believe the Luftwaffe base is located near the town of Gardermoen, about 22 miles northeast of their main base in Oslo."

"Okay, then if we know where they might launch this attack, why can't we bomb this place and be done with it?" the President again asked.

"Well Mr. President, first of all, we don't have any hard evidence that the bomb is actually there at this time. Maybe on August 5 or a couple of days earlier, but there now, who knows? Second, if we bomb this place, what's to say they don't simply launch a second bomb from another base, one that's closer, and this time, they drop it on London?" responded General Marshal.

The President was losing his patience. "Gentlemen, I assembled you all here this morning to come up with a solution to this bit of intelligence I've received. I will not let this country be hit by this Nazi 'wonder weapon'. I need an answer to this problem, and by God, I'm going to get it!"

Off to the side, seated directly behind Stimson, Jerry Sherman raised his hand.

"Sir, I might have an answer to your problem," he said sheepishly, unsure where he stood with all the political and military heavy weight seated around him.

Stimson turned around to face the young scientist. "And who are you and who do you represent?" the Secretary of War asked.

"Sir, I'm here representing General Grooves – you know, the Manhattan Project. I was instructed by the General to provide the President with a full report on our recent detonation at Los Alamos, and somehow I was roped into this meeting. As I said, I believe I have a solution to your problem."

Stimson scowled at Sherman. "Son, Why not leave policy and strategy to the big boys here. After you brief the President and me, we'll take your suggestions and...."

"Henry, let him talk," Truman interrupted. "I've listened to all of you for the past ten minutes and haven't heard so much as a 'tinker's damn' as far as a solution." Looking straight at Sherman, he said, "Let's hear what this young scientist has to say!"

All eyes in the room were now focused on Jerry Sherman. He opened his brief case, selected a pinkish colored folder and then pulled out a lengthy report, bound by a single paper clip that seemed ready to pop.

"Mr. President, have you considered using our newly developed and tested bomb on the Germans, specifically on Hitler's Command Post at Zossen? We have discovered that the blast is massive enough to demolish this place, as well as destroy all lines of communication in and out. Additionally, the Army Air Corp's 509th Composite Group is presently in Britain. We can have a special plutonium designed bomb dispatched within a few days to their location, which is well within range of their modified B-29 bombers."

Stimson started shaking his head. "And what if this 'bomb' doesn't kill Hitler? Suppose he survives and manages to get a radio message out attesting he is still alive just as the *Valkyrie* boys are pulling their coup. They get smashed, and Hitler has his bomb sent over special delivery," said Stimson, scanning the room for a consensus on his commentary.

Sherman was a little rattled by Stimson's comment, but Truman nodded his approval for him to continue.

"Sir, what you don't understand," Sherman started, "is when a blast occurs, there's a phenomenon known as EMP that occurs. This might be the answer you're looking for."

"EMP," uttered Truman. "Son, I'm not a scientist, so you're going to have to explain to all of us here what this 'EMP' thing is, in common everyday layman's talk."

"I'm sorry Sir – EMP stands for *electromagnetic pulse*. We found that by detonating an atomic device, a pulse is generated that basically shorts out anything electrical within a specific range including radios. In our report, we mentioned we did not have any radio communication with anyone for a few days as most of them were fried."

"Do you think the same things could occur over Hitler's command post, this 'EMP' as you call it?" asked Truman.

"I don't see why not." Sherman responded. "As long as you have shielded equipment like that on the 509th bombers, they will be fine. For everyone else though, Sir, that's a different matter. Even if Hitler somehow survives the blast, which is extremely unlikely, there's no way he or anyone else for that matter can get a message out stopping the coup from taking place."

Truman slapped his hands down on the desk. "Well gentlemen, I think we are starting to form a plan." He looked over at Generals Marshall and Reynolds.

"General Marshall, go ahead and have this 509th ready to receive its special package from General Groves. Have the Army Air Forces over there prepared a plan to strike both the Norway base concurrent with the dropping of this 'atomic bomb' on the Zossen headquarters. Sherman, have Groves immediately assemble another 'atomic bomb' and make it available for General Marshall's use."

Marshall and Sherman both acknowledged the President's directive.

"General Donovan," the President continued, "I need you to make damn sure we have the latest intelligence on this base in Norway, and if possible, find out when the Germans ship their bomb up there and where they might store it. Pass on all your information to General Kruger in London so that his boys get the latest scoop."

Truman then turned to his Secretary of War. "Henry, I want you to give them anything they need, whether it is manpower, planes, whatever. This mission is the priority. That's your job! Now, if there aren't any more questions for me, gentlemen, let's get to it!" finished the President smiling – pleased they now had a workable plan developed and he'd had a major hand in it.

Truman and Curry headed to the elevator and back to the President's Oval Office.

"Jerry, you seemed pretty quiet back there. You didn't say much and you're supposed to be my advisor. Is there anything on your mind?" Truman asked.

"No Sir, I'm fine, just a little preoccupied these days. I believe the plan has a reasonable chance for success, just a lot of Germans are going to die when that blast occurs," Curry replied.

"Well, better that a few Germans die in the short run, than a whole lot of Americans in the long run if you ask me," the President quipped. "This war's got to end sooner than later."

As they entered the Oval Office, Curry noticed a cardboard box filled with reel-to-reel tapes.

"Jerry, these are Roosevelt's tape recordings of various phone conversations he's kept all these years. Damned if I knew he kept a recording of nearly all the phone calls he made and received in case he was misquoted by politicians or reporters. I figured, since you worked closely with him, you might want to screen these before I have them turned over to the National Archives.

Curry grabbed the box from Truman's desk and headed back to his office, where another batch of messages and inter-office memos once again littered his desk. He sighed as he sat down; placing the box on his desk in hopes it might cover up all the little notes, each and every one requiring a response of action.

He grabbed a handful of the reel-to-reel disks, each meticulously numbered and labeled with the dates and times of the recording. There was over sixty of these reels, each one covering approximately 10 hours of phone recordings by President Roosevelt. *What a treasure trove for a future Presidential archivist,* Curry thought, looking at all the disks.

As he looked over the recording dates he noticed a disk labeled "23 February, 1945". *Hmmm, this is the last date FDR made a recording,* Curry thought to himself, reminiscing about his many Oval Office conversations with his past boss over the past four years. For old time's sake, he picked up his phone and asked Alonzo Fields to bring a tape player over to his office as soon as he could. Within ten minutes, Alonzo came through, bringing a large, bulky tape player in on a cart.

With a little assistance from Alonzo, Curry fed the audio-magnetic tape into the machine, put on the head phones and turned it on. He then sat back and listened to the former Chief Executive on the phone, giving instructions to cabinet members, sharing his all too common 'homilies' with congressmen and senators, or just making small talk with the numerous callers he received. After an hour and a half, he started to grow bored with the tedious array of recorded calls.

But just when he thought he'd had enough, he heard a call that sent chills up his spine. He was now listening in on the very call that the President had received with Jerry listening in on the President's extension, which had sent FDR into a convulsion, followed by a coma and ultimately, his demise. There, recorded for all, was the President's blackmailer, making his latest threat to reveal FDR's secret.

Curry sat back reflecting on that day in general and the blackmailer's call in particular. He thought it was strange no one in the White House, including President Truman, had heard from the blackmailer since that fateful day.

He played the tape over again and again, carefully listening to the caller's voice; it had a familiarity to it, but he just couldn't quite place it. He knew he had heard the voice before, and then he sat straight up in his chair as if a thunder bolt out of the blue had struck him.

Curry now knew with reasonable certainty the identity of President Roosevelt's blackmailer. The question now was how he would go about confronting this man with the truth.

At 15:45 hours, barely two hours after Truman's ad hoc strategy planning meeting broke up, the telexes at the United States Army Air Force (USAAF) HQs at Bushey Hall clattered to life, each one spewing paper off its roller at a high rate of speed as if it was hooked up to a New York Stock Exchange ticker tape machine. Written in bold letters across the transmission was written, "*Top Secret — For the Eyes of the Commander only*", and signed by the Army Chief of Staff himself — General George C. Marshall. Two G-2 Intelligence officers quickly scooped up the paper rolls and immediately made their way to the Commander's office — General Carl 'Tooey' Spaatz.

As luck would have it, Spaatz was conducting a call with his senior Air Force Commanders also present - Lieutenant General 'Jimmy' Doolittle, made famous by his raid on Tokyo in April 1942 and now commanding general of the Eight Air Force; Lieutenant General Nathan Twining, the Commander of the Fifteenth Air Force; and Lieutenant General Lewis Brereton and his recently arrived Ninth Air Force.

The two G-2 officers interrupted Spaatz's conference to hand him the top secret papers. Spaatz initially appeared annoyed at the interruption; his operations officer was briefing the assembled commanders on the latest results of *Operation Crossbow* — the bombing of the dreaded German V-1 and V-2 sites along the Northeastern European Coast. Spaatz had long complained to his superiors in Washington and London that *Crossbow* was a 'diversion' from the main task of wearing down the Luftwaffe and bombing German industry into rubble. He continually recommended instead that this operation become a secondary priority since even the 'days of bad weather' over Germany's industrial targets would still allow him enough resources to provide sufficient weight of attack for the rocket sites and the lesser crises. Until this moment, he had been overruled each and every time he asked.

After carefully scanning the documents, Spaatz's facial expression clearly revealed something of monumental, if not history making importance. In the orders from General Marshall, it was clear that *Operation Crossbow* was suspended temporarily for the moment.

Spaatz stood up and instructed all personnel to immediately leave the room with the exception of his three Air Force Commanders and their Operations Officers. Once the last person left the room, he instructed one of his two G-2 officers to stand guard outside the conference room door and bar entry of anyone including the "King of England himself", until cleared by the General personally. Spaatz then instructed the other G-2 officer to find Colonel Tibbets of the 509th Composite Group over at Royal Air Force (RAF) Base Honington and have the colonel immediately report to him regardless of what he was doing, even if it meant flying one of his bombers over to Bushey Hall.

"Gentlemen," Spaatz started "We have been handed a mission that I believe if successful, might end this damn war and we can all go home!" All three Air Force Commanders immediately sat upright at their Commander's comment, while the Operations Officers each reacted with a wide eyed, jaw dropping silence. This had to be big.

Spaatz continued. "I have summoned the commander of the 509th Composite Group over from RAF Base Honington because of his special capabilities, details that I cannot go into at this time, but, suffice to say, each and every single one of you will have a mission that ultimately supports his and our nations."

On the General's signal, Major Jeffrey Lawrence, General Spaatz's Operations Officer rolled out a large map of Europe over the conference room table, covering the various ash trays, Stars & Stripes newspapers, magazines and other assorted reading paraphernalia scattered all over the table. Lawrence then handed a large pointer to the General as he stood up to address his commanders.

"Okay gentlemen, here it is. We have word from very credible sources that Hitler is going to launch some sort of bombing attack against the United States sometime on August 5, launching this attack from an airbase located north of Oslo." Spaatz pointed out the general location on the map. "What's the name of this base Jeff?"

"Gardermoen," Lawrence replied.

"Right. *Gardermoen*. This target goes to you Nathan and your Fifteenth Air Force boys."

"One target for an entire Air Force to attack Tooey?" General Twining responded using the General's nickname. "What kind of target is it?"

"An important target that is highly guarded with probably the best the Luftwaffe has, so don't be conservative and hold anything back. It is absolutely essential this base and all its planes are destroyed!" Spaatz looked Twining dead in the eye to emphasize how serious he was.

Spaatz then looked over at General Doolittle.

"Jimmy, while Nathan is kicking the shit out of the Norway base, you will concurrently conduct a diversionary bombing mission over the cities of Dusseldorf, Hamburg, Wilhelmshaven and Berlin. Your mission basically is to serve as a diversionary force – saturate the German air defenses and keep as many of their fighters tied up chasing your Eighth Air Force boys over Germany. Same thing for you General Brereton and your Ninth Air Force, except all of your targets are over the Northern French coast. You job is to make the Germans believe we are conducting a massive bombing preparation strike as a prelude to a cross channel invasion."

"Is this what this is all about Tooey?" Doolittle piped up. "Is the invasion what this is all about?"

Spaatz let out a short chuckle. "If only..." he responded. "This is much larger than that by far!"

A knock at the door brought the conversation to a halt.

"Who the hell could that be?" Spaatz said, incredulous of the interruption given he had given strict orders not to be disturbed.

The intruder responded, opening the door to reveal Spaatz's G-2 officer, Major Thompson.

"This better be good Major," said the General, embarrassed at the interruption of his classified meeting with his commanders.

"Sir, we've located Colonel Tibbets and we're in luck. He's in the air on a training mission and we were able to divert him here to see you as per your orders," responded Thompson. "He should be here within 15, maybe 20 minutes max!"

"Have a vehicle waiting for him on the tarmac when he lands and have him brought immediately to this conference room on the double – understand?"

"Yes Sir," saluted the red faced Thompson, who immediately departed, closing the door behind him.

Spaatz returned to his subordinate commanders. "Gentlemen, as I mentioned before, Tibbets and his 509th Group is what this mission is all about. Everything you do on August 5 is in support of his overall mission. As a matter of fact, Jimmy, I want you to turn over operational control of the 364th Fighter Group with its three fighter squadron, which is co-located with Tibbet's 509th Group at Honington. This will ensure he has sufficient fighter escort heading to and from his target."

"Doesn't leave me with very much fighter cover left over to protect my bombers heading to north central Germany Tooey," replied Doolittle, a little miffed that a mere 'Group' was getting a three fighter squadron escort."By the way, just what exactly is his target?"

Spaatz looked over at Major Lawrence, who shook his head, a distinct sign this information was not releasable at the present time.

"Sorry gents, but the 509th's target is classified for the time being. Major Lawrence, is there anything you wish to add?" asked Spaatz.

Lawrence stood up while Spaatz returned the four foot pointer to him.

"General Brereton, your groups are first, lifting off to hit your targets starting at 0500 on August 5. General Doolittle, your Eighth Air Force will commence operations, departing from your airfields at 0900. The 509th will depart RAF Honington shortly thereafter on the same flight vector until this point," Lawrence pointed to a spot in the middle of the North Sea. "From here, the 509th will depart on a classified vector, returning pretty much on the same path."

Both Doolittle and Brereton looked at Spaatz, their facial expressions in agreement.

Lawrence continued. "General Twining, you mission is second in importance behind the 509th. The Eighth and Ninth Air Forces are acting as diversionary strikes to draw off sufficient Luftwaffe resources away from you and the 509th. Your Fifteenth Air Force bomber and fighter groups will take off from your airfields at 1030 hours along this path across the North Sea towards Gardermoen. It is important that you destroy everything on that base – every facility, bomber, hanger, everything!"

Spaatz then took over. "Gentlemen, I don't have to tell you that you shouldn't approach this as just another bombing mission over the Third Reich. At Gardermoen, the Nazis will throw everything they have at you Nathan – including the kitchen sink if they have it. As for Brereton and Doolittle – the more you can put into the air, the more Luftwaffe we can tie up and kill; and trust me, your missions won't be a cake walk either, not since they're using these new 'jet' powered fighters. It will be a long and bloody day, but if successful, we might just end this war sooner and save a lot of American and British boys in the long run."

When Spaatz finished, Major Lawrence told each Air Force Commander to have their Operations Officers to see him after the conclusion of the meeting in order to coordinate development of their respective target folders and other planning documents.

Another knock at the conference room door was greeted by Spaatz in a much the same way as before; with a short, obnoxious "Yes!"

Major Thompson immediately opened the door, announcing "Colonel Tibbets reporting as ordered", stepping aside to allow the 509th Composite Group commander entry into the secret conference.

Tibbets stood directly in front of General Spaatz and saluted smartly. He was still in his B-29 flight suit, failing to change because of the urgency of the request for his presence at the conference. Tibbets had flown for the better part of five hours and his body reeked and he desperately needed to bathe.

"Take a seat Paul," said Spaatz. "We were just wrapping up the mission for these gentlemen." Tibbets could see from the number of senior generals present, this mission was big, thinking perhaps it was the invasion of France and his unit would finally see action.

Again turning back to his three Air Force Commanders, Spaatz continued.

"Nathan, one last thing, and this is a specific instruction from the Joint Chiefs of Staff and the Office of Strategy Services. Once your last plane has lifted off, you are to make radio contact with an OSS man code named *Prairie Dog*. The frequency is identified in this telex. Now, do any of you gentlemen have any further questions?"

That was the signal for the Eighth, Ninth and Fifteenth Air Force Commanders that their meeting with Spaatz had concluded and to begin their planning actions. Lawrence directed the respective Air Force Operations Officers to see him in his office. Tibbets remained seated – Spaatz still had to deal with him.

Once the last commander, General Twining, had departed and closed the door behind him, Spaatz pulled his chair up close to Tibbets, much like a school kid desiring to share a deep secret without anyone else overhearing.

"Paul, the moment you and your group have waited for appears to have arrived at last," said Spaatz in a low voice. "In a separate telex, I received word yesterday that your 'package' is scheduled to arrive within the next 48 hours, under extremely heavy armed guard, under the cover that this is a new type of 'block buster' bomb. General Grooves is also sending a technical arming package along to assist with the fusing and arming process."

Tibbets smiled. Finally, everything he and the 509th had trained for over the past 18 months was about to be tested, and, if successful, would herald the dawn of a new form of warfare.

"May I ask what and where the target is?" asked Tibbets.

Spaatz quickly looked around the room, more out of forced habit than necessity since they were the only two present. He looked through the telex, then used his pencil to circle the answer to Tibbets's question.

"The target city is Zossen, just north of Berlin. The specific target is the OKW bunker complex located at this latitude-longitude." Spaatz showed the telex information to Tibbets as confirmation.

Tibbets sat back in his chair incredulous. "All this about destroying a command bunker complex?" he asked. "Forgive me saying this, but why can't this mission go to one of the other Air Forces you have here?"

Spaatz leaned closer to Tibbets. "Because we have hard intelligence to confirm Hitler himself will be there on the day of your mission. According to the Joint Chiefs of Staff, they wanted a mission that would virtually guarantee his death."

Tibbets immediately raised his right hand to his chin in wonder. Not only was this a major mission to take out the very command post running the Nazi war effort, but they were going to attempt to take out the top leadership of the Third Reich once and for all.

"I'll have Major Lawrence provide your operations officer with all the coordinating information, specific dates, times, the works. Is it still Major James Hopkins?" Spaatz asked.

Tibbets nodded.

Spaatz continued. "As insurance, I've instructed General Doolittle to make the 364th Fighter Group available to you for escort. That should give you around 80 F-51 Mustangs for protection. Do you think that will be enough or will you require more?"

"No Sir," Tibbets responded. "Getting there will be challenge enough, but the problem is once I drop the damn thing. This bomb generates quite a shock wave. If I don't turn right there and haul ass out, it could take me and everyone else out who came along for the trip, and I mean out!"

Spaatz stood and extended his right hand to Tibbets.

"Colonel, I trust you will know what to do when the time comes. If there's anything else I can do, call me anytime. I wish you luck!"

Tibbets stood and returned Spaatz's handshake. "Thank your Sir." *I'm going to need it*, he thought as he departed the conference room and returned to his plane.

Major Frtiz Spangel took one last drag on his cigarette, then flung the expended butt out onto the dark runway that served as the main thoroughfare of Luftwaffe Base – Gardermoen. Dawn was an hour away and morning twilight began to slowly illuminate the German airbase on what looked to be a pleasant August 4. Off along the eastern edge of the tarmac were silhouetted at least two dozen fighters, many of the type Spangle had flown earlier in the war, bringing back a few bittersweet memories of his fighter days during the *Battle of Britain*, four summers ago. On the western side of the tarmac, dwarfing the fighters, were five massive Ju-390 heavy bombers, all part of the Luftwaffe's secret bombing group assigned to attack special targets specifically at the Führer's directive. To maintain secrecy as to their true mission, the unit masqueraded as a maritime reconnaissance squadron, attacking British convoys coming within five hundred miles of the Norwegian coast. Missing from the bomber unit lines was Spangel's pride and joy – the '*Honey Bee*', which at that moment was inside a specially configured hanger receiving modification to her bomb bay.

As Spangel turned towards the *kantine* for a cup of coffee, he noticed a convoy of trucks, with what appeared to be three 88mm anti-aircraft 'flak' batteries, lined up outside the main gate under an extremely heavy SS guard detail. As he watched this unusual activity outside the main gate at this early time of the morning, he was joined by his co-pilot, Captain Hans Pancherz.

"What the hell do you suppose that's all about?" Spangel asked Pancherz.

"I don't know, but I suspect it will have to do with our orders which the squadron just received. The commander sent me to go fetch you for a briefing and I'll bet you a week's leave in Paris it doesn't have anything to do with '*fishing boat*' spying," replied Pancherz referring to their practice of flying out over the ocean in search of British vessels, as he grabbed his colleague's arm.

Fifteen minutes later, along with the '*Honey Bee's*' navigator Lieutenant Strossel and the 50 plus crewmen of the other five bombers, they were seated in the flight operations debriefing room.

What the hell can be in that convoy that's so important?, Spangel thought to himself, instinctively reflecting what was going on in the minds of most of the crews assembled. Many of whom were barely awake due to the early morning nature of this sudden squadron officer's call. Their wonder was soon shattered with the announced '*Achtung!*', causing everyone present to snap to immediate attention as a be-medaled SS officer entered the room accompanied by Squadron Commander Colonel Koenig and four men in white coats – obviously technicians of some sort.

"Gentlemen, please be seated," ordered Koenig, who then turned to the high ranking SS officer.

Scanning the room thoroughly to make sure only Luftwaffe and SS personnel were present, he stepped over to the conference room podium, his facial appearance completely devoid of any expression that might convey what the meeting was about.

"Gentlemen, I am SS-Brigadeführer Kurt Sturmer and I am in charge of the detail that has just arrived at this airbase. My orders come directly from SS Obergruppenführer Kammler, who works directly for Der Führer. I am here to accomplish two objectives; one is to deliver a weapons package to this squadron along with providing technicians who will assist in arming it. My second objective is to provide the targeting instructions to those crews selected by your commander, Colonel Koenig, as to who will deliver this weapon to its intended target." Sturmer stopped short to take in the assembled crew's reaction to his comments – noticing a mixture of bewilderment and utter stunned surprise. Seeing he now had their undivided attention, he smiled and continued. "I will now answer your questions."

Captain Haushofer, the pilot of the 'Grey Wolf', stood up. "Sir, the obvious question is who has been selected for the mission?"

Colonel Koenig stepped in to answer for the SS officer. "Since you asked the question, it's only right to tell you that three crews have been selected. They are Major Spangel's 'Honey Bee', Captain Kurstin's 'Birdwatcher', and your Grey Wolf, Captain Haushofer." A rush of wonderment filled the conference room at the selected crews.

Haushofer still remained standing. "Are we at liberty to ask where the target is?"

Koenig looked over at Sturmer. Since the room was secure with his SS men, Sturmer nodded his approval to Koenig.

Clearing his throat, Koenig announced, "Your target is New York City. You will all fly tomorrow morning. As of now, this base is secure. No one is allowed to leave this base until further notice without the express approval of SS-Brigadeführer Sturmer. Is that clear?"

Spangel raised his hand. "Sir, my plane is in for maintenance. How am I going to fly tomorrow?"

"Your plane is being fitted with a special device that will allow you to load this 'bomb', and it's expected to be completed by this afternoon. This evening the bomb will be loaded with the assistance of the technicians you see here in the back of the room," replied Koenig.

The Squadron Commander then handed the targeting pouches to Spangel, Kurstin, and Haushofer. "Study the details carefully," Koenig instructed the three pilots. "Take your instructions from the technicians this afternoon. Pre-flight is at 0700 tomorrow morning."

Looking at the remaining crews, Koenig then brought the room to attention. "You all will assist where you can. Remember, the base is closed until further notice. Dismissed!"

Jerry Curry walked down the long hallway of the U.S. Capital building until he came to the object of his search, the door of a U.S. Senator. As the daily traffic of the senate buzzed about him, he thought about what he would do and say when he confronted the man inside. He took a deep breath, then opened the door and entered the office.

As he stepped in, the Senator's secretary looked up the visitor.

"May I help you?" she asked Jerry.

"I've come to see the senator, is he available?" Curry responded, hoping he didn't seem as nervous as he felt.

"The senator is busy right now, but if you care to make an appointment..."

Curry had come all this way and wasn't going to let a secretary deflect him. Seeing the senator in his office, he brushed past the women and entered.

"We're old friends, I'm sure he won't mind a quick get-together," Curry called over his shoulder, entering the senator's office and shutting the door behind him.

The object of Jerry's Capitol Hill visit was standing behind his desk with a drink in his hand, looking out his window across the Washington landscape.

"I think it's time you and I had a talk, Senator Wheeler," said Curry, as the man turned his attention from the window to his office visitor. "A talk that's long overdue."

Wheeler looked Jerry up and down, then sat down behind his desk, looking as if he had finally been caught.

"Can I fix you something Mr. Curry?" he asked, pointing to the corner table of his office that served as an ad hoc office bar.

"The only thing you can fix is the mess you've put yourself in," replied Curry, pulling out a chair and taking a seat directly across from Wheeler. "I finally figured out that it was you behind all the calls to FDR, blackmailing him all these years."

Wheeler knocked back a chug of his drink, then stared directly at Curry.

"Is that so?" Wheeler asked. "What makes you think I had anything to do with 'blackmail', especially blackmailing a president?"

Curry smiled, leaning back in his chair. He suspected Wheeler would deny it, but he was prepared.

"Well senator, let me lay it all out for you. First of all, I found out that Hopkin's assistant, Jay Hill, used to work for you until Harry hired him away. This was around the time you and the President had a major falling out in policy. Hill then turns up dead by Ford's Theater. Suddenly, the President starts receiving phone calls shortly after the Japs bombed Pearl

Harbor, calls causing the President to uncharacteristically begin to look soft on the Germans."

Wheeler continued to stare directly at Curry without any expression at all. "So what?" Wheeler retorted. "What does that prove?"

"Well Sir, it establishes motive. If Hill had the letters, you couldn't very well use them against FDR, and if he sold them for profit, which is what it looks like he was trying to do, there went your ace in the hole, and the letters may or may not ever be exposed."

Wheeler still tried to play coy."You still haven't connected me to any blackmail scheme."

Curry smiled again. "Oh, but I have my friend, I have," said Curry. "You see, what you may not have been aware of was Roosevelt kept tape recordings of all his calls and I happened to listened in on one such call, the one you made his final day in the Oval Office. I'm sure the FBI would have no trouble matching it up against your voice."

The senator knew once and for all the jig was finally up, pushing his glass across his desk, then leaning back in his chair with the look of a defeated man.

"Were you planning on using them against Truman? Because if you thought you would, it would be a tragic mistake. This President isn't one for blackmail, and couldn't care a less if this had occurred on Roosevelt's watch," said Curry. "If you don't mind, I'll take those documents and see that they're destroyed."

"I wasn't planning on it," responded Wheeler. "After my favorite nephew was killed at sea by the Germans early this year and with Roosevelt gone, I no longer had the heart for it, or this job."

"What are you saying?" Curry asked. "Is this why you abstained?"

"Yes, how could I vote 'no' against going to war against the Nazis when they killed him? If I voted 'yes', I would have looked like a hypocrite," Wheeler uttered looking down at his desk as if ready to cry.

"So what will you do now?" Curry asked.

The senator reached inside his coat jacket and handed an envelope to Curry. "Go ahead – open and read it," replied Wheeler.

Curry pulled the letter out, glancing over the one paragraph narrative, then laid the document down on the senator's desk.

"Senator, I believe the sooner you hand this letter of resignation in to the Senate President pro tempore Kenneth McKellar, the better for this country."

☆ ☆ ☆

0800 hrs, 5 August, 1945 Northeast of London

Early on the morning of August 5, the skies of England were a pilot's paradise, with warm temperatures and a crystal clear sky that invited all aviators to partake. The early morning fog, so typical for this time of the morning, had disappeared earlier than usual, as if divine intervention had played a hand.

In an arc radiating from London across northeastern and southeastern England, hundreds of bombers and fighters took to the skies towards their pre-arranged targets, starting with northern France, followed shortly by targets in Germany and Norway. With so many planes taking off from the numerous airfields that sprinkled the English countryside, the windows of dozens of cottages in the villages surrounding the numerous air bases violently shook or outright shattered from the loud vibrations from the immense bombers, heavily loaded with explosive ordnance.

In Berlin, the *Valkyrie* conspirators also began fanning out to their pre-arranged locations throughout the city in anticipation of the day's planned events. 'Prairie Dog' Steege remained in a small house near Schöneberg, listening in on the radio for the pre-arranged signal from the Eighth Air Force indicating the strike was on its way. Across town, Stauffenberg and Hoffman met General Tresckow at the War Ministry Bendlerblock building to re-check with Massar if there were any changes to Hitler's schedule of the day. Quickly calling Der Führer's valet Heinz Linge, Massar was able to confirm Hitler was still scheduled to visit the Zossen OKW Command Post to promote a senior Wehrmacht officer as well as initiate a new operation *'that would have earthshaking consequences'*.

Massar quickly relayed the information to Tresckow, Stauffenberg, and Hoffman; yet the group still had disquieting concerns.

"Did Linge say when and how long Hitler would remain at Zossen?" Tresckow asked Massar nervously. Turning to Hoffman and Stauffenberg he then asked, "Are the American bombers still on schedule to hit the command post at 1300 hrs?"

"That's the plan," Hoffman responded. "At least the last time we talked with *Prairie Dog*. He's supposed to let us know when they've lifted and if they're on schedule."

Lieutenant General Olbricht, the Chief of the Armed Forces Replacement Army Office, entered the room and joined the group. From their facial expressions, he could see the plan was more or less on schedule, but clearly there was angst within the group.

"Alright, here's a change in plan," said Stauffenberg. "Inside my briefcase I have two one kilogram blocks of plastic explosives along with 'pencil' detonators for just such an occasion. If for some reason the Americans do not show up, or it looks like Hitler is leaving early, I will set the detonators, leave them within my briefcase, then place it close to Hitler and his gang, after which we'll get the hell out of the building. Hoffman, I will require your assistance with arming them."

Hoffman nodded in agreement."We'll take your car then Claus," replied Harold.

"Once we've seen the explosion and know that Hitler is dead, I'll contact Olbricht to initiate *Valkyrie*," said Stauffenberg. Everyone present agreed with the backup plan.

"For what it is worth," responded Tresckow, "This assassination must be accomplished today, *coûte que coûte*[57]. Even if it fails, we still must take action in Berlin. For the practical purpose no longer counts; what matters now is that our resistance movement must take the plunge before the eyes of the world and of history. Compared to that, nothing else matters!"

✳ ✳ ✳

Flight Operations Office, VIII Air Service Command
RAF Base Honington, 73 miles NE of London.
1100 hrs, 5 August, 1945

Captain Ed Donovan finished his tenth game of solitaire, then leaned back and watched through the window as the last plane 'Freddy's Folly', a B-29 belonging to his former group, the 509th Composite Group, lifted off the runway of RAF Base Honington, headed for God knows where. Only three other planes, including its commander, Colonel Tibbets' plane 'Enola Gay' took off shortly after dozens of Eighth Air Force fighters took to the skies.

Since being reassigned out of the elite group for insubordination and conduct unbecoming an officer, his life had continued in a downhill spiral. Busted by Tibbets for buzzing the control tower with a B-29 to impress an English gal he was having an affair with, Donovan turned increasingly to drink to ease his sense of failure as an Army Air Force pilot. A recent drunken fight, his third in a month with a number of other Army and Royal Air Force officers at an English local pub, ended up in him being grounded,

---

57 "Whatever the cost"

and landed him in confinement facing court martial charges. Since the local fighter group commander needed everyone available to support the Eighth Air Force and 509th's mission preparation, Donovan was temporarily released and assigned to flight operations, with the added task of making radio contact with an OSS man once the last Eighth Air Force plane had departed.

As he watched 'Freddy's Folly' depart from sight, he picked up and threw the deck of cards across the room, starling the other flight controllers present.

"I should have been in the mission," he muttered. "I'm ten times the flyer Fred Hutchinson is," referring to the pilot of 'Freddy's Folly'.

"Still got a case of the ass?" Lieutenant Sterling asked Donovan as he returned to his seat.

"So I broke a few rules, what's the beef?" Donovan asked the other flight controllers present. "What do they want — top rated pilots, or those who can't fly worth a crap, but obey all the rules?"

Sterling tried to ignore the question and was rapidly becoming annoyed at the busted Air Force captain making noises of self pity. He looked at his watch and noticed it was 11:10a.m.

"Hey Donovan, weren't you suppose to call someone when the last plane of Easy Eight's 364th Fighter took off? That was over 40 minutes ago," asked Sterling.

Donovan looked at his watch. *Holy crap*, he thought. Looking over to Lieutenant Sterling, he replied, "Well, whatever this guy needs to know can be a few minutes late, what the hell!" He then stooped to pick up the scattered deck of cards lying about the floor.

"Captain, I highly advise you to make that call. That order came down all the way from General Spaatz himself. If he finds out you blew him off, I guarantee you won't see daylight for some time to come," retorted Sterling.

"Fine, have it your way," said Donovan, dropping the few cards he'd picked up. Heading over to the radio already preset to the desired frequency, he picked up the sheet of instructions next to the mike and studied it for a moment.

"*Prairie Dog, this is Almighty. Terminator is en-route — over*".

Within a minute, came the response *"Almighty, this is Prairie Dog — roger. Why is Terminator running late — over?"*

✵ ✵ ✵

Maybach II Complex
OKW Command Post, Zossen, 13 miles south of Berlin.
1145 hrs, 5 August, 1945

Heinrich Hoffman was standing impatiently outside the Maybach I check point. Der Führer was due at any moment and required his favorite photographer present to snap all important propaganda photos of readying to launch the ultimate vengeance weapon against the impertinent Americans.

Where the hell is my brother? he wondered, all the while holding his access badge allowing Harold entry into the high security compound.

As Heinrich was about to give up and head inside, a black Mercedes sedan with two occupants pulled up to the access check point. Heinrich immediately recognized Harold as the driver, with a Wehrmacht Colonel with an eye patch alongside him.

"It's about time you got here, I was about to give up on you," Heinrich scolded Harold. "Here's your access badge," he said as he handed Harold his temporary credentials for entry. "I am to escort you through the complex at all times. Who is this Colonel and what's his business here?"

"I am Colonel Stauffenberg, Chief of Staff for the Home Army," replied the Colonel. "Herr Hoffman was kind enough to give me a ride since I too have business with Der Führer."

Heinrich looked the Colonel over. "Very well, you might as well accompany me through the check point." All three presented their identification and orders to the Security Detachment Commander, then proceeded through the SS checkpoint into the complex. Wehrmacht officers and soldiers were also present throughout the complex in large numbers, getting ready for Hitler's arrival as well.

As the three strolled down the bunker hallway, Heinrich asked Stauffenberg if he had ever met Hitler before.

"No, I have not had the opportunity but I'm looking forward to meeting him today," replied Stauffenberg. "Has he arrived?"

"Der Führer should be here momentarily, but with his schedule and security needs, you have to be flexible," said Heinrich, picking up the pace in order to get to the main command center. "I do know that Reich Marshalls Goering and Himmler are here as well to partake in this historic moment."

"I completely understand," responded Stauffenberg. Stopping for a moment, he asked the senior Hoffman if there was a phone nearby in order to make a call back to the War Ministry.

"Certainly Colonel, use this office here. The command center is just down this hallway, second door on the right. I will see you there shortly."

Harold stayed with Stauffenberg, watching the hallway as the Colonel called Olbricht for the latest news from *Prairie Dog*.

Once Stauffenberg received an update from Olbricht, he let Harold know the Americans were on their way, but would probably arrive later than expected.

"Somehow, we have to delay Hitler as long as possible," Stauffenberg told Hoffman as they walked into the Maybach command center.

As they entered, both were awestruck by the vast array of large well illuminated maps, clacking telexes and phones that fed into the large room. In front of Hoffman and Stauffenberg were literally dozens of solider technicians, each wearing headsets with microphones, collecting information from the far reaching venues of the Reich. Anything and everything that was of a military nature occurring within the Third Reich was projected on screens for the military leadership of Germany to view and take action on. In essence, the two of them had entered the very nerve center of Oberkommando der Wehrmacht – 'OKW'.

To their left they noticed a number of senior officers, most noticeable Field Marshall Keitel and General Jodl congratulating another General for some accomplishment. Stauffenberg thought he recognized him, but with so many other officers all about, it was difficult.

Entering from another doorway came Field Marshall Goering, looking highly stressed if not outright agitated, followed by half a dozen senior Luftwaffe aides. On the screen before him was a large map depicting northern France, Belgium, the Netherlands, and northern Germany. Stauffenberg and Hoffman could see dozens of incoming lights illuminated, each one indicating radar tracking locations of American and British bombing missions saturating German air defenses. Not only were the Allies on their way, but in a big way.

Near the map was a large scale tracking board indicating each side's tentative losses. The Americans so far had lost 250 bombers and another 75 fighters over France alone, while the missions hitting northeastern Germany seemed to indicate a frightful number of losses.

Stauffenberg pulled Hoffman out into the hallway to converse away from the noise of the room.

"Where the hell is Hitler?" he asked Harold. "Find out from your brother when he is due to arrive!"

As the two continued their discussion in the hallway, a Wehrmacht General suddenly bumped into Stauffenberg. Looking at the officer, Stauffenberg saw it was none other than the newly promoted General of Panzer Troops Johan Bernatz.

"What the hell are you doing here?" Bernatz asked the stunned Stauffenberg.

"I have business here with the General Staff that does not concern you," the Colonel retorted to the indignant General.

Bernatz was not satisfied with the answer. "Somehow, I don't believe you – Colonel. I think you're here conducting business for that traitor, General Tresckow," he shot back.

Stauffenberg went on the offensive. "Oh really? And what is your purpose for being here today. Being decorated for killing more unarmed civilians you call partisans?"

"I am here Herr Colonel, because Der Führer summoned me here today for consideration regarding my appointment as the new Army Chief of Staff, replacing General Kurt Zeitzler. Then I will be able to sweep scum like Tresckow and you away."

Suddenly Bernatz felt something poking him in his back, causing him to lunge slightly forward.

"I don't think so," said Harold, pointing a pistol in the General's back. "Now be a good boy and follow the Colonel here to a nice, quiet room."

The three of them headed for an empty office and locked the door behind them.

"What do you plan to do with the General here?" asked Harold. Stauffenberg found a lamp, pulled the cord out and proceeded to tie Bernatz up.

"How long do you think you can keep this up?" said Bernatz before being gagged with Stauffenberg handkerchief.

"Long enough, Herr General, long enough." Harold handed the pistol to Stauffenberg.

"Go find out what's keeping Hitler while I keep our 'guest' on ice," Stauffenberg said to Harold, who quickly departed in search of his older brother.

✻ ✻ ✻

Gardermoen Luftwaffe Base
22 miles north of Oslo, Norway.
1230 hrs, 5 August 1945

The blaring of air raid sirens heralded to everyone at the base that intruders in the form of enemy aircraft would soon hit within 15 minutes. Acting with extreme precision and training, Luftwaffe fighter pilots quickly scrambled into their fighters and were soon aloft in search of the American bombers. Meanwhile, anti-aircraft crews rapidly assembled by their guns, taking aim towards the western skies in search of any enemy aircraft that escaped the German fighters sent to hunt them down.

In the meantime over in Hanger #10, Major Spangel and his crew had just finished their pre-flight checks of the '*Honey Bee*' and were ready to be pulled out the hanger on to the runway. On board the device had been loaded and checked by the accompanying technicians and was ready to be armed. Ahead of them, '*Birdwatcher*' and '*Grey Wolf*' were already on the runway awaiting the signal from Zossen to proceed to their target.

With the sounds of the sirens, technicians and crewmen alike scrambled to the various bunkers and shelters found within the base. Within minutes came the tell tale sound of 'pom-pom-pom' as dozens of German 88mm anti aircraft flak cannons fired towards the sky, the noise now competed with the sound of the wailing air raid sirens.

Lieutenant Strossel looked at Spangel. "Now what?" he asked the pilot, who was as unsure as everyone else what to do.

"Try to raise Koenig," Spangel ordered Captain Pancherz. Suddenly, the crew of the '*Honey Bee*' was startled by the loud explosion occurring on the runway – '*Grey Wolf*' had just been destroyed. Within seconds followed three different sounding explosions announcing the crash of three large American bombers – B-29's in all - immediately followed by five more in succession.

"Can't raise him," replied Pancherz. "Can't seem to raise anyone over at the flight ops' shed."

A technician ran over to the plane waving his arms. "They've hit the special ammo bunker," he yelled before ducking the shrapnel whizzing throughout the area.

Spangel breathed a short sigh of relief. They had loaded the last 'bomb' from the bunker only two hours ago.

Another Luftwaffe crewman entered the hanger. "They've hit *'Birdwatcher'* and most of the other Ju-390's!" he yelled before falling down, seriously wounded from all the various blasts.

"We got to do something," yelled Pancherz. "We're sitting ducks here!"

Spangel turned and ordered one of his crewmen to go get a tug ready to pull the plane out of the hanger. Three other crewmen joined him, hopping out of the various hatches more out of fear of being caught inside the plane if it was hit, than in assisting in finding a tug. Within seconds, a tug was found and hooked up, slowly pulling the plane out.

As suddenly as the raid started, the Americans had departed, leaving the base heavily damaged with all the Ju-390's destroyed, except for one – the 'Honey Bee'. In their haste to leave, the Americans left behind 15 burning B-29 bombers scattered all over Gardenmoen in their wake.

As the crew pulled 'Honey Bee' into position, Spangel yelled out the window to another set of confused airmen to find whatever they could to push the burning remains of 'Grey Wolf' off the runway.

"You can't be serious?" Pancherz asked Spangel as he started up the engines. "We don't have the orders or the authority to fly this mission!"

Spangel revved up the final two engines of the six engine giant bomber, as he began to taxi towards the runway. Seeing a clear way around the burning 'Grey Wolf', he thrust the throttle to full power and sped down the shattered runway.

Looking over at Pancherz, he proclaimed "I don't need orders for this..."

✳ ✳ ✳

Maybach II Complex
OKW Command Post, Zossen,
1245 hrs, 5 August, 1945

After a short search, Harold found his brother and to his surprise, Heinrich, while nervous, was in good spirits.

"Hitler will be here in five minutes, can you believe it?" yelled Heinrich, who already had three cameras adorned around his neck, looking somewhat like a lost tourist within the military complex.

After making a small excuse to use the rest room, Harold made his way to Stauffenberg, still holding General Bernatz captive within the small office.

Hoffman relayed the news to Stauffenberg, who while relieved to hear his target had finally arrived, still faced the problem as to what to do with Bernatz.

Handing the pistol over to Harold, Stauffenberg instructed him to cover Bernatz while he checked over the communications center.

As he entered the nerve center of the complex, Stauffenberg was surprised at the amount of chaos present. Reports were coming in that the secret base at Gardenmoen had been hit by American bombers, but the reports were inconclusive as to the amount of damage sustained. Other reports indicated more American attacks occurring throughout northeastern Germany as indicated by the large air defense tracking map. As he quickly studied the map, he noticed a small series of blips heading toward the Berlin Air Defense zone – the American strike on Zossen, now approximately 15 to 20 minutes away.

Stauffenberg realized he only had minutes to get clear of the complex. Turning to depart, the entire room came to attention as Der Führer, leader of the Third Reich, entered the communications center.

Reich's Marshall Goering, realizing that the main purpose for Hitler's visit had just been attacked in a pre-emptive strike, immediately tried to make excuses, citing a leak within the Army General Staff.

"Traitors!" Adolph Hitler yelled, turning a deep red in the process while curling his hands into fists. "I should have the entire army staff shot at once!" Looking back at Goering, Hitler then asked, "How did the Luftwaffe allow the Americans to get so close to the base?"

As Goering and a number of other General Staff officers attempted to explain the impending situation in Norway, Stauffenberg was able to slip back to the office and inform Hoffman the Americans would be there in less than 15 minutes.

"What do we do now?" Hoffman asked. "If we let him go, we're blown. If we stay, we're killed and neither of us can signal Tresckow."

Stauffenberg took the pistol from Hoffman still covering Bernatz. "You go, get far enough away from here, then contact Tresckow at this phone number and have them initiate *Valkyrie!*" Harold couldn't believe what he had just heard but the Colonel handed him a piece of paper with the number scrawled on it in pencil.

"Go, go now!" Stauffenberg instructed, waving the pistol at Harold, who opened the door to depart.

"God save our sacred Germany," said Stauffenberg as Harold departed, wondering if he would ever see the Colonel again.

As Harold departed along the Maybach command post corridor, he could hear Hitler screaming loudly at the senior officers present, yelling obscenities and invectives against them.

Bursting into the bright light, he was momentarily blinded. Regaining his vision, he coolly made his way to Stauffenberg's sedan, parked outside the SS check point. Within a couple of minutes, he had made his way down the command post access road, through two more security check points, then towards the main street leading back to Berlin.

About four miles down the road, he decided to stop at a local gasthaus to call Tresckow and let him know what Stauffenberg was up to. As he brought the car to a halt, he heard the sounds of a flight of American bombers nearby. Looking up into the sky, he could see the faint vapor trail of four large bombers – B-29s, almost directly over Zossen. *Only four?* he thought. *What were the American's thinking? Four bombers aren't near enough to scratch the paint off the command post bunkers much less devastate the complex.*

Harold called the number Stauffenberg handed him. Tresckow immediately answered with a "Ya, Staffenberg."

"This isn't Stauffenberg," Harold responded. "This is Hoffman, letting you know that the Americans are here with only four bombers..."

Suddenly, came the largest explosion Herald had ever heard, followed by a huge shaking as if an earthquake had taken place.

"What was that noise?" asked Tresckow. "Was that the bomb going off?"

Harold tried to answer, but the line suddenly went dead. Looking back towards Zossen, he was immediately transfixed at purple-reddish mushroom cloud rapidly rising from the ground.

I've got to get the hell out of here, he thought, dropping the phone and heading towards the sedan. Jumping in, he immediately floored it, racing down the street as fast as it could travel. Looking behind in the rearview mirror, he could see what appeared to be a shock wave, emanating from what was left of the Zossen Command Post, causing everything in its path - structures, vegetation, and people - to burst into flames.

Faster, faster, he thought, attempting to outrace it. Coming to an intersection, he slowed long enough to avoid hitting any other traffic. As he cleared the intersection narrowly missing an army truck, he suddenly felt the car lift up from its rear and begin to spin end over end towards a nearby building, smashing it and the car in the process.

At Bendlerblock War Ministry building, many of the military conspirators nearby with opened windows were shocked by an immense bright light immediately followed by a loud blast and a tremor coming from the south of Berlin. As they gathered by open windows, they too observed the tale tail sign of a reddish mushroom cloud ascending into the skies. All along the base, smoke and fires could also be observed, leaving all within the building wondering exactly what the Americans had dropped if they were the ones responsible.

General Tresckow and Olbricht both grabbed phones to find out if Zossen was taken out, simultaneously finding out the telephone lines were dead. They headed to the building's communications room, only to find out that radio communications were out as well.

As they headed upstairs to work this unforeseen situation, Tresckow and Olbricht were immediately confronted by General Fromm, commander of the Home Army. It was under his name *Operation Valkyrie* could be initiated.

"Who and what is going on here?!" demanded Fromm as he confronted Tresckow and Olbrict.

"Der Führer is dead, blown up at Zossen by an American bombing attack. We're initiating *Operation Valkyrie* immediately in order to ensure law and order," retorted Tresckow. "You can either be part of the solution or part of the problem – you choose!"

"You have no authority!" exclaimed Fromm. "I want proof Hitler is dead!"

Suddenly, a voice came from behind the excited General. "Here's your proof."

Fromm turned around to see Colonel Massar aiming a P-38 pistol directly at him. "Is this proof enough? Hitler is dead. Take a look in the direction of Zossen. Do you think anyone could have possible survived a blast like that?" Massar asked.

"Take him away," Tresckow ordered Massar as he and Olbrict headed back to the Chief of Staff's office.

Once back in his office, Olbrict and Tresckow were met by General Beck along with a few others from the Kreisau Circle.

"So it begins," said Beck, looking southward at the raging conflagration enveloping Zossen.

Tresckow emerged with two copies of the plan, handing one to two senior Wehrmacht Majors standing by.

"Major Zeiber, take this order over to Major Remer, commander of the Greater German Guards Battalion, and have him secure all these objectives within the government sector, arresting all the SS and Nazi Party officials he comes across. Let him know that with the Führer's death, we are activating the *Valkyrie* plan. Major Kirn, you will drive north to the Defense Group III headquarters, and use whatever means possible to include their communications facilities and initiate *Valkyrie* across Germany as per the same instructions I just gave Zeiber. Now, the both of you go – and God speed!" Both officers saluted Tresckow, then turned and immediately departed.

Tresckow then joined General Beck, still observing the burning town of Zossen, nearly obscured from view due to the massive fires and smoke emanating from the blast area.

"Do you think we did the right thing Henning?" Beck asked his conspiratorial colleague. "Did it have to come down to this to rid Germany of such a tyrant?"

Tresckow turned to Beck. "An English philosopher Edmund Burke once said, *'All that is required for evil to prevail is for good men to do nothing'*. Ludwig, I can truthfully say today, we did something to stop this evil."

Beck shook his head in agreement, then added, "Let's get a hold of Agent Steege and let him know that Germany will soon be ready to negotiate an end of this war madness once and for all."

A year later off the coast of Newfoundland, a French fishing boat pulled their net in after a long day's fishing off the Grand Banks. As they pulled their net in, they immediately noticed it weighed far more than normal, nearly halting the electric winch. As the fishermen began looking into the large net, they noticed what appeared to be a seven foot wing section from an airplane – a large one at that. Spying the distinctive green camouflage usually associated with the Luftwaffe, they struggled to retrieve the broken wing, pierced with bullet holes. As they removed the wing fragment from the net, they noticed a second aircraft fragment - a small piece of the forward cockpit with the faint words '*Honey Bee*' written across it.

"Ah – war junk," said the captain as he ordered the fragments to be tossed back into the dark green waters.

Epilogue

With the end of the Second World War, many of the combatant nations – Axis and Allied alike - faced daunting challenges as they began their transition from a six year national war effort to one of a peace time economy. For the former European Axis nations, recovery varied from the Italians, who sustained minimal damage to their country's infrastructure but underwent a significant loss of prestige with the loss of their colonies in North Africa, to Nazi Germany, thoroughly devastated by the continual bombing of her cities and ultimately, the recipient of the world's first atomic bomb strike. But in the ashes of their defeat, the military still maintained control of their respective governments, ensuring that the chaos each country experienced at the conclusion of '*the Great War*', a generation prior, would not be repeated.

From the Allied perspective, both Great Britain and the United States took a deep breath in the knowledge that a de-Nazified conservative government, under General Beck as President and Dr. Carl Goerdeler as Chancellor, had taken root in the wake of the *Valkyrie* coup d'état. Those senior Nazi officials that weren't killed outright with the Zossen atomic blast were rounded up and put on trial (heavily supervised by the Allies) for War Crimes, with many being hanged or receiving life imprisonment. It was firmly understood by Churchill, Truman and the new German leadership that Germany, aside from maintaining a peaceful co-existence with her former enemies in the west, would serve as a 'bulwark' against the spread of communism from the east, still keeping in mind Stalin and his Soviet Russia.

Since the Soviets had quit the war in 1943 after signing an armistice, the Allies saw no need to reward the Soviets in negating the shameful armistice and handing the German spoils back to her. This kind of action would have fostered a strong backlash by the Russians towards the west in general, and the Germans in particular. The Soviet leader mandated that the Red Army be modernized, while the dreaded 'NKVD', soon transformed into the 'KGB', would focus its massive collection efforts on obtaining the latest military technology. This would start with the secrets of the atomic bomb, much of which had already been obtained from American sources embedded within the 'Manhattan Project' at Los Alamos, and missile technology from the Germans at Peenemunde. The seeds of a post World War II 'Cold War' between Germany and the Soviet Union had been planted and were taking root, with an eventual showdown foreseen within the next two generations. Unfortunately for the emerging central European countries like Hungary and Czechoslovakia, each became the objects of attention between the two sullen behemoths vying to make 'satellites' of them to their way of thinking.

Other Allies had far different issues to deal with aside from reconstruction with the advent of peace. Following Germany's negotiated surrender, her occupation forces soon departed from northern France, allowing the Vichy French to re-establish control over the former fortified zone. Within six months, a fierce debate would rage throughout the country as former 'Free French', Frenchmen who did not desire to live in what they regarded as a collaborative regime working side-by-side with Nazi Germany, clashed with incumbent Vichy proponents. French governments came and fell as the country debated her future. With French politicians focused on left versus right politics, Paris' attention waned from the colonies as one by one, they tested the waters seeking independence. First to declare independence was French Indo-China under Nationalist Ho Chi Minh, soon followed by North African colonies starting with Algeria. As the government debate sharpened, French citizens were faced with pro-colonist versus anti-colonist issues as well and over the next decade they would careen close to civil war.

As was the case with France, Great Britain also began to feel the ever increasing 'pangs' for independence from her colonies. Broke from over five years of continual warfare across the globe, the British needed to borrow increasingly more from America who in turn put pressure on her foreign and colonial policy to cut her colonies loose. Before long British India morphed into an independent Hindu India and Muslim Pakistan. However the resultant internal problems in each country led to open conflict as each sought to gain the upper hand and the largest mass migration in history across the Indian sub-continent. Other colonies soon followed in Asia and Africa, as the British Commonwealth transitioned from a monolithic imperial entity directed from London to that of an economic trade block.

In the Far East, clearly a 'Pax Americana' policy prevailed across the Pacific, in many ways reflecting a contemporary relationship Rome had established throughout the Mediterranean Sea in the wake of the Punic Wars. If the United States could identify with ancient Rome as the victor, there was no doubt Japan was reduced to a modern day 'Carthage'.

When Japan started the war with the United States, she endured almost singularly the massive brunt of America's might and blood. With her capitulation in early 1945, Japan's citizenry (those who survived to final assault) began to starve by the thousands. Her cities and nearly all her industry were laid to ruin by General LeMay's firebombing; her countryside reduced to thousands of acres of heavily contaminated land as a byproduct of the chemical weaponry used by the Americans on fanatical military and citizen militias. Japan would therefore begin its era of peace as a proto-feudal state. She may have kept her emperor, but lost everything else in the process including, most importantly, her prized possession across the Straits of Tsushima - 'Chosen' - now referred to by her post annexation name as 'Korea'.

Korea had been an independent kingdom prior to Japan's annexation in 1910. With the landing of American occupation troops and the establishment of a civil administration, various Korean politicians began to arise, organizing independence committees and scores of political parties. Within a short time, two key politicians; 70 year-old Syngman Ree and Chinese favorite Kim Ku, would vie to be the top leader of an independent Korea, while often times working at odds with the American occupation, who at best were ill educated about the development of a functioning Korean government. With the election of Ree within a few years, the newly independent Republic of Korea was formally declared, and the Americans headed home, leaving a somewhat united, though highly dysfunctional government, in its wake.

The situation in China, though equally dysfunctional, was far more manageable. With the landing of thousands of American troops in Shanghai as part of *Operation Longtom* in early 1944, Chiang Kai-shek was finally able to gain and maintain the momentum against the Japanese, concurrently fighting the communists whenever the opportunity presented itself. Upon Japan's complete collapse a year later, Chiang was able to focus his forces and deliver a decisive blow against Mao Tse-tung, breaking the Chinese Communist Forces and forcing them to flee to the mountainous areas of western China where they would resume their life as a small irregular 'guerilla' force against the victorious Nationalist armies. The Generalissimo may have won the battle, but his war against the corruption of his forces and his government was far from over.

For many of the individual lives caught up in this cataclysm, adjustment became a challenge. President Truman continued many of Roosevelt's policies such as the G.I. Bill to ease the transition of American forces and her economy from war to peacetime footing. Defense budgets were slashed, and within a few years, the 15 million man armed forces shrank to less than a million, while maintaining a short lived monopoly of the atomic bomb.

While economically, the Americans controlled the world; her policies would turn inward, focusing on the American people.

Truman's triumph in leading the United States into war against Germany in the wake of Roosevelt's death was truly a milestone for his administration and he never forgot those who helped; in the 1948 Presidential election, Senator Fletcher was approached by Truman to be his Vice Presidential running mate, allowing the Democratic ticket to easily sweep the Republican contender Dewey to defeat.

Jerry Curry opted not to stay and help the Truman administration with its peacetime transition plan. He decided he'd had enough of Washington D.C. and all the back room politics, instead heading back to resume his business that his family had controlled during his absence. Immediately prior to his departure he married his friend Alice and the two of them lived together in Kentucky.

As the American armed forces shrank in size, many soldiers faced decisions whether or not to continue their military service. Major General John Reynolds soon left his post at the War Plans Office to accept command of an Army Corps in the Far East under General MacArthur, largely through his friendship with General Eisenhower. After a few years, he retired from the army, settling in Los Angeles to begin a long career teaching. Colonel Butch Watts would also leave the HQ's General Staff to join General 'Wild' Bill Donovan's Office of Strategic Services as it transformed in a couple of years into the Central Intelligence Agency – the 'CIA'. In the early 1950s, Allen Dulles became CIA Director, bringing Kirk Steege in as his Deputy Chief of Intelligence or 'DCI'. Captain Sam Posavec opted to remain a career man, rising through the officer corps eventually commanding the 11th Airborne Division before retiring from the army as a Major General. Other military men were less fortunate with the coming of peace; Captain Donovan was court-martialed by General Spaatz for his actions and discharged from the Army Air Force, eventually settling in the Toledo, Ohio area where in the succeeding years he would hold a series of low paying menial jobs before meeting his end as a skid row derelict.

In Germany, General Tresckow became the overall Chief of Police, with General Olbricht becoming the new Minister of War. Colonel Pierre Massar became a politician within the new government, rising to succeed Olbricht as Minister of War in the following decade. In this capacity, he would become instrumental in preparing Germany for her future conflict with the Soviet Union.

However the final note is reserved for the occupant of a yellow taxi that had pulled up to a small pale green bungalow just a few miles east of the Port of Long Beach in California. The sole passenger checked to make sure he had the correct address, then exited the taxi, collected his bag from the driver while leaving him a five dollar bill for his fare and tip. He noticed the small mail box off the porch with a single name painted on it – 'Kate' - confirming he had arrived at the right place.

Taking a deep breath, he reached down, grabbed his bag, then slowly walked up the small concrete steps onto the porch, then rang the doorbell. From behind the screen door, a woman in another part of the bungalow called, "Yes, who is it?"

Harold Hoffman responded, "I told you, I would see you again…"

www.ingramcontent.com/pod-product-compliance
Lightning Source LLC
Chambersburg PA
CBHW051932020726

47501CB00001B/95